THE OCCASIONAL JONAS KEMBLE

Finding another self wasn't as arduous a task as Marcus had imagined, perhaps because the difference between him and his creation was barely perceptible to others.

At the end of the autumn term, Damiani took Marcus to a London pub where they ordered the house wine. Damiani reacted to it much as he had done to the tea from RADA's new machine. Eventually, he said,

"I saw him in the play, your other self. He is the man you would like to be, huh? Some of the time. What is his name?"

"No, please..."

Damiani threw up his arms. "We had an agreement. I tell you mine, you tell me yours. Mine is called Rocky."

Marcus smiled. "Mine's Jo."

"Just Jo, huh?"

Marcus lowered his voice. "Jonas Kemble."

"Tell me, does he talk to you?"

"Not so far."

"Ah, he has something to hide? Something which lurks that he doesn't want us to know?" He smiled. "It's good. It is what every actor longs for, and only some achieve. Your Jonas Kemble is not just bolder and braver... he is dangerous, huh?"

Other books by Douglas Watkinson

THE NATHAN HAWK MURDER MYSTERIES:

Haggard Hawk
Easy Prey
Scattered Remains
Evil Turn
Jericho Road
White Crane

THE OCCASIONAL JONAS KEMBLE

DOUGLAS WATKINSON

Published in the UK in 2022 by Quartermain Press

Paperback ISBN: 978-1-915497-00-0
eBook ISBN: 978-1-915497-01-7

Cover design and typeset by SpiffingCovers

PROLOGUE

A friend of Marcus Lawlor once said to him, "Does everything you touch turn to gold?"

A week earlier Marcus had received glowing reviews for his Prince Hal in a BBC version of *Henry IV.* He was then cast as Hamlet up at Stratford, which led to him being offered a lead role in a film about Marco Polo.

Marcus hadn't objected to the slight resentment in his friend's question. If their situations had been reversed, he would have felt the same way. However, every time he was praised or envied it brought to mind his father's words when an agent signed him up after a student massacre of *Cat on a Hot Tin Roof*. Henry Lawlor, even then considered to be acting royalty, had said, "You have the talent, inherited from me, along with the looks, and that's five per cent of what you need. The other ninety-five is luck, and luck's a capricious bastard."

The remark had steadied Marcus from that day forward, but had his father really found it necessary to make it in front of eighty people at a first-night party?

* * *

Luck was definitely on Marcus's side the day he first saw Golden Meadow. He and Teresa had four children by then, aged between three and eight, and they were desperately in need of more space than their rented cottage could provide. He saw the advert for the house one morning and rang to make an appointment to view. No problem, the receptionist told him. The estate agent wasn't available that day but he had a window early next week. Marcus said he would check his diary and call back. He left a note for Teresa, who was doing the school run, went straight out to his car and within twenty minutes was turning off the main road down the lane towards Aston Merrick.

It was a steepish incline and the village could be seen from nearly a mile away, set out on the far side of the valley, the farmland around it jigsawed into fields of rapeseed, grazing and bare earth. He pulled over and gazed at the place, perhaps for as long as five minutes, spending the first two of them dealing with the guilt that he could afford to live in such a village. Once that was out of the way, he accepted that Aston Merrick was where he would move his family to. On perfect cue, the sun broke through as if to light the opening scene of the rest of his life.

He drove through the village, down dead-end lanes and back again, all fanning out from an Elizabethan manor house and its sidekick of a church. Eventually he asked an elderly woman who was curled over her vegetable garden for directions to Golden Meadow. She straightened up and pointed towards the end of the village with a trowel. As he drove away he fancied he could see her thinking: "I've seen that young man somewhere before..."

Marcus parked some distance from Golden Meadow

and walked the remaining four hundred yards so that his first impression, the one that would stick in his mind forever, would be flawless. It was a wise move, since the closer he got, the more he could see that the house, for all its splendour, needed work. Or, as the estate agent's advert had said, it had been 'a much loved family home'. He pulled on the cast-iron handle and a series of clangs took him the possibility that no one was at home.

He turned and looked across the courtyard at a 'much loved' barn which, like the house itself, was built of local stone mellowed over centuries with roof slates as thick as books. Facing it was a swimming pool with a plastic cover gently biodegrading beneath last autumn's fallen leaves, weeds reclaiming the space between the surrounding slabs. In front of him, and falling away into the valley, was the reason for the house's name: five, maybe six acres of emerging buttercups. Beyond that was a woodland, a mass of arms and hands with hazy green fingers reaching for the sky.

As he was about to pull on the bell again, though God knows whoever had failed to hear it the first time was either deaf or dead, the door opened and a tall gangle of a man in his mid-eighties stepped out followed by a rush of tobacco-laden air. He was dressed in grey flannels that had seen better decades and a tweed jacket that was no doubt the reason he had taken so long to answer the door. He had had to locate it, struggle into it and even then had buttoned it up askew. Unlike most people, who invariably gave Marcus a second look when they laid eyes on him, this old boy simply asked if he could help. As the clean morning air caught his lungs he followed up with a coughing fit that turned his yellowing skin orange. He apologised.

"My name is Marcus Lawlor," said Marcus, extending a hand.

There was still no recognition.

"I'm Jack Relph," said the elderly man.

"The house is still for sale, I take it?"

"Oh, I see! You've come from... what's their name?"

"Carters? The estate agent?"

"Yes, them."

"No."

Jack's face clouded. He had one eyebrow that frowned more deeply than the other.

Marcus took a breath. "Sorry, I meant, no, I didn't come from Carters direct. I saw their advert in *The Free Press* and called in on the off-chance."

Jack Relph dithered a little, but at least the frown softened into a wince of embarrassment.

"It's a little awkward, to be honest. My cleaning lady isn't due for another hour and the house is a bit of a tip."

"I'm used to tips. I have four children."

"Oh, they would love this place. Mine did." Jack chuckled and brought on another coughing fit which he tried to speak over. "If you promise not to look at the dust, would you care to take a shufti?"

Marcus followed Jack into the house and closed the door behind them. He was even more relieved that his first sight had been from a distance, since the up-close details were in danger of belying Golden Meadow's inherent beauty: its perfect Georgian beams, the plaster mouldings still intact, the wide oak staircase mellowed by three centuries of feet. God, it even had a cellar that wasn't just a damp hole in the ground but a fully fitted wine store. However, the place had been lived in by an elderly widower who smoked heavily and there wasn't much his cleaner could do about the ground-in smell of cigarettes, any more than she could flick a duster and modernise the Stone Age kitchen and bathrooms. Teresa would need careful briefing, but surely no reasonable person would turn down such a magnificent house simply because it needed rewiring, fully re-plumbing, a new heating system, new kitchen, new bathrooms and then decorating from top to bottom? After all, if she held her nose and turned a blind eye to the stained walls, the estate agent's blurb would ring true. It had been a much loved house. The memorabilia on display said so, mainly in the shape of family photos. Marcus counted one imperious-looking wife and three children, recorded from birth to graduation, marriage and grandchildren via holidays in the sun and Christmases at home. Jostling for priority on the crowded walls were just as many pictures of insects, some of them quite beautiful, others petrifying.

"The insects, Jack...?"

"It's my trade. Entomology."

Marcus paused on the stairs. "Professor J.D. Relph?"

Jack stopped and turned to him. "You've heard of me?"

"You made a documentary on fleas."

Jack was clearly delighted that someone knew who he was. "A friend of mine once joked that most people wouldn't recognise me even if I stung them on the nose." He lowered his voice. "I suspect the majority doesn't know what entomology *is*. What line are you in, Mr, er...?"

"Lawlor. I'm an actor."

Still no recognition, but then there was only one

television set in the house, twenty years old at least.

"That must be very interesting work," said Jack with forced gravity.

He ducked under a cobweb and carried on down the stairs.

"I'm imposing one condition on whoever buys the place," he said when they reached the main hall. "Nothing legal, more scout's-honour sort of thing."

He opened the door to a side room and Marcus followed him into a library, the only room in the house that didn't reek of tobacco. There was even a carved sign on the wall that said 'No Smoking', as if Jack occasionally needed reminding of his own rule. He gestured for Marcus to browse, then went to the French windows and opened them. They gave onto a classic English garden, neat and precise. Jack surveyed it for a few moments before bending into another bout of coughing. He stepped out onto the terrace and lit a cigarette to bring it under control.

Along the left-hand wall of the library ran volumes of classic fiction, poetry, plays and modern writing, while across the room the shelves heaved with history, atlases, dictionaries and encyclopaedias. Some of the books were early editions going back to the mid-eighteenth century, worth more as solid objects than as sources of knowledge and inspiration.

"What's the condition?" Marcus called out.

"I'm leaving the books. Whoever buys the place must promise to pass them on to the next owner." He smiled. "I'm sure few people agree but books will always be an essential to life; computers are a passing fad."

Marcus didn't argue the point. He joined the professor

on the terrace and asked him how much he really wanted for the house. Jack seemed puzzled by the notion that anyone might name their price and then accept a different one.

"Exactly what it says in the estate agent's advert."

"I'll buy it."

Jack looked at him for a moment, eyebrows raised. "I take it there's a Mrs, er..."

"Lawlor."

"Won't she need to see the place first?"

"No." He paused. "On second thoughts, I'll bring her over this afternoon, if I may."

"Splendid! My cleaner will have been by then and worked her magic."

* * *

"I've just bought a house called Golden Meadow," said Marcus as he entered the kitchen.

Teresa looked at him over the top of her coffee mug and said quietly, "Don't be daft."

"No, really, I've said I'll buy it."

"That's not the same as actually buying," she nitpicked.

"The current owner went on about Mrs Lawlor needing to see it first. I agreed I'd take you over this afternoon."

Teresa set down her mug and folded her arms.

"What about Imogen? You said you'd pick her up from play-school and give her lunch."

"Don't worry, I'll see to all that..." He smiled and drifted away for a few moments, back to Golden Meadow. "You know, this could be one of the most important days in our lives. There's something about the place." He added casually, "Needs work, of course."

"How much work?" she asked, quickly.

"Usual sort of thing, nothing major. Word of warning. It's a bit cobwebby. Like going on one of those ghost train rides…"

"I love it already," she said, drily. "I'm going for a shower. Imogen. Fish fingers, broccoli, chips."

As it turned out, and largely because Marcus guided the phone conversation in that direction, a neighbour offered to pick up Imogen from the Montessori, give her lunch and keep her for as long as necessary. It meant that by 1:30 he and Teresa were on their way to Aston Merrick. He stopped short of Golden Meadow to give her the same initial view he had had.

"What do you think?" he asked.

"Very nice," she said in an all-purpose manner, easy to expand on later if she liked the house, just as easy to contradict if she loathed it. He took his frustration out on the steering wheel with a Chinese burn.

Jack Relph's cleaner had done her best, though for all her efforts she hadn't been able to hide the house's shortcomings. In fact, for being cleaner they were all the more obvious, but Teresa smiled her way round them and soon warmed to Golden Meadow's owner. As they began to chat amiably about bugs, she succumbed only once to the urge to scratch herself.

In the downstairs toilet, a real spider had been stranded in the chipped sink and was desperate to escape. Jack lifted it out as one might a tiny child.

"*Eratigena atrica*," he said, as if blessing it.

He placed it on the floor, held his visitors back and

watched it scurry away from its potential new landlords.

When the tour was over and they finally sat down in the kitchen, Jack whipped off the serviette covering the tray his cleaner had laid out for afternoon tea. As he boiled the prehistoric kettle Teresa eased him towards the only question that seemed to bother her.

"Where are you heading, Professor?"

She had expected the answer to be a care home or secure accommodation or, given his cough and the amount he must have smoked during his life, something worse.

"Montana," he said. "I have a sister there. Her husband died last year and, well… family, you know." He smiled. "I'm rather looking forward to our second childhood. The insects will be a bonus, of course. I shall miss this place, but it is just a place."

Whether he believed that or not was difficult to tell. Teresa reached across the table and laid a hand on his arm. "I love your house, Professor. I'm sure we'll enjoy living in it as much as you clearly have."

"I'm sure we will," Marcus added with relief.

They never saw Jack Relph again. They exchanged Christmas cards with him for the next ten years until one day the inevitable letter dropped onto the doormat. It was from Jack's sister, informing them that her brother had died in his sleep and hopefully had been flown to paradise on the wings of some exotic insect.

* * *

By coincidence, the day Marcus moved his family into Golden Meadow was also Henry Lawlor's fifty-seventh birthday. Like most things to do with Henry, there was a problem. When he bought his first computer and it asked him to declare his age, he knocked seven years off it. Consequently, friends, fans, directors and producers had been wishing him a happy fiftieth all week and assumed he would be having a party to celebrate his half-century. Sadly not, Henry told them. Damn nuisance, but he was helping his son to move house that weekend.

When Marcus and Teresa arrived at Golden Meadow with The Others, Teresa lowered the driver's window, the better to hear her own tyres swish on her own gravel. She parked with a crunch. The children burst from the car and ran towards their grandparents, shouting excitedly, "We're moving, we're moving, we're moving," everything said three times to be sure of being heard.

"Really?" said Margot in a grandmotherly voice, the one that asks questions it already knows the answer to. "Where are you moving to?"

Zack and Imogen hadn't fully grasped the concept of moving and tagged along with their older brother and sister as Ethan pointed to the house and shouted, "There, there, there!" Carla, forward-thinking even at the age of eight, asked if Henry and Margot were going to live there as well.

"Regrettably no, my sweet," said Henry. "But today I've been charged with entertaining you while the grown-ups move your goods and chattels into this magnificent house."

They didn't understand much of what he'd said but, like millions all over the world, in theatres and on screens large and small, they were held by the mesmerising voice. He raised an arm and the children danced round him as if he were a maypole. He'd been doing some research on the house, he said, and legend had it there was a cave somewhere in the golden meadow itself. He produced a map of the field from his inside pocket, promising that by the end of the day the cave would be marked on it. Somewhere along the way they would stop for tea, juice, milk and whatever else their grandmother had provided. How did that sound? It sounded great, great, great, went the chorus and they set off, Henry with an heirloom shooting stick tied to the picnic hamper, the children circling him as if drawn by some magnetic force.

Margot watched her husband with a mixture of affection and stoical forbearance. His power over the children was similar to the spell he had cast on too many lovers to count in their thirty-odd years of marriage. Almost as if he had heard the thought and felt an apology was overdue, he turned and blew her a kiss before herding the children through a wooden gate. Their voices faded as they morphed into an advertiser's dream, a picture that could sell anything from soap powder to expensive wristwatches: an adoring man of indeterminate age, smiling, athletic, handsome, strolling across a field with his four grandchildren. The removal vans arrived and brought reality with them.

As the day wore on, Teresa became increasingly overwhelmed by the size of their new house. When they'd arrived that morning, the rooms had an echoey sound as every word, every footfall bounced from wall to wall. By four o'clock not much had changed. She hadn't expected her three-piece suite to look so agoraphobic in the vast living room, or her aunt's dining table to be a faraway island in a sea of oak planks. Upstairs was the same. In the main bedroom, the dressing table, wardrobe and chest of drawers she'd picked up as a job lot for £10 resembled the last few pieces on a gigantic chessboard.

Margot read her mind. "By this time next year, my love, you'll be crying out for more space. I'm about to make tea for the children in that disgusting oven that hasn't seen a spray since the place was built."

Teresa glanced at her watch. "God, it's been five hours! Marcus, darling, go and find them, will you?"

"Once again the old devil's had all the fun and done none of the hard work," Margot muttered. She corrected herself with a smile. "But since when was occupying four children a doddle?"

"And it is his birthday," said Marcus. "Fifty, so we're told: difficult age for a man, no longer young, not yet old."

His mother smiled and flapped him out of the house with both hands.

He set off across the golden meadow, his shoes gradually yellowing with pollen, and had to remind himself that he wasn't the trespasser he felt like. He was the owner of the house, the field and the wood beyond. There was no need to have a snappy answer ready in case an aggressive landowner asked him what he was doing there. He was walking in his own back garden.

He could see his father in the centre of the meadow, perched on the shooting stick, apparently gazing down in front of him. He was alone. Within a count of one, two, three, Marcus broke into a run as panic took hold and his imagination ran riot. Had The Others been abducted, or met with some horrific accident? Had his father lost his sanity and murdered them? Henry turned and raised a finger to his lips. He pointed down at Imogen, asleep on his Burberry.

"She couldn't quite stay the course," he whispered as Marcus drew near. "Though by God she tried."

"Where are the rest?"

He turned to see them in a… hole, a scooped-out hollow, its sloping sides covered in buttercups. The Others had been scratching away at it with sticks cut from the nearby wood.

"Daddy, Daddy, Daddy!" the cry went up.

"We found the cave," said Ethan, as he crawled up the sides of the hole.

"Where?"

"Here, here, here. This is it!"

Carla emerged clutching a stick in one hand and something far more precious in the other. "Look at this!" she said.

She unclasped her fist to reveal a copper coin, a twopence piece dating all the way back to 1993.

"Grandad says if there's money it's proof someone lived here hundreds of years ago."

"And how many coins does he say you'll find?" Marcus asked.

"I know of at least four," said Henry. "Carry on searching, my loves!"

"Actually, I came to call you in for tea."

"Another five minutes won't make much difference," his father said, holding up five fingers, a sure sign that he had spent the day with young children.

The Others returned to the hole, sliding down the sides on their backs, their clothes streaked yellow and green when they stood up.

"So, how does this cave work?" Marcus asked. "It

looks more like a dried-up slurry pit to me."

"A chap called John Bigg lived in it, so the story goes." Henry gestured down to Ethan to explain.

"He wanted the king to get his head chopped off," Ethan explained. "Only once it was done he felt sorry, so he came to live here."

Henry nodded. "Beautifully put. He was a signatory to Charles the First's death warrant and his subsequent remorse forced him to live the rest of his life as a hermit."

"Where had he lived before?"

"He was a steward at the manor house." He chuckled. "But history is written by people who weren't there at the time, so you pays your money and you takes your choice."

"It was all bloody, the head when they chopped it off," said Ethan, enthusiastically. "All the blood, they let people dip their hankies in it and take it home with them. They smeared it over the sores on their arms."

"I worry about that child sometimes," Marcus whispered.

"It's true, though. They believed it would cure everything from smallpox to syphilis, a detail I should have skipped over, perhaps."

A shriek of pure delight came from the hole in the ground. Zack's perseverance had paid off and he'd struck 'gold' in the shape of a fifty-pence piece from 1989.

"You see, you see, you see," Carla said to her father as if he had ever denied it. "Someone lived here in our garden, in this cave!"

At Henry's feet, Imogen stirred. He stooped to gather her up, drew her close and kissed her on the top of her head. "You've woken up in time for tea, my darling. Marcus, bring the hamper, will you? Children, we're leaving."

They clambered out of the hole immediately.

"How do you *do* that?" Marcus asked. "Make them co-operate so readily?"

Henry smiled. "I'm able to because I am *not* their father."

He set off with the children. Marcus packed away the picnic debris and followed in his own good time.

***

That night, Marcus and Teresa sat in bed, their clothes all around them, hanging on makeshift rails or still in boxes stacked unevenly on the floor. A couple of suitcases lay open-mouthed, with towels, dressing gowns and toiletries spilling out of them.

Teresa was making a list in her A4 diary. Occasionally she would circle an item and move it up or down the priority ladder, then change her mind and move it back again. Marcus had once appeared on *Desert Island Discs,* a radio programme that tinkered at the edges of its guests' lives. The presenter had asked what he would miss most, were he ever to be marooned. His wife's lists, he had said. They had a mystical power. If a task had a place on one of Teresa's lists, it was as good as done. He slipped a hand under the duvet and stroked her thigh.

"Maybe give it a rest now?" he said.

She closed the diary and dropped it onto the floor beside her.

"Pity your father can't come back tomorrow," she said, eventually.

"Did Mum say anything?"

"Did she mention a current distraction in his life, you mean? I don't think they discuss it anymore, just take it for granted." She squeezed his hand. "Why have you never been like him?"

"All that effort to be charming? I couldn't bear it."

Teresa turned and stroked his face. "And you'd have to shave every day."

"That's the killer."

She smiled and glanced round the room. "Do something for me, first thing tomorrow? Put the poster up?"

The poster she was referring to was huge. Teresa had found it in somewhere as unlikely as W.H. Smith, mounted it on plywood and hung it over the bed in their first flat. From there it had followed them to the cottage, and would now apparently overlook their every night-time move in Golden Meadow. It portrayed a knight on a white stallion, clutching a damsel with flowing hair, grossly out of proportion to her face. She was looking up at her rescuer with unfettered adoration. Marcus had always tried not to read too much into it.

It wasn't long before Teresa closed her eyes, though she still managed to hold a conversation. Inevitably it was about tomorrow – what needed doing and by whom. Just before she fell asleep she muttered, "We have done the right thing, haven't we? Buying?"

He settled the duvet around her chin. "I'm usually the one with doubts," he said.

"Will it be alright?"

"Of course. The Others will grow up in this idyllic place, their friends will come to stay, the house will come alive and you and I will stay young…"

She purred. "That's why I love you. Always so sure, so confident…"

"You think so?"

He heard her breathing become long and deep as she tipped over into sleep and he wished he could join her. In truth he was wide awake, troubled by the very doubt Teresa had expressed. The last two months had rushed by, almost without pause, and here he was at midnight on moving day wondering for the first time if he'd over-reached himself. Actors had a way of spending their way through the good times and being forced to beg and borrow through the lean. His father maintained that doubt was an asset, a means of seeing a problem from all sides. It was an odd belief for such a self-assured man to hold, but confidence was an overrated commodity, Henry insisted. Without fear and uncertainty, how should we test our courage? It sounded compelling in daylight but in the middle of the night it lost some of its power.

Marcus decided to lay his uncertainty before his other self.

Just after his nineteenth birthday, a July day near the end of his first year at RADA, his tutor had called him to his office. Every student had an annual assessment, a review of progress so far. Zoltan Damiani went through his kindly routine of providing a plastic cup of tea from the new machine. It was pure displacement on his part. If rough things needed saying he could suddenly lighten the conversation with his disparaging view of the cup's contents.

"Marcus, sit down. Make yourself comfortable, tell me how things have been?"

"Things have been fine, I think." He smiled. "What do *you* think?"

Damiani pointed, to nowhere in particular. "I like that. You go straight to the point."

He set down his own tea and leaned forward on folded arms. He was a slightly built man with fierce dark eyes and pale skin. Black hair in a schoolboy cut. Late thirties, Marcus thought, and therefore old enough and wise enough to be his tutor.

"I think somewhere within reach of you there is a fine actor. At the moment you are afraid. Chicken."

"What the hell...?" Marcus blurted out.

"There is bulletproof wall between you and the audience. You see each other but cannot reach. I saw it in the Dürrenmatt. You need to break it."

The end-of-year production had been Friedrich Dürrenmatt's *The Visit*, chosen not for its dramatic appeal but because it had a huge cast, something for everyone to get their teeth into. Marcus abandoned his own tea and shifted in his chair. He had often thought there was something of the wizard in Damiani and here was the proof. He had seen right through Marcus to his fear of performing.

"It is not a reason to quit," Damiani added.

"Who said I was thinking of quitting? My father would die."

Damiani shrugged. "In Budapest, during the revolution, I was afraid. Many times."

"Really?"

Damiani snapped his fingers to regain his student's attention. "Ask me how I coped."

"How did you cope?"

"I invented another me who wasn't scared of anything. He has stood by me ever since. Go home for the summer, Marcus, and create another you. Make him bolder, braver, two inches taller than you, someone who will break through the glass to reach his audience, sing them a lullaby or put the fear of God in them, whichever you... you, Marcus his master, choose. Give him a name, as I did, to make him real. Then come back September, we talk." He took a sip of his tea and curled his lip. "This is not tea."

He stood up, went over to the large fern by the window and emptied the plastic cup into it. He invited Marcus to do the same.

"What was his name, your other you?" Marcus asked.

"I will tell you if you tell me yours, when you have him."

Finding another self wasn't as arduous or disturbing as Marcus had imagined it would be, perhaps because the difference between him and his creation was almost imperceptible to others. At the end of the autumn term, after a studio performance of *Desire Under the Elms*, Damiani took Marcus to a London pub where they ordered the house wine. Damiani reacted to it much as he had done to the tea from RADA's new machine. Eventually, he nodded slowly and said,

"I saw him in the play, your other self. He is the man you would like to be, huh? Some of the time. What is his name?"

"No, please..."

Damiani threw up his arms. "We had an agreement. Mine is called Rocky."

Marcus smiled. "Jo."

"Just Jo, huh?"

Marcus lowered his voice. "Jonas Kemble.

"Tell me, does he talk to you?"

"Not so far."

"Ah, he has something to hide? Something which lurks that he doesn't want us to know?" He smiled. "It's good. It is what every actor longs for, and only some achieve. Your Jonas Kemble is not just bolder, braver… he is dangerous, huh?"

And twelve years later, at gone midnight on the day Marcus moved into Golden Meadow, Jonas Kemble answered any lingering doubts. Of *course* buying this house had been a good idea, he said. It would also be smart to get some sleep, so lie down, turn over and close your eyes.

Within five minutes Marcus was dead to the world.

-1-

"Like most of you, I have hundreds of stories about Imogen that she would rather I didn't tell, but this being her twenty-first birthday I'll allow myself just one. It's a tale of courage, determination and revenge, and it occurred five years ago to the very day…"

The Others groaned in a good-natured heckle, having heard the story so many times. Marcus pointed across the marquee at them. "Quiet in the gods! Yes, it was the night of her sixteenth birthday where she had probably drunk" – his voice changed to fluttering, girly innocence – "her first glass of wine ever. She was relaxed and giggly and someone made a joke. Imogen laughed, that big fruity laugh we all love. When she tried to close her mouth again, she couldn't."

The gathering laughed and Marcus swept his gaze across the guests in actorly fashion, appearing to take in each and every one of them, his eyes coming to rest on none. Except for the young woman who was wearing a silver dress that seemed to have been painted onto her. She had tilted her head and tossed a wealth of black, black hair forwards across the front of her body where she held it with both hands, as if offering it. She smiled at Marcus. He smiled back.

"Anyway, we bundled her into the car and headed for A and E where a young doctor examined Imo and said, 'Dislocated jaw.' Dislocated jaw? Wouldn't such a thing prevent you from talking? Not if you're Imogen Lawlor." He opened his mouth, held it there and continued in a Neanderthal grunt. "Er, ugh, er, ugh, ugh, er. She was trying to tell us something, but since we couldn't understand, we ignored her. The doctor sat her down, took her jaw in his hands and" – he mimed a gentle wrench – "there it was, back in its socket. I asked her what she'd been trying to say for the last hour. 'I'm going to be sick,' she replied, and true to her word she threw up all over me."

The guests applauded and Marcus looked round the marquee again. His gaze settled on the girl in the silver dress. She was still cosseting the hair, still smiling at him. She seemed to be on her own, no young man laying claim to her. Maybe that was why she had stood out from the crowd. He turned to Imogen.

"So, ladies and gentlemen, this is my beloved, beautiful, witty and talented daughter who, with no bias on my part whatsoever, is set to become a brilliant actress. Happy birthday, Imo."

There was more applause and foot stamping as Imogen went to him and draped her arms round his neck.

Teresa stepped in with the practicalities. The music was scheduled to begin at eight o'clock, she told everyone, introducing a local disc jockey. With it now being just after six, the guests had two hours in which to demolish the hog roast, the salmon en croute, the vegetarian quiches, the… whatever else the caterers had prepared, and finish off with one of their famously evil desserts. The bar would be open till eleven, she added, which brought a whoop of approval from the younger guests. This fed Teresa's anxiety that it would be a party of several factions: her stuffier neighbours in one corner, family friends in another, the children's friends roaming at will. Her fears were groundless. The guests began to mingle, to talk to each other, even to enjoy each other's company.

As the evening progressed, the light outside faded, the music began to blare and conversation first became shouted, then mouthed. Finally it petered out. Some of the Lawlors' less youthful neighbours began to leave, and Imogen insisted on being there to wish them goodnight. She played the role of a gracious hostess with great style. Was it his imagination, Marcus wondered, but had Imogen suddenly become the woman she'd been insisting for years that she already was?

She thanked departing guests, most of whom she had known all her life. They had enjoyed the party, they said, though some were still wondering why they had been invited in the first place. The reason was simple: having accepted the invitation, the crustier element could hardly object to the noise, the cloud of marijuana above the dance floor or the music playing beyond the Parish Council's allotted time.

Henry had taken his place at the bar, a glass of whisky in front of him, and spent much of the evening being gazed at. He was currently appearing as King Lear at the National Theatre. At the end of each performance, when he hung up the ragbag costume and stretched out the madman wig on its stand, he returned to being the man he always was, with one slight exception. He was now *Sir* Henry Lawlor, knighted for services to drama. At well over seventy he stood straight at six feet two, his silky hair swept back and as white as the collar it touched. His eyes were dark, clear and still, but able to change in a flash from gentleness to fury as the dialogue demanded.

Not far away, keeping a watchful eye on him, sat 'Henry's new wife', as Marcus still called her. Jenny Ballard had been a dancer, with a host of excuses as to why no one had ever heard of her. She and Henry had met ten years previously and were married a year later.

After a tour of the guests, Marcus approached Teresa at the table where she sat with a farmer friend and a stringy-looking actress who played a nurse in a hospital soap opera. He leaned down and whispered in Teresa's ear,

"How do you fancy a stroll in the moonlight?"

She looked up at him with a smile. "How very Noël Coward of you."

To his family's amusement, Marcus had spent the last week at the mercy of the BBC's weather app, worried about its prediction of a cold, wet August day and an even worse evening. Was he annoyed with forecasters for getting it wrong, Teresa asked, or happy that they'd made a mistake?

He led her from the marquee, and she looked up in astonishment at the perfect night sky. Before she could tease him further he pulled her towards him and kissed her on the lips. She had once said that when he did that with enough matinee idolness, she became 23 years old again with but one objective in mind: to have him all to herself. He pointed across the golden meadow, beyond the array of warning lights around Biggs Cave, to the wood beyond.

A few months after they moved in, when the wood had been more jungle than forest, Teresa had hired a man to clear it of everything but trees and wildflowers, then to lay a Celtic knot of wood-chip paths. From that day on, if ever she went missing, the first place to look for her was here in this gathering of tall trees. Her thinking space. If she could have nailed a sign to the outermost tree saying 'Rest of the world keep out!' she would have done so.

Marcus led her to an old carved seat, product of her weakness for buying things to sit on, an odd indulgence for someone who rarely took the weight off her feet. It was matched only by her collection of gilt-framed mirrors on every wall in the house, again an odd fetish for someone who seldom looked at herself. Teresa sat down and leaned into him, trying to stifle a yawn. She had every reason to be tired, Marcus thought. Gone were the days when she could party all night and appear next morning without a hint of damage to her beautiful face.

They could see the marquee from here, less an oversized tent, more a recently descended spacecraft powered by heavy metal engines glowing in time to the beat. If the throbbing had ceased, a creature from a distant star would surely have emerged through the front flap to warn of the end of the world. But the music played on, the warning was never given and now the engines hummed to the music of the 80s and 90s while the lights projected strange, writhing life forms onto the canvas walls.

"So, you've enjoyed it?" Teresa asked.

"It had its moments."

"I saw some of them flapping round you."

He smiled. "I only noticed their minds."

She nodded. "Such beautiful minds – not a wrinkle, not a sag, not a surplus inch anywhere. In spite of the desserts."

He kissed her on the lips again as over in the marquee the late Eddie Cochran tried to break down love into three component parts.

"You ogled the brains and left your poor father to struggle with the beauty?"

Marcus stretched out in a straight line, like a petulant schoolboy, hooking his thumbs in his trouser pockets. "Did you see Jenny as he trawled the talent? Afraid he might run off with a twenty-one-year-old?"

"In her shoes I might feel the same."

Marcus shook the bubbling images from his mind of his father trying to bridge a fifty-year age gap in a bedroom. The twenty-year difference between Henry and Jenny had been difficult enough.

"We should have made a detour to the house," he said. "Fetched a bottle of that Château La Lagune Jack Relph left. God help me! Eighteen years ago and it's not been drunk. Which reminds me, did I lock the cellar door?"

Teresa flinched, startled by the snap of a twig on the other side of the wood. Laughter followed, then overlapping voices, young, frivolous and wrecked on Tesco's finest. As they batted their way through low branches, one of the boys was criticising the DJ for playing ancient music. A girl with a gentle voice said she rather liked the oldies. Fancying the girl more than his own opinion, the critic rethought his argument. Maybe it was just the way the DJ presented them, full of reverence and overstatement.

As the sweet smell of marijuana reached them Marcus stood up and held out a hand to Teresa.

"Back to the house. I'll make us a cup of middle-aged tea instead."

He waved to the approaching party guests and, alarmed by their hosts' presence, one of them flicked away the joint he'd been sharing. It spun like a throwing knife, shedding sparks, and landed in the undergrowth. Marcus made to go and retrieve it, to stand in full view and draw on it, but Teresa beat him to it, crushing it underfoot.

They walked back across the meadow and on reaching the swimming pool revisited the slight argument of a few days ago. Marcus had insisted the pool be closed off, the winter cover installed, even though it was still August.

"A swim might have been nice," Teresa said.

"It might also have been tomorrow's headline. *Coked up friend of acting dynasty found face down in swimming pool.*"

"Something snappier."

"'*An Inspector Calls... on Marcus.*"

It was a reference to the J.B. Priestley classic which he was due to star in, with rehearsals beginning in three weeks' time.

There must have been twenty or so partygoers dotted around the living room. As Marcus and Teresa entered, the conversation ceased and the music was turned down while the room waited for Richard Salter, the lead character in TV's *Salter's Edge,* to speak.

"Good party, everyone?" Marcus asked.

A young man with brown hair, tinted blond at the tips, and a bony, jutting face, but good-looking for all that, let go of his droopy girlfriend and sprang to his feet.

"Terrific, sir! And what a great place this is! How old is it?"

Was he really interested or just well brought-up, Marcus

wondered. He was certainly well dressed. The invitation had stressed smart casual but this boy had on a dinner jacket, a dress shirt and bow-tie. He was either a relic from a bygone age or modern youth trying to be eccentric.

"1720, according to the deeds," said Marcus. "Built by a gentleman farmer called Alfred Tweak. Not *quite* the silliest name I've ever heard."

The boy turned his attention to Teresa. "Would you like us to…?"

She waved aside his offer to leave and went through to the kitchen. As Marcus made to follow, a girl on the far side of the room, wearing little more than a net curtain hung by two shoelaces, said in a jolly-hockey-sticks voice,

"Mr Lawlor, my mother simply loves *Salter's Edge.*"

"How wonderful. Be sure to give her my regards."

"And she and dad went to see Sir Henry in *King Lear.* They talked about it for a month!"

Marcus stifled a sigh. Even when he wasn't in the room, his father had the knack of upstaging him.

"Mmm, he is pretty good, isn't he? Why not ask him to get you free tickets?"

She raised a nervous hand to her mouth, showing garish transfers on long fingernails. "Do you really think…?"

"Oh, I'm sure he'd be delighted to help."

He escaped into the kitchen, where a runner bean of a girl was halfway through making coffee. Teresa was surreptitiously closing all the cupboard doors she had opened in her search for coffee beans.

"Would you like some, Mr Lawlor?" the runner bean asked.

"No, thank you. And it's Marcus, please." He reached

across the unit for the kettle. "You are?"

"Sorry. Amy."

"Hi, Amy."

He turned to see the girl in the clingy silver dress, perched on a kitchen barstool, hands clasped around one knee, leg drawn up into a Z shape. She smiled and he smiled back, almost as if it was now a mutual habit.

"We haven't met," he said.

She stepped down off the stool and offered him her hand. "Isabella. I'm a friend of Ethan."

He gazed at her, editing his first impression, which admittedly had been formed in a crowded marquee. He had thought she was beautiful. Here in the glare of kitchen spotlights her face couldn't hide behind the magnificent hair. In stark contrast to it her skin was almost ghost-like in colour. Her dark eyes were unnervingly still, even when she smiled.

Zack entered the room with his usual hurricane force.

"Where's this coffee, then?" He pecked his mother on the cheek. "Teresa, Marcus, how's it going?"

Allowing the children to address them by their Christian names was one of many regrets they had about their parenting. At the time it was a trendy means of bonding with offspring, but by the age of five or six it sounded more like rudeness than respect. Zack went over to the girl making coffee and put an arm round her waist, a move that told his parents where she fitted in to his ever-changing social life.

"This is Amy, by the way."

"We've met," said Teresa.

Whereas Ethan had inherited his looks from his father's side of the family, Zack was a taller version of his maternal grandfather, broad and muscular with gentle, pale blue eyes and fair hair worn in a ponytail.

"How about this for luck, Marcus? Two months out of drama school, she turns up at Freebooter to voice Miss Twinkletail opposite my Hector Hedgehog."

Isabella laughed. "You might have to explain."

"Freebooter's the animation company, *Tales from the Hedgerow* is a kids' cartoon. Miss Twinkletail's a dormouse, I'm a rebellious hedgehog."

Marcus turned back to Isabella. "You know Ethan from Oxford? Which college were you at?"

"Somerville."

Teresa slipped an arm round Marcus's waist and dug her fingernails in.

"Some of the most beautiful minds in the world went to Somerville," she said. "Indira Gandhi, Vera Brittain... Margaret Thatcher."

"You know, I think I will have that coffee, Amy. Where shall we take them?"

"The room with all the books in it?" Amy suggested.

He couldn't help himself. "We call it the library."

* * *

The library was almost as Jack Relph had left it. The same books stood on the same shelves in roughly the same order. Jack had even gifted them the leather-topped table, the chairs and the 'No Smoking' sign. Teresa had re-carpeted the place and added a couple of sofas, but that was about all. As a library, a source of reference, it had become virtually redundant, but it still served an important purpose. This was where the family gathered for so-called 'clan meetings'.

These were strange affairs where those present sat around the table and considered their arguments before advancing them politely. Phones were switched off, and no one fidgeted or flopped over the table as discussions lengthened. Marcus believed it was the effect of Shakespeare, Shaw, the Brontës and Thomas Hardy looking down from their leather bindings. Who would want those people to consider you an ill-mannered fool?

As they settled to drink their coffee, newcomers and natives alike observed library etiquette, at least for a while, as if there were a sign on the wall saying 'Quiet please' and an iron grey librarian watching them. They were distracted by tapping on the French windows. Imogen was out on the terrace, pointing down to the lock, an overacted look of desperation on her face.

"The woman herself, come of age!" said Marcus, going to the doors and unlocking them. "Yesterday she wasn't allowed to fly helicopters or drive lorries over seven tons. Today, God help us, she can."

Imogen entered with her escort of the evening, a young man from the next village called Kieran Hart who had recently qualified as a doctor. Could it be, Marcus had wondered when he saw them kissing earlier, that Imogen was defying rumours about her sexuality and turning her hormones on this offensively handsome young man? Ethan and his long-term girlfriend Gemma Blake were right behind them.

"It's over, Marcus!" said Ethan. "The DJ's taken his woofer and tweeter home, and the bar is no more."

Imogen went over to her father and hugged him.

"You'll smell bud and booze on me, Dad, but thanks for a great party. Thanks Mum. Mum?"

Teresa returned from wherever she'd drifted off to, disguising her absence as tiredness. "Sorry, darling, yes... yes, you're welcome. We'll need more coffee by the look of it." Amy stood up but Teresa raised a hand to prevent her following her out of the room. "No, dear, stay and talk."

Ethan went to Imogen and drew her towards him. "Happy birthday. Again. Have you seen Carla and Matt the Mutt? She short and bossy, her boyfriend tall and biddable?"

"Last I saw they were by the pool," said Imogen, raising two spliff-smoking fingers. "And no, Marcus, no one has taken the cover off and dived in."

As Marcus hammed up relief at the news they heard the distant rumble of a coffee grinder.

"I'll go give her a hand," said Zack.

***

In the kitchen Teresa was setting out a tray with biscuits, milk, sugar and spoons as if for a village coffee morning.

"You must be knackered," said Zack as he entered.

She smiled. "I don't do knackered."

"You're alright, though? Nothing..."

"I'm fine."

He asked again, different words with the same meaning. She shook her head.

"A silly flashback, that's all."

She wanted to tell someone, though preferably not one of the drama queens or kings in her immediate family.

That said, Zack was more grounded than the others and if anyone could reduce her fears, it would be him.

"When Ethan came in through the French windows, I just happened to be watching Isabella. I could see as clearly as if it had been written on her forehead ... what was going on in her mind."

"Which was?"

She looked at him, steadily. "That boy, Ethan Lawlor, is gifted, handsome, charming, comes from a good family. They have money, fame, prestige. I'm going to have him."

Zack laughed. "You got all that from the way she looked at him?"

She nodded. "Because I saw myself, twenty-eight years ago, looking at your father in exactly the same way."

He stepped behind her and put his arm round her neck, her chin in the crook of his elbow.

"Where did that look take place?"

"The King's Head, Islington. I'd been with a friend to see him in *Look Back in Anger* and I waited in the bar afterwards until he noticed me."

"I'm glad he did, otherwise we'd both be talking to someone else." He let go of her. "You really think she's here on some kind of recce? Why has she passed on me?"

Teresa could hardly tell him that he wasn't the easy touch she feared his brother might be. That was why she liked Ethan's girlfriend. She was grounded, sensible, safe: all those words she would have hated being applied to her in her early twenties.

"You aren't so easily impressed," she said.

Zack smiled and looked down at the tray. "Let's go."

As they entered the library, Zack in the cameo role of

a po-faced butler, it was clear that Isabella hadn't exactly clubbed Ethan and dragged him away as his mother had feared. She was sitting on a library stool beside Marcus.

"I'm sure I'm right," he was saying. "There's an accent there, a slight lilt, but I can't quite place it…"

"Guess," she mouthed.

"Is the clue in the name? Isabella, Isabella…"

"Who wants coffee?" Teresa called out.

Isabella rose from the stool, straightened the clingy dress with a rock of her hips, and took her mug over to the tray.

* * *

The after-party chatter continued for another half-hour, during the course of which Teresa convinced herself that Zack was right. She had spooked herself into imagining a dark purpose where none existed. Isabella was no more than a natural flirt, something Teresa herself had often been accused of. She could hardly condemn a young, attractive woman for behaving in the same way.

At around one o'clock Teresa realised she wouldn't need to allocate bed spaces as if this were a kids' sleepover. The guests who had remained were beginning to fade, in spite of their youth and the coffee, and were making camp all over the ground floor of the house. Marcus caught Teresa's eye and pointed above his head. She nodded gratefully and they wished everyone goodnight.

* * *

Isabella found a pokey room on the top floor of the house, reached via a winding stair that gave onto a small landing. She imagined these were once servants' quarters, now a series of junk rooms, although this particular one seemed far too clean for that. Maybe Teresa was a woman who vacuumed her house every day, regardless of whether it needed doing. She slipped out of the silver dress and let it drop to the floor beside her. She took a silk dressing gown from her overnight bag and put it on slowly, as if she was being watched.

Who would she choose to be the voyeur, she asked herself. Whose tread would she like to hear on the stairs right now? She was spoiled for choice. Zack was top of the list – Zack with the locker-room body and a neck she could happily sink her teeth into.

Marcus, maybe? He certainly wouldn't be her first older man. All that masculinity packed into such a pleasing shape and a willingness to succumb, she was sure of it. The grandfather? She laughed silently. He was certainly a challenging prospect but, like as not, beneath the wouldn't-you-if-you-could arrogance there'd be wrinkly skin and a libido that was more talk than action.

Ethan, then. Cleverness over raw sexuality every time. Not that Ethan was a dog in terms of looks. And there was much else in his favour. Friends who had been at Trinity with him had made a judgement after he'd gained a double first. He was clever, certainly, but also neurotic, volatile, oddly unsure of himself, easily swayed… easy to pull.

She lay down on the floor, using her towel as a pillow, and closed her eyes. She imagined an adoring Ethan beside her watching her every breath, wanting her but afraid to make the first move. Far from helping her to drift off, the image aroused her. The moonlight from the sloping window overhead made it worse. It gave objects in the room a silver appearance, and after an hour struggling to ignore it, she stood up, tied her dressing gown tightly around her and headed to the door.

As she made her way down the creaking stairs, each tread threatened to give her away. At the first-floor landing she was suddenly confronted by her own reflection in one of Teresa's army of mirrors. She paused, retied the dressing gown more loosely and carried on down the stairs.

The hall and the living room had the feel of a ghost ship whose crew had been struck by a deadly fever, such was the stillness of the bodies slumbering in the half-light. One of them was Kieran Hart, a doctor with a bedside manner to match his beauty. Why hadn't he made a pass at her, she wondered. Earlier on, in the marquee, he was seated at a nearby table and hadn't so much as glanced at her. He had eyes only for the birthday girl.

Isabella sidestepped the moment and watched herself raise her bare foot. She hovered it above Kieran's head and held her balance like a ballerina waiting for the next phrase of music. On hearing it, she drove her heel into his face and heard gristle being ripped away from bone as his nose parted company with his skull. His hands rushed to his twisted face. Blood began to pour from his nostrils and escape through his fingers. He held up his crimson hands as if offering a sacrifice to a pagan goddess...

Back in reality, she smiled and brushed the hem of her dressing gown against his face. He flicked it away and turned over, still sleeping.

She made her way to the kitchen. Here in the dresser would be a wealth of oddments, items to remind her of this nighttime prowl. She opened the apothecary drawer and peered in. A small penknife, a rolled-up tape measure, dental floss, a laundry marker, a blunt pencil, a ball of string, odd screws, an open packet of chewing gum. Too commonplace. Something from the cutlery drawer, then? Knives, forks, spoons? Nobody would miss them either, so where would be the fun?

The adjoining dining room might be more promising. Entering it she caught sight of a man's jacket, draped over the back of a chair at the table. Bomber in style, the leather was dark brown, expensively soft. She stroked it, then felt in the pockets. As she leaned down she caught the faint aroma of something she recognised. When chatting with Marcus in the library, she had noticed his cologne. Like the jacket, it was expensive. She lifted one sleeve to her face as if an imaginary hand might reach out and caress her cheek.

At the cuff was a button. She felt the familiar rush that, just for a moment, blanked out the rest of the world. She bit through the thread attaching the button and, as it came loose, she finished the job with her fingernails. She placed the button in her mouth.

-2-

As usual, Teresa woke next morning ten seconds before the alarm went off. She reached out for the digital version of Beethoven's Fifth and prodded it into silence.

"Are you awake?" she asked.

Over the years Marcus had pared his answer down to, "Mm."

"The big clear-up," she said. "It'll be a piece of cake if everyone plays their part."

She stepped into the shower and ran her hands over her body, checking there was no spare flesh to push down over her hips, no price to pay for that second wedge of cheesecake she'd polished off last night. She dressed as she always did ahead of a full day: jeans, a flowery cotton top and running shoes. She followed up with a whisk of makeup, then opened the curtains to discover the forecasters had got it wrong again. Instead of rain hammering at the windows, sunlight streamed in through the glass. Marcus mumbled that he would join her downstairs in a minute.

The kitchen was much as Teresa had expected to find it, with the decent china from the dining room scattered across every surface. Her mother's silver cutlery lay at odd angles across the remains of a late-night feast.

She went through to the living room, drawn there by the sound of snoring. It was Kieran Hart. She watched him for a moment, his head flopped back over a cushion, mouth open: a picture of the man he would be at eighty. She clapped her hands twice. When her mother used to do it, the whole class sat bolt upright, but Teresa had never perfected it. The carpet heaved in one or two places, the leather armchairs groaned, and so began the business of sending the party stragglers on their way.

She went back to the kitchen and cleared the table. As she turned to make coffee, she saw Henry standing in the doorway, watching her. Bathed, shaved, his hair unruffled, clothes without a crease, he might have been the hero of a thousand films, the man who had risen after a night of passion or action without a mark to show for it. Jenny would doubtless be five minutes behind him and would start picking nonexistent fluff from his lapel or fiddling with his perfectly knotted tie.

"Splendid party," he said. "How do you do it, my dear, and manage to look so radiant throughout?"

"Thank you, Henry."

She reached up to a high cupboard and took down the only cup and saucer in the house, a Crown Derby combo kept purely for Henry, who thought mugs were for builders and gardeners.

"Would life have been any easier if you hadn't married... us?" he asked, gently.

"If I'd made use of my law degree, you mean? Easier, probably. Boring, almost certainly."

"No regrets, then. Do you have a copy of this week's *Spectator* to hand, by any chance?"

"*Spectator*? And you the original champagne socialist?"

He lowered his voice. "I've changed political horses. Apparently, they've given my *Lear* a glowing review."

"It'll be in the library."

When Marcus finally appeared, he was looking pretty heroic as well, Teresa thought, no doubt conscious that young women were still in the house. He glanced round and said what he usually said when he entered a room.

"Where is everyone?"

"Your father's through in the library. And the walking dead are about to invade from the living room."

As he drew her close and was about to kiss her, Carla clomped into the room wearing clog-like slippers that claimed to be the answer to all posture problems. She opened the fridge and was about to reach in for a slice of leftover apple tart when she sensed her mother's eyes roaming her body. She straightened up. It didn't need Teresa's critical eye to remind her that she'd put on weight lately. She turned away and settled for muesli.

They were soon joined by Henry's new wife, wearing the demented look of a mother who has mislaid a child in a crowded supermarket. She asked where Henry was and began to quarter the room. Before she could pick up the scent Teresa took her arm and led her to the table.

"Library," she said, gently. "Take a pew, Jenny. I'll pour you some coffee."

Jenny squeezed onto the bench between the table and the stone wall that backed the inglenook in the next room. She was almost as performance ready as Henry, Teresa thought. The makeup repair was first rate, the hair coiled and piled, elongating the bony face. Still lithe and supple, as ex-dancers tended to be, there was just one telltale sign that age was taking its revenge. Her hands. The fingers were becoming spindly, the joints craggy.

The dossing partygoers drifted in, plundered the cornflakes and coffee with one hand, sent text messages with the other and returned to their pitches in the living room. It was a good hour before all of them had disappeared down Golden Meadow's drive, the last four in a dangerous-looking old Peugeot. They all thought it had been a wonderful party, it was awesome to have met Teresa, and cosmic to have actually seen, touched, shaken hands with Sir Henry. Oh, and Marcus as well. Teresa went to the hall and yelled, "Family! Kitchen! Now!"

They didn't exactly come running, but when finally assembled she picked up her diary and was about to assign jobs when Marcus raised a finger. "Listen!"

His bat-like hearing was a family joke, along with his bloodhound sense of smell. They inclined their heads in the direction he was pointing.

"Water, running down a drainpipe. Not the one over the kitchen, the other side of the house."

Gradually, most of them heard it.

"Someone's left a tap on," said Teresa. "The hot, no doubt."

Marcus patted Imogen on the arm. "Run up and turn it off, love. Your legs are still the youngest in the family."

Imogen groaned and set off and half a minute later, according to Marcus's ears, the tap was turned off. Teresa went back to the business in hand. Her list was short but demanding.

Phone Mike Travis re marquee. Remove.
Living room, clear – Imogen. Vacuum
Kitchen, utility – Carla
Garden, woods, clear – boys
Dogs. From kennels – Jenny?
Lunch, leftovers (check salmon)
Dinner tonight?

There were no dissenters. Golden Meadow would be back to its old self by nightfall, she insisted. As they rose, Imogen reappeared and paused at the door as if about to introduce a bill-topping act.

"It wasn't a tap. It was a shower."

She turned and Isabella entered, her silk dressing gown all but flapping, a towel wrapped around her head. She was holding an apologetic hand to her mouth.

"I am so sorry," she said, casting round for words to meet the situation. "That Perry Stanton, he promised..."

Teresa glanced at Ethan.

"Spiky hair, blond tips," he said.

"He promised he'd give me a lift back to Oxford," Isabella complained. "But Imo says he's gone."

Teresa smiled. "Never mind, you can help us clear up. Someone'll drive you back later."

"I would love to," said Isabella, her face creasing. "The thing is..." She looked down at her wrist. Her watch was still in the bathroom.

"Half nine," said Marcus.

"I have a conference call at twelve, a prelim interview for a job." She gestured hopelessly in the direction of the long-gone Perry Stanton. "He *knew*..."

"I'll run you back," said Ethan.

She closed her eyes in relief. "Thank you."

Teresa glanced over at Zack, who didn't dare look back at her. She had watched Isabella from the moment she entered the room. Her eyes had flitted from face to face, landing on Ethan at the critical moment. How could he have refused? How could Teresa leap in now and say she had a better idea? Why didn't Jenny run her home, or even Matt?

"I'll pop back upstairs and get dressed," Isabella whispered.

* * *

Forty minutes later, Teresa was struggling to keep her temper under control. The Others and their partners, plus Marcus and Jenny, had gathered in the hall to say goodbye to Isabella as if she were a cherished friend. Her thanks, directed mainly at Teresa, contained every superlative in the book. It had been a wonderful, awesome, fabulous party, it had been brilliant, amazing, incredible to meet them all. When she had finished gushing, Ethan led the way out to his car, carrying her bag.

"Who in their twenties goes to a party with an overnight bag?" Teresa asked quietly. "Complete with dressing gown, towel, range of makeup, change of clothes?"

Zack reached out to her. She shrugged him away.

"Back to work!"

-3-

As they drove out of Aston Merrick, Isabella looked around the car. "Very nice."

"Graduation present. Second-hand," said Ethan.

She laughed. "No need to apologise."

"Seatbelt?"

She pulled the strap across her body, tightening the close-fitting sweater even more.

"Do you remember when we first met?" she asked.

"A lecture in the Sheldonian. Some feminist saying men have been emasculated."

"You brought Gemma with you." She frowned. "She won't mind if you drive me back?"

He shrugged. "Isabella. Sounds exotic. Where are you from?"

"Argentina."

He turned to her, laughing in surprise.

"I thought you were going to say Chipping Camden or Hay-on-Wye. Where did the Spanish accent go?"

"Escuela de Inglaterra, in Buenos Aires. Your father spotted it, though. Got a fag anywhere?"

He nodded at the glove compartment, where she found a packet of Marlboro Lights, lit two and passed one to

Ethan.

"You should thank me for getting you out of the big clean-up," she said. "I'm not sure how pleased your mum was."

He smiled. "God help those who come between her and her plans. I take it there's no interview?"

"Was it that obvious?"

"So, Isabella from Argentina, linguist, liar… legs."

"My best feature, after the hair. Your grandfather thought so, anyway."

"Oh, Christ, he didn't come onto you, did he?"

"No, he just looked. And looked again." She smiled mischievously. "Does Gemma tell lies, make up interviews, wriggle out of chores? What *does* she do, by the way?"

"Teaches at a primary school."

Isabella laughed. "Of course she does. Kind, patient, dedicated."

"My parents love her. They think she's a steadying influence."

"You need one? That sounds promising."

***

He pulled up outside Isabella's house, at the end of a row of Edwardian monsters down an Oxford side road. Like its neighbours it was originally of red brick, but smoke and traffic had turned it brown. The windows, with their stone surrounds, were tall enough to walk through, though Ethan doubted any had been opened in years. The front garden boasted half a dozen forbidding fir trees that reached almost to the gutters.

"Who do you share with?" he asked.

"Three other postgrads; two lads, one girl, all of whom take life far too seriously."

She unbuckled her seatbelt and waited for him to make a suggestion. When it became clear that he was waiting too, she laughed.

"My bag is so, so heavy."

He heaved an exaggerated sigh. "I'll bring it up."

He followed her into the house. The tiled hallway was the kind people hurry through to get away from. Two bikes leant against the stairs, one with a basket on the front, the other a macho mountain bike with a helmet clipped to it.

Isabella's room was on the second floor and was twice the size of any that Ethan had ever rented while at Oxford, yet it felt cluttered. It was the clothes that made it so: rails and rails of them, together with two chests of drawers, too full to close. At least thirty pairs of shoes were lined up against a skirting board as if, at the sound of a starting pistol, they might race across the room. Not quite so easy to smile at was the dirty laundry, dumped in alcoves, waiting to be washed.

She flopped into a baggy, balding sofa that changed its shape at the slightest touch.

"So, what's your master's in?" asked Ethan.

She winced slightly. "I signed on for an MPhil, got fed up halfway through. Officially I'm under notice to quit, but I say they've taken my father's money, so what's their problem?"

At the mention of Isabella's father, Ethan looked round, expecting to see at least one photo of her parents. In his mind Dad would be a dead ringer for Juan Perón, with a harsh yet smiling face, Mum would be Evita in her prime. But there was no photo. There was only one picture, eight feet long and three feet high at least, fixed to the far wall. He went over to it. In the background was a snow-capped mountain range, presumably the Andes, set against an ice-blue sky. In the foreground was grassland, and a massive herd of cattle being moved across a river by mounted gauchos in high boots and wide-brimmed hats. She rose from the sofa and went over to stand beside him.

"Home," she said. "Estancia Sobromente, the most beautiful place in the world. Almost the size of Yosemite National Park."

"Is that big?"

"A million acres."

He laughed. "I thought Golden Meadow was big at ten. What's the river?"

"Rio Salado, runs straight off the Andes." She shivered. "Lifeblood of the ranch, my dad says, but always freezing. You must come and see it one day."

"Where did you actually live?"

She went over to a wooden desk and booted up her laptop. She clicked on a photo then turned and beckoned Ethan to join her.

"A village called San Antonio de los Aguilas. There... there's my parents' house."

She tapped a creamy white building with an adobe tiled roof, curved crenellations running along the top of the walls and a porch with a heavy, studded door. Set all around was an army of terracotta pots, five or six feet tall, spilling over with bright flowers and exotic grasses.

"You lived there all your life?"

She nodded. "I went to the village school for a while but then, like the other bright kids, off to Buenos Aires." She looked up at him and pulled a face.

"You weren't happy?" he said.

"I missed my horses, friends in the village, Mama, Papa."

They both knew what would happen next: they'd known ever since they got into his car at Golden Meadow. They would go to the bed in the corner and undress slowly or in a rage, depending on who made the first move. Meanwhile, holding off the moment with smalltalk was almost as charged as the sex would hopefully be. Ethan placed his hands underneath her breasts, moved aside the downpour of hair with his face and kissed her neck. Suddenly she turned and pushed him backwards towards the bed where she told him to strip off. As he did so, she looked him up and down as if approving the goods, then smiled and slid out of her own clothes.

***

They had left the cigarettes in the car and joked about who should go and fetch them. Isabella leaned up on one elbow and whispered that it didn't really matter, since before he left for home she intended to have him at least twice more, if only to prove that life was more fun without a steadying influence.

He raked his fingers through a handful of the hair and laughed. "In one word, tell me what I should see when I look at you, Miss..." He broke off. "Christ, I've known you for two years, but not your last name!"

"Morales."

He laughed. "As in morals?"

"That would be *moralidad*."

"One word."

She stretched up and bit him on the neck. "*Vampira*. Now tell me more about Gemma." He shifted where he lay. "Don't say she's a schoolmarm, even in bed. Does she mark you out of ten, write encouraging comments on the pillow?"

She settled her head on his chest and her hair cascaded over their bodies.

"We've been friends since we were six. We kind of lived in the same sentence, if you know what I mean. Bread and jam, needle and thread, Ethan and Gemma. Then the day we got our A level results we ended up in bed."

"What happened when you went to uni?"

"I had other girlfriends there, sure, just as she had blokes at college." He shrugged. "But come the holidays we always got back together."

"No questions asked?"

"None."

She smiled and leaned up on her forearm. "I've got a question. How are you going to explain to your mother why running me home took so long?"

"That jackknifed lorry just outside Thame?" he suggested. "Remember how we crawled for over an hour?"

She laughed. "More difficult is the love bite on your neck."

"I met this vampire..."

She pulled herself up his body, bared her teeth for a moment, and kissed him.

-4-

Teresa had always planned to move The Others into the London house, and when she finally named the day they gave her a standing ovation. It had been a difficult decision to make. It would mean that all four of her children had finally left Golden Meadow. Left home.

So far, Carla was the only one who had become anything like independent. She had worked for Marquis Auctions in Richmond since leaving university and lived in a small flat in Twickenham with a girl who led a suitably tidying-up, dishwashing, hoovering life.

Zack and Imogen had rooms in a house near Central School of Speech and Drama. They came home most weekends, usually bringing a crowd with them. Ethan had left home and returned. When he finished at Oxford he went straight to work for Jubilee Films, a production company owned by Adrian Stepley, who had been at school with Marcus. Ethan described his job as 'an assistant to an assistant of an assistant' in the making of a wartime drama documentary and, like Zack and Imogen, he preferred the comforts of Golden Meadow to the flophouse his workmates were renting.

Number 19 Ashbury Road was the house Teresa had

grown up in. It was a Victorian terraced affair in Acton – almost Chiswick, Marcus said, Chiswick being the English version of Hollywood Hills, with famous faces visible in its shops and cafés. When her mother died, Teresa found herself with a dilemma. To have sold the house would have felt disloyal to her parents, to have somehow denied their very existence. Her mother had been a teacher in Preston who came south for a better job and within a week met Teresa's father, a junior doctor at St. George's hospital. Five years later they bought 19 Ashbury Road and for the rest of their lives it was their pride and joy, proof that they had made it. But it lacked the fizz, the whirling emotions, the noisy intimacy that Golden Meadow was alive with. As a child Teresa had felt as if she and her parents went for days without seeing one another, each pursuing their own interests in the privacy of a far-flung room. Teresa's was in the attic conversion, so far away that, rather than call up three flights of stairs, her mother would buzz her on an intercom when dinner was ready. They would eat quietly and listen to the six o'clock news, perhaps *The Archers* afterwards. When it was over, her mother would return to her marking, her father to classical music on his stereo, and Teresa to her homework. Home life had a hair-tearing dullness to it, overlaid with a mystifying sadness.

Once rehearsals for *An Inspector Calls* were underway Teresa visited the house alone one evening, ostensibly to check that the carpet fitters had done a satisfactory job, in reality to close a curtain on her childhood. She barely recognised the place as she moved from room to room.

As she climbed the stairs to the attic she felt her pulse begin to race with regret, guilt, apprehension... such a cocktail of emotions that she could barely separate one from the other. She opened the door carefully and made her way through to her old bedroom. She ran her hand along the empty shelves, which thirty years ago had been crammed with soft toys, books, knick-knacks, all now boxed up and stored in Golden Meadow's loft. This room was where she had made the most momentous decision of her life.

One evening she had summoned her parents to the attic, to her domain, believing it would give her an advantage. Her mother was nervous, her father merely irritated at having been called away from Mahler's 5th on Radio Three.

"I'm moving in with my boyfriend," Teresa said.

The stillness which followed was broken by her father scratching his chin.

"Someone at the office?" he said, hopefully.

"No. He's not a lawyer, he's an actor."

Her mother was flabbergasted but soon composed herself, enough to nod at Teresa's abdomen and ask the obvious question,

"You're not…?"

"No!"

"And you'll be staying on at Pickett and Royle, finish your articles?" said her father. "I mean three years at uni and now…"

Teresa shook her head. "I'm giving up the law. It's no fun and it's making me very unhappy."

Her parents glanced at each other and her father eventually asked, "Well, can we at least meet him?"

"He has long hair," warned Teresa, singling out her father's main objection to young men.

Oddly enough, he laughed. Her mother followed suit.

And Teresa now laughed as she recalled the incident. She turned in a flash as she heard a delicate cough behind her.

Isabella was standing in the doorway. Teresa had never believed in blood running cold. How could it, unless you were dead? At which point it wouldn't run at all. But she did believe in fear masquerading as a lump of rock that drops into your stomach whenever you sense it. Isabella smiled and came forward as if greeting a friend she had known for years but had lost contact with. Before Teresa could prevent it, the two women were embracing.

"Teresa, how wonderful to see you," said Isabella.

Teresa took a step backwards. "What are you doing here?"

"Ethan and I are attending some alumni event at the Café Royal. He asked me to meet him here."

"Does he have a key?"

"I presume so. Oh, I see, you're wondering how I got in. The carpet layers were clearing up downstairs. I persuaded them I wasn't a burglar."

You mean you flashed everything you had at them, Teresa thought, and they fell for it. And Isabella certainly wasn't dressed for an evening at the Café Royal. The hair was huge and the blouse beneath the jacket too revealing, the makeup so provocative she looked more like an escort than a suitable companion for her son.

"So, you've had a good look round?"

"The house is just wonderful. You grew up here, Ethan tells me."

"When are you expecting him?"

Isabella took out her phone and held it up like a courtroom exhibit. "He's just texted to say he's been held up and will I meet him there."

"I'm leaving soon. I can give you a lift."

"Thanks, but it's out of your way. I'll call an Uber."

"Don't let me keep you."

"Oh, it doesn't start till seven."

"You're early, then."

"I'm early everywhere."

"Then be early at the Café Royal!"

Isabella smiled before stepping away and watching herself follow Teresa, down the stairs, out through the front door and into the street. It was suddenly dark, the middle of the night and cold enough for breath to hang in the air. Teresa turned into an alleyway and a moment later heard the footsteps behind her. She broke into a run but Isabella was younger, faster... more beautiful. She spun Teresa round and grabbed her by her throat, her white, sinewy, perfect throat. She squeezed and felt the bones crush in her hands, blood seep out from where her fingernails had pierced the skin. Teresa began to weaken, then to buckle as she struggled for breath. Isabella let go of her and she fell...

"'Bye," said Isabella with a smile, as she turned and left the attic.

What had that bloody girl wanted, Teresa wondered. Had the carpet layers really let her in? Had she picked the lock, or maybe...? She waited until she heard the front door close, took out her mobile and dialled Ethan's number. It went to message. Isabella had got to him first, no doubt.

-5-

The day of the Ashbury Road relaunch began badly for Marcus, thanks to a visit from the chair of the Aylesbury Archaeological Society. Marcus hadn't seen Colin Simpson approaching the house, otherwise he would have thrown himself to the floor and stayed put. Colin came to the window, cupped his hands to his forehead and peered in. Marcus looked up, their eyes met and the next forty minutes of his life went up in smoke.

"Need to chat about Bigg's Cave," Colin said.

Bigg's Cave was a tribute to Henry's ability to persuade an audience that everything that came out of his mouth was the truth. Over the last eighteen years a simple hole in the ground had been elevated in status to the dwelling of a guilt-ridden, regicidal signatory. When news spread that Marcus intended to fill it in and plant a mature oak tree there, the Archaeological Society obtained a temporary preservation order and began the task of proving the unprovable.

Marcus hurried to the front door, where Colin was already unlacing his muddy boots.

"Who are you today?" Colin asked, with his usual attempt at humour. "Inspector Goole, Richard Salter or that bloke in *Marco Polo*?"

Marcus settled in the captain's chair and left Colin standing. He was a scrawny creature who fiddled constantly with a curly beard whose purpose was to give his face much needed character. It was difficult to believe that he had once been a high-powered salesman for a drugs company.

"Bigg's Cave?" Marcus prompted.

"Just to say we've done a top-layer scour of the... a surface scrape of the, er..."

"Surface?" Marcus offered.

Colin nodded. "Most revealing."

He dug into a pocket and fished out two coins, a 10 pence and 5 pence, both from the 1980s.

"Colin, I've told you before, my father was the one who..."

"That's the contention we hope to disprove. We need your permission to dig down a further six inches."

"Why?"

"Because there is more to that hole than just, well, a ruddy great hole in the ground. The committee believes it was once inhabited, and to prove that requires more digging. You can't refuse, actually – the council's given us an extension."

Marcus laughed. "Can't refuse? That is my field!" He stopped as he heard himself being drawn into the esoteric world of trowels, hand rakes and elderly pensioners whose pleasure was in validating a harmless fantasy. It wasn't a million miles from his own line of work.

"How long will it take?"

"Into next spring I would say. Any hurry?"

"My oak tree."

Colin laughed. "You plan to live another hundred years

to see it grow?"

Marcus gave him his Richard Salter stare, the one he used when finally confronting the killer, rapist or trafficker.

"I intend to do a Capability Brown and plant a fully grown one. Go dig around in your hole, Colin, before I bury you in it."

***

When Marcus and Teresa arrived at Ashbury Road for the launch, the christening, the official opening – the event was gaining titles by the day – they found a surprisingly well-ordered house, although a mere week of The Others living there was hardly a test of time.

Being house mother was a role Carla relished; indeed, sometimes felt she'd been raised for. If she was going to take charge of her siblings, the place would run like clockwork. At the first sign of the 'creative chaos' her mother had relished at Golden Meadow, Carla would come down hard. In quiet moments images of hair in plug holes, unflushed toilets, pans left to soak overnight ran through her mind. There would be none of that. They would cook individually, unless otherwise arranged, and each would be responsible for clearing up after themselves. Finance? A weekly clan meeting would be held to work out contributions towards toilet rolls, kitchen towel, dishwasher tablets…

Matt embraced Marcus in a sumo hold and would have done the same to Teresa had she not complained of rheumatism in her left shoulder. Matt had a recipe to cure it, a concoction of herbs rubbed in and garnished with arnica seeds. With a leer he offered to apply it.

"Do shut up, darling," said Carla.

She knew what her father was thinking from the pasted smile on his face. He had never understood why his beautiful daughter had picked Matt from a crowd of admirers, most of whom would have jumped at the chance to be on her dance card, as it were. In time they might have presented a challenge to her, however, whereas Matt would remain highly biddable and slightly afraid of her in spite of being six inches taller than her. Ethan, Zack and Imogen had made a fair pretence of liking the man, even admiring him. He had grown up in a family without a penny to spare and he now owned a canal barge. It was moored in Paddington at the moment, though to avoid long-term charges he moved it up and down the Grand Union at regular intervals. He advertised himself as "a personal power coach". Whatever that was he seemed to earn a living wage from it. He also understood Thai takeaway menus.

Teresa had hoped to see Kieran Hart among those in the kitchen, but in the weeks since Imogen's birthday he had announced that he was off to South Africa to work as a junior registrar. He'd already been interviewed by the charity which owned the hospital and the signs were good, Imogen said. But who had taken his place in Imogen's affections? Her name was Anna Macey, tall and leggy, the latter encased in jeans that surely impeded the blood flow to her feet, Teresa thought. She had a rather lovely face, with an openness that many of Imogen's friends didn't possess. Her only immediate fault was in being a branch manager for Lamb and Cotter, the London estate agent.

Zack was there with the far distant Amy, and Marcus felt an immediate pang of guilt when he saw her. He had told fellow cast members that she had referred to the library as 'the room with all the books in it' and he now felt cruel for having done so. He leaned towards her and pecked her on the cheek, a gesture which stunned her with delight.

"No Ethan?" said Teresa.

Ethan, Ethan, always bloody Ethan, Carla thought. No wonder he was the problem child, and yet still they all favoured him. Not just his parents, but Zack and Imogen too. That was going to change. There would be no favourites under her stewardship of 19 Ashbury Road.

"He was in Oxford yesterday," Zack explained. "Hooking up with a friend doing a postgrad."

"But he's bringing Gemma?" Teresa asked casually.

"I think all that's cooling down, Mum."

Was that why Isabella had been casing the joint a week ago, Teresa wondered. She was planning to step into Gemma's shoes? Before she could sink too low at the possibility, Marcus said,

"Matt, if you'd be so kind, we'll order the Thai now, under your expert guidance."

-6-

That same evening, Isabella and Ethan went late-night shopping in Oxford. She had seen a pair of shoes she couldn't live without and Ethan had lent her the money to buy them. Afterwards, they made their way to a noisy, studenty café in Jericho, where coffee was served in cups the size of soup bowls. Isabella watched Ethan as he tackled a doorstep sandwich.

"Impressive," she said, thoughtfully. "No, not the sandwich. You and your balancing act. This is the fifth time we've spent the whole day together. How do you square that with Jubilee Films?"

He ran the back of his hand across his mouth and smiled. "Funny old business, film-making. They tolerate bad behaviour, so long as they know your father."

"Have you told Gemma about me?"

"Not yet." He winced slightly. "I'd like her departure from my life to be a gradual fade, not a sudden reveal."

Isabella laughed out loud. "What the fuck does that mean?"

"I guess I'm waiting. For her to meet someone who'll knock her dead."

"In the world of primary school education?" She shook

her head. "You can't just let it roll on."

"I think she knows."

"She *doesn't* know, because she doesn't *want* to know."

* * *

Back at Canterbury Road, Ethan collapsed onto the sofa, raising a cloud of fine dust, and for the umpteenth time in the last hour he checked his phone messages.

"You're expecting her to call?"

"Gemma? No. My mother. Or more likely Carla."

She sat beside him, looped her arms around his neck and whispered in his ear. "The other women in your life?"

He chuckled and told her about the Ashbury housewarming, which was taking place at that very moment. He was pleased to have missed it but offended that none of his family was bothered by his absence.

"You should have gone," she said. "You should have taken me."

"Yes, but not..."

She suddenly pinned him back in the sofa and stared at him. Her facial features seized up and the stillness of her eyes made them seem almost black.

"Maybe there's another reason you're putting it off," she said in a voice to match her face. "Are you scared of ditching the girl who steadies you? Or ashamed of the one who's taking her place?"

She leaned away from him and smiled.

"Your face," she said. "You were feart, admit it. Did you think I was going to smack you?" She went over to a pile of laundry, took a towel from it and threw it at him.

"Go and shower."

As she listened for the hot water to start thumping through the pipes in the wall, she cast her mind back to a school counsellor who had once asked her if she knew the difference between a plan and a strategy. A plan was a series of actions set in mental concrete and all too often predictable, she said. Strategies were pliable, open to change and sudden surprises. Those who used them were cunning, mercurial and dangerous.

She went over to Ethan's work satchel, unfastened the straps and made a mental note of where the contents were placed. His phone was in the front pocket, screen facing inwards. She took it out, unsurprised that the home page was a photo of Gemma – short blonde hair, perfect teeth, just a touch of cleavage to her River Island dress.

Isabella found her phone number, went out onto the landing and called her.

"Hi, babe," Gemma said, believing the caller was Ethan.

Isabella could picture her, hair tied back, lambswool cardigan, perhaps even a playground whistle still dangling from her neck.

"Gemma! It's Isabella Morales. We met at Imogen Lawlor's twenty-first?"

"Oh, hi!" said Gemma, in what sounded like genuine delight. "How are you?"

"Fine. Gemma, do you think we could meet up?"

"Well, super, yes."

"How about after work tomorrow, say four thirty-ish at Traders in Thame? It's about Ethan."

That wiped the smile out of Gemma's voice. "What

about him?"

"Nothing to worry about, really, it's just that... Can you make it?"

"Yeah, but..."

"Great!" Isabella turned to a nonexistent fellow student. "Sorry? I'll be there in a sec... Gemma, I have to run, I'll see you tomorrow, four thirty."

Back in her room she could hear the water still running off Ethan's body, slapping the shower tray as it fell. She cleared the recent calls list on his phone and returned it to his satchel, then slipped her hand into the main pocket and ran her fingers through the wealth of trophies to be taken. There were memory sticks, a pencil sharpener, an eraser, a metal bookmark, a tiny Swiss army knife. Pins and needles ran back and forth across her scalp as she took out the knife and held it tightly, as if trying to connect with its owner.

She carried it over to a chest of drawers and opened one. Behind the crushed underwear was her treasure trove. An antique walnut smoking box, the label had said when she bought it. She unlocked it, lifted the lid and slipped the knife inside.

* * *

Isabella arrived at Traders half an hour early. It was a trick an old tutor had confessed to using against his students: get there first and whoever you are meeting will feel uneasy for having kept you waiting. The place proclaimed its Tudor origins with low crooked beams, salvaged from a shipwreck in 1601, a wall plaque declared. The central beam dipped so much it had been padded and a warning sign attached advising customers to mind their heads.

Isabella chose a central table, itself a relic from a distant age. Over at the bar the staff were taking advantage of the afternoon lull and it was five minutes before a young waiter came over to her. He gave her an impersonal smile, more duty than pleasure, and asked what he could get her. She looked at the name tag on his T-shirt.

"I'll have a latte, Donny. And a caramel slice."

"No problem."

He went back to the main counter and asked the girl behind it to make the coffee. Isabella watched him over the top of her iPhone. He was pretty: silky black hair cut just long enough. Tanned skin, almost the colour of the latte she had ordered, and smooth for his age, free of scars where spots might once have been. He was laughing with a couple of girls who probably felt the same way she did about him. But he was dawdling. Her coffee had been made, the caramel slice set down on a plate, but he was still talking, flirting...

She glanced round the restaurant. Four couples, middle-aged shoppers who offered no distraction to ease her boredom while she waited for Gemma to arrive. There were no assignations afoot, no conspiracies being shaped, no crimes being planned. She reached into her bag and felt for her door key. With the square-cut corner of it she began to carve her initials on the leg of the table. *I.M.*

Gemma arrived on the dot of 4:30 and, on seeing her, the waiter's manner changed from casual disinterest to nervous delight as he took her anorak and bike helmet from her. She was exactly as Isabella remembered, dressed in a knee-length skirt, cardigan and the sensible shoes of her profession. Isabella rose to greet her and the two women embraced. Behind Gemma, Donny had arrived with the coffee and cake.

"Just put it down," said Isabella.

He did so and immediately turned his attention to Gemma. "What can I get you, Miss Blake?"

"Cappuccino, please."

"No cake today?"

"No thanks."

She sat down and between the three of them they settled the rickety table.

"Busy day?" Gemma asked Isabella.

"I've been chairing a forum on maritime law, about which nobody knew a thing. Especially me, so it became a bit of a dogfight. How was *your* day?"

"Kids of seven and eight, you're up on the ceiling one minute, down on the floor the next, but..."

"Somewhere in between it's worth it?"

"Oh, yes. Isabella, why did you...?"

Isabella was employing another trick the tutor had shared with her. Never let the person you're trying to get the better of finish a sentence. It pares down their confidence, gives them a sense that what they're trying to say isn't worth hearing. She leaned across the table and lowered her voice to a dramatic whisper.

"Gemma, I am really sorry. He still hasn't told you, has he?"

Gemma laughed. "Told me what?"

Isabella closed her eyes and sat back in the chair, struggling to compose herself. She gentled her voice, one caring woman to another.

"He promised me he would, promised me a *week* ago."

"You've been seeing each other?"

The waiter brought Gemma's coffee, placed it in front of her and smiled.

"How are you, Donny?"

"Oh, great, yes, great," he answered. "Yes, thanks."

"I'm pleased to hear that."

He hurried away, more in love than ever.

Isabella wondered if she had slightly misread her adversary. She'd assumed that, with her being a demure teacher, news of her unfaithful boyfriend would have her reaching for an embroidered hankie to wipe away tears. Instead, Gemma said,

"What a feeble bastard. I knew something wasn't right, but..."

"I'm sorry."

"It isn't your fault. I just wonder why he didn't tell me." She gazed at Isabella, hoping she might have a suggestion beyond the caring smile.

"I'd like to think he was afraid of hurting you. You're right, though, it is cowardly. You say you knew things weren't right. Did he ever give you a hint?"

Gemma sipped the froth from her cappuccino. "If he did I didn't notice. Maybe I should have done."

What on earth did the young waiter see in this plain-faced, pathetic martyr, Isabella wondered.

She stepped aside from the moment and watched herself rise from the table. She leaned forward, clenched her fist and drove it into Gemma's face. The blood burst from her nose and lips as she fell backwards in her chair. The room shuddered as her head hit the flagstone floor. She lay there, mouth open, the perfect teeth shining scarlet and white...

Isabella sighed with friendly irritation. "There you go, blaming yourself instead of him. He didn't mention anything about..." She stopped herself. "Here, try some of this slice, let's both have a sugar rush!"

"You sound like you know more than you're telling me."

Isabella drummed her fingers on the table, annoyed with herself. "Me and my big mouth," she hissed. "No, no, you've every right to know, because it's nothing you've done. He told me that when he was with you he just couldn't get Teresa out of his head. His actual words?" She lowered her eyes. "Fucking you was like fucking a younger version of his mother."

Gemma grimaced and a moment later her eyes began to redden, not with distress but with anger. Self-pity or jealousy had never been emotions she gave in to. If she had any concerns at all they were for Ethan, who had always been easy prey, a perfect sucker for flattery.

"Are you okay?" asked Isabella.

"Fine."

"I'll walk you to your... to your bike?" She smiled. "That sounds so quaint. So Miss Marple."

They left Traders together, with Isabella paying the bill and the waiter helping Gemma on with her anorak; so attentive, so smitten by the willowy blonde, though uncertain what to make of her reddened eyes.

When they reached Gemma's bike, Isabella took her by the arm.

"Promise me you'll be alright," she said.

Gemma nodded, unlocked the security chain on her bike and fastened her helmet. What would she do now,

Isabella wondered. Confront Ethan? Would he deny he'd said such a thing about his mother? Would he question Isabella? She smiled and waved as Gemma pedalled away.

-7-

The days leading up to a first-night performance had always been a mystifying business for The Others. Marcus would wander round the golden meadow mumbling lines, eyebrows squeezed together in agony. All of a sudden he would reach for a copy of the script he always carried in his pocket, refer to the misremembered line, curse and carry on. At other points he would address the air, demanding to know why he had ever agreed to take the job in the first place, asking the children, himself and finally Teresa the same barmy question.

By their early teens The Others had begun to mock him. Didn't he know by now that once the first-night show was over and the air-kissing, the champagne back-slapping had begun, he would wonder why he'd dreaded the days leading up to that first night?

The run up to *An Inspector Calls* followed the same pattern. Marcus slumped over the kitchen table one evening and waited for Teresa to ask him what was wrong. A horrendous run-through had brought out the worst in everyone, he said, especially the director Charlie Burgoyne who, incidentally, was becoming more explosive, more unreasonable and fatter by the day. He reached down to

Troilus and Cressida.

"Be ready, guys, it's going to be a dog's breakfast."

Troilus and Cressida were Golden Retrievers. It had been another parental gaffe allowing the children to name them, and even though they were known as Troy and Cress, the pretentiousness of giving them Shakespearian names in the first place lingered.

"I'm sure it'll work out fine," Teresa said.

"Why do you always say that?" he asked, tetchily.

She couldn't recall the last time she *had* said it, but that was beside the point.

"Because it always does. It's just been a bad day at the office."

"Your platitudes are as bad as Jack Priestley's. Today showed every boil and blister in the bloody play. He was a humourless, simplistic, moralising old sod with a knack for breezeblock dialogue."

She tried again. "I thought you'd decided to give Goole a tongue-in-cheek attitude, not the self-righteous copper nemesis thing."

"*There's* an example of him writing by numbers. Goole. Sounds like ghoul; the graveyard monster feasting on dead bodies. And I'm sick of bloody policemen. I've played so many in my time, it's a wonder I don't stop and search people in the street."

"Marcus."

"What?"

"Enough."

He paused before sliding back the chair and rising. Troy, Cress and Teresa stared at him until he turned and walked out.

"Supper in half an hour!" she called after him.

He went to his office. It was a room off the hall and must have been built as a cloakroom by Mr Tweak, the aspirant gentleman farmer of the early seventeen hundreds. There would have been carriages arriving at the door, ladies in scuttle-shaped bonnets and high-necked cloaks being helped down steps by men in top hats with silver-handled canes. Or had he mixed up his styles and eras? He smiled, recalling classic dramas he'd been in where viewers had tweeted their hobby-horse niggles about the wrong shaped beard, wrong parasol, wrong lavatory seat. However, no one ever said that, far from being dazzling and straight, the hero or heroine's teeth should be rotten or plain missing, with hideous breath to match. The truth is one thing, but you have to lie about it sometimes.

A photo of The Others on his desk stopped his mind racing. It was a snap taken just before Carla's twenty-first. Inset was a smaller photo from ten years earlier, with the children posing in the same positions. All four looked as if they could see right through him.

He opened up his laptop, and as the white apple gave way to a wedding photo, him and Teresa outside the register office in Brixton, he opened his email. His agent handled most of his fan mail and only a few friends knew his personal address. Even so, some trashcan fodder had found its way to him. One of them stood out. It was from somebody called Juan Morales. The strap heading was a long photo, a mountain range in the background, cattle crossing a river in the foreground and the words 'Estancia Sobromente' in a stark typeface with a web address below it. The email ran:

Estimado Señor Lawlor
Allow me to send to you my every good wish for the production of *An Inspector Calls*.
It may surprise you that I know of it 7,000 miles away in Argentina! My daughter Isabella is a close companion of your son Ethan.
Once again, please accept my best wishes for a successful production.
Respetuosamente
Juan Morales

He leaned back in his chair. There was something vaguely sinister about the message, a between-the-lines attempt by the sender to sidle up, to ingratiate himself. Marcus had received many a dodgy tweet about past performances, but they had all been somehow anonymous. He took his laptop through to the kitchen.

Teresa was closing the Aga on a dish of cauliflower cheese and bacon.

"What is it?" she asked immediately.

"I've had an email from the father of one of Ethan's friends. That girl with all the hair. Isabella. It's not just that he's got my address from somewhere, but he's five days too early. I mean protocol, you don't start sending first-night messages a week in advance..." He stopped. "Oh, for pity's sake, what does it matter! Hey, I'm sorry for moaning and groaning when I came home. I'm sure you're right. I'll be brilliant."

Teresa clicked the link to the Estancia Sobromente website. Across the top was the same long photo that headed the email. Down either side of the homepage were pictures of never-ending grass, cattle galore, gauchos, all under a blazing sun.

"The time stamp, 9:15 this morning. Is that when it was sent, or when you received it?"

He shrugged. "You're asking *me* a technical question?"

Marcus had by now transferred his attention to the cauliflower cheese and put two plates in to warm. Teresa googled the time difference between London and Buenos Aires and smiled. "They're four hours behind us, which means he wrote this at five this morning. An early riser?"

"Shall I answer him?"

She thought for a moment. "Yes, but make it simple. Thanks for your kind wishes, M.L."

Marcus suddenly startled and cupped a hand to his ear. "You hear that?"

She listened intently, perhaps for the dogs wrestling on the hearthrug in the living room. "What?" she eventually asked.

"That deathly hush. That's how it'll be forever now."

She patted his arm. "Welcome to middle age, my love, at long last. When you feel a crisis coming on, let me know. I'd like to be there when you buy the Harley-Davidson."

* * *

The day *An Inspector Calls* opened at the Cavendish Theatre Marcus rose in what Teresa had always considered to be an altered state. It was most noticeable over breakfast, which on first-night mornings was always bacon and eggs followed by two cups of coffee. He would then butter his toast and spread marmalade with such precision, such delicacy, that she wondered if the change was a matter of rising blood sugar. They never discussed it, so she could never put the theory to the test any more than Marcus could ever introduce her to the real reason for his newfound confidence: Jonas Kemble. Teresa simply thanked God for the change in him and left well alone. Yesterday, having moaned and groaned about the forthcoming end of his career, today he was full of the confidence, even the arrogance which an actor requires to do the job.

***

Later on that day Teresa drove them to 19 Ashbury Road, which seemed to freeze at their approach. No rogue lights were burning, the curtains were all drawn, even tomorrow's bins had been lined up on the pavement. How long would that good order last, Teresa wondered fleetingly. Marcus phoned for an Uber and they exchanged their usual adieu.

"Be wonderful," Teresa said.

He smiled. "If you insist."

They kissed briefly and off he went. She paused to savour the moment. This must be how a bird feels when it's released back into the wild, she thought. She turned and was about to ring the bell when Carla opened the door six inches.

"Has he gone?" she asked cautiously.

"Yes."

"Everything okay?"

"Fine. Can I come in?"

"Sorry, sorry."

Carla stepped back and Teresa entered.

Being greeted by The Others with delight whenever she appeared was one of Teresa's few vanities. This afternoon, however, spoiling the effect was the dormouse Miss Twinkletail, seated at the kitchen table. She'd been crying. Zack signalled his mother not to concern herself, but she ignored him.

"Whatever's the matter?" she asked Amy, hoping Zack hadn't chosen today of all days to move on to pastures new.

"Ethan's been telling me about Marcus's pain before a first night," Amy said.

Teresa looked at Ethan disapprovingly, knowing the pleasure he took from winding people up.

"I feel for him," Amy went on in a blubbery whisper.

She reached for another tissue and dabbed at a fresh outbreak of tears.

Teresa slipped off her coat and folded it over a chair. "Show of hands, all the actors in the room," she said.

Imogen, Zack and Amy responded instantly.

"It is pure affectation," said Teresa. "Marcus Lawlor is no more afraid that he'll give a bad performance than I am of breathing in and out. Don't be fooled. And do *not* imitate."

"Grandad's just the same," said Ethan.

Teresa laughed. "Father and son are two of the most self-assured... heavens, I nearly said self-*possessed*... men I know. Hopefully, the other two are standing here in this kitchen. Yes, and you too, Imo." She took a deep breath and turned to Carla. "How's the house going?"

"Brilliant!"

"Brilliant-ly," said Zack.

"*That's* the only thing we're sick of," said Ethan, drawing his brother towards him with one arm.

"I am brilliant. I act brilliant-ly," said Zack. "Adjective, adverb. The house is going brilliant-ly."

"Was he always this pedantic?" Carla asked her mother.

Teresa smiled. "I'd say you've… bought it on yourselves."

"Don't encourage him," said Carla.

Imogen went right up to Zack and flicked his chin. "And wait till he starts on 'neither' replacing 'nor' or his latest 'should of' versus 'should have'."

Amy was glancing from face to face, clearly distressed by the passion they were showing over the mere corruption of language.

"My love, they're playing," said Teresa, reassuringly. "It may sound rough, but it's the way they've always been."

The conversation moved on by unfathomable means to the man next door and whether he had two wives, or one of the women had a husband and a female civil partner. At hawklike speed they swooped and soared over the complications, the legalities, the day-to-day living arrangements of those at number 21. They progressed from street gossip to current affairs via past memories and future plans in a seamless flow. Amy made to join in at one stage, but quickly abandoned the attempt. Teresa knew better than to even try.

The free-for-all was halted by the first few chimes of Big Ben – the doorbell.

Carla hurried to answer it and the electricity in the room followed her out and didn't return. Matt entered in his usual manner, as if those already there would stagger at the raw power he exuded. Every time Teresa saw him she hoped he would have turned into a suave, handsome intellectual, but there he was, as inconsequential as ever.

"How's the rheumatism?" he asked.

She winced. "Worse."

Instead of crushing her in a bear hug, he pecked her on the cheek.

He had brought Anna Macey with him, thereby putting paid to Teresa's secret hope that Kieran Hart had failed to get the job in South Africa and elbowed his way back into Imogen's life. That ship had sailed, quite literally.

"I'm going upstairs to change," said Carla. "I suggest everyone else does the same. Except you, Teresa. You look gorgeous."

"I second that," said Matt.

One day, Zack thought, I will stick that man's dick in a door jamb and slam it.

Teresa beckoned to Ethan just before he left the room. He knew the question she was going to ask, she knew the answer he would give.

"Gemma's meeting us at the theatre, then?"

"Gemma isn't coming," he said, gently.

"Oh, that's a shame."

"But Isabella is. Remember Isabella?"

For the next hour or more Teresa's hopes rose and fell as Isabella failed to materialise while Ethan assured them she would soon be there. When the time came to leave, still with no sign of her, they went out onto the pavement in Ashbury Road to meet the Uber that would take them to the theatre. As it drew up to the kerb, so too did a black cab from which Isabella emerged, cool as you please. She reached into her shoulder bag, apparently searching for her purse, until Ethan took the hint and hurried over to pay the driver.

"Am I late?" she said. "I am so, so sorry. One hell of a day."

Ethan slid back the door of the people carrier and hustled them into it.

At least one of Teresa's fears had been groundless and he sighed inwardly with relief. Isabella was dressed – almost underdressed – in a grey, cottony overcoat and sensible, low-heeled shoes.

Once they were on the move, Ethan asked her, "Your hellish day?"

"You remember Tom Morley?"

"History at Keble." He turned to The Others. "If you eat Brussels sprouts at Christmas, the chances are his dad grew them."

"Sounds a real gas," said Zack.

"You mustn't make fun," said Isabella, anxiously. "I met him for lunch today in Blackwell's and he had some kind of seizure. Then I remembered he's got this nut allergy thing. I called an ambulance and he was hauled off to the Radcliffe. I mean, obviously I stayed with him till he came round."

"Will he be alright?" asked Amy.

"Well, yes, but if I hadn't..."

Teresa smiled. "If you hadn't acted the way you did he might have died?"

"It sounds dramatic, I know, but..."

Could no one else see it, Teresa wanted to ask. The story of a nut allergy had a dramatic hollowness, but they all seemed to believe it. Captive audience. Easy enough to check Tom Morley's condition, of course, but who would bother? And even if Isabella was caught in a lie would it faze her? Unlikely. Would it bother the other passengers in the vehicle? No, they would laugh at it. Even so, a lie is a lie is a lie. It isn't a fantasy or an embellishment, it's the downright opposite of the truth. Tell one lie and you will tell a thousand. Some of them will not be so harmless.

***

The foyer at the Cavendish Theatre was already busy when they arrived and, in spite of being the lead actor's wife, Teresa insisted on her party joining the cloakroom queue of 'real' people. Those lovingly taught good manners were tossed aside when Henry descended on them with his new wife.

"My darlings," he said, taking Teresa by the shoulders and kissing her on the cheek.

The Others swarmed round him as they had always done, and the sea of people within twenty feet instantly realised who this must be – the family of Sir Henry Lawlor – and stood back to allow them through. The cloakroom attendant came out from behind the counter to take their coats and, in spite of her embarrassment, Teresa surveyed her children with pride. The boys were looking superb in evening suits, bowties, pressed shirts. Who had done the ironing, she wondered. Carla, of course, who also looked pretty fetching, the better for having shed a few pounds. Imogen looked as beautiful as ever. Anna was smart, if a touch severe. Amy Wotsit was... Teresa hated herself for thinking it... barely noticeable.

"Where's Isabella?" she suddenly asked.

Imogen nodded towards the ladies toilet in time for them to see Isabella emerge. She was carrying the grey overcoat as if it were a wet towel she was about to drop. The dress it had been covering up was shimmering red, the hem as high as it could go, the neckline just about clinging to the rim of her bra. She had changed into a pair of red stilettos, the heels of which were almost as high as the shoes were long. She handed her coat and shoulder bag to the attendant and shook the mass of hair to draw attention to herself. She went over to Henry and smiled up at him, certain he would recognise her. He took her hand and leaned forward to kiss it, a paramour from a bygone age. A camera flashed, then another, then another, and people began to ask each other who she was. Henry wasn't sure either, but pretended otherwise before turning away to a skeletal, time-ravaged actress who had approached him. They embraced in the manner of true friends. No cameras flashed, no one bothered to ask who she was. They knew.

Having taken their seats, five or six rows back in the centre of the stalls, Jenny touched Teresa on the arm. "Who the fuck does that little bitch think she is?" she hissed.

It was the first time Teresa had heard Jenny swear, and for some odd reason it had brought her to life.

"My mother would've said she's no better than she ought to be," said Teresa. "It sounds more vicious in a Lancashire accent."

The lights dimmed and the curtain rose. During the first ten minutes of the play Teresa sensed the first-nighters beginning to twitch at the moralising self-congratulation of the family on stage. Then Marcus entered and an indefinable charge ran through cast and audience alike.

For Teresa there had always been something disturbing about watching him pretend to be someone else. The man on stage was the same one she had shared her life with for thirty years, loving, handsome, gentle, yet she had often sensed a dark, unreachable otherness to him. It wasn't the simple bravado most actors use to fool their audience. It was a genuine air of menace. Was it there in his Inspector Goole, she wondered. Yes, it was, even though he was playing a mouthpiece, a means of giving a bunch of despicables their comeuppance and then sparing them by revealing that his character didn't exist. His Goole was subversive, scary, dangerous, all achieved with a smile in his voice as he relished the task of tearing the Birling family to shreds.

-8-

When the play was over, Teresa and her party waited in the foyer, tuning into snippets from the audience. By the sound of it they had loved every moment. One particular critic told her, in his custard voice, how breathtaking she looked, how the children had blossomed, and how insightful Marcus's performance had been. More trendy profiler than Priestley prig, he said, no doubt wondering how to fit such a mouthful into his review.

For the next half-hour the usual theatrical courtesies were observed, with a trip to Marcus's dressing room where the Lawlors congratulated everyone in sight on a 'superb, wonderful, fabulous' production. When the orgy of praise began to break up and visitors had been kissed and better kissed, James Gray, who had played Arthur Birling 'superbly, brilliantly and powerfully', knocked on Marcus's door to say there was a fleet of people carriers outside the... even he, a late middle-aged, unadventurous man, paused and drew breath at Isabella's dress... outside the stage door waiting to take everyone to Chelsea for the first-night celebration.

The party was being held at Prospero's, on the eighth floor of a steel and glass deformity. Marcus remembered it for its height above sea level. Last time he was there, he had left feeling queasy and on the journey home Teresa had pulled onto the hard shoulder of the M40 so that he could be sick. It was one of his most convincing performances in front of a camera, he insisted. The memory of it faded as the invitees applauded his entrance.

When the applause died down, Marcus thanked everyone, including Teresa, for an outstanding production. It was all down to team effort and the imagination of the director, he said, and led a round of applause for Charles Burgoyne, who nodded graciously. Within minutes the whole room was afloat on a sea of champagne, picking at the flotsam of canapés.

Two things had annoyed Teresa. The first was Henry, and it wasn't really his fault. During the interval he had been fawned over by several journalists, and here in Prospero's a young female critic was asking how he'd felt about his own appearance in *An Inspector Calls*, fifty years ago.

He smiled at her. "You certainly know how to wound a chap. Is it really half a century?"

"You played Eric," she said.

He turned to a cluster of admirers. "Next you'll tell me that Ralph Richardson played Birling."

"Well, he did."

"I'm teasing you, my dear."

She wanted to ask more, but he pointed at the young actor who had played Eric that evening. "That boy made a fine job of it. I must go and congratulate him. Excuse me."

That 'boy', Richard Damon, was deep in conversation with the other thing that had irritated Teresa. Isabella.

"That bloody dress is barely naked to the visible eye,"

said Carla, turning to her mother. "She's sticking her tits in that poor sod's face, but if he stares at them she'll call him a perv, if he doesn't she'll be offended. A real catch-36C situation."

She giggled, looked down at her glass and handed it to her mother.

Teresa drifted over to the side of the room. Her feet were killing her, thanks to a pair of shoes she intended to bin the moment they arrived home. Marcus approached, glass in hand, and sat beside her. It was the first time they'd spoken privately since he'd come off stage.

"What did you think?" he asked quietly.

"Do you really need to ask?"

He was about to fish for a fuller compliment when he caught sight of his father heading towards him. For a moment Jonas Kemble deserted him. He was no longer the star who had just given a brilliant performance, but the fearful boy awaiting his father's approbation. He stood up quickly.

"You were excellent," said Henry, then gestured to himself, top to toe. "Then why wouldn't you be? By the way, I was talking to Jim Gray. I didn't know his father had succumbed to the bane of my generation, losing his marbles." He turned to Teresa. "Hamilton Gray was Laertes to my Hamlet. He's in Bungay Hall, the retirement home for stricken actors. Marcus, would you be kind enough to drive me down to see him one day?"

"Certainly. And thanks, Dad."

Across the room, Isabella had deserted Richard Damon in favour of the gawky Jane Sillitoe, who had played the cheated-on Sheila Birling.

"I thought you were *awesome*," Isabella said.

"How kind of you," said Jane, extending a hand. "I'm sorry, I don't think we've..."

"I'm a friend of the Lawlors. Isabella Morales."

Jane paused to make sense of the hair, the dress, the shoes. "Isabella Morales," she said, smiling. "What a simply *fabulous* name."

Jane was distracted by another admirer, and Isabella pulled Ethan away from a group of elderly actresses.

"So, when are you going to do it?" she whispered.

"I hadn't quite..."

"You're having second thoughts?"

He glanced over at his parents and waved at them. "It just seems a bit of an ambush."

"You were the one who suggested it. You want *me* to ask them?"

"No, no."

She straightened his bowtie. "I'm doing a Jenny Ballard on you. Sorry."

"The old man'll be fine," he said. "Teresa's another matter."

Isabella smiled. "Believe me, she'll do anything to keep you close. She's scared that I'll haul you off into the night."

She held her smile to assure him it was a joke. He took her hand.

A group of flatterers had descended on Marcus, and Ethan hovered with Isabella at the edge of them. As a waiter topped up their glasses, Ethan raised a hand. "Kudos on the performance, Dad. Brilliant!"

Isabella fluttered her hand, as if to calm her racing heart. "I was so... *so*... I mean, like... wow!"

Marcus smiled. "I take it you liked it as well. And Isabella, my darling, you look absolutely divine."

Christ, he thought, it was ages since he'd used that vacuous luvvy line. Was it the booze or a side-effect of the flattery talking? Regardless, he sealed the compliment with a kiss on her cheek.

"Mum, Dad, Isabella's got some good news!"

"Tell us," said Marcus. He hoped it wouldn't take long. He had spotted the producer of *Salter's Edge* and his minuscule wife heading towards them.

"She's applied for a job with M & S. Their European Development arm. They've given it to her!"

"Well done!" Marcus signalled for the *Salter's Edge* producer to approach.

"Four minutes by Crossrail to Paddington, two minute walk station to office. We wondered if you and Mum had plans for those attic rooms?"

"You mean, can Isabella have them? What a good idea. Talk it over with your mother. Excuse me."

He turned away from them and fell on the compliments of the pocket-sized wife. Ethan sat down beside Teresa and pecked her on the cheek. "What do you reckon?"

The condemned shoes pinched her again, but at least the pain had sharpened her senses. "We're not really the people to ask," she said.

He laughed. "Who else, then?"

"Carla, Zack, Imogen? If they don't fancy the idea, what then?"

"We'll look for a flat somewhere, I suppose," Isabella said, sadly. "We were going to do that anyway."

"And then you remembered the attic."

"Ethan did."

"Is that why you went to see it the other day?"

Isabella smiled, coyly. Ethan closed his eyes and rubbed them with the heels of his hands, suddenly feeling ashamed. He had deliberately caught his father off guard on a night when he would say yes to anything. He had allowed Isabella to make a veiled threat to his mother. Teresa had taken it badly. When he opened his eyes again, she was staring at him.

"Clan meeting," she said. "See what everyone else says."

* * *

The next morning, and in spite of the favourable reaction to *An Inspector Calls*, Marcus indulged one of his favourite eccentricities. In a blue sky of five-star reviews there was a single wisp of cloud in the shape of *The Post* critic's lukewarm reaction and Marcus referred to it on an almost hourly basis. What a useless bastard that James Barrington was. What did he know about drama anyway? Teresa hoped the clan meeting would provide a distraction, something for her husband to think about other than himself.

Unfortunately, the clan meeting three days later rapidly deteriorated into a scrappy affair, largely because it took place in the Golden Meadow kitchen, not in the library under the watchful eye of Jane Austen and her companions. There was no motion formally presented for discussion – there seldom was – and on this occasion the question was hardly a question at all.

"Do we mind Isabella moving into Ashbury Road?"

Teresa asked from the head of the table.

There was an exchange of glances that asked why this hadn't been dealt with on Zoom to save them all hacking down to the country. The main voice of dissent was Carla's.

"Let me get this right," she said in a manner that suggested everyone else had got it wrong. "You refurbish the house you grew up in for us four to live in, and because there are two spare rooms in the attic, Ethan suggests we bring a cuckoo into the nest?"

Ethan sniggered. "Cuckoo! She'll love that."

"Suppose I'd asked if Matt could take the room?"

"He wouldn't want it."

Carla turned to Zack. "Okay, then, how about Amy?"

"I wouldn't want her that near."

Carla sighed irritably. "Imo, what's your excuse?"

"Anna? Christ, I've only known her for two weeks."

Carla pointed at Ethan. "*He*'s only known Isabella for a couple of months."

"Wrong. I've known her for two years."

They all knew why Carla didn't want another female in the house. At worst she would be a challenge to her role as house mother, at best another attitude for her to manage.

"Just tell me how it'll work," she said to Ethan. "You'll live in your room, she'll be the ghost in the attic, never seen, never heard, apart from the odd creak on the stairs?"

Marcus asked them to avoid hackneyed analogies. If Isabella was going to take the top rooms, what difference would it make to anyone? Carla dropped the passive tone from her aggression.

"Dad, be your bloody age! 'We're just good friends.' Is that the line you're falling for?"

"So what?" Ethan said.

"I think we have a right to know just where she fits into your life," said Teresa.

Ethan drummed his fingers on the table. Teresa could hear as well as see that he'd started biting his nails again. True, he was under stress at Jubilee Films, working long hours in far-flung places. As far-flung as Oxford, apparently. Ethan sat back and thought for a moment, emerging in an altogether different frame of mind.

"We just hit it off. I can't predict where we'll be in a year's time and I know it sounds like something Dad would say, but I can have a proper conversation with her. Gemma just soaked it all up."

Zack the peacemaker stepped in. "Is this such a big deal, guys? If things work out, then fine. If they don't, she can leave."

"The boy talks sense after all," said Imogen. "Can we vote and get back to our lives?"

A vote wasn't really necessary, but they took one all the same. Teresa abstained and everyone else but Carla was in favour of Isabella moving in. She scraped back her chair, stood up and left the room in a huff. A minute later they heard gravel fly and her car screech off down the drive. Always chary about upsetting Carla, the other three fell into a sombre mood and left shortly afterwards, Zack and Imogen together, Ethan on his own, heading for Oxford with the good news.

"Why did you agree to her moving in?" asked Teresa once she and Marcus were alone.

"Did I?"

"The opening night."

"Ah, yes. Little buggers caught me off guard."

"You could've said no at the meeting."

"Well, why did you abstain?" He stopped himself and softened. "Terri, we're talking about a girl moving in to Ashbury Road, not whether to bring back hanging."

"You like her, then?"

"Is there any reason not to?"

She turned away, her fists clenched. "Can't you see beyond the plunging neckline, the dresses up to her fanny, the simpering smiles? She's dangerous."

He shrugged, puzzled by her sudden ferocity. "What I *can* see is you fretting over your favourite child."

She stared at him. It wasn't the first time he'd accused her of cosseting Ethan. She could stay and fight with him, and probably win, or give him a shrivelling look and walk out. She settled for the latter.

-9-

Zack handed his documents to the manager of Proustie Van Hire, a man with an overhanging belly and a moustache you could swing on. The card reader bit down on his credit card and Zack knew he would never see the ninety-five quid again. When had Ethan ever paid him back?

As he drove to Oxford he tried to fend off more doubts, the main one being why Ethan wasn't with him. Had he really been called into Jubilee Films that morning for some catchup shots, so he couldn't drive to Oxford to pick up Isabella's stuff? Or had he become the family scrounger? He chuckled affectionately. What a guy Ethan was! All his girlfriends were great-looking, smart, sexy and well up for it. And this time he'd found someone whose family was loaded. A cattle baron. Amy's dad worked for a local builder in Herne Bay, while her mum was a care worker.

He approached Oxford via Summertown and turned into Canterbury Road. There was a space right outside Isabella's house, a large enough gap in the tapeworm of studenty cars lined up nose to tail. He parked and went to the front door, which was ajar.

"There's three flights of stairs," Ethan had said. "Sorry, bruv. Be thankful you're carrying stuff down, not up."

"Until we get to Ashbury."

"I'll be home by then, Imo and Carla too." He had laid a hand on Zack's shoulder. "I love you for this."

Zack heard raised voices coming from the second floor, and paused on the stairs. An argument was heating up, three voices bullying a fourth who was pleading with her attackers.

"I'm sorry, guys, but my allowance hasn't come through."

"That's what you said last month, Bella," a harsh male voice complained.

Zack took the rest of the stairs two at a time.

"The time before that, your dad transferred it to the wrong account!" added a girl.

"He did! He's old, he forgets, but it will come and then every penny I owe..."

Zack opened the door and strode into the room. Two men and one woman had Isabella cornered.

"Problem?" he asked, forcefully.

Isabella hurried to his side and clung to him as he put an arm round her shoulders. The hair was tied up in a scarf that stretched across her forehead, leaving only her face on show. It was an odd moment to notice such a thing but something Amy had said was right: the face would not be worth looking at but for the hair.

The two men in the room began sizing up Zack for trouble, leaning towards caution, but the girl wasn't so bothered. She was mid-twenties, with crinkly auburn hair and a thin face spattered with freckles. Pretty, Zack thought, despite the hacksaw nose. Student wear. Denim jeans, sweater.

"Who are you?" she asked, as he looked her over.

"Zack Lawlor. What's your beef with my friend?"

"You don't understand," said the fitter of the two men.

He was Zack's age and probably the owner of the mountain bike down in the hall, since the other guy was nerdy skin and bone.

"Not that it's any of your business, but she owes us rent and utilities," said the nerd. "£2742·00 to be precise."

Zack looked down at Isabella, who sobbed into his shoulder, dampening his favourite leather jacket.

"I've said I'll get it to them when my allowance comes through."

She stepped out of the moment and watched herself become the wispy, fearful victim of evil designs. Zack understood immediately. In a surge of vengeful anger he grabbed her abuser's arm, wrenched it up behind his back. His body dangled at the shoulder like a speared animal. Zack straightened the arm and bent it back. She heard the bone snap. The shattered end pierced the skin. Blood ran down to the lifeless hand. Its owner looked up, eyes begging her for mercy…

Zack went back to the door and opened it wide. He could see the mountain biker considering whether to take the argument to the next level, then deciding against it. At his signal, he and his housemates left the room. Isabella closed her eyes and sighed with relief.

"Thank you. You're a star."

"You okay?"

She shrugged and turned to the job in hand. "Yes, yes, I'm fine."

An archipelago of stacked boxes stretched across the

room, the largest island in the group being labelled 'shoes'. Others read 'glass', 'china' and 'kitchen'. Beyond them were three rails of clothes, puffed out at the sides from overcrowding.

"All this is to go?" Zack asked, cautiously.

"Amazing what you collect in four years."

He drifted over to the window and looked down at the van. He clapped his hands together, like his mother did when summoning purpose, and suggested they start with the clothes, one of them at each end of a rail.

Isabella laughed. "I've got a nasty feeling Ethan hasn't told you everything. I think the furniture should go in first."

"What furniture?"

She tried to stifle amusement behind a hand. "The stuff with a blue sticker is mine."

He shook his head. "It won't all go in."

"Two trips, then?"

After a lifetime of being conned by his brother he should have known there would be a hitch. Today's caper, billed by Ethan as 'collecting a few things from Isabella's house', would mean at least six hours on the road, and did that bloody sofa really have a blue sticker on it? Yes, and so did the matching armchair.

"Furniture first," he said. "You'd better ask biker boy to lend a hand. Good job I didn't pick a fight with him."

She shuddered with fear. "He's such a nasty bastard. Can't we do it ourselves?"

"What's his name?"

"Jason Dorner. Ground floor."

When Jason opened his door, Zack said straightaway, "Mate, I'm really sorry, but it's the sofa. Could you give us a hand with it?"

Jason toyed briefly with the idea of making Zack beg, but to what purpose? His lying, thieving housemate was going and that was all that mattered. He nodded and followed Zack back upstairs to her room.

The two of them manhandled the sofa down to the street, then returned for the armchair. As they tied the pieces down in the van, Zack asked,

"Mate, they do belong to her, don't they?"

Jason nodded. "I helped the John Lewis driver get them up the stairs." He lowered his voice and asked politely, "Is she going to live with you?"

"Same house. My brother's girlfriend."

"Ethan? Yeah, I met him." He glanced round as if he had more to say, but reservations about saying it.

"What is it?"

"Watch that you don't become her gofer. I was, for a whole year. Not just the odd lightbulb or blocked toilet, it was more... bodyguard. I was fending off people she owed money to, who'd lent her stuff and wanted it back. I even threatened a bloke she said was stalking her."

"This money she owes you lot...?"

Jason turned to go back into the house. "I'm not holding my breath for it."

"Even so, our address is 19 Ashbury Road. Ashbury Road, W12."

Jason nodded. "I'll help you with the rest of the stuff."

Within an hour they had folded, squashed and jammed everything into the van. After a final check of her room Isabella handed Jason the keys and gave him a quick smile. Zack thanked him and shook his hand.

Five minutes later he and Isabella were stuck in the Summertown traffic, hemmed in by local mothers in a hurry to collect their children from school in mock Range Rovers. Rough terrain, these Oxford side roads, Zack mumbled.

As the traffic started to flow, somewhere on the Headington bypass, Isabella began to prattle, talking as much to herself as to Zack. She was so relieved, so happy to be sorting out her life, earning her own living. She was starting the new job on Monday, looking forward to it and dreading the prospect at the same time. Did Zack know that weird combo of feelings? She was also grateful to be rid of people who thought she was scamming them. Jesus, her father was one of the wealthiest men in Argentina. Did they really think she would screw them for such a piddling amount? She squeezed out a few tears and leaned forwards in her seat to make sure Zack had noticed.

Zack kept his eye on the road. He was beginning to feel guilty now. Not only had he swallowed Jason's take on Isabella, he had even thanked him for the warning, then given him her new address. All Isabella had wanted was for this day to be over, and instead of wishing her good luck for the future her housemates had bullied her for money.

When he reached the Thame exit he signalled to pull off on to the slip road.

"Where are we off to?" she asked, as if they were starting a new adventure.

"Service station. I'm starving!"

At the Costa Coffee checkout Isabella insisted on paying for what they had ordered, only to go overboard with apologies when she realised her purse was in the van. Zack fished in his inside pocket for a twenty-pound note.

They sat opposite each other in the corral of tables and Isabella leaned forward on her elbows, watching Zack rip into a ham sandwich. She had never looked at him face on before, not up close anyway, but she had been right. He had the edge on Ethan for looks with his chiselled face, curious blue eyes and chestnut plait. But she sensed a staid and old-fashioned streak in Zack, an intractability born of his high regard for himself. What fun it would be to knock that out of him. How would she do it? Run both brothers at the same time, perhaps? It wouldn't last long, of course, not in a family whose members knew each other's business down to the last detail.

She dipped her chin to draw his attention.

"Why are you smiling?" he asked.

"I don't know. Watching you murder that sarnie, I suppose."

"Tell me something. Why England when you could've gone anywhere?"

Oh, God, she thought, does he really want conversation or can't he read the signs?

"My father thinks Oxford's the only university in the world worth going to. Mum had never heard of it." She drifted away for a moment. "It's nice to get away from them. Like you guys are doing."

He stopped chewing. "Are we?"

She laughed. "I don't mean you'll never see them again. But the house? The move to London? You can let yourself go a bit."

He looked at her steadily. "Assuming I want to."

She laid a hand on his arm. "Don't you? Only I was thinking... if that van wasn't jam-packed... I mean there's a sofa, for heaven's sake."

She smiled in an obvious fashion and waited for the offer to be taken up. He could hardly ask her to clarify, but was in no doubt that she'd just hit on him. With a club hammer.

"What do you say?" she whispered.

He downed the remains of his coffee and stood up. "I say if the van wasn't so full, there'd be less to do when we get to the house. Let's go."

***

When they reached Ashbury Road, Zack was relieved to find his three siblings already there, plus Matt and the ever mystified Amy, all waiting for Isabella's arrival. He had expected to have to chase them to help lug her possessions up to the top of the house.

To everyone's relief, Carla was making a huge effort to welcome the newcomer. She had repaired any damage to her relationship with Ethan, if their hugs and jokes were any indication, and she had planned a spaghetti bolognese supper for that evening.

Meantime, she arranged the unloading of the van while coping with the fact that their new housemate didn't carry a single item up the three flights of stairs. Carla tried to justify it: Isabella needed to be in the attic deciding where the army of dresses would be hung, the shoes billeted. It could all have waited, of course, but people had different ways of doing things.

Teresa phoned Carla halfway through and made her own kind of effort.

"Say hello to Isabella for me, will you? I'll pop in at the weekend, bring a welcome present. You don't happen to know what perfume she wears, do you?"

"Clive Christian Number One, I think."

Teresa pretended to gulp. "I'll get her a box of chocolates."

* * *

Isabella had always hated the first night in a new room, be it student digs, a hotel room, even a cabin on a boat, but the studio flat, as she'd decided to call the attic, was different. She felt curiously at home. Half an hour earlier, when the last of the wine had been drunk and the leftover spag bol bagged up for the freezer, Ethan had given her a 'shall we, shan't we?' look and she'd briefly shaken her head.

She sat up in bed, pillows against the wall, and looked round at the boxes she would live out of for the next two or three weeks. She felt no urgency to unpack them and get the job done. A tutor lover had once said it spoke of her dissatisfaction, her constant search for a new direction, her doubt that she would ever find one. She had thought at the time it was penny-dreadful psychology, but the sex had been so great she pretended to take his opinion on board.

All in all, she rated the move to Ashbury Road a success. The attic was a perfect living space and showed no signs that Teresa had ever inhabited it. There were no scuff marks on the furniture, no holes in the plaster where posters of idols or faraway places had been pinned, no marks on the desk where Teresa might have carved a claim to it. There was nothing in the drawers, no telltale page from a magazine going all the way back to... how old was Teresa? It was hard to tell since she'd taken such good care of herself.

She reached down beside the bed and took a notebook from her bag. It was such an old-fashioned thing, unlike her in every way, precise, discreet and grey. It represented one of the few consistencies in her life and she updated it regularly. It wasn't a diary, though the entries, if decoded, would inform the reader of her movements for the whole year. On the relevant page she entered the date and the amounts: £2742·00, rent, £8·45 Costa Coffee, Thame, and then £95·00 van hire. She'd heard Zack and Ethan discussing it over the spaghetti bolognese. Totted up with other entries for the month it amounted to £5274·81 with a whole week still to go.

And there was no reason why the rest of the financial year shouldn't be just as productive. This family met her headline requirements, from the flamboyant grandfather right down to baby Imogen. They were clever in their artsy way, successful, wealthy and famous. She had invited herself to Imogen's 21st, seduced Ethan the following day, dispatched his former girlfriend and had now moved in with them. It had taken her just eight weeks. It hadn't required any particular skill, only the hair, long legs, a revealing dress or two, and above all recognition of a suitable target. Was Ethan more than that, perhaps even the love of her life, as romantic fiction would have it?

She replaced the grey book, switched off the bedside light and cosied down. Mhac Na Galla! Just as she was about to close her eyes, certain that life could not be going any better, a galaxy of luminous stars lit up the vaulted ceiling. They were the kind of thing a young child might have found in a Christmas stocking. They hadn't been painted over in the refurbishment and, even though their brightness faded as she counted them, it felt as if Teresa was looking down on her through a host of tiny windows.

-10-

Contrary to Carla's fears, there were no major problems in the first three or four months that Isabella lived at Ashbury Road, and in many ways she was the perfect housemate. She never brought friends or colleagues to the house, didn't play pounding music like Zack and Ethan were inclined to do and, most important of all, she rarely left a trace of herself in the kitchen or bathrooms. Imogen was seldom seen at Ashbury, having joined a pro-am theatre group alongside her course at Central. Zack had taken up a hobby, though in Carla's opinion Nam Pai Chuan had less to do with a passion for kung fu than a means of avoiding Amy.

As for Carla herself, she saw less and less of Matt, which gave her a guilty sense of freedom. She was working long hours at the auction house, barely noticing the increased demands on her time. She did fret occasionally that she might no longer be her siblings' main resource, their confidante and confessor. She needn't have worried.

One day, a month after Isabella had moved in, Carla was summoned to the Mayfair auction room by the blustery head of the firm, Jean-Pierre Marquis. A sale entitled Royal & Noble was taking place that week, consisting of heirlooms from such European family names as Bourbon,

Hohenzollern and Habsburg. Jean-Pierre wanted her to prod the cattle, feed and water them with caviar and champagne and then herd them into the cleverly lit sale room. She would then take charge of the telephone bidders and charm them into parting with their cash.

The first lot for sale was a pair of Meissen wine coolers, beautiful and impractical, Carla thought. She had checked them that morning, holding them up to the light without fear and guessing correctly that the hammer would fall at nineteen thousand pounds.

As the bidding started, she looked across the room at the buyer, a man she thought she recognised, but didn't. However, she certainly knew the guy sitting behind him. It was her brother, Ethan, smiling at her with… yes, pride. He texted her quickly, asking to meet her after the auction.

* * *

In the auction house foyer Ethan hurried over to his sister, intent on hugging her. She fended him off for the sake of appearances and they changed their greeting to a businesslike kiss.

"How did you get in?" she asked, quietly.

"I told the doorman I was your brother. You're very popular here."

She laughed and led the way up a curved flight of stairs and into what was modestly called the Marquis tea room. Like most people seeing it for the first time, Ethan gasped. With its floor-to-ceiling faux tapestries, polystyrene mouldings and plastic chandeliers it had very little of the works canteen about it.

"Versailles?" he said to Carla.

"On the cheap. You want tea?"

She led him towards the ornate service counter. Jean-Pierre Marquis spotted her from across the room and headed them off.

"*Ma cherie*, you did such a perfect job," he said. He took her by the shoulders and gazed into her eyes. "I shall not forget this, believe me, I shall not."

"My brother Ethan," she said, introducing him.

"*Enchanté*." Jean-Pierre shook Ethan's hand quickly and turned to address the room. "Half an hour, *mes amis*. Then work. Sooner we do, sooner we get rich."

He winked at Ethan and moved on to deliver more compliments to individuals.

Ethan followed Carla over to a mock Louis XV chaise longue, conscious that the room was at least half full. He had hoped for a little more privacy to make his confession. She smiled.

"I've known that guilty look for twenty years. What's up?"

"Need your help, your advice, your... you." In a strangled voice he managed to add, "That bastard Stepley has fired me."

Carla groaned with relief. "Is that all?"

He had guessed that she would dismiss it as trivial. It was one of the reasons he had come to her.

"Trouble is, the guy was right to heave me out."

He described with grudging irony how he'd fallen short in his duties as an assistant to an assistant to an assistant. Carla easily guessed the main reason for that. When he should have been working, he'd been with Isabella. Not her fault, Ethan insisted. In fact, she'd tried to persuade him to get back on the workhorse and ride, but he hadn't been inspired by the project. Diseases of Medieval London.

"Smallpox, syphilis, gonorrhoea and the plague, they aren't the reason I did a history degree."

She laid a hand on his arm and tried to coax him through his options. Could he go back and plead with Adrian Stepley? No, and he didn't want to. Were there other companies, doing stuff that he fancied, that he could talk his way into? Yes, but he'd need a reference from Jubilee Films.

"There's something else," he said. "Stepley reckons I've done too much... more than he'd like, anyway." He sniffed, twisting one nostril, then the other. "Threatened to tell Marcus."

"Someone in the film business doing coke?" said Carla, wearily. "I'm so shocked."

He smiled. "It's not me I'm worried about, it's the papers, the gossip journos." He drew the headline in the air. "Drug-addict son of Marcus fired."

She looked at him, bemused. "The vanity of the men in my family. All of you believe your world will crumble if you're caught so much as ... spitting in the street. When will you accept that nobody really gives a damn?"

"Easy for you to say. You're wrong..."

"Then why do you all carry on spitting? Does Isabella know you've been fired?"

"Didn't feel right, laying it on her, whereas you, you always know..."

He looked her in the eyes. They were fourteen, fifteen again, him in some dreadful scrape with a girl, a teacher, once even the police. Carla had rescued him every time.

"What am I going to do, Car?"

She pursed her lips. "You are going to get a list together."

"Not a Teresa list..."

"A list of companies you'd like to work for. Push and shove. Ram the Oxford bit down their throats. And when it comes to Adrian Stepley, lie about him if you have to."

She looked round at her tea-drinking colleagues to make sure no one could overhear.

"The guy's a slimeball anyway, started perving over me when I was thirteen. How many film companies are there?"

"Thirty, forty."

"Hit them all. Use a bit of charm. You've seen Henry do it, you've seen Marcus do it. It's in the genes."

"Right."

She thought for a moment. "There's a client of ours, wasn't here today but... Ralph Erdun. I mean, talk about irons in fires: property, casinos, a football club, a film company."

He smiled for the first time since they had entered the tea room. "Ethix Films? I know them."

"You want me to...?"

This was also part of the ritual. Carla never put an offer of help into words, anxious not to belittle him. She hung it in the air to be grabbed at.

"Talk to him for me," he said. "I'll love you forever."

* * *

Ethan crept up the stairs to the attic, even though there was no need for secrecy. He'd been sleeping with Isabella ever since she moved in and everyone in the house knew it.

He knocked on the door and leaned in. She was sitting on the bed with her feet up and her iPad in her lap. She beckoned him to come in. He settled beside her and leaned back on one elbow.

"Busy?" he asked.

"Catching up with some friends on Facebook."

He smiled. "Seeing how wonderful their lives are?"

"Some of them think mine is. Handsome boyfriend, famous family."

She showed him her new Facebook page, her profile photo digitally scalloped, her hair billowing. She jabbed the Friends button and scrolled down the gallery of faces, a blur of sameness, most of them South American by their appearance.

"Am I there?" he asked.

"No, but your brother is."

"I thought he hated Facebook."

"*Says* he does."

She found Zack's Facebook, the photo the same one he'd placed in Spotlight, the actors' directory. From the timeline it was obvious he and Isabella had been posting to each other and Ethan tried to read the exchange. She snapped the iPad cover shut.

"I've got a problem," he said. "I've been with Carla today. She sorted me out. Pep talk, plan of action..."

She turned to him, her face frozen, her eyes deathly still. He remembered where he'd seen the expression before. In her room in Oxford when she asked if he was afraid of ditching the girl who steadied him or ashamed of the one who'd taken her place.

"I got the sack, three days ago," he said. "I'm not sure

whether to be pleased or hacked off, but… you don't seem bothered."

"Just wondering why you told Carla first, not me."

"That's what she said." He smiled. "Habit. Next time I get fired, you'll be the first to know."

She rocked herself off the bed and looked down at him.

"You three – Imogen, Zack, you – can hardly breathe without getting Carla's approval."

He waved her criticism aside. "She'd be lost without us."

"Can't you see how dangerous that is?"

He laughed. "No."

"If you were standing on Beachy Head and Carla said jump, would you do it?"

She began to unbutton her blouse. Her fingers were slow and sure, working in time with her thoughts. How long would it take to get Carla out of their lives? She dropped the blouse onto his face, unfastened her bra and covered her breasts with her hair. She would need to play a long game and that wasn't her preferred method. Seizing opportunities was her way, not sitting back and waiting. She slipped off her pants and watched his eyes follow as the flesh between her legs began to tingle. She reached down to cover it with her hands. She would need to get close to Carla. Easy. But could she keep up the pretence of being her best friend? Long games need long lies.

She knelt on the bed and beckoned him to reach up for her.

-11-

Carla hated shopping, more so since the clocks had gone back and brought a psychological chill to the weather. After a long and arduous week at Marquis she steeled herself for the chore and went out into the hall, struggling into her biker jacket. It gave her a kind of toughness with which to face the dreaded task.

As she closed the door to her room, Isabella came down the stairs, garnished with expensive new gloves, matching hat and scarf and carrying two empty shopping bags. They looked at each other and laughed.

"Morrisons?" said Carla.

Isabella nodded, as if in pain. "Do it together? Halve the hell?"

Despite what Carla had feared, it turned into quite a pleasant experience. They even stopped for a coffee in the Morrisons café and chatted for nearly an hour, breaking the ice over something as unlikely as apples. There had been none of Carla's favourites on the shelves since God knows when, a fact she blamed on people who believed that red meant ripe. Where were the hard, crunchy and to hell with what colour ones? Isabella agreed, in spite of Argentina being one of the world's biggest exporters of apples! They giggled and moved on to the latest film releases and a list of must-read books.

The same thing happened a couple of Fridays later. As Carla put the finishing touches to her list and went out into the hall Isabella called out from the landing above.

"Car, are you...?"

"I am."

"Give me two minutes. We should make it a regular thing. Seven thirty every Friday, you and me against the world."

"Coffee afterwards?"

* * *

When the drudge of shopping was over, they went through to the café and while Carla ordered two cappuccinos, Isabella bagged a table. She sat and watched Carla chatting to the women serving behind the counter, all smiles and smalltalk, as if they were old friends. Far from being the hard nut of her siblings' wishful thoughts, she was a pushover, a perfect target.

As Carla set the coffees down on the table, Isabella's phone must have buzzed.

"Sorry, Car, I have to take this."

She turned slightly away and said to the caller, "John, we've been over this a dozen times now. It's in the *blue* folder, salaried staff. Green is for cash payments." She rolled her eyes at Carla. "No, they're not online, they are paper receipts... Look, I'll meet you at the office tomorrow morning, nine thirty... yes, I know it's Saturday."

She finished the call and groaned. "New intern. Thick as a brick."

Carla smiled and wondered if Isabella might be the best person with whom to share her own problem. She decided she was. Jean-Pierre Marquis had offered her the position of Assistant Director of Operations in their Mayfair office, she said. Her parents would say grab it and jump, but it wasn't that simple. Matt wasn't happy about her taking it and she knew why. He would have felt emasculated by earning considerably less money than she did.

"Take it," said Isabella, shrugging. "If he doesn't like it, too bad."

***

A week later, Isabella texted Carla to say that she couldn't make Morrisons that evening and embellished her apology with a string of sad-faced emojis. Work to catch up with, she explained. Next Friday? Smiley face. Carla replied with a thumbs up.

Isabella sat by the window that overlooked Ashbury Road, a strange place at one o'clock in the morning, with slumbering cars leaning into both kerbs, but no lights in windows, no people passing by. The only sign that the world hadn't come to an end was a fox slinking into a front garden through the bars of a wrought iron gate. It toppled a bin then jumped the wall and ran back the way it had come, with a chicken carcass in its mouth.

At around one thirty the light at Ashbury's front door was triggered, which meant that Matt was leaving. He had crept out of Carla's room like a thief and closed the front door without a sound. Isabella could almost see him squirm as the security light gave him away. She watched as he walked over to his car, pulled rather than slammed the driver's door shut and drove away.

She glanced across at Ethan, lying naked on his front, dead to the world. This was the perfect time to do it. Middle of the night with Carla having drunk too much, sleepy, vulnerable. She went to the tall mirror and checked the makeup. Perhaps a few final touches? She decided against.

She trod carefully down the stairs and on the next landing went across to Carla's door. To her surprise, Carla recognised her knock and called out her name in a low nighttime voice.

"Isabella, hi!"

"I knew you'd be awake," said Isabella as she opened the door. "I heard Matt leave and… is it okay if I come in?"

Carla beckoned her. "Is everything alright?"

"Yes, yes, and this is just a quickie."

She entered and looked round, expecting to see a few signs of Carla's evening with her lover… crumpled clothes, mussed-up hair, even scratches, but there was nothing. Carla was dressed in a cotton nightdress that plucked at her curves and her hair was perfect. She was replacing a cork in a half-drunk bottle of red wine. Isabella's hands were gently churning the air in front of her as she summoned the words.

"Small thing… well, maybe not small. Rent."

She had set up a direct debit with her bank, she said, but there was no money in her account. Yet. Her salary from M & S hadn't gone through and her father was so busy at the moment he'd probably forgotten her allowance. Had Teresa mentioned it? Carla raised a reassuring hand to stop her worrying.

"She'll understand. Here, let me move that crap."

Carla scooped up the pile of oddments she had spread over the sofa, the contents of her handbag. She had intended to weed out the frivolous from the essential before work tomorrow, but it could wait. She dropped it back into her bag and Isabella sat down, perching on the edge, unsure of where to settle her hands. She clasped them together and finally dropped them into her lap.

"Did you take the job?" she asked.

Carla smiled, awkwardly. "I did, and Matt was cool about it. Cooler about the extra money than the principle of it."

She found a clean glass for Isabella and divided the remains of the bottle between them.

"He always seemed like a good man to me," said Isabella. "Respectful."

"Well, yeah..."

"Not the sort to raise a hand to you, or... you know..."

Carla laughed. "Thump me? And get his balls ripped off?"

Isabella looked away. She took a few sips of wine and waited, avoiding Carla's eyes.

"Why do you say that?" asked Carla after a pause.

"It's nothing. Really. I'm just so... pleased for you."

Carla moved slightly, to look at her face on. Her eyes had reddened and she blinked.

"What is it, Bella? Tell me."

Isabella shook her head, as if she hoped the subject would go away. Carla set down her wine glass and took Isabella's from her hand.

"You've got me worried. I've missed something..."

Isabella blurted out. "Carla, when you were kids, was

Ethan ever...?" She winced and seemed to struggle for the right words. "Ever violent?"

"Of course he wasn't!"

Carla waited while Isabella tried to soften the question.

"Maybe violent isn't the right word," she said. "Rough? Unpredictable? They don't really explain it." She reached out and Carla took her hand. "Promise you won't say anything?"

"If that's what you want..."

"He explodes over the silliest things, accuses me of not understanding their importance."

"He's got a mouth on him, yes, but..."

"You haven't heard us arguing? The other night I was late back from somewhere. He was still up, waiting for me, and accused me of all sorts."

She stopped herself and looked into Carla's face, which had clouded in disbelief.

"He's your brother. I can't..." Isabella started giggling, nervously, breathily. "I really know how to pick men. My husband was an absolute bastard."

Carla was aghast. "Your husband?"

She nodded. "I was married before and no, I haven't told Ethan and yes, yes, I'm terrified of doing so. His name was Ricardo and he began as a dream... kind, gentle... and then gradually he changed." She lifted the hair above her right ear to reveal a scar. "He gave me this, caught me with the buckle of his belt. My father was livid and he's not a man to upset."

"Where is Ricardo now?"

"He's dead," said Isabella, simply. "But I seem to have a gift for repeating mistakes."

Carla looked on in horror as Isabella slowly opened her dressing gown and lifted her nightdress to show her lower ribs. There was a patch, the size of a hand, yellow at the edge, purplish at the centre. Isabella retied the gown quickly. She could see Carla's mind spinning off in the desired direction, her forehead breaking out with sweat.

"That isn't him!" said Carla. "That's not the real Ethan. It's the weed, the coke, whatever else. I thought that was over and done with."

Isabella shook her head quickly. "I don't know which of them is the bigger sucker for it, Ethan or Imogen. Please, please don't say anything. I had to tell someone and... I must go."

She stood up. Carla grabbed her arm and pulled her close.

"Hang on, we can't just forget..."

Isabella wriggled free and hurried from the room.

As she climbed the stairs to the attic she wondered what would happen next. This was the reward for waiting, for having taken her time. Uncertainty galore and all the excitement that goes with it. Who would Carla tell first, in spite of being asked to keep it a secret? Matt? Just thinking of him conjured up the smell of his wide-boy deodorant. Zack or Imogen? Possibly, but they wouldn't believe it. And she certainly wouldn't tell her father. Which left her mother. Would Teresa swallow it, just as Carla had done? Certainly not. For a start, there was nothing to swallow.

She closed the attic door behind her, went over to the underwear drawer and opened the walnut box. She slipped into it the tiny key that Carla had missed when gathering up the contents of her bag. Across the room Ethan was still sprawled across the bed face down, unlikely to move for another six hours. It was the wine they'd drunk earlier, or rather the wine he had swigged and she had sipped. She untied the dressing gown, slipped off her nightdress and knelt beside him. She lowered her head and let her hair fan out over his back. He didn't move. She reached up and kissed him on the neck.

***

At four o'clock in the morning, when Isabella was sleeping soundly, Carla lay wide awake. Her thoughts leaped from horror to catastrophe: from Ethan's aggression to his drug use, to him encouraging their baby sister to join him in getting high. She hadn't recognised the description of Ethan as a man who might lash out at the slightest provocation, but how frightening it would be to wake up one morning and find Isabella with a black eye or a broken jaw. Raise the fear a degree or two and he might even kill her. Maybe he and Carla had been too close for her to notice the change in him, the shift from loving brother to Oxbridge lout. Sure, he had always been sharp and emphatic in his views, intolerant of others whose minds didn't match his own. People like Matt.

That was the trouble with four o'clock in the morning. Morbid ideas seemed all too plausible. If she had to make a spot judgement she would blame the booze, the weed, the coke, three items that had crept into their lives along with burgers and chips and refined sugar. Everyone knew they would kill you in the end, but shrug, shrug, you had to die of something. Did that inevitability lay waste to Ethan quitting... agreeing to drug counselling if necessary? The chances of him taking the suggestion on board were zero. At best he would fast talk her into feeling stupid, at worst... who could tell?

-12-

Teresa's telephone behaviour was a rich source of amusement to The Others. At the beginning of any phone conversation with their mother her voice was soft, secretive and nervous while she gauged the mood at the other end of the line. She would often move around the house, away from Marcus, and ask for things to be repeated. When the line broke up, thanks to Golden Meadow's walls being three feet thick, she would immediately call the caller back. Following protocol, they would redial her and get the busy signal. As would Teresa. Today, Carla was in no mood for delay.

"Mum, listen, I need help from you and Marcus. Urgently."

Teresa had been brushing the dogs and there was a mist of hairs floating in the air. She leaned out and glanced down towards Marcus's study to check that the door was closed.

"What's wrong?"

"Mum, it really is a small thing, but it needs nipping in the bud."

"Is it you? Ethan? Zack? Imo?" She always listed them in date-of-birth order.

"Mum, I swear it's something and nothing. It's Ethan. Look, how about we meet at Westfield?"

"What's wrong with him?"

"Tomorrow lunchtime, the sushi bar on the first floor. You needn't bring Dad if you don't want to."

"I can. The Cavendish is dark for three days, some problem with fire regulations, but we're not supposed to know that."

"Bring him! Twelve thirty tomorrow."

Carla ended the call and Teresa made the absurd theatrical gesture of glancing at the phone, almost accusing it of cutting short the conversation. She headed down to the study, calling out Marcus's name as she went.

"Who was on the phone?" he asked as he turned to her.

Usually, her answer would be the impossible 'nobody' which would draw comic reproach.

"Carla," she said.

He nodded. "I've had another email from Juan Morales."

At least it steered her mind away from the possibility that Ethan had contracted some terminal disease or murdered the bigamist next door. Marcus found the email and turned his laptop towards her.

> Estimado Señor Lawlor
> My daughter Isabella informs me you have graciously given her accommodation in your London house. She has not yet received payment for her first month of work so I will transfer to her money to pay you. My heartiest thanks for your kindness.
> Respetuosamente
> Juan Morales

"What do you make of it?" he asked.

The email came as no surprise to Teresa. In many ways it was reassuringly obvious, with its timing and deliberate awkwardness of style. Was now the time to voice her suspicions to Marcus? And for that matter, why hadn't he realised it for himself?

"It bothers *you*, I can tell that," she said.

"That sense of him spying on us from the next room." He smiled. "You decided to charge her rent, then?"

"I'm charging *all* of them. The sooner they learn…"

The sentence wasn't worth finishing and he began to pick dog hairs off her jumper. Any moment now he would pull her towards him and suggest they go upstairs and, frankly, she didn't have time. She turned away.

"We're meeting Carla tomorrow at Westfield. Lunch."

He groaned. She turned back to the door and made her escape.

* * *

Marcus loved being recognised, though he claimed he couldn't bear it. As he strolled across the main concourse of Westfield shopping mall, heads turned towards him. It used to be young women who pointed him out. Now it was their mothers, or rather the same young women grown older. And it wasn't Inspector Goole they recognised, it was Richard Salter of *Salter's Edge,* whose character combined every dramatic cliché a leading man could bear. Marcus's good looks were instrumental in the show's success, though the BBC in its politically correct prissiness would never concede that.

Having the same forbidding stature as his father, people never rushed over to Marcus as if he were a long-lost friend. If he smiled they might take it as an invitation and step closer, at which point he would drawl the slowest, luvviest "Hi!" imaginable. Occasionally they would say they knew the face but couldn't quite place him. Was it the gym, the accounts office, the golf club? He would walk away, mortified.

In the sushi bar Marcus and Teresa took their food from the conveyor belt buffet and went to a corner table that looked across the millpond of fake marble to the Apple store. Shoppers and sightseers crisscrossed in the intricate, delicate way human beings do, good manners in motion, Marcus liked to think. Carla arrived soon afterwards, only twenty minutes later than agreed, but still her father glanced at the watch he never wore.

"Yes, I know and I apologise." She stooped to kiss each of them. "I'll get some grub and be with you."

When she returned with her sushi, toasted seaweed and Highland Spring she sat down next to her father and poured herself a glass of water. Marcus turned the bottle slowly where it stood until the price tag became visible. Water and coffee were his new favourite moanabouts: £1·60 for bottled water which cost 2p from the tap, coffee 19p from bean to cup, £4·50 from cup to lip. Carla was too fraught to care. She was about to divulge a secret which Ethan had asked her to keep, and to break a promise she had made to Isabella. In the process she would rat on Imogen. Carla rested her elbows on the table and sipped from her glass.

"Ethan's been fired from Jubilee Films," she said.

Marcus sighed. "I knew that. Stepley phoned me weeks ago."

Teresa glanced at him. "You might have shared it!"

"I didn't think it was that big a problem." He turned back to Carla. "Sacked why, do you know?"

"All the coke he's shoved up his nose might have something to do with it. More worrying is that he's taking it out on Isabella."

"What do you mean 'taking it out'?" Marcus asked.

"What does *anyone* mean by that, Dad?"

She had raised her voice and it had carried. Marcus glanced over the plastic ivy at the audience of onlookers. If his daughter was about to entertain them with family secrets then he had two choices. He could try to stop her, for fear of being unmasked as just an ordinary father dealing with domestic issues, or respond to it as Jonas Kemble would when faced with an audience. He leaned back in his chair, speaking softly,

"You sound very sure, Car. Some details would help."

She took a deep breath before rehashing the conversation she had had with Isabella. When she finished she leaned back in her chair and shrugged the responsibility over to her parents. Her mother seemed concerned, but her father's attention had veered away to a couple at a nearby table who had recognised him. They were sophisticated, mid-thirties and unlikely to be outwardly starstruck. The woman was also pretty, with stylishly unkempt blonde hair falling round a fashionable face. The young man was a perfect match for her, tanned and gelled, jacket over the back of his chair, shirtsleeves rolled up to show off tattooed biceps. Marcus smiled at the woman before turning back to Carla.

"You reckon the cause of him being violent is cocaine?" he asked.

"Whose word is 'violent'?" asked Teresa. "Yours, Isabella's?"

Carla's response was written in her sneer. Christ, Teresa was going to defend the little bastard all the way. Raise a hand to a woman? Unthinkable. Cocaine? Forced on him by some unscrupulous acquaintance.

"The booze doesn't help either," said Carla. "He could never handle it. And Isabella reckons it'll get worse."

"Now she's a psychologist?" said Teresa.

"How long's it been going on?" asked Marcus.

"I don't know."

Marcus had tried cocaine himself once, when he'd been working in Los Angeles. A fellow actor had asked, one evening, if he fancied a line. Marcus snorted it, messily, pretending it was nothing new to him. He had liked it. In fact, he had liked it just a little too much so he never touched it again.

"Who buys it?" asked Marcus. "Isabella?"

"Why blame her?" said Carla.

"Why leap to her defence?"

"Because it's *his* nose it's going up, not hers!" Carla paused, lowered the volume. "Sorry, yes, I reckon that's where Isabella's rent has gone. Mum, she asked if you can wait for it."

"So she's using too?"

"No, Mum, chances are she gives the money to Ethan."

Marcus smiled at Teresa. "I have her father's word the rent'll be taken care of."

"That is *not* the bloody point."

She was about to explain why that was so when across the concourse she saw Ethan step off an escalator, appearing to drag Isabella behind him. He strode towards the sushi bar, the anger in his face creasing it, making him seem ten years older than he was. He knew exactly where he was heading, where to find them. Teresa gestured to warn Marcus and Carla of his approach. When he reached the table, Marcus said,

"Hello, mate."

Ethan looked down at Carla. "You may want to take this somewhere else, Dad."

"We're fine here."

"Suit yourself. Shift up, Mum."

Teresa did so and Ethan and Isabella squeezed in beside her. Isabella was modestly dressed for once; even the hair was pinned up, albeit in an elaborate swirl. Marcus started to greet her, but she looked down at her lap, clearly apprehensive about the conversation ahead.

"So you don't think Isabella and I are right for each other," Ethan said to Carla, in a splintery voice. "Or more correctly she shouldn't spend the rest of her life with a man like me."

Carla screwed up her face in bewilderment. "What?"

"Your advice in your middle of the night conflab, to which I say what business is it of yours? And while we're on the subject of partners, what the hell are you doing with some throwback who calls himself a personal power coach? What *is* that by the way?"

Carla brought her hands to her mouth as if to pray through them. "I didn't say that about you."

He gestured to Isabella. "You mean she drew it out of the air?"

With a mind to the future, or rather five minutes from

then, Marcus said, "Mate, whatever needs saying, we're trying to keep the levels down."

"I said it about her first husband," said Carla.

She glanced at Teresa as if she had made a defining point, but Ethan didn't give his mother the chance to react.

"You think one of them's going to bend me over the table and slap my arse? I *know* she was married."

"Who to?" asked Teresa.

Ethan took his eyes off Carla for the first time and turned to his mother. "Does it matter? A bloke called Ricardo who is now dead. Back to why I'm not the right person for her."

"I did not say that."

The smug tone of a point scored crept into his manner. "Is it because I'd knock her about like he did? Well, Matt the mutt may not leave any physical signs of abuse" —he tapped his temple with his forefinger.—"but he's beating your mind to a pulp."

He looked over at his father.

"I take it you know your friend Stepley fired me? Yes, I can tell from the 'old news' look on your face. You should thank me. It means you no longer owe him anything, a free voiceover for some pathetic series or other."

"Have you tried to get another job?" asked Marcus.

"Yes. In fact my big sister here said she would help."

"I'm fucked if I will now!"

"What else has she told you?" said Ethan. "As if I couldn't guess."

Carla jolted forward in her seat. "Listen, shove as much coke up your nose as you want, but you know what's really shit? Dragging Imo into it. You should be looking out for her!"

He paused and then began to laugh, a fair impression of true amusement, which threw some of the onlookers who had tuned in to the argument.

"Our innocent little baby sister has been snorting great fat lines of chop for two years or more." He translated for Teresa's benefit. "Cocaine, Mum, she's a dab hand."

"How does she afford it?"

"Have you ever been to your purse and were sure you had more than *that* in it? Mislaid a credit card, found it a day or two later? Missing any jewellery? Well, now she's started nicking from Isabella: clothes she keeps in the spare room, stuff with a value."

Marcus tapped Ethan's arm to get his attention. "And you've said nothing?"

"To you, Dad? What would have been the point? Your head's been stuck up the 1930s for the last four months with that moralising prick..."

"Let me remind you of something. That moralising prick and his ilk have allowed you to live in Aston Merrick, not on the twelfth floor of some high-rise. They sent you to Oxford, bought you a car..."

Ethan squeezed his face in painful recognition of the rest of the speech. "Send us a bill, Dad."

Marcus smiled. "Perhaps I should."

Carla suddenly grabbed Ethan by the arm.

"How did you know where to find us today?"

"What's that got to do with..."

"I only told one person I was coming here." She glared at Isabella. "I told *her* yesterday I was meeting here at twelve thirty to sort things out. She told you?"

"It's a loyalty thing."

"Everything I've said about you came from her! The drugs, the violence, how she was afraid of you." She shifted her stare to Isabella. "Show them!"

Isabella held out both hands as if fearful of the sudden lunacy which had struck Carla. "What do you mean?"

"The bruises. When she came down to my room the other night she had bruises, right here, lower ribs. Show them!"

Reluctantly, Isabella opened her jacket and slowly began to roll up her top as if unveiling a work of art. There wasn't a mark on her. She held her pose longer than she needed to, tears beginning to well up, and then she slowly covered up again.

Ethan prodded his head again, tap, tap, tap. "God knows what's gone on up there, Car. Sure, I'm pissed off at getting fired. Who wouldn't be?" He gestured to embrace the argument they had just had. "But this... you saw this as a chance to get rid of her."

Carla turned to her parents. "Help me!"

Ethan was on a roll. "The idea of another woman ruling the Ashbury roost, you couldn't bear it. Well, here's a bit of lateral thinking: bugger off and live on a canal boat with Captain Jack. Rule *his* life."

He turned to walk away, to exit in grand family style, but he mistimed his flounce and bumped into a woman carrying a coffee. It slopped but didn't fall. In a quick shift of character, he apologised to her, then stomped off across the concourse. Before following him Isabella looked from Marcus to Teresa.

"I'm sorry," she whispered, through the tears.

It had played out just as Isabella imagined it would, all

the better for being so public. She reached out and laid a hand on Carla's shoulder, then hurried away. Marcus rose to follow, with what purpose he didn't know. He paused and turned to his new audience, twenty or so nearby faces and their poised iPhones. He smiled and said the words that explained away all trouble between parents and children.

"Families, eh?"

He knew that social media and some of the trashier papers would explain it very differently, but his own performance had been nigh on faultless.

-13-

Zack arrived at the Spotlight offices for a casting session only to discover that twenty young actors had already been through the mill that morning and he was one of twenty more. From an objective point of view most of the forty could have played the role, quite a hefty one in an upcoming television drama series called *Conshie*, set during World War II. He was an hour early in order to give himself time to look up 'conscientious objector' on Wikipedia, as a result of which he doubted the subject would thrill too many people. He could imagine the outrage that thought would provoke in both his father and grandfather. Drama, they maintained, could emerge from the slightest event: by the same token large canvas epics could bore the viewer rigid. It depended on the writing. With that in mind he fixed a rictus smile, put his head up, shoulders back and went to meet his inquisitors.

The producer was a smart Indian lady in her early forties, as ex-BBC as they come and wildly enthusiastic about the project. The director was neither as beautiful nor as full of beans as his producer. He had, after all, seen thirty-two young actors already that day, and would be hard pressed to tell one from the other this time tomorrow. The third person lined up against Zack was an unforthcoming man in his late thirties, with shifty eyes and in need of sunlight and a decent meal, by the look of him. The writer.

"Hi!" said Zack, brightly, and perched on the edge of the chair the director had nodded to.

"Hello, Zack," the producer purred. "Thanks for coming in, so glad you could make it."

"My pleasure," said Zack.

"It says here on the sheet 'Zachary'," said the director flatly. "Are you Zack or Zachary?"

"Mainly Zack," he replied.

The producer handed him a script. "We'd like you to read for Charles Mantle. It's a pivotal role, he'll be in every episode, so..."

"Just a second," said the director. "Zack Lawlor. Are you one of the Lawlors – Sir Henry, Marcus?"

Zack looked down at the floor in appropriate modesty. "Dad Marcus, grandfather Henry. Please don't hold it against me."

Hold it against him? The director could have bloody kissed him. The dreary load of tosh which was *Conshie* needed *something* to make the bastards watch and a name like Lawlor might just do it. The producer was equally delighted, but for different reasons. She was in the presence of a theatrical dynasty, albeit the tail end of one, and now she looked at Zack she could see the family likeness. And also picture the PR blurb. Dishy, famous, talented, in that order.

"Okay, Zack," said the director. "If you'd be kind enough to wait outside in the greenroom."

"You don't want me to read?"

"Oh, er, yes, but it's the look I'm after as much as anything. Page 17."

They read a scene together, after which the producer asked him to wait. An hour later they offered him the part of Charles Mantle, subject to agreement with his agent and contract thereafter. Genuinely thrilled, Zack thanked them several times.

***

When he walked in through the front door of Ashbury he called out, "Carla! Carla?"

She wasn't just the person they all went to with their problems; she was also the first to hear of their triumphs and good fortune.

"Car, you in?"

He opened the door to her room and took an actor's breath to speak. He paused, mouth open, the door handle still in his hand, and for a moment couldn't make sense of the scene before him. Had she said she was going on holiday? Had she written it on the blackboard in the kitchen? She must have done, for here was all her luggage, suitcases, boxes...

He stared down at the unfamiliar sight of his older sister in tears, cowered into the corner of the sofa. Her hair was a mess, her features puffy, her mascara clowning its way down her cheeks. Beside her was a box of tissues: those she had used had been wedged between two cushions. He slammed the door behind him and hurried over to her.

"What the hell is it?" he asked, accusingly.

He knelt down on the rug in front of her and turned

her face towards him.

"You and Matt?" he said, fearing one of their emotional collisions had gone too far.

She shook her head. "Ethan."

"What's happened to him?"

Christ, she thought, they all think he's a fragile, breakable little doll, at the mercy of everything from a grazed knee to a nervous breakdown. It never occurs to them that there might be another side to him.

"There's nothing wrong with him, except that he's an arsehole!" Her lips began to quiver with rage. "Almost as bad as his new girlfriend. They deserve each other."

Zack knelt up in shock and she began to review the one-act drama that had aired in the Westfield sushi bar. Sensing it would be a lengthy critique he sat beside her on the sofa and took her hand, but she soon reclaimed it in order to chop the air in front of her into chunks of anger. When she had finished she turned to him for his reaction, correctly guessing what it would be.

"Well, don't worry, Car. Honestly, it's bound to blow over."

"No, it bloody won't!" she yelled. "That is what he thinks of me. I'm some unbearable control freak. And he's so bewitched by that scum baguette he can't see that she set me up!"

Zack nodded and then asked quietly, "Did she, though?"

She glared at him. "She wanted me out. She's *got* me out!"

"Steady on, kid." He gestured to the packed suitcases, the boxes, the folded rugs. "You mean she got you out as in… you're leaving. Where are you going?"

"Matt's boat. He's always saying I should move in."

"Carla, it'll be like living in a bloody corridor."

"Nonsense. Bags of room. I was waiting for you to get home. To help."

Zack allotted just five minutes to dissuading her from the move, not that he timed himself. It wasn't worth it. When Carla made up her mind the likelihood of anyone changing it was minimal. He saved his best card till last, hoping it would encourage her to fold.

"What about the rest of us?" he asked in a whiny voice. "Me, Imogen, Ethan?"

She scoffed at the last name and told him there was no need to whisper it, he hadn't come home yet. He was probably out with Isabella, celebrating. Besides, she added, she was moving onto Regent's Canal, not a canal on Mars. She'd still be available.

She turned back to her belongings and picked up the silver box that her grandmother had bought as a christening present. No woman ever remembers her christening spoon, Margot had said, but she'll always need a jewellery box.

"Taking the diamond necklace with you?" Zack asked.

"Lost the key to it and the bloody thing's locked. You haven't got one that might fit?"

"Oh, I've got so many jewellery boxes, one of the keys is bound to."

She smiled at long last. "Where were you this afternoon, anyway?"

"Went to a casting, that's all." He stood up. "Come on, I'll drive you to the boat."

* * *

Matt's policy of chugging up and down the Grand Union Canal, tying up at a fresh mooring every few weeks in order to avoid charges, had paid off. His fellow boatman George Charrier, a man in his late fifties, had a mooring on Regent's Canal for which he paid an obscene fee per annum. Matt resented George's ability to afford it, the more so because the money came from a family fortune that George and his two sisters back in the Dordogne were in the process of spending. George had a problem, however. He wanted to take his wife, Justine, on a leisurely cruise up the Grand Union, destination Birmingham, taking in several arms of the canal – Buckingham, Oxford, Northampton. In his absence he was afraid that some mooring hopper would tie up in his place and then be difficult to shift. He solved the problem by offering the mooring to Matt for the duration, free of charge. Matt had jumped at it. Indeed, he joked that George should be paying *him* for guarding the domain and tending the garden which ran up the bank.

Zack parked half on the pavement and instantly drew a tin-pan alley blasting of horns from the traffic behind. He went to the iron railings separating pavement from towpath six feet below and looked up and down the canal.

"Which one is it?" he asked.

"There, the red and green," she said.

He squinted and read the name. "*Landmark*? Odd name for a boat. You stay here, keep your eye on the car. I'll go dig him out. If a traffic warden appears, we've broken down, right?"

Carla opened the padlock on the railing gate with her

spare key and watched Zack haul one of her cases down the concrete steps to the towpath. Beyond *Landmark* there was a brick building, no bigger than a garden shed, with a striped canopy covering a gaggle of Chinese tourists at a hatch. They were buying tea and sandwiches, taking them to flimsy tables and wobbly fold-up chairs. Farther along was an iron footbridge, painted blue and white, and poking through the angled struts more young tourists were taking photos of the boats below. Zack smiled, recalling something his grandfather had recently read in *The Spectator*.

"Stand on any London bridge at midnight and you can smell three things above all others," Henry had declared. "Diesel fumes, marijuana and chicken tikka."

From the towpath on Regent's Canal, the only thing Zack caught a whiff of was raw sewage, in his mind if not his nostrils. Reaching *Landmark*, he set the case down and climbed aboard at the stern. The boat shifted under his weight and he froze; it dipped a little, causing a faint stirring on the otherwise calm water. The door opened and Matt appeared, ready with a devastating quip.

"Permission to come aboard, is it?"

"I've brought her."

Matt's face stiffened. "Brought who?"

Zack nodded up to the iron railing thirty yards back where Carla, standing guard over the rugs and cardboard boxes, was waving to them.

"You didn't know she was coming?"

"No."

He waved back at Carla with as much enthusiasm as he could muster.

"She's had a fight with Ethan. Don't worry, they'll be

back to normal a week from now."

Matt nodded, trapped by his own open-house offer, having believed Carla would never take him up on it. He went quiet, clearly working on an excuse for not putting her up, but nothing came to him. Zack was already heading back to the steps.

-14-

Isabella was fond of the bathroom on the middle floor of 19 Ashbury Road. She had made it her own, feminising it to the point where Ethan and Zack preferred using the one on the ground floor. Even Imogen seemed put off by its array of oils and lotions and its aura of being someone else's private domain.

She lit the three scented candles and ran the bath, then turned and gazed at her body in the mirror. The mirror was the kind that didn't tell the truth, made of the same glass used in lifts that turns fat men into athletes and smooths out wrinkles on faces. Courtesy of this mirror, Isabella's body had every classic feature that men and women down the ages had desired. Long legs, tapering thighs, uninsulated hips that drew the eyes upward to the curve at her waist. Rising from there, her upper body was the shape of some exotic vase, overflowing with hair. The steam from the water began to mask her reflection and she stepped into the bath.

Beyond the door she heard Imogen calling up the attic stairs to Ethan, the words unrecognisable above the sound of the immersion heater refilling. It would be a mutual sympathy visit, a vapid discussion of whether their big sister had deserted them for good or merely a week or two. Would

Imogen take her sister's place, Isabella suddenly wondered. She was self-willed and gutsy enough to try and, by dint of being the youngest, she had a greater sense of entitlement than her siblings. Would Ethan turn to her for support, now that Carla had gone? She smiled. Another long game was called for. More pawns, more patsies, more casualties.

***

Marcus woke earlier than usual, at a time when even the BBC's morning news magazine was still in bed. Financial guff was pouring out of the kitchen television and a reporter in Hong Kong was being politely familiar with his female London counterpart. Marcus muted them and brought up Twitter on his phone to discover that he was indeed trending, though hardly starring, in a minor disaster. Hashtag 'lawlorgobs' had a following of sheer delight that Ethan and Carla had been witnessed blasting each other with both barrels. But as bloody usual, his father had stolen the show. 'Poor Henry,' one of the tweets read, 'How dare these brats cuss and swear in public?' One of the few that did mention Marcus was unflattering to say the least. 'Watch the #lawlorgobs go for each other, best thing their father's been in for years.' It included a link to a piece of video of the event, taken from an angle that suggested it was shot by the pretty blonde or her muscled boyfriend. Another link showed Marcus in a state of ill-disguised embarrassment giving the feeble apology, 'Families, eh?' He switched to Mail Online and out leaped Henry, a fine photo of him, bottom right, taken the previous year at the Cannes Film Festival. No picture of Marcus, no reference to *An Inspector*

Calls, just drivel: 'Ethan and Carla Lawlor, grandchildren of Sir Henry Lawlor (pictured) caused a rumpus yesterday in the Westfield Shopping Centre when...'

Marcus had been wondering how the press would deal with it and was now miffed that so little had emerged. He flopped into the kitchen armchair, suddenly exhausted, and his thoughts wandered briefly towards cocaine, the drug of plenty. They were quickly dragged away to Carla and his fear that a nasty spat with her brother would drive her deeper into the arms of the personal power coach.

With the Cavendish Theatre dark until the chief fire officer decided otherwise, Marcus had time on his hands. Later that day, he filled it by taking Troy and Cress for a long hike. Returning via the golden meadow, he saw the outriders of the Aylesbury Vale Archaeological Society packing up for the day, standing on the rim of Bigg's Cave and placing various items into a sack. He veered away immediately, skirting the meadow to avoid Colin's waffle about this pinprick of history.

It was dusk by the time he reached the house. The bats were dogfighting around the eaves and lights were blazing money from a few downstairs windows. He paused to shake off the sudden fear that a few left-on lights would bring his finances crashing down. Would that in turn see them moving into a bungalow in the next village, probably in the pitch black, whimpering about the good old days when the...? He switched on an outside light, then filled a bucket from the garden tap and swilled the dogs' legs. Teresa, arms folded against the early evening chill, came to the back door while he stooped to dry off Troy and Cress. She usually chose her moments carefully, but not on this occasion.

"Carla's gone."

He straightened up. "Gone where?"

"To live with Matt on his boat. Zack's been on the phone, asking if it'll be for long."

Marcus leaned on the door jamb and removed his boots, then followed her through to the kitchen.

"No one could live with that moron for more than a week," he declared.

"Carla could."

"Out of defiance?"

She turned on him, fiercely. "Because we didn't believe her."

He raised a warning finger. "Why do I get the feeling that you're blaming *me* in some way?"

The dogs had already withdrawn to a corner of the dining room, sensing turbulence ahead.

"You didn't exactly support her."

He was genuinely taken aback. "We both know Ethan'll calm down. As for his remarks about Carla, he's right, she's always thought she ruled the roost."

"So yet again you defend this tart from God knows where!"

"Tell me what 'this tart' has done and I will listen."

"Imogen snorting cocaine for the past two years? Adrian Stepley sacking Ethan? Thanks for telling me about that, by the way." She was getting into her stride, pacing the kitchen as if it were a cell and her parole had just been refused. "All you were worried about in that wretched sushi bar was your image!"

"Well, I did give it a passing thought."

"When those phones began flashing, recording the

whole shindig, the first thing you should've thought about is how to spare your family! But you went into actor mode!" She parodied his voice. "Oh dear, what will the Twitterati yap about tomorrow? Me, me, me!"

He chose a surface on which to bring his fist down. "That is unfair. You may not think it's important that I protect my image, as you sneeringly put it, but remember what it's given us." He gestured around him. "This!"

It was developing into an argument where one party would have to storm out of the room, neither of them willing to back down or able to change the other's mind. They were spared by the phone ringing and both turned to where it sat, trembling on an upright oak pillar. The display told them it was Ethan. Teresa snatched it and tried unsuccessfully to change her manner.

"Hello, darling," she said, in the same tone she would have called her husband a bastard. Zack would have picked up on it and asked what was wrong. Ethan seemed to already know.

"Mum, I'm sorry," he began, his voice low with shame.

With a jabbing finger, Marcus asked that she put the phone in speaker mode.

"I shouldn't have done that," Ethan went on to say. "Tell Dad I'm sorry, will you?"

"We're not the ones you should apologise to."

"Carla's gone. Didn't Zack tell you? I said some pretty harsh stuff."

"You can put that right," she said. "But be honest. Are you in trouble? Drugs? The job?"

His voice lifted a little, finding some spirit. "No. And nor is Imo, before you ask. I'm getting it from all sides,

Mum. Isabella's furious that I opened my trap, didn't talk it over with her first. Will Carla come back?"

"I can't say, but..."

"Mum, why do you never give the answer I need?"

"Go round to the boat. Say sorry. How is Zack?"

Ethan chuckled. "Moody, gloomy, asking what's wrong with this fucking family."

She smiled. "His usual cheery self, then. Listen, I didn't... we didn't want kids who'd make life easy for us."

"So long, Mum. Thanks for being so predictable."

Teresa hung the phone back on its cradle and turned to Marcus.

"No mention of the part Isabella played, that she set him and Carla against each other."

Marcus shrugged. "Are we sure she did?"

She sighed angrily and flopped down at the table. "She's wormed her way into the family, best rooms in the house, then got rid of the person Ethan turns to when he's in the shit."

"Alright, then, kick her out of Ashbury."

Teresa gripped the air in front of her in despair. "And have her take him with her? To Argentina, maybe? Christ, he's already made enough mistakes. The drugs, getting the sack, falling out with his sister. Did Isabella object to all that? No, she encouraged him."

"Why the hell would she do that?"

"Some women don't want their partners to be successful in case they make a break for it. It's a risk we take. Your mother took it with Henry, I did with you."

"So it's all about the wicked men?"

"No, it's about your son being easily impressed. The

irony is that when she's flushed his career down the pan, saddled him with children, debts and all the bloody rest of it, she'll despise him for not standing up to her."

"Are you sure you aren't reading too much into it," Marcus offered, quietly.

She chuckled sourly. "It wouldn't be so bad if she brought something to the table herself: a promising career, a consuming passion, something other than her father's money and big hair!"

-15-

Christmas sneaked up like the seasonal mugger it had become, bringing with it the usual invitations to drinks parties in Aston Merrick. 'Oh, I'm so disappointed,' Marcus would say with a Henry boom in his voice, 'but I'm working this year.' An innocent neighbour, a genial man more tolerated than liked, made the mistake of asking if he was doing pantomime. Teresa heard the question from across the shop they were in and rode to the rescue, insisting they hurry home because the dogs would have their legs crossed. In the car Marcus brooded on the man's faux pas and asked Teresa if he had the face of a pantomime dame. No, she assured him, more the back legs of a horse.

Right up until Christmas Day, and even as Marcus carved the first slice of turkey, he believed that Carla might sweep into the room in dramatic style and take her place at the table beside him. It wasn't to be, and without her the celebration became a lacklustre affair.

Knowing that he was the cause of her absence made Ethan almost as morose as his father, but he chose to blame his moodiness on Isabella being in Argentina. She would be away for three weeks, which suggested to Teresa that her boss was just as susceptible to the voluminous hair and plunging necklines as many others were. They heard from her via the magic of Zoom and a flood of photos on Instagram. At this time of year Argentina presented an enviable picture, with blossoming trees and the natives walking the streets in T-shirts and cotton slacks. Her father, she said, was 200 miles away, down in some far-flung corner of Estancia Sobromente wrangling beef. He had returned for Christmas Day and left early the following morning, and from all the evidence was camera-shy. There wasn't a single photo of him, yet plenty of Isabella's mother, who didn't live up to Ethan's preconceptions. Señora Morales was not Evita by any stretch. She was overweight with brown hair, whereas Ethan had expected black, black, black like her daughter, or even dramatic white, the colour of choice for premature greyness. The photos were taken in the garden at the family house: the woman was smiling as she tinkered with exotic plants and delicate trees. The weather had been balmy enough to spend Christmas Day outside, Isabella told the Lawlors, and there were several shots of friends and family to prove it. When Ethan zoomed in on some of the faces the pixels objected and blurred the images.

Late on Boxing Day Marcus checked his emails and found the usual greetings overkill from his agent, various friends and producers. Tucked among them was a message from Juan Morales.

> Estimado Señor y Señora Lawlor
> Feliz Navidad!
> May I and my wife wish your family a very happy Christmas with much joy and success in the new year.
> Respetuosamente
> Juan Morales

Marcus wasn't sure why it offended him. It might have had something to do with the words Feliz Navidad, reminding him of the annual surfeit of a Christmas song by that name. More reasonably he considered it to be unwarranted familiarity and another encroachment into his life. He archived it and tried to forget about it.

* * *

When Isabella returned from Argentina in the first week of January, she came laden with presents for her Ashbury Road housemates and tales of New Year celebrations at Estancia Sobromente. She had bought Ethan and Zack gaucho knives with carved bone handles and lethal blades. Ethan quipped that should one of his tyres ever get a stone in the tread he now had the perfect means of removing it. For Imogen there was an expensive waistcoat in tooled leather, a perfect fit, and for Amy a colourful T-shirt with a map of Argentina printed on it. For everyone there was yerba maté, a traditional Argentinian beverage drunk from gourds and passed round a circle of friends like some liquid spliff. There was also wine, which they drank that same evening with a communal takeaway. It was Zuccardi, Isabella explained, produced on the slopes of a neighbouring ranch. When she said 'neighbouring', she meant sixty miles away.

Softened in their attitude towards her on account of the peace offerings, they believed her when she said again and again how pleased she was to be back at Ashbury Road, how much she had missed England, how next Christmas she would join them at Golden Meadow. They retired to bed having eaten and drunk too much. Only Zack was mildly troubled. He wondered how Isabella had managed to get the knives through customs.

Early the next morning Ethan woke with a start as he heard the pistol-shot creak on the stairs. He sat up quickly and his head swam with revolving pain. He untangled himself from Isabella, who stirred but stayed put. There was a gentle knock on the door.

"Isabella, you there?" Zack asked.

"What you want?" Ethan mumbled.

Zack entered apologetically and hovered. "There are two men downstairs, want to talk to Isabella."

"What about?"

"Wouldn't say. I'm making breakfast, if you fancy some."

"Yeah, thanks."

Zack turned slowly to leave the room, head still thick from the Zuccardi, but Ethan called him back.

"Hang on, mate. Two blokes? How old? What like?"

"Forties. One fit, the other flabby. Londoners."

"Tell them I'll be down in a minute," said Isabella from somewhere under the duvet.

Zack had parked the two men at the big pine table, still piled with the remains of last night's meal and the plates and cutlery they had used. One of the men had turned away from it, not out of squeamishness but interest in the run of wall tiles behind the kitchen sink, which became the subject of a one-sided conversation with his companion. He wondered if they were the genuine article? Victorian tiles fired in some Staffordshire pottery – Sowerby's, he thought – and worth a fortune each. Twenty-five quid to be exact, so forty-three tiles here added up to £1075·00. But he had a nasty feeling they were repro, forty quid a box. He turned and smiled as Zack entered and went over to the porridge he was making.

"I gave it a stir, save it burning," he said. "Where'd you get these tiles, mate?"

"Tile shop," said Zack bluntly. "She'll be down soon as."

The man at the table had cleared a space for himself. He leaned back in his chair and yawned. This was the first day back on the job since New Year and he planned on making it a successful one. He had a warm glow about this first call of the day. These kids were young, there was money in evidence, he would probably get what he'd come for.

"Hi!" said Ethan, coming into the room.

The man at the table looked up. His companion dragged himself away from the tiles, folded his arms and became the sullen threat he was meant to be.

"What do you want Miss Morales for?" asked Ethan.

"Let's wait for her to come down, shall we?"

When Isabella appeared she was dressed in a tight white sweater and jeans that groaned at the seams whenever she moved. Her hair billowed with every turn of her head. The two visitors regrouped to less aggressive positions. The one at the table stood up to shake Isabella's hand.

"My name is Kevin Dunstan," he said. "My colleague is Mark Pooley."

Pooley unfolded his arms and leaned away from the kitchen unit while Dunstan showed Isabella an ID card in a leather wallet.

"We represent Far Side Collection Service. Our job is to

recover unpaid debts in a friendly and businesslike manner."

"Well, sorry to have kept you, but you can now leave," said Zack.

"You invited us in."

"I'm inviting you out."

Isabella intervened. "Just a moment..."

She gestured for Dunstan to sit down at the table again, which he gratefully did. Isabella glanced from one face to the other in perfect innocence.

"Explain the problem to me," she said.

Dunstan opened a folder and ran the backs of his fingers down a list.

"There are 17 claims against you here, Miss, for sums ranging between £500 and £3300. Let's say that you've forgotten to pay these debts and before any more..."

"How much altogether?" Zack asked.

"£16,372."

Isabella smiled at him and asked sweetly, "And who am I supposed to owe this money to, Kevin? Gas, electricity, phone provider?"

"Friends and acquaintances, mainly."

She looked at the list of names, becoming more and more horrified as she did so.

"These are people from uni. I can't possibly owe..." She turned, wide-eyed, and pleaded with Ethan, tapping a name on the list. "This guy here, I definitely paid him back. And Jason Dorner, God, he's the richest man I know, but I still paid him back."

"We've sent you several requests for repayment, Miss. Perhaps you didn't receive them?"

"They will have gone to my old address."

"Canterbury Gardens, Oxford? No, they were sent here."

He showed her a copy of the latest letter with its underlined threats and fistful of exclamation marks.

"How did you get this address?" she asked.

Zack had known the answer to that the moment Jason Dorner's name was mentioned. Biker Boy. Had the people she owed money to clubbed together and hired Far Side Collection Service?

"Did I sign contracts or letters of agreement with any of these people?" she asked. "Did they issue me with IOUs? I mean, for you to just swoop in and..."

"Miss, Jason Dorner's father is a barrister and he will take this matter to law if he has to."

She stared at him. "That is appalling! You're threatening me. In front of friends, witnesses."

She stepped away from the moment and watched herself go to the stove and lift the pan of porridge from the hotplate. It was still simmering as she approached Dunstan. She stood beside him, then slowly tipped the contents over his head. She spooned out the dregs and dropped them onto the wig of Quaker oats. It began to slip down his forehead, scalding the skin as it went. When it reached his eyes he tried to claw it away. His eyelids were already blistering. He opened his mouth to scream...

"I'm passing on the information I was given," he said. "Why don't we see if we can reach an accommodation?"

"Have you got any legal powers in all this?" Zack asked.

"No, but I'm authorised by the parties to inform you of what will happen should their claims be ignored."

"Sixteen grand?" said Ethan, finally taking in the enormity of it. "Nobody borrows that much from friends."

"I know what's happened," said Isabella, closing her eyes in grim realisation. "I did borrow now and again, then asked my father's secretary to reimburse people. She's either forgotten or, more likely, written cheques in Argentinian pesos."

She sighed and explained that she'd had the same problem herself just before Christmas at a bank in Ealing which refused to accept her allowance cheque. She promised she would tackle her father again, if Kevin cared to leave the list, or as a backup he could take Juan's email address to pass on to his clients.

"I'd rather have a bona fide cheque from you, Miss Morales. Post-dated, if necessary, to give your father time to..."

She smiled. "Certainly."

When she returned from the attic with a blank cheque and a biro, she was all flirty smiles and playful charm, mainly aimed at Dunstan, who wasn't entirely immune.

"It's been so long since I wrote a cheque," she said. "I mean can you remember the last time you actually wrote one out, Kevin?"

She waited for Pooley to pull out a chair for her and sat at the table.

"Shall we say two weeks from now? Oh, would you believe it!"

The biro she was using had dried up. Dunstan reached into his jacket and handed her his own.

"Far Side – two words – Collection Service," he said. "One, six, three, seven, two."

When she'd finished he took the cheque and scrutinised

it. Her account was with Banco Galicia, who had an address in Buenos Aires. Would they honour a cheque like this, for such an amount and written in pounds, or was it more baloney? Dunstan didn't really mind. By writing it out and signing it this slippery bitch had admitted that she owed the money. That would do for now.

Ethan escorted Dunstan and Pooley to the front door and watched them depart in their ancient BMW. He committed the registration number to memory and turned to Zack, who had joined him.

"You need to get a grip on that, mate," said Zack quietly. "Easier said than done, I know, but…"

Ethan sniggered. "Rein her in, you mean?"

"She hasn't borrowed money; she's squeezed it out of people with no intention of paying them back."

"Will they die without it?"

Zack looked at him, puzzled by his callousness. "No, but five hundred quid here, a grand there – some people can't afford it."

"Then they should've been more careful." He nodded at the departing BMW. "Two debt jockeys bowl up, accuse her of stealing, threaten her with…"

Their voices were rising. "I didn't hear accusations, I didn't hear threats," said Zack. "Okay, one of the fathers is a barrister."

"Let's all quake together, shall we? Isabella's old man has screwed up and now she's written them a cheque. Anything else I can help you with?"

He pushed past Zack and went back upstairs.

In the attic Isabella was standing by her underwear drawer. She turned as Ethan entered. He was frowning, part hangover, part concern.

"Zack reckons you owe that money. For real."

She smiled. "He's right. I do."

He laughed briefly, unsure whether to believe her. "Now you've paid it back."

"Not really," she whispered.

"You mean...?"

"I mean exactly what you're thinking. Those two parasites have had a wasted journey. The cheque will bounce. Oh, don't look so shocked. You must owe people money, surely."

"Not to the tune of sixteen grand."

She shrugged. "Aren't I wicked? But it isn't their reputations, or their self-esteem or pride I've taken, it's just money."

She kissed him on the cheek. He felt the lipstick she'd applied for Dunstan's benefit stick to his skin. She stared at him, waiting for his response. He nodded. There was a logic to what she had said. It was just money. Two months ago he would have been terrified by not paying his debts, to say nothing of dreading his parents' disapproval. At last he was starting to believe, as Isabella had always done, that money is the easiest thing in the world to come by. Any fool can make it.

He returned to the bed and threw himself across it, face down. Isabella opened her trophy box. She reached into her bra and took out Dunstan's pen. It was an expensive one, if a bit flashy. Gold. She slipped it into the box and closed the lid.

-16-

Imogen went carefully up the narrow stairs to the attic. It was the only place in the house where she felt uneasy. When a stair creaked she imagined the tread shifting, throwing her off balance. In black and white, rather than colour, she would reach out for the handrail to steady herself, cut, her hand would slip beneath it, cut, and she would fall to the landing below. How her mother had coped with it as a girl was beyond her.

She tapped on the attic door and called out for Ethan. It was no secret that he had moved in with Isabella, which was one more thing Teresa and Marcus were pretending had never happened. It was a detail, of course, and yet... yet for Imogen there was something frightening about Carla's departure. 'I'm just popping to the postbox,' Teresa would say when they were kids. 'Carla, you're in charge.' For five minutes the teenage Carla ruled with a rod of iron.

Now she was gone and the structure they had known since childhood was beginning to crumble. That at least was Imogen's middle-of-the-night belief. Her daylight text messages were simpler and more to the point. '*Carla, I miss my big sister. I love you. Please come back. x*'. She received cursory replies, but nothing to suggest Carla would change her mind.

Ethan came to the door, a spliff in his hand, his manner slow and bleary.

"Hi, babe, come in."

Isabella was on the sofa, leaning on the arm of it, legs drawn up beside her. She was smoking a cigarette and now watched as brother and sister embraced with a warmth she didn't comprehend. Where she came from people weren't in the habit of displaying affection, but every time these two met on the stairs, or in the kitchen, or when one of them walked in through the front door, they hugged as if they'd been apart for months. She had asked Ethan why that was. He had never denied Imogen time, he said. As children they spent so much of it together, hours on end in the pool, emerging with skin wrinkled like walnuts. Together they watched the same films over and over, shared the same sense of humour, even the same friends.

"Hello, sweetie, how are you?" said Isabella.

"I'm fine, fine."

"You want?" Ethan asked his sister.

Imogen nodded and he started to roll her a spliff. She collapsed backwards onto a beanbag she recognised from childhood. It had been pensioned off to the loft at Golden Meadow five years ago and hauled back into service when Ashbury was furnished.

"You heard from her?" Ethan asked, lighting the joint and handing it to her.

"Not for a week."

"Bugs you, huh? Bugs me. We should send a gunboat down the canal, sink the *Landmark* and drag her away."

Imogen drew on the spliff and held it.

"Something else on your mind?" Ethan asked.

She nodded. "Three months from now, it's all over for me at Central. Choices to make. This theatre group, they've asked me to join them."

"Who are they?" asked Isabella.

"They're called Cross Curtain. All female. They reckon it's their USP, which in case you didn't know..."

"Unique Selling Point," said Ethan. "Sounds desperate."

"I know why they've asked me," Imogen went on. "Lawlor's quite a name to have in their monthly blog."

Ethan groaned. "My advice? Wait till your end-of-course production. You're bound to get some takers. Christ, Zack's in this *Conshie* thing simply because Dad's who he is."

He turned to Isabella, expecting her to agree.

"Depends if the female-centric thing has legs," she said. "I say yes. Men have had it their way for so long."

"Exactly," said Imogen.

She screwed up her face and lowered her voice, presumably in case it reached as far as Turnham Green where the company was based.

"Trouble is, most of them aren't very good."

"Then you'd be mad..." Ethan began.

"They are committed, though. And they're not *all* crap: one or two are pretty reasonable."

Isabella leaned up, swung her legs round and reached down for her ballet pumps. She had sensed an opportunity to solve the Imogen problem.

"When did you say they've asked you to join?"

"They're putting on two new plays and they've wangled a three-week run at the Cockpit."

Ethan clucked like a chicken, but the girls ignored him.

"Hour-long pieces," said Imogen, pushing herself farther back into the beanbag. "The one they've offered me is a three-hander and it's good. Have you guys got any coffee up here or do I have to go down to the kitchen? Amy's still doing that giant jigsaw puzzle."

Isabella leaned forward and whispered to Ethan. "Darling, go and make us all a drink."

He stretched out and got to his feet with a display of being much put upon, then staggered out of the room and down the stairs. Isabella smiled and crushed out her cigarette.

"You know what bothers me?" she said, quietly. "Some are good actors, you say, others not quite so."

"Yeah."

"Ever thought of asking a name to take a part?"

"I think Dame Judy's booked that month."

"I don't mean a big star, I'm thinking more, well… you remember Jane Sillitoe?"

Imogen laughed and abandoned the spliff. "She may not be *big* big, but she's big. Getting her to agree might be…"

"I kept in touch with her, after *An Inspector Calls*. We meet up occasionally." She reached for her phone, which had slipped down between the sofa cushions. "I had a text from her the other day saying why don't we do lunch some time. What if I asked her?"

As the idea took hold Imogen began to flap with excitement. "I'd love it, but would she be up for playing with an all-female group?"

Isabella smiled. "Oh, Jane wouldn't mind. Quite the opposite, I'm sure."

She found the text message she'd been referring to and showed it to Imogen.

"If she likes the idea, we'll meet up and go from there."

***

When Isabella arrived at Beralini's in Henrietta Street, Jane Sillitoe was already seated at a corner table. Her profile was unmistakable, the face long and equine with a 'neck any hangman would die for', as a witty critic had once said. She took the remark as a compliment, but wished someone would occasionally mention her startling eyes or gravelly voice, two attributes that had certainly helped her love life over the years. She was nearly forty and for years had looked much younger, but her mother all too often had said that her youthful appearance would suddenly dip, and reached up and plucked at the loose skin on her own neck by way of emphasis. Partly to counter this Jane always dressed immaculately, expensively and, yes, alluringly. Always on show as the actress, never the slob in jeans and T-shirt, the ploy had served her well. She was rarely out of work.

She rose to greet Isabella and they air-kissed.

"Isabella, darling, how wonderful to see you." She turned to the waiter who had been fawning over her ever since she arrived. "Mario, bring us a bottle of the Barolo, if you'd be so kind."

The waiter smiled and hung Isabella's coat on a bentwood stand next to Jane's while the two women took their seats. Isabella glanced round at the other customers. Most were from the City, she thought, the men with fashionable stubble and garish waistcoats, the women in buttoned-up jackets and matching stilettos. One or two had noticed Isabella's arrival but quickly returned to their smartphones.

"Tell me everything!" said Jane. "The job? The house? How was Argentina?"

"It was big, as always, and I know you love the outdoors, Jane, but too much of it and I begin to feel—" she smiled, coyly "—insignificant."

"Is Ethan still…?"

Isabella laughed. "Yes, we're still on."

"Oh, good. I am so pleased for you. I miss his father, you know. Those nights he spent at our house, when it was too late to drive home, we would play silly boardgames, or Jenga and we would…" She stopped herself. "We were always groggy the next morning."

Isabella smiled. "He stayed over?"

Jane played along. "The best-looking man on the London stage spent at least one night a week with us at Greenwich."

The waiter came with the wine and poured each of them a glass. He left the bottle and departed at a smile from Jane.

"You wanted to see me?" she said.

"Yes, about Imogen, strangely enough." The name didn't strike an immediate chord with Jane. "Marcus's daughter."

"Oh, the one at Central."

"She's been paged by a company called Cross Curtain."

"I think I've heard of them…"

"They want her for something called a scratch night? New writing, two plays, an hour long each. At the Cockpit."

"They're going up in the world."

"It's a big ask, Jane, but would you read the one Imo's doing and consider being in it?"

Jane was instinctively hesitant. "Er, yes, of course. I mean I do have a part looming in a series, but... yes, with pleasure."

Isabella heaved a sigh and leaned forward in her chair. "There, that's my good deed for the day. She's absolutely nuts about you, Jane. Nothing short of a crush, really."

Isabella hadn't expected Jane to say anything other than yes to her request. Even well-established actresses are susceptible to flattery.

"The steak," said Isabella to the hovering waiter. "Medium. That should get me round the National Portrait Gallery."

"That's where you're heading?"

Isabella looked away and struck a serious pose, the better to be believed.

"It's a crazy story, really. My mum started looking into our family tree. My dad's people were extremely dull. Bandits and farmers who emigrated to Argentina from Catalonia in the eighteenth century. My mother's side was almost a straight line. Her family travelled from Seville to Buenos Aires in 1723. They were shopkeepers, bakers, tradesmen, but what really excited me was the name Pacheco."

She paused, making Jane feel the name should mean something. It didn't.

"I followed it right back to 1618 when Juana Pacheco, my great, great, ad infinitum grandmother married Diego Velasquez."

Jane's own experience of genealogy was mainly

through actor friends who traced their ancestry on television programmes and wound up in crocodile tears at the revelations. Most of them, apparently, were related to people like Anne Boleyn or Oliver Cromwell, never an ordinary member of the peasantry.

"Why the trip to the Portrait Gallery?"

Isabella reached down into her bag and took out a printed postcard. Jane recognised it as *The Toilet of Venus*—a reclining nude, her back to the audience, as it were, looking at her own face in a mirror held by Cupid.

"Juana modelled for Diego," Isabella went on, excitedly. "And that picture is my mother in her prime! The waist, the hips, the thighs, they're hers, they're mine... don't you think?"

"The face in the mirror's a little blurred," Jane said.

"That's the reason I want to see the original. I'm hoping it's more revealing."

Jane smiled. The story could be true, of course, but as a fantasy was it harmless wishful thinking, or something dottier?

"Good luck," she said.

"What are you doing the rest of the day?"

"I have to see my agent, three o'clock. Money, contract, boring stuff."

When they finished the meal Jane signalled the waiter to bring the bill and Isabella began a well-practised rummage through her bag, her face tensing up as she turned over a purse, a packet of tissues, receipts, keys, a face-repair kit. Jane waved her anxiety aside.

"Darling, my treat."

Isabella sighed with relief. "That is so sweet of you.

Oh, here it is…"

Jane smiled and handed over her debit card.

* * *

When Isabella arrived back at Ashbury, it was almost dark and she could see Ethan and Imogen through the front window. Brother and sister were laughing, giggling, overtaking each other in their banter, finishing each other's sentences as if in some well-rehearsed comedy. The sweet smell of marijuana was seeping out under the door and into the hallway.

Isabella climbed the stairs to the attic, dropped her coat and shoulder bag onto the bed and carried on through to the bathroom. She crept up to the mirror, wondering what facet of her would be gazing back. She smiled and greeted the arch strategist, who had resisted the urge to seduce one of the theatre's better known actresses, sacrificing the pleasure of doing so for the longer game of being rid of Imogen. There was still a trace of the elegant fantasist in her reflection, the one who had sat in the National Gallery, room 30, staring at her invented heritage, admiring the perfect woman, the unblemished skin and voluptuous curves. She knew why she had chosen *The Toilet of Venus*. You could almost reach out and touch Juana's shoulders, and yet the full face was a mystery. The reflection in the hand mirror, held by Cupid, was so cleverly indistinct that an onlooker could readily imagine their own lover in its place. The longer Isabella had looked, the more she had imagined her mother, the more she had seen herself.

She poured herself a glass of last night's wine and

stretched out on the sofa. She reached down to her bag for the grey cashbook and made an entry, £75 for lunch. She had, after all, drunk most of the wine and her main course was the more expensive of the two. The tally for the month so far amounted to £2540.

An hour later, she sent Ethan a text message, knowing he would respond immediately, in spite of Imogen's agreeable company. *'I'm upstairs and desperate'*, she said, adding an emoji of a face with its tongue hanging out. *'And tell Imogen it's on! JS will read the script and consider!'*

Two minutes later Ethan appeared at the door and looked across to where she lay naked on the bed, just as Juana Pacheco might have done while her husband committed her to posterity. Ethan undressed as he approached, saying he'd barely managed to stop Imo tearing up the stairs behind him. Isabella rolled over onto her back and pulled him down close beside her.

"A good day, then?" he whispered, taking a swathe of hair and letting it run through his fingers and flow around her body.

"An *excellent* day. But I need this to round it off."

She took his head in both hands and stared at him. She had noticed it before, but here in the half-light it was even more pronounced, the similarity between father and son. Both as handsome as you could wish, one of them rich, famous and, as yet, untried, the other as feckless and besotted a lover as she'd ever had.

"Open your mouth, just far enough." she said.

He smiled, parted his lips, as she grabbed him by the hair and kissed him.

-17-

"They're cool about you taking the day off?" said Imogen casually as she drove Isabella to Greenwich. "Your bosses, I mean?"

Isabella chuckled. "They can hardly refuse. I have this 'kidney problem'. I need regular hospital check-ups. Life and death stuff."

Imogen turned to her, frowning. "Seriously?"

"Oh, you sweet girl, of course not."

Imogen smiled, horrified by the ploy yet secretly admiring Isabella's gall in using it.

Jane Sillitoe lived in a street of small terraced houses with a flight of steps up to her front door and another down to the basement window. It was as close to Greenwich Park as she could afford when she bought the place, but she had promised herself she would move closer when finances allowed. When that time came, she was so in love with the house that she decided to stay put. The only problem with her particular street was that car parking was by resident permit. As her visitors neared their destination, Isabella texted to say they were close by. Jane emerged through her front door waving a windscreen pass, which Isabella took charge of and tucked behind a clip on the windscreen.

"How is your father?" Jane asked as she pecked Imogen on the cheek. "Your mother too, how are they?"

"Fine," said Imogen, taken aback by the sudden familiarity. "Yes, they're fine."

She was conscious that Isabella and Jane, in their designer casuals, were far better dressed than she was. As usual it was jeans and a scuffed denim jacket for Imogen, worn over the Oxfam sweater that had faded from cerise to pink in the year she'd had it. Nevertheless she twitched her shoulders back, lengthened her neck and took the script from the back of the car. She carried it like a ticking bomb into the house.

The interior of the place was a delight and quite in contrast to its yellow brick facade. All the furniture, from the dining table and its accompanying Z-shaped chairs, the stepladder bookcases to the dresser in carved oak had been made by Jane's partner, Billy, she told her visitors. Was that Billy or Billie, Imogen wondered. Her question was answered by a wooden sculpture in an alcove. It was of two idealised, entwined female forms, each with her face buried in the other's body. The grain of the wood was so pronounced it might have been veins under their skin.

They took their coffee into the living space and settled at a low teak table shaped like a sunflower, petals and seeds carved into it. Too delicate to put cups and saucers on, Imogen thought.

"So, you've got something you'd like me to read?" Jane said.

"And be in," Imogen blurted out. "I'm sorry, I mean if you think it's good enough, I'd love you to think about being..."

"Cross Curtain. And they've grabbed a two-week gig at the Cockpit?"

Imogen nodded. "They've asked me to be in this when I leave Central."

"How flattering."

Imogen shifted in her chair, which might have been beautiful to look at but was impossible to relax in. "Oh, I know it's the Lawlor name they want and I feel really bitchy saying this..."

Nervousness was the last thing Jane had expected in a child of Marcus Lawlor and she found it endearing. Most young actresses she knew were unbearably confident and full of themselves. She reached out and laid a hand on Imogen's arm.

"Be as bitchy as you like."

Imogen smiled and looked at Jane properly for the first time since they had arrived. Marcus had described her as having a characterful face, his way of saying that in some aspects she could be stunning, even beautiful, but all of a sudden her features could harden and become witchlike.

Imogen lowered her voice. "Some of the company aren't very good."

Jane laughed. "That isn't bitchy, darling. Just wait till you've been out there a few years, then you'll know bitchy."

Isabella was beginning to feel slightly left out. "To be fair, Imo, they've had great reviews. A whole paragraph in *The Guardian* about their cut-down version of *The Tempest*."

"Maybe the critic was just grateful for it being short," said Jane. "Kudos, though: tackling Shakespeare, long or short, is quite something." She nodded at the script Imogen was clutching. "So, what's the play called?"

Imogen wiped nonexistent dust from the front cover. "*Ships*. By a guy called Luke Duval. It's his first, so you won't have heard of him."

"What's it about?"

"You want me to read the half page at the…?"

Jane smiled. "I'd rather you told me in your own words."

It was a kind of test, Imogen thought, and shifted slightly as she focussed.

"It's set in the 1920s. A newly married couple seem to be living an idyllic life, but the woman knows something is missing and it worries her husband that she can't say what it is. He invites his sister to stay, to see if she can help, and the two women discover much in common. And then even more as they begin an affair. They eventually decide they'll go off into the sunset together, but come the moment of truth, all three on the verge of their lives being changed forever, the women realise they can't do it. Each of them loves this man in their own way, for their own reasons, and to leave him would destroy him."

There was a pause while Imogen waited for Jane to comment, or at least put life into the deadpan expression she'd adopted. She eventually took the script from Imogen and promised to get back to her as soon as possible.

The brief awkwardness which followed was broken by Billie arriving home after a morning's work at her studio. She had a whiff of ageing goth about her, with marks on her face where elaborate piercings had once been and a violent tattoo rising from under the collar of her shirt. Isabella stood up to greet her, but Billie raised a hand to fend her off, gesturing to the sawdust in just about every crease of her clothes. She and Jane distance-kissed and Billie dumped her holdall on the bar linking the room through to the kitchen.

"Hi," she said to Imogen.

"This is Imogen Lawlor," said Jane. "Daughter of Marcus. Inspector Goole?"

"Right," said Billie, trying to bring Marcus to mind. "Billie West. And before anything else, I need a shower. It's been a dusty day."

* * *

Imogen and Isabella left Greenwich an hour later with Jane waving them off from her front door. During the drive back to Ashbury Road, Imogen imagined a host of reasons why Jane would hate *Ships* and turn down the idea of being in it. It wasn't until she nearly clipped a throbbing Audi as she negotiated Chiswick roundabout that she uttered a word, and that was to call the driver a twat. She was even more annoyed that he didn't respond but instead zoomed off ahead of her.

"How do you think it went?" Isabella asked.

"Badly," Imogen muttered.

Isabella smiled. "I think she was flattered."

"Also, look at me. I mean she's dead stylish – the house, the clothes, the furniture. And I turn up dressed like a bag lady." She slammed the driving wheel. "Why the hell didn't I make an effort?"

"I thought you played it just right."

"There's a bigger problem. Say Jane agrees to do it. The three-week run at the Cockpit clashes with my end-of-course production."

Isabella shrugged. "Abandon the course, do *Ships*."

"My father's on the board of Central, one of their big names. If I duck out he'll be wrecked."

"You'd rather keep Marcus sweet than further your own career? Crazy. Especially since Jane clearly likes you."

Imogen turned to her for a moment. "You mean she…?"

"Couldn't take her eyes off you. She'll say yes just to get to know you better."

"I want her to do it because she likes the play!"

"You know your trouble? Carla's and Ethan's too?"

"You missed out Zack."

Isabella rocked her hand in front of her. "Jury's still out on him, but the rest of you? Freedom of choice from birth, but you don't know how to use it. Opportunities galore, there for the taking, yet you defer to Marcus and Teresa before grabbing them." She turned to Imogen and lowered her voice. "You should have grown up on an Argentinian wasteland, as dead in its way as a New York or London high-rise. Two options in such a place: you jump from a window or walk down the stairs, out the door and never return. So, if an actress of Jane Sillitoe's calibre doesn't mind kissing you on stage, why hesitate to kiss her back?" She laid a hand on Imogen's arm and said, as if it were a matter of life and death, "Promise you won't hesitate."

"I promise."

"As for joining Cross Curtain, that'll spare you the stupid business of coming out to your family or, God forbid, having a clan meeting about it."

Imogen laughed. "Jane hasn't agreed to anything yet."

"She will, believe me."

***

Isabella held the demon's head up to the light in the attic bedroom. It was the size of a walnut, hardwood and exquisitely carved with a knife that must have been as delicate as a scalpel. Billie's handiwork, almost certainly.

She hadn't been looking for a memento of the trip to Jane's house, but there it was in the most unlikely place, the downstairs toilet. It had been on the end of the cord by which the window blind was raised or lowered. If it had a voice it would have called out, she mused, if it had arms it would've beckoned. She had untied the knot which held it in place and slipped the carving into her bag. Would they miss it? One day soon, no doubt. How would they explain its disappearance? Had it been flushed away, dropped in the bin, stood on and crushed into dust? Surely no one would have stolen a wooden knob.

She unlocked the walnut box and added it to her collection.

-18-

As Marcus and Teresa sipped their morning coffee the doorbell clanged and the dogs went berserk. It was one of many jobs Marcus had been promising to do ever since they moved in: change the doorbell from the yank-down triangle Alfred Tweak probably installed to a push-button purr the dogs wouldn't react so violently to. Teresa hollered the dogs into silence and went to greet the early-morning visitor. It was Colin Simpson and he insulted her immediately.

"Lord and master not up yet?"

She had no idea why she responded in kind to such an inane greeting. "Can his lady and mistress help?"

He almost let fly another witticism but something in her glare prevented him.

"We think we know... well, we're pretty certain, 95 percent, we know the secret of Bigg's Cave. Shall I come in and wait or would it be better if I..."

"Come through," she said, brusquely.

He entered the kitchen carrying a holdall with a Czech logo on it. Slazenga. Whatever the bag contained was heavy. Teresa gestured him to take a seat at the kitchen table and offered him coffee, which he declined.

"Between jobs, I hear?" he said to Marcus, inviting

comment which never materialised.

"Bigg's Cave," said Colin, eventually.

"Not another extension, I hope."

"We know its secret. There isn't one. Well, there is, but it's not a cave." He looked at Marcus expectantly. "I thought you'd be keen to know what we'd found."

"I assumed you'd go right ahead and tell me."

"The evidence is all in here," Colin said, pointing down at the holdall.

He took the bag to the stone hearth and upended it. Out fell an assortment of charred ironwork and at first gawp Marcus could identify crude hinges, door latches, square forged nails, hooks, the blade of a scythe, a knife, tines of a rake, rivets, handles.

"These artefacts are from a wooden dwelling. Cottage? Hovel? Cross between the two, I imagine." He turned to try and enthuse Teresa. "What do you think of it?"

"Rusty," said Teresa.

"The verdict?" asked Marcus, now showing a modicum of interest.

With the romance of finding something beyond his wildest dreams shattered, Colin began to speak in nigh on proper sentences.

"It isn't a cave. Caves don't have doors and windows, never mind hinges and handles thereon. A bit of research up at the manor house did the trick. Funny people those Van Aalsbergs. He's alright but she's a bit Dutch, if you know what I mean. A touch of the winged bonnet and a dress you could camp under."

Marcus glanced at his nonexistent watch.

"I asked to see the family records. There it was. Your

man Alfred Tweak was a good friend of the then owner, Lady Mary Clissold. Friend as in a D.H. Lawrence kind of friend, I surmise, because when she died in 1710, she left him £3000. Close on a million quid in today's money. Life-changing. And boy, did he change his. He was living on this site in a cottage, mainly wood and thatch. He pulled it down, had it dragged across the field and burned. Then built this place."

Marcus nodded. "Started over. Lucky man."

"So the hole was already there?" said Teresa.

"Yes. Could be anything. Meteorite falling to earth, subsidence due to a dried-up watercourse, even a hand-dug slurry pit far enough from the house so as not to offend. Or it could just be a hole in the ground which they used as a fire pit." He stooped to grab his empty holdall and in the manner of a superhero said, "My work here is done."

When Teresa returned from seeing Colin off the premises she found Marcus kneeling at the hearth, sifting through the heap of iron oddments. He stood up and transferred the rust on his hands to the seat of his jeans. He went over to his computer and typed into the search bar, 'Oak Tree, mature, for sale'. As with most things he tried to buy on the internet, up came a thousand choices, none of them what he was after. He was offered puny 20-year-old trees, five metres tall. He wanted *big* as in *enormous*: surely such a tree must be available? If Capability Brown could obtain hundreds in the 18th century, surely Marcus Lawlor could find just one in the 21st?

***

Jane called Imogen a few days later to say, without resorting to effusive compliments, that she thought *Ships* was excellent and she would be happy to appear in it. Could the two of them meet to discuss it further? Imogen made all the right, bouncy noises and arranged to go over to Greenwich for supper, but somewhere in her mind she began to regret having approached Jane in the first place. Not even Isabella with her shrieky delight at the good news could fend off the unsettling prospect of informing her parents.

She would do it at Easter, she decided. Even without Carla there would be enough covering hullabaloo to soften the grand reveal of her quitting drama school ahead of schedule. She would mention Cross Curtain, but probably not add that it was a female-centric company. If the subject came up, she knew there would be questions, hurt glances and stifled sighs from her mother as she wondered what on earth had happened to Kieran Hart.

* * *

On Easter Sunday, after the obligatory morning hike, the party returned to the house and sat down to a lunch that would have fed twice their number. As usual on these occasions, Henry carved the beef joint while Marcus went round the table filling glasses. Just as he had done at Christmas he had laid places for Carla and Matt and right up until dessert there was an air of expectation that they might rush in, apologise for their lateness and dive on the food. As it became more and more certain that this wouldn't happen the table banter began to lose its fizz and the silences grew longer. Imogen broke one of them by gently slapping the table and saying,

"Mum, Dad, everybody, I've got something to tell you. Dad, please, sit down and listen to this."

His face was a picture of theatrical innocence. "I *am* listening."

"Grandad, is he?"

Henry smiled, confirming the general belief that in his eyes Imogen could do no wrong.

"No, my sweet, his mind is firmly on the latest script for *Salter's Edge.*"

Marcus held up his hands in capitulation and sank back into his chair.

"I'm in a bit of a quandary," Imogen said. "I've been invited to join Cross Curtain."

They expected her to follow up with more information, but Isabella had schooled her in this type of revelation. The trick was to get those on the receiving end to ask questions as soon as possible: that would leave her in control of the conversation to follow.

"Who or what is Cross Curtain?" Teresa asked.

"A theatre company in West London."

"Never heard," said Marcus. "Dad?"

Henry shook his head and silence fell again.

"Haven't they got a three-week run at the Cockpit?" Isabella prompted.

"That's what they want me for."

Marcus warmed to their existence. "Well, that's fantastic. Or at least it can't do you any harm. What's the play?"

She told him it was called *Ships*, a period piece about a young married couple: the wife getting unhappier by the day so her husband calls in his sister to lift her out her decline. Marcus nodded, suitably unimpressed.

"Thing is, Jane Sillitoe's agreed to play the sister, opposite me," said Imogen.

"Now you are talking," said Henry. "When's it on?"

"May 10th to the 31st."

He raised his glass. "Two seats, five rows back."

Marcus looked at her, slightly puzzled. "End of May. Aren't you appearing in the Tennessee Williams at Central?"

Imogen glanced at Isabella for courage. "I'll have to let them down. Three weeks at the Cockpit is too good a chance to..."

"Just a second."

"Dad, I've made up my mind."

"Good for you," said Henry.

"I disagree," said Teresa, sharply. "You can't just walk out on a course."

"With only six weeks left of it?"

"I don't care. You've agreed to be in *Camino Real*, the lead no less."

Isabella chose that moment to nudge Ethan, who stood up and lifted his glass as if he would make a toast to his sister's decision. He smiled down at Isabella.

"We also have an announcement," he said.

Teresa had always understood the power of an unfinished sentence. Deferred announcements were almost as dangerous.

"Why don't you tell them?" said Isabella.

"No, you."

She smiled, coyly. "I'm expecting a baby."

Teresa's fingernails scratched the tabletop as she

clenched her fists. Her beloved, jobless, feckless, coke-snorting, gifted son had been well and truly snared by this woman about whom she knew so little but suspected so much.

Ethan looked round at the stunned faces. "Don't all holler at once. Your first grandchild, Marcus, Teresa. Henry, you'll be a great-grandfather."

There were a few half-hearted congratulations but no extended followup, no questions about the due date, the sex of the new arrival or possible names. Taken aback by his family's lack of enthusiasm, Ethan added that his son or daughter would be born a Libran, just like Teresa.

Imogen had her own view of the breaking news. For a moment she thought Isabella had chosen to make the announcement in order to draw fire from Cross Curtain and speculation about Imogen's waywardness. A second later she realised that the opposite might be true, that she herself was the cover for the pregnancy news. Either way Isabella had stolen the day, since Jane Sillitoe's involvement in *Ships* would be history come June 1st. Isabella would soon be giving birth to a new family member who would outlive them all.

-19-

Ethan felt, rather than heard, Isabella crying. He had woken to find her body shaking gently beside him and turned to see her holding a ball of tissues to her face. He leaned up on his forearm, suddenly wide awake.

"What is it?" he asked, anxiously.

"I'm sorry, I didn't want to wake you. It's the baby."

He was none the wiser. "You mean being pregnant is making you... what?"

She shook her head. "Today at Golden Meadow, I thought they'd be pleased."

He sat up and switched on his bedside light, blinking at the alarm clock. It was 3:20am.

"So did I, to be honest."

"Maybe with it coming on top of Imo leaving drama school... but you'd think a new baby would..." She turned to him. "I want us to be a family. With them. And, yes, Henry too and Jenny and their friends."

She took a quaking breath and summoned a fresh outbreak of tears. He took her hand.

"Give them time, maybe?"

"What if they won't accept me, to say nothing of our baby, I mean maybe we should think of striking out on our own somewhere?"

He frowned. "We can't afford it. I haven't got a job and you'll have to quit yours."

She struggled to sit up beside him, reached out for a tissue and blew her nose.

"What happened with that project? The documentary about the graveyard they dug up?"

"I haven't heard back from the producer, which is a bad sign," he said, bleakly. "Listen, half three in the morning isn't the time to talk about this. I'll speak to Mum and Dad, I promise."

* * *

It took a week of persistence on Isabella's part for Ethan to keep his word. After another night of tears he rose early the next morning and phoned Teresa from the landline extension in the attic. She was feeding the dogs when the phone rang and jammed the phone between her shoulder and ear while she carried on spooning their breakfast into bowls.

"Teresa, how's it going?"

"Fine. What time is it?"

She could see perfectly well from the kitchen clock that it was seven thirty.

"You mean why am I phoning so early? It's about the other day, when we told you we were pregnant."

She could tell from his dry, slightly belligerent tone that a complaint would follow.

"The response was tepid to say the least. From everyone. It's been bothering me ever since."

Teresa wondered if that was the flunky 'me' talking, meaning Isabella. She put the phone on speaker.

"Well, I certainly didn't mean it to sound that way. Is Isabella there? Let me speak to her."

"She's asleep still." He slowed down and his voice warmed a little. "Look, Mum, she feels cut off, maybe because her family's thousands of miles away and the least she expected from you lot was to be overjoyed that a sprog was on the way."

"I hate the word sprog. Baby or child."

"Don't change the subject."

Marcus had drifted into the kitchen, still in his dressing gown. She pointed to the dog bowls, which he placed on the floor, and put the phone on speaker.

"You'd like me to set the record straight?" Teresa asked.

"A bit more than that, hopefully. An apology maybe?"

She felt the blood rush to her neck and face. "An apology for not going wild at the news?"

"Well, a show of..."

"You must be mad, the pair of you. You're living in a shared house and you've no income. How can you provide for a family?"

"Hell, Ma, don't you start as well."

"Which means you're living on Isabella's salary and if you think..."

Ethan cut her off. She tossed the phone to Marcus, who replaced it on its cradle.

"Bit harsh," he said.

"That cheeky little bitch is now policing our reactions."

She sat down quickly at the table, realising that she had

just raised her voice at Ethan for the first time in over four years. Could that possibly be true?

"Would it be so hard to just say sorry, we were taken aback but we're delighted?"

"It would be a lie on three fronts. I'm not sorry, I wasn't taken aback and I'm not delighted."

He turned away, trying to avoid a head-on collision. "I agree it's a bad time to get pregnant, no job and..."

"It's deliberate on her part. I should have done something much sooner..."

He laughed emptily and the dogs decamped into the living room. "You need a refresher course in basic biology. It takes two. Male, female."

"So what's she doing without birth control?"

"What's *he* doing without it?"

She got to her feet again and closed in on him.

"What is it with you and that girl? Is it the flattery, the come-and-get-me smiles, all the hair? The perfect tits, always on offer? Can't you bloody see?"

"No, I can't."

"Is that why you've done nothing?" He opened his mouth to protest. "You're great at playing the tough cop who can put the fear of God into a family of prigs, but a girl smiles at you in real life and you're lost!"

Marcus shrugged. "Terri, what do you suggest..."

"You can stop behaving like some pathetic luvvy liberal who's afraid to rock the boat. I want that bloody boat sunk! Not only has she nailed Ethan to the wall with fatherhood, I say she got rid of Carla."

"Well, I..."

She slapped the table. "And I'm not sure how but I think

she's moved on to Imo. You saw her at Easter, prompting her, asking the right questions on cue."

She had run out of breath and leaned forward on the table, looking sideways at him with disdain.

"You know what's wrong with you?" he finally said. "They are growing up; they *have* grown up and you can't bear the thought of it. Get yourself a life."

* * *

They hardly spoke to each other over the next few weeks and not because either of them was sulking. They took pride in being able to blow up in each other's face and call it quits twenty minutes later. Other things in their lives, besides Isabella's existence, took precedence.

In the run-up to the production of *Ships* Marcus resigned from the governing body of Central in order to spare the school principal embarrassment at his daughter quitting. He had expected the decision to be vaguely traumatic, but the moment it was done he felt liberated and vowed to resign from other honorary appointments in the coming months.

To the forefront of their concern was Zack's first read-through of *Conshie*, which took place a week prior to the first day of filming on *Salter's Edge*. Father and son spent much of early summer texting each other, Zack picking Marcus's brains about filming protocol, the pecking order on set and on one occasion they even discussed Zack's role. Charles Mantle was a gift of a part, overflowing with emotional baggage. Having lost most of his family in the First World War, by 1940 he was committed to deterring young men from signing up. For a storyline about people who were opposed to war on principle, there was a great deal of physical violence woven into it. Counterpoint, the director had insisted. Those with a problem with that should keep it to themselves and get on with their jobs.

Richard Salter, the part Marcus was universally known for, was an altogether different kettle of fish. His department, the Special Operations Unit of the National Crime Agency, held him to be a man of high IQ and breathtaking perception as he roamed the English-speaking world solving crimes which had baffled others. The crimes were usually bloodcurdling and complicated. Evil, the producer maintained, was a gift that kept on giving, at least in terms of television drama.

Marcus arrived home one evening after a pleasant day's filming where there'd been no tantrums, no stammering guest stars who didn't know their lines and the location caterer had been on top form. He and Teresa had supper together, after which he went to his office to glance over the following day's scenes. On his private email there was a message from Juan Morales and as usual his stomach began to knot up. Odd, Marcus thought, that a man he had never met could have this effect on him. Maybe that very anonymity was the reason for it.

> Estimado Señor Lawlor
> I am recently informed by my daughter that she is to bear a child in the early summer. This is good news for my wife and for me!
> I understand that you knew of this for some time and perhaps have forgotten to forward it to me. No matter.

However, can you please confirm that your son is to marry Isabella? In my country we take a poor view of families who do not honour their responsibilities.
Respetuosamente
Juan Morales

Marcus rolled his chair back away from the laptop. There was something not simply intrusive but… menacing about the email, a veiled threat hiding behind the restrained delight. He decided not to show it to Teresa. Given how she felt about Isabella and the idea that she might one day bear the family name it would lead to a long night of harsh words, followed by Marcus arriving on set next day looking like death. He turned instead to the business of finding a mature English oak to fill in the hole in the ground formerly known as Bigg's Cave.

-20-

Before moving on to the Cockpit, *Ships* opened at the the Tabard theatre, which occupied the top floor of a pub in Chiswick. The auditorium was reached not through the bar, as with most pub theatres, but via a covered stairway set at an angle to the building. It had all the charm of a railway bridge, complete with a corrugated roof and metal handrails on either side. To set it apart from Clapham Junction, however, it had a red carpet and one wall strung out with posters of past productions.

Marcus and Teresa went straight to the pub to rendezvous with Henry and his new wife. They found him leaning at the bar with a complimentary double scotch in his hand, talking to Anna Macey. She was laughing at something he had said and even in the boozy Friday evening hubbub his voice could be heard above all others. He greeted Marcus and Teresa and gestured to an ever watchful barmaid to serve whatever they asked for.

They took their seats up in the theatre, a venue which held less than a hundred seats, raked at a steep angle. When Isabella entered she seemed, for once, to be indistinguishable from the crowd, partly because of the subdued lighting, but as she climbed the gangway steps under Ethan's steerage, she tripped and fell to her knees. There was a concerted gasp, followed by muttered concern as Ethan and Zack helped her to her feet. Teresa smiled. Had she tripped by accident or taken a deliberate dive? Either way, in her interesting condition, the fall was a success. At various points throughout the rest of the evening people asked with puckered looks of anguish on their faces how she was. And if they hadn't realised she was pregnant they were soon informed.

When the lights went down in the auditorium and up on the stage, Teresa's eyes widened as she took in the set for the first play. Strapped for cash, Cross Curtain had borrowed most of what they needed from Ashbury Road. Having been in the loft for over twenty years certain items suddenly took on the status of treasured mementoes, especially a writing desk once used by her father and a gilded mirror belonging to her mother. That would be taken back to Golden Meadow and hung on a wall: Teresa had the very spot for it.

The first piece of the evening was called *The Tick*, which Ethan and Zack, seated behind their parents, agreed must be the story of the parasite which attached itself to Cressida's back leg when they took both dogs to Coombe Hill at Christmas. A tale of bloodsucking and murder. It was, in fact, a period piece about the enfranchisement of women. Three Edwardian ladies returned to a London house late on June 8th 1913. They had witnessed their friend and fellow campaigner, Emily Davison, throw herself under the King's horse at the Epsom Derby and were divided in their reaction to it. The younger two were in shock and believed it had been a bizarre accident, the third held that Emily had intended to kill herself and thus enliven the campaign.

Accident or self-sacrifice, somewhere along the line the two younger women wound up declaring their secret love for each other and sneaked off to paradise while the militant third returned to the fight.

At the interval, after checking that Isabella hadn't damaged herself or her baby, Henry had nothing but praise for *The Tick*—the writing, the performances, the direction. Marcus knew his father was exaggerating. The three actresses had gabbled and folded their arms far too much on stage.

Ships was a far superior piece of work, with the same furniture shifted into a different configuration but still reminding Teresa of home. Imogen set out her stall in the first few minutes of the play, portraying with humour and pathos a young woman in 1940 going mad in a marriage to a dull, unmemorable husband. Jane Sillitoe entered and the audience shifted to the edge of its seats. Teresa hadn't noticed it before, certainly not in *An Inspector Calls*, but Jane, with her sharp featured beauty, was an actress who could fill the stage, demanding that her presence be registered.

About a third of the way through, Jane and Imogen's characters reached a dramatic high point. After a long, emoting exchange they paused, met centre stage and kissed, at first rather chastely and then again with passion. No one in the trendy West London audience so much as faltered in their breathing, save Anna Macey, who remained perfectly still, her profile towards Teresa, before reaching into a pocket for a tissue. She held it to her eyes to prevent tears smudging her makeup. The kiss she had seen – that the whole theatre had seen – was no dutiful interpretation of the script. It was proof of something Anna had been denying for three weeks.

The play meandered to its mawkish conclusion when Jane's character left the house, sacrificing her love for Imogen for the sake of her brother. There was restrained anguish from both women, true to the period, no doubt, except that Imogen dissolved into sobs creating an uncomfortable blur between fiction and fact. Even Henry twitched, and his new wife reached out to lay a hand on Anna's arm. A moment later the audience applauded wildly.

In the bar afterwards, Henry ordered drinks for both casts and the stage crew, congratulating all and sundry on a splendid evening and wishing them well for their futures. He then went in search of Teresa, who had retreated to a corner seat.

Across the bar Jane Sillitoe was smothering Imogen with long embraces and gushing praise, the usual prattle of a first-night celebration, but more than just delighting in her protégée, Jane gave the impression of somehow owning her.

Henry rose as Jane and Imogen approached.

"My dears, you were superb," he said, as if merely stating the obvious.

"Cheers, Grandad."

"Thank you, Sir Henry," said Jane, flushing like a girl. She turned and gazed at Imogen. "Wasn't she terrific?"

"Both of you, simply wonderful," said Teresa with a bolt of enthusiasm from nowhere. Imogen looked round the bar, frowning.

"Seen Anna, Mum? She said she'd be here."

"Had to dash off. Some problem with her sister's new baby."

Jane whisked Imogen away to meet an actor with dyed

blond hair, a cheap jacket and vulgar jewellery in both ears. Teresa followed them with her eyes.

"Tell me I'm wrong, Henry," she said.

He knew exactly what she meant and squeezed her hand. "I know the difference between acting and real life. It's kept me sane all these years. What those two young women gave us this evening was the real thing."

-21-

By mid-August the razzmatazz of Imogen's success had died down and Teresa decided to take action. She wished she could sit Marcus down to discuss her plans like normal people, ordinary parents, but he was now heavily into the new series of *Salter's Edge*. Besides, he would have fobbed her off, no doubt, with accusations of gross interference in their youngest child's life. The Others weren't children any longer, he would argue, their goings-on were essentially none of their parents' business and why… why had she so taken against Isabella, who in a few months' time would present them with their first grandchild?

There was truth in all of that, of course, but leaving well alone had always been his chosen domestic policy. A little corroborative proof might help to change his attitude and to that end she arranged to meet Anna Macey one morning in a crowded Starbucks near her office in Richmond.

Anna was her usual, businesslike self, dressed in the Lamb and Cotter house colours, black trouser suit over a frilly white blouse. She was pleased to see Teresa, if a little wary about why she was there. They took their coffees out to the pavement area and Teresa slopped hers into its saucer as she sat down. It was an ice-breaker. Anna piled in with a fistful of napkins and mopped up. When they settled and faced each other, Teresa said,

"You and Imogen..."

"You haven't come all this way to get us back together again, I hope?"

"No, no."

That was one question answered. Anna seemed to have no frayed emotional ends as a result of the breakup.

"You were hurt the night of the play, I could see that."

"It's happened to me before – will again, I'm sure."

"That is sad."

Anna brushed aside the sympathy and gestured for Teresa to carry on.

"When I left Golden Meadow this morning, I knew exactly what I wanted to ask you. Now it sounds pathetic, but here goes. In the last six weeks or so, did you ever feel you were being manipulated?"

Anna was puzzled. "By whom?"

"Isabella Morales. Did you ever feel she was pushing Imo and Jane towards each other and you out of the picture?"

Anna smiled, wryly. "As an estate agent, I know something about manipulation. At its best the client shouldn't be aware of it happening." She thought for a moment. "Isabella was... determined, shall we say. I put it down to her wanting the best for Imo."

She took a sip of her coffee, chin way forward to prevent a rogue drip falling onto her blouse. Teresa began to feel silly, over-protective... all the things Marcus would have accused her of had he been there.

"That said, I did have Billie on the phone several times," said Anna.

"Who's Billie?"

"Jane Sillitoe's ex, asking the same thing you are. Did Isabella know what she was doing? Splitting up her and Jane, me and Imo? Did she do it deliberately? I tried to play it down. I should have stepped in, maybe. They'd been together for six years."

"Where did they rehearse?"

"Oh, Greenwich, Jane's house." Anna frowned. "Now you mention it, Isabella went with her, at least to begin with. Like a chaperone."

"Or a matchmaker. How did Jane feel about it all, I wonder?"

"Best guess, she was flattered. She's forty plus, a brilliant actress and a lovely person, but she's hardly love's young... well, no need to be bitchy about it."

Teresa smiled. "No, but you're right. She isn't."

***

Teresa persuaded Marcus to accompany her to Jane Sillitoe's house more by what she left unsaid than by giving him a real reason. It still hadn't occurred to him that there might be more to Imogen and Jane than had met the eye of the Tabard audience.

He had an afternoon when he wasn't called for filming and Teresa picked him up at midday from a housing development in Battersea. Fortunately, he had had a slight altercation with the director of the latest *Salter's Edge* and spoke of little else for most of the stop-start journey. Eventually he asked about the purpose of their visit.

"I'm worried about Imo."

He laughed. "Worried? That she's had a minor success?"

She slammed the steering wheel and yelled at him. "Are you really thick or just pretending to be?"

His eyes widened. "Jesus, where did that come from?"

"Or so bloody PC you daren't look, never mind criticise."

"Criticise who? Stop the car!"

"No! Ten minutes and we're there."

He sighed and pretended to be distracted by a woman with a pushchair, her shopping strapped into it and a toddler walking beside her.

"Criticise what?"

"You daren't say a word. You turn a blind eye to everything – the dope your children smoke, the coke they snort, the booze they were downing at fifteen years old! You say yes to the bad language. Or is it free expression? Yes to them screwing their partners in my house, unmarried, not even committed. My mother would have died!"

He laughed. "She *did* die, but not as a result of The Others' behaviour. More a result of ours."

The satnav told them that King George Street was three minutes away. He glanced at his nonexistent watch.

"Why don't you wear one of the three you've got?" Teresa asked.

"You still haven't told me why we've come here. When's she expecting us?"

"She isn't."

He turned to her. "You mean we're ambushing her?"

"Keep an eye out for a parking meter."

When they found one Marcus paid with an app on his phone, and felt a momentary sense of achievement at having done so. They walked the hundred yards or so to Jane's house, passing shops that on any other day would have pulled them through their doors: one selling exotic fruit and veg, another jewellery, a third the inevitable health food. Reaching Jane's front door, Marcus rang the bell and nodded down the steps to the basement.

"My room, when I used to stay here."

She nodded. Christ, he thought, it hadn't even crossed Teresa's mind that he might be getting the occasional back rub here.

"Doesn't look as if she's in," said Teresa, with a hint of relief in her voice.

He nodded down the street to a low-slung sports car. "Her motor's there. She won't be far away."

The door opened to the length of the safety chain and he turned to it.

"Janey, hi!"

Jane slid back the chain and opened the door far enough to appear sociable. She was wearing a richly embroidered dressing gown, which she pulled tighter around her body. She smiled.

"Marcus, how lovely."

They stood gazing at each other, Marcus on the top step, Teresa on the pavement.

"We were just passing and wondered if we could skive a coffee, or even some of that carrot cake you excel at."

"Yes, yes, do please."

She opened the door fully and ushered them in, saying loudly, "Teresa, how lovely to see you as well."

It was meant as a warning, but it didn't work. A sleepy voice from upstairs called out, "Janey, you okay?"

Marcus and Teresa froze and a moment later the owner of the voice tiptoed down the stairs, unmistakable legs appearing first, followed by the rest of her. It was Imogen, dressed only in bra and pants. When she saw her parents she woke fully.

Fight or flight. She chose the latter, turned and hurried back up the stairs.

"Coffee?" said Jane, brightly. "I'm afraid I've run out of carrot cake, though."

"I'm sure you have," said Teresa. "Imogen loves it."

***

Imogen eventually appeared, fully dressed in clothes which her mother hadn't seen before. A silky top with glittery buttons, designer jeans with a velvet plush to them, a new belt. Expensive. Painted toenails on bare feet. She sat down opposite her parents at the table while Jane laid out mugs for coffee and tinkered with sugar and spoons to stave off the inevitable.

"What the hell are you doing?" Teresa growled at her daughter.

"If you've something to say, Mum, go right ahead, but don't speak to me like I was twelve."

"What are you doing shacked up with this woman?" She looked up at Jane. "While we're at it, what the hell are *you* doing?"

"I can understand your surprise," said Jane, calmly. "But with respect I'd say it's obvious. And since we're both adults, I think..."

"Don't give me the grown-up woman stuff. You're old

enough to be her mother."

"Does that have a bearing?"

Marcus put an arm round Teresa's shoulders, apparently to comfort her, in truth to hold her down. He looked at Jane, then Imogen. "I'm sorry, I had no idea about this."

"What are you apologising for?!" said Teresa.

"Yeah, just tell us what you feel about it, Dad. Disgust? Unbridled joy?"

The coffee machine gave its final hiss and Jane asked, "Black or white?"

Teresa glared at her. "Whatever colour it is, I'll throw it against that bloody wall! Where's your partner of six years, Jane?"

"I can't say Billie and I were ever joined at the hip, but we'll remain good friends, I'm sure."

Teresa closed her eyes tightly, distorting her face. "Can't you see you've been played?" She turned to Imogen. "You think Isabella had your best interests at heart? No, she's been playing human chess, shoving pawns and patsies round the board from the day we met her."

"Are you jealous or something?" Imogen shrieked. "Without her input, *Ships* would've fallen flat. Have you seen the reviews, Dad? *Time Out*?"

She reached out for the magazine and stopped when he raised a hand. "I have."

Teresa slapped the table. "She did it because that's what she does. She breaks things up and my family seems to be her current target. Anna and Billie killed by friendly fire, but that doesn't make them less of a casualty."

She hadn't expected Jane or Imogen to collapse into a Damascene fit, recover and jump on the phone to their previous partners, but a wince of recognition from either of them would have been nice.

"It isn't really the point," said Jane.

"You like people making a fool of you?"

"Fools or not, here we are." She gestured to Imogen. "Do you think I've grown close to Imo against my will?"

"She is 21 years old!" Marcus growled.

"Dad, at 22 you were living with Teresa. How old were you, Mum?" She clapped a hand to her mouth in mock surprise. "Oh, that's right, you were 21."

Teresa looked at her, this suddenly different person who used to be her daughter. "So this... arranged marriage will succeed, will it?"

"Right now it's what I want; it's what I'll have."

"Generation Entitlement," said Teresa.

Imogen's face puckered into a sneer. "You use that all the time, Mum. So boring."

Jane pushed a mug of coffee across the table to Teresa. Marcus intercepted it and pushed it back.

"I think we'll skip coffee," he said, rising.

Teresa looked up at him. "Is that all you can do?"

"Quite frankly, I think it is."

-22-

During the drive back to Golden Meadow any mention of a name – Jane Sillitoe, Isabella Morales, Imogen herself – would have brought Teresa's rage to the fore with slamming of the steering wheel or changing lanes without indicating. If Marcus so much as winced he would be accused of proxy driving. Left to her own devices they stood a reasonable chance of getting home in one piece.

When he got out of the car, he looked across at the meadow, which was currently living up to its name. Everything was late this year, or so local gardeners had been telling him, and a long winter followed by a cold spring had held everything back. The forecast had promised that today would be the warmest of the year so far and the buttercups had responded by bursting into flower. He turned to Teresa, hoping she would at least acknowledge the sheer dazzle of it, but she had hurried into the house.

The dogs greeted her with their usual delight. She ignored them and filled the kettle, turning the tap full on until it sprayed her. She swore.

"Do you think Imo'll leave Ashbury?" Marcus asked, as she dried her top with kitchen towel.

"Why ask me?"

She threw teabags into the Lordship and Ladyship mugs and tried to hurry the kettle along.

"I say she'll come to her senses," he offered.

"Meantime you're not bothered that your daughter's now shacked up with a woman twice her age?"

"Is there any point?"

"It's *The Killing of Sister George*. Will you be happy if Jane's career goes down the pan the same way George's did? With Imogen just a footnote?"

"I'm supposed to be the one who can't tell drama from real life."

"You know sod all about either!" She broke off and turned away. "And we... this family, we know *nothing* about this woman. We've taken her word on everything. She has that ability to simper and men fall for it. No, she's not stabbing anyone, poisoning them, chucking boiling water in their faces. Something far more insidious. Isolating them. She's thrown Imo and Jane Sillitoe together, not to help Imo's career, but to remove her from the family. Along the way she's ruined two other lives, Anna Macey's and Billie's."

She paused to draw much needed breath.

"Ruined is a little harsh," he said.

"She's wormed her way into Ashbury and, incidentally, hasn't paid rent for three months out of the seven she's been there. Not bad, eh? She got rid of Carla, pitched her into the arms of Moron Matt to the point where my own daughter refuses to speak to me on account of me 'favouring' her brother. That would be Ethan, who she's trapped for life by getting herself pregnant. She should have been pushing, pushing, pushing him to get a job, but instead she stands by as he smokes more and more dope and drinks a bottle of wine every night."

Marcus winced. "How do you know this?"

"The bloody bins. Empty bottles. And the house reeks of marijuana."

She turned away and he tried to follow her, but she signalled him to keep away.

"Why?" he asked, in genuine bewilderment. "Why is she doing all that?"

"Maybe no reason at all. But I'll tell you this: Zack and Amy are next in line. Full house."

"What'll she do to them?"

"I don't know. All I'm sure of is that you're letting it happen."

He opened his mouth to retaliate, but took a deep breath instead. He turned towards the back door and the dogs scurried after him.

* * *

Imogen was in two minds, the one that knew her mother was right, the other that wished she wasn't. To help fend off any self-doubt she had told the outside world, her brothers and friends, even Carla in a text, of her plans to go and live in Greenwich. As she lined up her worldly possessions in her room and packed her clothes into boxes, she hoped someone would burst in and argue the case against her leaving. She had even considered phoning Anna Macey that morning, not to beg forgiveness or anything so feeble, but simply to explain and then wait for Anna's opinion.

Her door was slightly ajar and she heard Isabella come

down the stairs on her way to the kitchen. She paused at Imogen's door as if to rest from a long walk. Their eyes met.

"How are things, Imo?"

"Fine."

Isabella entered the room and perched on the arm of the sofa. "You know, I do admire you for what you're doing. It can't be easy, but I've never seen a couple like you and Jane so meant for each other."

Imogen carried on wrapping her collection of framed photos, using old T-shirts to protect them.

"Tell that to my parents."

"It isn't their life, I know, but I do feel responsible for hurting them." She paused and became slightly tearful. "Anything I did regarding Jane was for the play, your career. It seemed so right at the time."

Imogen nodded to a packet of tissues resting on a box marked Useless Bits, containing things she'd made at school, toys from Christmas crackers, love tokens from a handful of crushes. Isabella pulled out a tissue and blew her nose.

"I shall miss you, Imo. Not that we can't meet up. I'm sure we will anyway. That pool at Golden Meadow, I haven't swum in it yet, and this summer you and Jane must come over. Moral support. When are you leaving?"

It was the first time anyone had voiced that. Imogen was going, leaving Ethan and Zack behind. She shivered as Teresa's suspicion jangled in her head for the fourth, fifth, sixth time that day. Had she and Jane been eased into a love affair at Isabella's behest? Was Isabella gloating over her accomplishment?

"I'm going this evening," said Imogen, quietly.

-23-

When demand for his talents had started to rise, way back in the last century, Marcus had signed up with a London agency in Golden Square. Carson Dooley was neither two separate people nor Irish American as his name suggested. He was a one-man band with a small clientele and an old-fashioned style.

Marcus drove to Ashbury Road and took an Uber into central London. At the front door to Carson's plush office Marcus paused, as he always did, to summon Jonas Kemble. He then checked his appearance in the glass door, pushed it open and climbed the shallow, blue-carpeted stairs.

As ever Carson was dressed in his trademark three-piece suit, white cuffs gleaming at the wrists and a perfect silk tie at his neck. He was 60 years old and the first thing people noticed was the large forehead, made all the more prominent by what little hair he had being swept straight back. He had a kindly face, for an agent. Many of them can smile and smile and be a villain, but Carson was a gentle creature and if, as he maintained, life is a performance, then he hadn't decided which role to play, but happily took 12.5% from those who had.

"Marcus, what a lovely surprise!"

Surprise, yes, Carson thought, but lovely? Marcus never dropped into his office for a friendly chat. There was always a problem attached.

"Family all well?" he asked.

"Turmoil."

"Oh, dear," said Carson, evenly. "By the way, they're talking about yet another series of *Salter's Edge*, you know."

"God help me, I can't."

"You say that every time. Tea?"

Instead of yelling from where he stood, Carson went over to the door and asked his assistant, Della, if she would be an absolute angel and make them a pot of tea. Maybe that would bring out the darker purpose of his client's visit.

"Jane Sillitoe..." Marcus began.

Carson closed his eyes, as if giving thanks to a higher being.

"An absolute dream of a girl," he said. "I'll be forever grateful that you steered her my way."

Carson's opinion was a stumbling block given that Marcus had come to London in the ill-conceived hope of persuading Carson to strike Jane off his books. It would be punishment for having lured Imogen away from her family and into a relationship with her. Marcus could then return home, not as the pathetic luvvy Teresa had accused him of being, but as a man who always did right by his family. It was Jonas Kemble who made him pause and bring the whole escapade into perspective. It wasn't Jane's fault that she had fallen in love with his daughter. And vice versa. It was the way of things. Surely, if there was blame to be apportioned it should be levelled at Isabella and her unscrupulous matchmaking.

"Listen, Hortense Farraway wants you to say yes to another Priestly. *Dangerous Corner,*" Carson went on.

Hortense was the CEO of Mazz Productions, a group which had a controlling stake in the Cavendish theatre.

"You can see her point given the success of *An Inspector Calls*. Oh, and she's lining up Charles Burgoyne to direct."

Marcus groaned, swivelled away in his chair and fixed his gaze on a photo on the wall, himself as Henchard in a forgotten BBC adaptation of *The Mayor of Casterbridge*.

"It's the friction between you and Charles that lights the fire beneath everything you do together."

Marcus smiled. "Give it a rest, Carson."

"They'd like an answer by the end of the month."

He opened the top drawer of his desk and took out a copy of *The Stage*.

"Have you read this week's edition?" he asked in an almost reverential tone.

"I haven't read *any* edition for 20 years."

"There's an item about your father. He's agreed to appear in a revival of Joe Orton's *Loot* at the Sherborne."

"To appear as what? The corpse?"

"Truscott. The bent police officer. Honestly, that man is theatrical gold. Whenever his career settles he picks a role that no one would ever *dream* of him doing and then bedazzles us."

"Doesn't he just," Marcus muttered. "Dates?"

"I've no idea... oh, you mean for *Dangerous Corner*. Early November through to Feb."

"Which part does Hortense think I'll be daft enough to play? Not that Priestley's characters are noticeably different from one another."

"Robert Caplan."

Marcus smiled. "Pompous, self-righteous, ends up blowing his brains out, not a laugh to be had anywhere."

Carson smiled and adopted the role of confidant. Every actor needed one, he believed, preferably with a degree in behavioural psychology.

"You seem downcast, my dear fellow. I assume Jane Sillitoe has something to do with it?"

"I came to ask you to junk her, to take her off your books. Pure retaliation on my part. Childish, nasty, desperate. My better self stepped in to counsel against it, so please forget I ever mentioned it."

Carson nodded. "Is there another angle to the problem, one that I can help with?"

Marcus picked up his leather jacket and shrugged himself into it.

"Like I said. Turmoil. Say yes to Hortense, will you?" He paused. "You're an agent, Carson, but even so you bring out the best in people."

Carson smiled. "A *trompe l'oeil*, I assure you."

Marcus left the office, passing Della on the way. She was carrying a tea tray, silver pot, bone china, custard creams. For some reason his mind fled back to the day he met Jack Relph. It must have been the custard creams, the biscuit of distant memories.

-24-

A week after Imogen moved out of Ashbury Road, Ethan woke early and offered to go downstairs and make Isabella tea. She suspected an ulterior motive, which became apparent as he sat on the bed beside her, watching her sip. Like a child asking a parent if they could visit a playmate, he said he wanted to check that Imogen was… all right. Imo was free all day and he was thinking of nipping over to Greenwich. If Isabella didn't mind.

"Not in your car, I hope," she said.

Her implied permission surprised him.

"Fair enough," he stammered. "Why not the car?"

She gave him an old-fashioned look. "You and Imo? Few beers, bit of this, bit of that?" She snorted imaginary cocaine from the back of her hand. "You'll be in no state to drive home. In fact, if I were you I'd stay the night. Your father's old room in the basement."

"Why don't you come with me?" he said.

She pretended to consider the idea. "No, no, thanks. It's family stuff. I'll be alright."

He looked down at the bump. "Sure?"

"Darling, there are four months to go, not four days. I'll be fine. Give Imo and Jane my love."

He left for Greenwich just before lunch, having ordered an Uber on Isabella's account and borrowed a wad of cash from her. At the front door she kissed him on the cheek and straightened the seams of his jacket along the shoulders. He asked her for the umpteenth time if she minded him leaving her.

"After all, it'll be the first time you've been in the house all alone. I mean..." He paused and smiled. "I don't know what I mean."

She pushed him playfully out through the door and closed it, then waited until she heard the taxi pull away. In the kitchen she took a pizza from the fridge, placed it on the top rack of the oven and set the timer. She stood back, holding the bump in both hands, still at a loss to understand why women were trampled in the rush of their own hormones during pregnancy. The thought of bringing her baby up didn't swamp her with dreams or dreads about its future. For a start, someone else would be doing the child-rearing donkey work.

She made her way up the stairs to the first floor. Zack's room would be locked in all probability. Amy would have insisted on that, surely. Isabella reached out to the handle, turned it. The door creaked open.

This was her first ever visit to Zack's room. It was fearfully neat, with an obsessive compulsive air to it. The bed was precisely made, the cushions and furry toys fussily arranged. Electronic cables were gathered and tied, the desk laid out as if for an inspection. Even the pieces on a chessboard, the knights and bishops, faced in the right direction, dead centre of their squares. Isabella turned a knight 45 degrees and smiled.

She would take a trophy, but more than that she was looking for a point of entry, a flaw in Zack's character that she could exploit. At that moment she felt as she often did when Zack was alive in her mind: the urge to grab him, push him back on the bed and fuck him to a pulp. She went over to a black and white photo on the wall, Zack with his perfect torso half in shade. It had been taken in his ponytail days, the long plait now removed for his role in *Conshie*. She reached out to it, as if to wrap her hand round and pull his head towards her.

She turned to the bedside table, opened the drawer. Pin neat and right at the front was a vibrator. A delicate toy for the delicate Amy? Too obvious for Isabella to make off with. Set beside it was a tortoiseshell box. She removed the lid. Cufflinks, assorted rings, even a tiepin. A diamond ear stud. That would be missed immediately, but what about the backing plate? Gold and perfectly crafted. Annoying rather than devastating when it can't be found. She took it and placed it on her tongue. The timer down in the kitchen told her the pizza was cooked. She closed the box and left the room.

She sat in the kitchen for the best part of two hours, rising occasionally to make tea, clear away the plate and cutlery she had used, or visit the bathroom. On any other occasion the minutes would have dragged by, her imagination would have screamed out for narratives to fill the time. But not today.

She heard the key turn in the front door and Zack muttering, repeating himself, as he closed it behind him. For a moment she thought he wasn't alone, that he had brought the insipid Amy with him, but then she realised he was practising lines. As he passed by the open door he caught sight of Isabella, seated at the table gazing down at her mobile as if she couldn't believe something she had just heard or seen on it. He went to the doorway and caught her attention. She smiled feebly.

"Hi, Bella. You two okay, you and the bump?"

She screwed up her face a little. "Yes, yes, I suppose."

"Where's Ethan?"

"Greenwich to see Imo."

She laughed and her gloomy expression changed to one of irritation, as she tapped her mobile. "This friend of mine from Somerville's been on, Grace Drayton. She married another student, nice enough lad, but not… to my taste. Nor hers, apparently."

Zack smiled. "Sounds complicated."

"As a matter of fact it's dead simple. He has a younger brother, quite the catch evidently. Looks, talent, going places. Her husband doesn't even come close." She stared up at Zack and her voice faltered. "She hooked up with the wrong brother, Zack."

Zack stood up, went over to the sink, poured himself a glass of water that he didn't really need and started to drink it. Isabella rose from the table and went over to him.

"What would you do in her place, Zack? Put right the mistake? Be honest with both of them? Or would you pass on the chance of a lifetime's happiness?"

Zack smiled. "What does the younger brother say?"

"He's just waiting for Grace to make the first move. Afraid that she won't. If you think about it, it becomes kind of scary."

He set the glass down on the drainer with a clink, then

stepped out of her reach, held up both arms and broke into a slow handclap.

"That was quite a performance, Bella. Not too full on, not too understated. Pity it didn't work." She looked up at him. "Carla, Imo, Ethan, even my father may have taken you at face value. Not me."

He wanted to say that he had seen through the buildup to this moment and was almost flattered to be part of Isabella's endgame. She had come on to him now to frighten him off. She wanted him and his two sisters out of the house, out of Ethan's life. She wanted Ashbury Road for herself. Did she believe that his father, in some sentimental fugue brought on by the birth of his first grandchild, would hand over the keys to Ethan? The house next door had sold last month for one point four million pounds! So would she then get rid of Ethan and somehow keep it for herself? He couldn't finish the scene in his mind. For a start, the house wasn't Marcus's to give away. It was Teresa's. Apart from that, wasn't Juan Morales as rich as Croesus?

Isabella closed her eyes. "Zack, sweetie, put it down to rampaging hormones."

She smiled and eventually nodded at the door as if dismissing a servant.

-25-

That evening, Isabella lay in the bath looking down at her abdomen, rising out of the water like an upturned ship. She tried to lower it but it wouldn't budge. She ran more water to cover it, turning the taps with her toes.

When the bump was submerged she speculated on the possibilities of the next few months. Would her feelings about motherhood change? She doubted it. People were bound to ask about the prospect of it as the weeks went by. 'Oh, I'm ecstatic,' she would have to say, but why on earth would a sane, red-blooded woman look forward to a lifetime of drudge? God knows, they moaned about it incessantly after the fact: the sleepless nights, breastfeeding, nappy changes, the food-covered clothes, the sticky hands on everything, the tantrums and the crippling boredom of staying at home with a creature who didn't understand a word you were saying. More importantly, how quickly would her stomach, her waistline, return to the scalloped shape she had worked so hard to achieve? Or would her hips never lose that girdle of fat they would surely develop? Would her breasts drop and stay forever where they had fallen?

She slapped the water and made herself a promise. This baby would be her one and only, her lifetime membership fee to join the Lawlor clan. Thinking of which, she wasn't used to not getting her way. This was the second time Zack had refused her advances and it grated. It would have been so, so nice to have rushed him upstairs, thrown him on his bed and screwed him to kingdom come. It would have been one in the eye, too, for the tragic Amy, who these days was spending more and more time with Zack. Defending him? Guarding him against predators? Maybe Isabella needed to up her game a little.

Her mind wandered around the problem and finally settled on Marcus. How would he feel, she wondered, about a mini affair with the mother of his first grandson? It was common knowledge that many men found pregnant women desirable, but how would he, the deep-down prig, react? With moral panic to begin with, she thought, but that wouldn't last, not if she'd read him correctly. The clean image and the real man were poles apart, and once the offer was made he would soon take it and beg for more.

* * *

Read-throughs for *Salter's Edge* took place in an old BBC rehearsal room in Blackfriars. Marcus always asked the Uber driver to set him down a mile or so distant so that he could walk his childhood memory of the Thames. As he approached St Paul's Cathedral he heard Henry telling him it had survived everything the Luftwaffe had thrown at it only to be suffocated, seventy years later, by the steel and glass monstrosities around it. More often than not he arrived at Granboro Studios in a melancholic frame of mind, not due to the modern development of the area but his father's sadness about it.

The latest script had rapidly overturned that feeling. It was the work of an experienced author who, unlike greener writers, didn't wince and shift at the actors' interpretation of his lines. It was a good story, to boot, in which Richard Salter mined the covert nastiness of an undercover operation, emerged with his man in a metaphorical headlock and marched him off to justice.

Marcus left the studio in the company of Phyllis Quilter, an actress he had known for centuries. They chatted as they waited for an available black cab to take them to a restaurant. As one drew up to the kerb Marcus was surprised, to say nothing of apprehensive, when Isabella stepped out of it.

She was clearly distraught, glancing from him to Phyllis and back again. Marcus reached out for her arm.

"Why are you here?" he asked.

She turned to him with a forced smile. "I hoped I'd be in time. I'm sorry, I didn't think. I wanted to speak to you alone."

"Who told you where to find me?"

"I rang your agent and someone called Della told me where you'd be."

"She shouldn't have done."

Phyllis Quilter began to sense a problem. "Marcus, would you like me to...?"

"No, I wouldn't," he said, forcefully. "Isabella, you still haven't said what you're doing here. Phyllis, this is Isabella Morales, my son's girlfriend. Bella, Phyllis Quilter."

"How nice to meet you," said Phyllis, her eyes wandering over the mass of hair which, in the riverside breeze, was veiling the face.

"Something really disturbing has happened and I must speak to you."

Her voice petered out and she looked away.

"Can't it wait?"

"Not really."

He sighed, irritably. "Get back in the cab."

Isabella slid back into the taxi, followed by Phyllis and Marcus, who barked their destination to the driver.

***

By the time they reached the Portuguese restaurant a mile south of the river, Isabella's demeanour had changed completely. No longer the timid, apologetic bundle of nerves who had ambushed Marcus outside Granboro Studios, she was a chatty, smiling fan of *The Cherry Orchard*, in which Phyllis was due to appear later in the year. Isabella was either making an incredible effort to be sociable, Marcus thought, or there had never been a problem in the first place.

As lunch progressed and a second bottle of wine was opened, it seemed abundantly clear to Phyllis that this young woman was besotted with Marcus. She laughed at everything he said, witty or not, and her touchy-feeliness was excessive. He tried to edge away from her, aware that Phyllis was imagining more than family ties between her old friend and this absurd little starfucker.

By the time their coffee arrived Phyllis was feeling downright intrusive and decided to leave. She stood up and reined in her possessions.

"Phyl, please…" Marcus said, with a hint of despair in his voice.

"It's okay, I've got shopping to do in town. Thank you for lunch and… er, nice meeting you, Miss Morales."

Isabella reached out to shake her hand but Phyllis ignored it.

"Good luck with *The Cherry Orchard*," Isabella called after her. "Maybe Marcus'll bring me to see it."

Ever since the incident at Westfield, Marcus's default emotion when in public had been paranoia. The fallout from the Ethan-Carla gunfight had passed fairly quickly but, as Henry had often said, once the press, social media, the talking heads, get you on the run they chase you to the cliff edge and push. He glanced round. Ten, twelve couples, mostly minding their own business, one or two pretending they hadn't recognised him. Phones propped up against sugar bowls.

"I hope she didn't leave because of me," said Isabella.

"I doubt it," he said, coolly.

"I mean, knowing that I wanted to talk to you…"

Was it his imagination, he wondered, or had she raised her voice a degree or so, the better to be heard by those at nearby tables? He lowered his own.

"How can I help?"

"I honestly don't know how to put this and I hope you understand…"

"Get on with it."

She took a breath. "Zack and I were alone in the house one afternoon and he came into my room and he said I'd made a mistake."

She dipped her head as if forcing herself to move on with the story. Marcus tapped the table and she looked up again.

"He said that I'd gone for the wrong brother. It should've been his baby I was carrying, not Ethan's. I'm sure he'll deny it if you ask him."

Marcus frowned. "What happened?"

"I told him he was wrong but he wouldn't have it. Had I missed the signs along the way, he said. And then he put his arms round me and tried to..."

She paused and shook the memory from her head. She waited for Marcus to react. All he said was,

"And?"

"He apologised and I suggested that he move out. For Ethan's sake, if not mine. And his own career, of course. I'd hate that to be damaged." Suddenly anxious, she reached across the table. "Please, please don't tell him I've said anything. I don't want trouble between brothers..."

She reached out for the wine bottle and a waiter stepped in to fill her glass.

"Sir?"

"Not for me. Cappuccino. Two."

"The other alternative is that Ethan and I move out," said Isabella. "A place of our own." Anxious again, she suddenly closed her eyes. "And don't you dare say anything to Teresa. She's anxious enough about the baby, I'm sure."

He nodded. "Will you get married, do you think? It would make your father happy."

"It depends.

She was suddenly alarmed. "Oh, God, you haven't told him about this! He can be so unpredictable. Volatile. Aggressive. Argentinian. It's the way we do life there."

She turned away and caught the eye of a nearby middle-aged woman whose husband had gone to the loo.

The woman smiled, clearly wondering how Isabella fitted into Marcus Lawlor's life.

Isabella whispered. "We always seem to be surrounded, or overseen by... someone," Isabella whispered. "It would be nice to be alone with you sometime."

The waiter returned with their coffees and set them down.

"The bill, when you've a moment," said Marcus.

"It's so strange," said Isabella, whimsically. "I always thought that second time around I would marry someone older."

"How old was your first husband?"

"Ricardo? Twenty-three when he died." She stared at him as if to share a confidence. "Whenever I feel wobbly or insecure I can always turn to you, I guess... for help?"

He nodded and looked away. Christ, she thought, how much more obvious do I have to be? Or is he simply scared of reading the signs?

She stepped away from the table and watched herself beckon him. She took his tie between forefinger and thumb and led him across the restaurant. Dog on a lead. She turned him and pushed him back against the wall, then grabbed his head and pulled it towards her. She closed her eyes and found his mouth with her tongue. She squeezed it inside him and for a moment he responded in kind. Then she bit down on his tongue, spongey and warm, held it for a moment and withdrew. She laughed. He didn't move. Blood began to drool from his mouth and congeal around his lips. Crimson and sticky. He reached up and wiped it on the back of his hand...

The skin on Marcus's neck had begun to crawl. He

was right to have been on guard, it seemed. Never mind her bleating about Zack's behaviour, but had she just made a pass at him? He flashed back over their bitty, broken conversation... indeed, over everything since their meeting outside Granboro Studios. Maybe Teresa's fears were justified.

He paid the bill and as they left the restaurant Isabella took him by the arm, almost as if he were a trophy for her walnut box. A woman on the far side of the restaurant took a photo. If she had snapped his father with a young woman drooping from his arm, stumbling from too much wine and pregnant to boot, Henry would have been trending on Twitter within hours. But the photo was of Marcus, a middle-aged man having lunch with his worse-for-wear, future daughter-in-law and, in spite of Phyllis Quilter's disapproval, the world graciously considered the man who played Richard Salter to be beyond reproach. Marcus wasn't sure how he felt about that.

-26-

Amy Tully had never learned to swim, in spite of a childhood spent in Herne Bay with the beach a stone's throw from her parents' house. Her lack of buoyancy hadn't exactly hampered her progress in life, it was simply embarrassing, especially with all the talk between Zack and Imogen about endless summer days by the Golden Meadow pool.

She decided to enrol secretly for swimming lessons at the baths in Wimpole Street. Within two short weeks she had cracked it and her delight at her success had given Miss Twinkletail, the dormouse she voiced in *Tales from the Hedgerow*, an extra squeak or two. The same grit which had allowed her to take both feet off the bottom of the Wimpole Street baths gave her the courage to visit Marks and Spencer's headquarters.

She took the overground to Paddington, crossed over Regent's Canal and down onto a wide, cobbled towpath. The narrowboats moored along it, far from being places to live, seemed more like a designer's counterpoint to the forbidding building towering over the area. Like most of new London it was tall, sharp cornered and made of glass and seemed a far cry from the shops where three generations of her family had bought their underwear.

At the main entrance she paused and checked her reflection in the glass doors: a girl with tied-back blonde hair carrying a four-square handbag, perfect for the job in hand. She checked the role she'd given herself: quiet, considerate, outwardly naive and with a ready smile for all who crossed her path. The pincer doors opened as if they would swallow her whole and she entered.

The oversized lobby had pretensions to being a jungle, with tall palms vying with spindly trees and exotic bushes for the available light coming from above. She felt an urge to touch them, to see if they were real or plastic, but she smiled at them instead. An overweight security officer's expression didn't change as she approached him for directions. He looked her up and down and pointed to a distant reception desk, behind which sat three smartly dressed women, partially hidden by the screens in front of them. Amy chose the oldest of them, a rather beautiful woman in her mid-forties, and smiled at her.

"Can I help you?" the woman said.

For a split second she thanked her lucky stars that Zack wasn't with her. He would have said, albeit with infinite charm, 'I've no doubt whatsoever that you *can* but surely you mean *may* I?' The woman would have carried on half smiling at him, no doubt, just as she was half smiling at Amy. Waiting.

"I'd like to speak with" – she clicked open her handbag and referred to her phone – "with Isabella Morales."

"Do you have an appointment?"

"Oh, yes."

The woman paused before asking, "What was the name?"

"Isabella Morales."

"Which department?"

"European Development."

Amy's face was beginning to ache from over-smiling. The woman turned to one of her colleagues.

"European Development?" she asked, quietly. "Isabella Morales?"

The second woman asked, "How are you spelling that?"

Amy handed her the phone and the woman typed the name into her computer. Whatever came up on her screen caused her to frown slightly whereupon she asked if Amy would take a seat, presumably while she sought help from higher up the chain.

***

Zack had been filming in the wilds of Ruislip and by the time he reached the Chinese restaurant that evening he was exhausted, starving, irritable and mono-syllabic. Amy was already there, being fluttered around by a young waiter who had brought her a glass of wine. He pulled the chair back for Zack, who smiled his thanks.

"Good day?" Amy asked.

"Fair," said Zack.

"Phillip Bray again?"

"The man can't remember his lines from one moment to another. Poor sod."

Would the news she had enliven him, she wondered, or have him flop over the table in despair? Either way, he was going to hear it, in spite of the excitement coming from the next table of Chinese ex-pats. It was somebody's birthday and three generations were celebrating it.

Amy had already ordered the meal and when the starter came Zack fell on it in his usual manner. To his family's bewilderment, he would always lean forward and curl an arm around his plate as if someone might suddenly snatch it away.

"Something you should know," she said.

Given that he was gnawing his way through the spare ribs, she half expected him to growl or snap, but he grunted dutiful interest.

"Isabella..." He groaned wearily. "Have you seen her Facebook page lately? Photos of her and your father which some knob has posted. Hoping it would go viral, I suppose. The pair of them coming out of a restaurant, her preggo and pissed."

Zack paused in his assault on the ribs. He hadn't told Amy about Isabella trying to seduce him the other night. In the grand scheme of his life other things took priority, things like his role in *Conshie*.

"So?"

"That's kind of how I thought you'd react," she said. "My guess is Isabella wanted to stir things up. Look at the chase-me-fuck-me way she's gazing at him in this one. '*Lunch in Clapham with the best-looking actor in London, my future father-in-law, Marcus Lawlor.*' "

Zack gestured for her to turn the iPad towards him. He glanced at the pictures and returned to the ribs.

"Right," said Amy, snapping the tablet cover shut. "Let's see how this grabs you."

She pushed her plate aside and leaned forward, the

better to hold his attention.

"I should be telling your mother. Not you, not your father, since I've no wish to ruffle the creative equilibrium..."

"Pardon?"

"...but I spent the morning at the M & S head office. Digging. You know Isabella works there?"

He nodded. "Yeah."

"Where exactly?"

"European Development... something."

"Wrong. No one called Isabella Morales has ever worked for Marks and Spencer. Anywhere."

He stopped eating. His eyes fell on her untouched spare ribs.

"You going to leave those?"

"Zee, did you hear what I just said?"

"Yes, yes, of course I did." He suddenly frowned. "But I've heard Isabella on the phone to people in her office."

"You're an actor, I'm an actor. How difficult is it to fake a call?"

She pushed her spare ribs across to him. "He's so out of it these days with all the weed it's hard to tell. Would he care? That's the other thing I don't like. She's making a fool of him when she should be kicking his butt to get a job."

"If she doesn't work, where does she get her money?" he asked.

"The rich father, presumably. That and she keeps borrowing from friends, never paying them back."

"Like the guys in Oxford. God, you'd need a lot of friends to support her lifestyle: rent, new shoes every week, clothes never worn twice, Ubers everywhere."

"Where do we go from here, Zack, given that nowhere

isn't an option?"

"Carla would know."

"To hell with Carla!" She caught herself and lowered her voice again. "Not literally, I just mean that you lot, you always run to Carla. I suggest we search her room."

He was baffled. "Looking for what?"

"I'm not sure, but isn't it the next step people take? And I don't think we should tell Teresa yet. She's taken a few knocks, so let's do some more..."

"Digging?"

"Digging."

Zack nodded and did exactly what his father would have done in a similar situation: he checked the time on a watch he wasn't wearing.

***

Patience had never been a Lawlor virtue, not even for Zack, the most pragmatic of the bunch. For the next week he checked his brother's plans daily until Amy suggested that his sudden interest in Ethan's schedule might arouse suspicion. He backed off immediately.

A few days later Ethan announced that he and Isabella would be heading out to Golden Meadow next Sunday. A goodwill mission. Did Zack and Amy fancy joining them? Amy wilted with pained regret. How lovely it would have been, the four of them moseying down to the country, but on this occasion they were due at a friend's party later in the day.

When Sunday arrived, Zack was out of bed by six o'clock, a complete waste of effort since Isabella wasn't ready to leave the house until gone eleven. With a firm grip on his irritation, Ethan hung around in the kitchen, occasionally calling up to her, wondering if there was anything he could do to help. For an hour she said she would be down in two minutes and finally appeared, dressed to kill. The hair was its usual self, contrived in its bid to impress and held with a floral headband matching the new dress. New shoes. Flat heels to cope with pregnancy.

They left the house and as Zack howled with relief Amy prevented him from dashing up to the attic. They should hold off for a bit in case Isabella had cunningly forgotten something and returned. Consequently, it was midday before they crept up the stairs, only to find the attic door locked. A pertinent detail, Zack thought: Isabella was the only person in the house who ever locked their door. He smiled, produced the spare key from his pocket and they entered.

They stood in the centre of the living area and looked round, and a hint of the more familiar Amy returned.

"We shouldn't be here," she whispered.

He laughed and kissed her on the cheek. Her courage returned.

"The place is a dump," he said.

It wasn't. Admittedly there were Isabella's trademark piles of dirty laundry all around, but that was the extent of the piggishness.

"No laptop," said Amy, glancing round. "Taken it with her."

"Any more thoughts on what we're looking for?"

"Anything that tells a different story to the one she'd like us to believe."

Someone had fitted shelves since Zack was last there. Ethan, presumably. He had always fancied himself with a power drill and a few rawlplugs and had made a decent job of it. The shelves were filled mainly with books, but these told Zack and Amy no more than they already knew of Isabella's past. Half were in French and Spanish, reflecting her degree course. Alongside them were ornaments, all of which might have come from the local Oxfam shop. There were no clay models from school art classes, no signed drawings, no soft toys that retained their appeal into adulthood. No photos. Not that she had brothers and sisters, admittedly, but what of her parents? Zack's own room was dotted with framed snaps of Carla, Ethan, himself and Imogen, the dogs, Marcus, Teresa, Margot and Henry. Even of Henry's new wife.

There was one exception to the soulless room and it stood out for being the only item on the far wall. It was a postcard-sized portrait of a woman in profile from the waist up, her dark hair tied back. She appeared to be holding some kind of clipboard, although surely not, as an inscription beneath it, etched into the silver frame, bore the name Juana Pacheco and a date, circa 1631.

In the bedroom on the wall facing the bed itself and therefore the first thing Isabella saw when waking, was the panoramic photo of her home, Estancia Sobromente. Zack recognised it from the house in Oxford. The splendid isolation of the place was at odds with the room, the house, the street, London itself and to that extent seemed unreal. He looked away. Amy had already gone to a chest of drawers, presumably one that Teresa had used all those centuries ago. At the top level were two half-drawers, left and right. Amy slid one open.

"You're supposed to start at the bottom," Zack said. "Work your way up."

"Only if you're burgling the place and have no intention of closing them. Honestly, this woman has more thongs, more bras, more knickers than Victoria's Secret!"

She fanned through the underwear with forefinger and thumb as one might a stack of paper.

"Not your style?" said Zack.

"Wedgies."

She opened the drawer beside it and lifted out the walnut box. She held it in front of her as if it might suddenly explode, so Zack took it from her. It was locked. He tried to force it, finger pressure only. He shook it. Jewellery, maybe?

"Bugger it," he said, replacing it. "Some other time."

Amy had gone to Isabella's side of the bed and opened the drawer in the bedside table.

"Strange," she said. "Nothing in it. I'd expect perfume, headache pills, tampons, girly stuff. But nothing."

"It's all in that bloody walnut box."

She ignored him and he turned away until he heard a familiar crack. Amy's knee joint as she dropped to the floor, head down, peering under the bed. She reached out and pulled a grey notebook through the dust. She stood up again and examined it, flicking through the pages, expecting, hoping it would be a diary or an old-fashioned address book. Zack peered over her shoulder.

"Some kind of cashbook," she said.

He took it to the window and went through it with increasing bewilderment.

"Expenses, laid out month by month. It goes back two

years, all the way up to yesterday. Everything from a cup of coffee to... God, there is big stuff here, two thousand pounds, three..."

He handed it back to Amy, who began to examine it thoughtfully. She suddenly looked up at Zack, her voice beginning to squeak as she gave way to excitement.

"These aren't expenses," she said. "They're income. Regular entries, £1000 on the first of every month. Sounds like an allowance."

Zack snatched back the book and turned the pages to the previous September. He ran his finger down the column and stopped at an entry for £95·00, below it £8·45 and right at the bottom the £1742 she owed her housemates.

"You're right," he said. "There's the van hire and coffee she screwed out of me when I moved her here. Look at the monthly totals! Twelve grand, fourteen... twenty-seven!"

He gave her the notebook and asked her to hold it open on the windowsill. He took out his phone and began to photograph each of the two dozen pages. When he'd finished Amy returned to the bedside, knelt down and slipped the book back into its place. She took out a tissue, dabbed dust over the giveaway trail marks and stood up.

They smiled at each other. The sums recorded by Isabella every month had fired their imaginations. One more thing caught Zack's attention as they left the room. A pile of mail on a shelf, weighted down by a polished stone. Among it he hoped to find correspondence addressed to Isabella – bills, final demands, threatening letters, perhaps even the odd County Court Judgement against her. There was nothing. Every letter was addressed to Ethan. Isabella either carried her mail with her, or more likely shredded it the day it arrived.

Down in his room Zack printed off the individual months, two copies, and they sat at his work table poring over the entries. Occasionally they drew each other's attention to a particular item, growing ever more horrified. A large proportion of the entries were in the £300 to £500 range and had names beside them… John S, Martin, Claudia… They assumed these were loans from people who would never see their money again.

Four or five entries stood out from the crowd for being life-changing amounts if you were a student or a struggling actress. Amy's imagination pitched her into the realms of high-class escorts or something to do with drugs. Given Isabella's South American connections, could she be the UK agent for some cartel back home? Ethan tried to let her down gently. If it was drugs they'd be talking about more than the £14250 here, back in January. By the opposite token she'd have to be a bloody good screw to command that price as a professional tart. He reached out for a pink marker pen.

"Highlight the big numbers, see if they've anything in common. £14250, January. With the letters MP beside it." He laughed. "Her MP's paying her for sex?"

"One here, P & P, February."

He looked across at Amy and screwed up his face. "£8000? Postage and Packing? What the hell…"

"Next page. £12500. NA. Not Applicable? I don't get it."

Zack shrugged. "Elsewhere she writes the full name. Richard, Kelvin, Kirstie. Hell, last November, £37,500! LJ!" He turned in his chair, flipped open his laptop and typed the initials LJ into Wikipedia, coming up with a few meaningless names. He batted the laptop closed and leaned back. "Who in God's name is LJ?"

"Someone who's a lot poorer since meeting Isabella."

* * *

Marcus was in his office when the phone rang.

"You've been on the phone for ages, Dad," said Zack.

"Well spotted. Do you want your mother?"

"Yeah, buzz through, will you?"

"I'm already here," said Teresa on the kitchen extension.

"Hi, Mum. Dad, you can go, mate."

Marcus breathed freely again and left them to it. He reached up to the shelf beside him and took down a copy of *Dangerous Corner*.

"Mum, I'd like to come over and see you both one evening."

"What's wrong?"

"Nothing! We've discovered something... about Isabella."

Teresa rose from the table and began to walk the length of the kitchen. The dogs followed.

"What kind of thing?"

"I'd rather not talk on the phone. When are you both there?"

"Darling, I'd need to vet it first before your father..."|

"Bloody hell, Mum, he doesn't need protecting!" He sighed as audibly as he could. "Sorry, but I'd like him to be there. Tomorrow night we'll be over, eight o'clock-ish."

"We?"

"Me and Amy." Clearly, Teresa needed a moment to

recall Amy. "Amy Tully, Mum."

"I know, I know. You've just got me worried, that's all."

"See you tomorrow. Big smacker of a kiss."

***

The dogs barked and then changed their aggression to yelps of delight as Zack pulled onto the Golden Meadow gravel. It was a clear, mild night and Teresa came out to greet her visitors, Troilus and Cressida charging ahead of her. She embraced Amy, who went as stiff as a board, then she turned to Zack with a full-blown hug.

"I swear the dogs recognise different car engines," she said. "When Ethan was here they did exactly the same thing. Come on in, it's chilly."

"No, Mum, it's lovely compared to West London, but lead the way."

They went into the kitchen and Marcus sauntered down from the study, tomorrow's lines rolling around in his head.

"All well?" he asked Zack, a shorthand enquiry as to how the *Conshie* filming was going.

"Excellent. You?"

Marcus nodded. "Been in Richmond Park today."

"Do you remember going there when you were younger and one of the dogs chased after a stag?" said Teresa. "Antlers the size of a tree and when he stood his ground Troy and Cress skidded to a halt and turned tail..."

She was prattling, her way of keeping bad news at bay.

"Ten years ago, Mum, long before Troy and Cress were born. But, yes, I remember."

Marcus turned to Amy, smiling. "You know, we bought a house with enough rooms to billet an army and spend most of our time right here, in the kitchen."

"That's rich, Dad, from someone who boasts he hasn't been to the top floor of his house for over a year." He turned to Teresa. "When is the baby due, by the way?"

Teresa laughed. "Don't you and Ethan ever talk? I suppose that's the trouble with your generation: you don't talk, you just text. Middle of October."

Amy nodded. "Libra."

"Why don't you both sit down?" said Zack.

"That bad, is it?" said Marcus.

His method of coping with possible bad news was to pre-empt it with a barrage of feeble quips. Teresa slid onto the bench and leaned on the table, arms folded.

"First biggish thing is this. Isabella does not work for M & S."

Marcus pulled out a chair for Amy then settled next to her. He looked up at Zack "So who does she work for?"

"Nobody."

Teresa turned away, not so much to absorb the news as to align it with her own suspicions.

"You know this how?" Marcus asked.

"Amy went to the headquarters the other day, asked to speak to her. There is no European Development section, and no Isabella Morales."

"Is that such a bad thing?" Marcus asked, carefully.

"Of course it is!" said Zack. "She has phone conversations with people 'from the office' which..."

"Sounds more like an elaborate game to me." He turned to Amy. "Are you sure?"

Zack bore down on him in mock despair. "I'll move on. We found a cashbook."

"Found?" asked Marcus, icily.

"Searched her room. Don't get high and mighty. When I was fifteen, you searched my…"

He let it go, reached down to his satchel and took out the copies he'd made of Isabella's cashbook. They were a record of her earnings for the past two years, Zack explained.

"Earnings?" said Marcus.

"Stop repeating everything."

He pushed the copies across to his father and pointed out the entry for £95·00 van hire and £8·45 for coffee.

"It isn't that she still owes me, it's proof that she earns a living this way. Look at the highlighted entries. Small amounts, big ones, each representing some poor sucker she's conned. Some have got initials by them, not that I know anyone called MP or NA… P & P? As for the biggy, LJ… Lionel Jeffries, Lyndon Johnson?… £37,000!"

"You should have nicked her phone," said Teresa.

"Bottom line is Amy and I now believe that what Isabella wants is the house."

"You mean Ashbury," said Marcus.

"All to herself. Carla, Imo, me gone."

Marcus wandered over to the kettle and filled it. Zack sighed irritably as he sensed his father backing away from the problem in favour of a cup of tea which nobody really wanted.

"Dad…"

"I need to think." He gestured to the mugs on the rack. "Anyone else?"

"Make four, love."

When the tea had brewed Marcus suggested they take it through to the library, the one place in Golden Meadow where calm and reason still prevailed. They decamped.

"So, what we've got is a young woman who's targeted us, via Ethan," said Marcus once they had settled.

Zack laid out the copies of Isabella's cashbook on the table. "The big question is where does all this money come from? Amy and I have been down the drugs route, the high-class tart thing and, tempting though they are, we're asking for input, ideas."

"The father, Juan Morales?"

"Then why doesn't she call it 'Allowance' or 'Dad'? It's NA, MP, P & P."

"What about the ex-husband, supposedly dead?" said Teresa.

"We only have her word that he's carked it. I mean is she a front for him in some business or other..." He broke off. "Amy?"

She was staring up at the books opposite her as if entranced. She smacked her lips once or twice to moisten them.

"Are you alright, dear?" asked Teresa.

"Yes, I am. Well, I'm not, but... no. It depends on your point of view."

She rose from the sofa, went over to the shelves and pointed up to where the books weren't as snugly arranged as elsewhere.

"*Mansfield Park*, *Northanger Abbey*, *Pride and Prejudice*. They're not there." She turned to them. "MP, NA, P & P."

Zack opened the library steps and scrambled up them to check.

"Jesus, she's right!" He turned to his parents. "Dad, weren't they first editions?"

"All the Austens were." He stood up. "How the hell has she done that? Most were in three volumes."

"One at a bloody time!" Teresa said, irritably. "Ever since Imo's twenty-first."

"Hang on," said Zack, in a moment of doubt. "Jane Austen, LJ?"

"That'll be *Lord Jim*," said Teresa. "A first edition signed by Joseph Conrad himself."

She went over to where it should have been, next to the author's other works. It was missing.

"How much do they add up to?" Teresa asked.

Zack made a quick calculation. "According to the grey book, about seventy odd grand."

"It couldn't possibly be someone else, could it?" said Marcus. "Imo, for example? Ethan, if he's been strapped for cash? Matt, even. I mean I wouldn't put it past..."

Teresa glared at him. "Anyone but Isabella?"

Zack shook the copied pages at him. "She wrote them down in her cashbook, Dad! So add us to the list of poor suckers."

Marcus perched himself on the corner of the table and covered his face with both hands. "I feel like I've betrayed Jack Relph's trust."

Zack snapped at him, "This isn't about Jack Relph, it's about *us*!"

"You think Ethan knows?" his father asked.

"Surely he'd have come to one of us?"

"Not necessarily," said Teresa. They turned to her and waited for more. "Am I the only one who believes he'll do anything she tells him to?"

"No, but I'm not sure why," said Zack.

"Because he's afraid of her, " his mother snapped. Zack scoffed in disbelief. "Please, Zack, if you knew how dreadful it makes me feel."

"What the hell is wrong with you two? Dad goes into spasm over Jack Relph, you think you're responsible for everyone's behaviour. The only villain in the piece is Isa-bloody-bella."

They remained silent for a moment or two, waiting for inspiration. Eventually Marcus stood up and said,

"Okay, I'll do something. Don't ask me what, just give me time."

Zack laughed sourly. "Sounds like No Further Action to me."

"I promise it isn't."

An hour later, when Teresa heard Zack's car reverse on the gravel and drive away into the night she realised that at least one positive thing had come from tonight's revelations. She would never again forget Amy Tully's face, or her surname.

-27-

Teresa supposed it was in the nature of family trouble that, no matter how drawn-out or harrowing a crisis was, daily life continued to flow around it. In the course of doing so the original problem began to take second, third, fourth place in a queue of other pressing matters. Hopefully, that explained why, two weeks after Zack and Amy's revelations, Marcus had failed to keep his promise to do something about Isabella.

To be fair *Salter's Edge* was still being filmed, though it was due to finish within weeks. That would be the ideal time for Marcus to act, except that as Richard Salter gave them back their real lives, Robert Caplan, the prig he had agreed to play in *Dangerous Corner,* would replace him.

Teresa timed her assault on his broken promise perfectly. She chose one evening when he was not called for filming the next day and settled him in the vast living room with a tray supper. They watched the first episode of a documentary about the American Civil War and were much impressed by its narrative style. At the end of it, Marcus glanced at his phantom watch and asked if she fancied episode two. She declined, saying that she wanted to discuss something with him.

He yawned convincingly. "If it's Isabella, I haven't had time recently."

"You swore you'd do something, in front of me, Zack and Amy Tully."

Obliging him to keep his promises invariably worked, but tonight she added a confrontational spur.

"You do know I read your emails, don't you?"

He smiled at her. "Do I send you any?"

"I was referring to the ones you don't. All of them."

He paused, mentally flicking back through his email account to anything he might have wanted to keep from her.

"Why?" he asked.

"I've read everything you've had from Juan Morales. They've all been creepy but the last was downright threatening. 'Can you please confirm that your son is to marry Isabella? Her uncertainty on this matter distresses me. In my country we take a very poor view of families who do not honour their responsibilities.'"

"More an awkwardness of style."

"*Deliberate* awkwardness." He looked at her, apparently concerned at last. "I don't think he writes them. In fact, I don't think he exists."

"So who...?"

"Isabella. I believe she's set up an account in the name of Juan Morales. Remember that first one? Wishing you well for *An Inspector Calls*? Time stamped 9:15 in the morning which meant he wrote it four hours earlier. Quarter past five? Nah!"

"Why did you never say?"

"I tried to think of ways to write back to him, with a

secret that would send her packing. An email saying Ethan is schizophrenic, or HIV positive, or has a congenital heart problem."

He was appalled. "Christ, Terri..."

"It's alright, I didn't follow through. The fact remains I believe Juan Morales is an invention. So what does that make her?"

"Crazy, possibly."

"I would've said downright dangerous."

He sighed heavily again. "I'll do something. Tomorrow."

***

He rose early, took the train to Marylebone and from there a cab to Mayfair. He loved the area for its ability to conjure up a horse-drawn world of Georgian wealth, romance and intrigue, bustling with maids and valets, top hats and silver canes. The buildings still evoked that illusion, but the ambience did not. Roadworks, the bane of most London streets, played against the din of honking traffic going nowhere fast.

He turned into Brook Street and sauntered past Claridge's, Teresa's least favourite hotel in London. Whenever she had been there for lunch she wanted to grab the fawning manager and his staff of flunkies and slap them into reality when they toadied to the likes of Henry or Marcus. On top of that their prices were an insult.

Reaching the Argentine embassy, Marcus stood below the blue and white flag with its emoji sunshine face, aware that half a dozen security cameras would be watching him, hopefully recognising him. To that end he had decided to play the charming, sophisticated thespian with but one question to ask and a determination not to leave without having it answered. He waited for Jonas Kemble to draw level with him, then rang the doorbell. He expected a disembodied voice to ask how it could help him. Instead, a besuited man in his forties opened the door and greeted him in perfect English.

"Good morning, sir. How may I be of service?"

"I'm looking for advice... help, really."

Help and advice were two commodities which, his father maintained, gave your target a sense of control over your future from that moment on. And thereby a willingness to assist.

"Advice upon what matter?"

This man was higher up the chain of command than a mere gatekeeper and would need careful handling. Marcus glanced up and down the street as if his enquiry was so diplomatically sensitive it couldn't be dealt with there on the pavement. The more-than-doorman opened the door wider and invited him to step in.

Marcus had expected to be overwhelmed by treasures plundered by conquistadors, or at least a high ceiling or two, hung with crystal chandeliers casting light on tapestried walls, but the reception area was more reminiscent of a middle-range hotel. The people in immediate view were also something of a disappointment. He had envisaged slim, olive-skinned creatures, not the two slightly podgy women seated behind the John Lewis desk. As for the two men, where was the Diego Maradona lookalike?

"May I see inside your bag, Señor?" the more-than-doorman asked.

He was referring to the satchel, which Zack had left hanging on a coat peg at Golden Meadow and Marcus now used to carry scripts. The doorman took out Marcus's phone.

"Please turn it off for me, then on and off again."

Marcus presumed it was in case he intended to blow the place up with a quick phone call and did as he had been asked.

"Now please, would you be so kind as to pass through…"

To pass through the phone booth of a scanner, he meant, a castoff from Heathrow airport, by the look of it. It tinkled rather than rang as he walked through it, the metal in the gold chain around his neck, maybe. He took his bag and was ushered towards the reception desk, where the elder of the two women adjusted her glasses in readiness. Her face was pale and blotchy behind the makeup, so un-Spanish-looking it made her native accent seem implausible.

"*Buenos dias*, Señor Lawlor, welcome to Argentina. My name is Luciana Davila."

He smiled the Lawlor smile. "I wonder if you can help me. I'd like to get in touch with an old friend who I believe is living in Argentina. I haven't seen her for 20 years, though it often seems like yesterday we were…"

The more-than-doorman nodded at Luciana, returned to his own desk close by the front door and refreshed his collection of monitors.

"Your friend, Señor, tell me something of her and I shall do my best. Her name?"

"Rosa Morales. At least, I assume that's what she's called now. She was so in love with Juan, and he with her. I heard on the grapevine they had married."

Luciana smiled. "Rosa Morales. Juan Morales. We are a nation of 43 million people, many with those exact names."

Marcus took a Post-it Note from his satchel and referred Luciana to the scrawl on it.

"Does this help? Juan owned a cattle farm, ranch… Estanc…"

"Estancia Sobromente," Luciana read. "If you will take a seat, Señor, I will find someone who can help you. Would you care for coffee?"

Marcus smiled. "No, thank you."

He sat in a spindly armchair at the side of the room and watched Luciana dial an internal number on a clockwork phone. The conversation with whoever picked up was in Spanish, but the names Rosa Morales, Juan Morales and Estancia Sobromente figured large and, almost inevitably, the name Richard Salter cropped up. When Luciana replaced the receiver, she walked across to him and said,

"Someone will be down." She held out the notepad she was carrying, open at a blank page. "Would you be so kind as to give me your autograph?"

"With pleasure. To Luciana?"

She nodded, aware that her colleagues were looking on. He wrote a brief message and then his name with a series of flourishes and handed back the pad.

"*Muchas gracias*, Señor. It is for my mother, you understand."

He had heard those exact words a thousand times and in every major language in the world.

"She is also called Luciana? How charming. Do give

her my regards."

It was forty minutes before anyone appeared, but when he did he was a young Julio Iglesias, heavier set but as handsome as his doppelgänger. He half bowed to Marcus, who rose to shake his hand.

"Señor Lawlor, I am Marcelo Viveros, the Administrative Attaché. If I am not mistaken you are the son of Sir Henry, is this so?"

Marcus took a steadying breath. Even in this outpost of some tinpot regime's empire his father could upstage him.

"I do have that honour," he said, with a plastic smile.

Viveros groaned with delight. "I have seen Sir Henry as *King Lear*. Believe me, he was... but you saw for yourself, no doubt. He was *magnífico*."

"Wasn't he just."

Viveros pointed to a door at the far end of the reception area. "Please, follow me."

Viveros led him into a large conference room which looked out onto a garden, heavily shaded by three lime trees. He gestured to a highly polished mahogany table. Viveros sat at the head of it, took out his laptop and placed it in front of him.

"You must forgive the time it has taken to answer your question. Your friend, Rosa, you know for certain she has married Juan Morales?"

Marcus had rarely played embarrassment more convincingly. "Well, actually, no. I mean, I found it odd that I wasn't invited to the wedding."

Viveros nodded. "She worked for him?"

"I'm not even one hundred percent sure about that. Rosa was a very skittish young woman, not so much a liar as a wishful thinker, but I liked her enormously and often wondered what became of her."

"Forgive my hesitation, Señor, but it seems an odd request to bring to an embassy."

"You surprise me."

"You could have enquired of the telephone companies, the postal service, the provincial government. There are no secrets in Argentina."

"I don't speak Spanish."

Viveros smiled, his lips as thin as razorblades.

"Shall we stop playing games, Señor? I don't believe you came here today in search of a friend. I would go so far as to say that Rosa does not exist."

"Then what exactly *have* I come for?" asked Inspector Goole.

Viveros typed into his laptop and turned the screen to show Marcus the webpage for Estancia Sobromente.

"This website is a fake. As for being the size of Yosemite Park, it is no bigger than Hampstead Heath."

"Well, I'm damned," said Marcus.

"The pictures here within it can be found on any tourist site. Facts about the beef industry are common knowledge. I shall inform the real owners of the estancia of the site's existence and leave them to take appropriate action."

"Who are they?"

"One of the most powerful companies in Argentina: Inversión Agrícola." He relaxed sufficiently to place his tongue in his cheek before adding, "There are three men named Juan Morales employed by the company. The oldest is 32, the assistant head of their IT department and his wife is called Maria, not Rosa."

He closed the laptop and stood up, indicating that their chat was over and Marcus should leave. He fastened up his satchel and followed Viveros to the door.

"I have a feeling that I have answered your question, Señor, and am delighted to have been of service. May I now know what the question *was*?"

Marcus smiled. "I've forgotten."

He left the embassy and walked back towards Claridge's. Unlike Teresa he was not averse to being fawned over and on reaching the hotel he went into the bar and ordered a double scotch with ice. Then another. He had hoped they would soften the doubts that were now plaguing him. Did Ethan know that Isabella had stolen large sums of money from friends and future relatives, albeit in the shape of Jack Relph's first editions? Was he aware that she had never worked for Marks and Spencer? Did he believe the lies she had told? Was he party to the moves she had made against his siblings in order to isolate him? Was she encouraging his weakness for marijuana and cocaine? And did he know that, far from being a wealthy cattle baron, Juan Morales was an ordinary... what?

On the train journey home Marcus decided to confront Ethan with what he had learned. It would be difficult, not least for Ethan himself. How would he react? By turning on Isabella? Unlikely. Disappearing from family view, maintaining that a great fuss had been made about a few lies, a handful of thefts and Isabella weaving an elaborate fantasy? Whatever Ethan's reaction, Marcus decided it was time for a face-to-face meeting.

-28-

As Marcus finished breakfast the next morning the phone rang. It was Zack, with news that Isabella had moved one step ahead of them all by using the nifty trick of going into premature labour at thirty-five weeks. Though secretly relieved that he could hardly challenge Ethan at such a moment, Marcus cursed Isabella's timing, saying it was typical of her. Thirty-five weeks was neither safe nor unsafe, an ambiguity which placed her centre stage.

Evidently, Zack had been asleep when the drama began and had woken to a piercing scream coming from the attic. He rolled out of bed and stood up. Ethan was calling him.

"Zack! Zack, I need you, mate. Zack, wake up."

Zack hauled on a pair of jeans and yesterday's top and hurried up the stairs, hugging the wall to get his balance. Bleary and stiff, he opened the door to find Ethan gibbering in panic.

"She's gone into labour."

"You said five more weeks."

"I know what I said!"

Isabella yelled Ethan's name from the bedroom and they hurried to her. She was seated on the edge of the bed, head down, hugging the cramp in her abdomen. Her nightdress and the bed she was sitting on were patched and smeared with blood. For a moment Zack saw it as an elaborate ploy, a hoax on her part to gain attention. A beat later he realised it was real.

"She's been leaking like a rusty tap for twenty minutes. Shit, blood, amniotic fluid… "

"You're pissed," said Zack, angrily. "I can smell it, you jerk."

"No, no, really…"

Zack pushed him aside and went over to Isabella.

"Help me, help me," she said and began to retch.

As she did so her face contorted in agony and she clutched at what presumably was another contraction. She tried to breathe as she had been taught, but it didn't help. She made to stand up and fell against Zack. He reached out to stop her falling.

"Dressing gown," he snapped at Ethan. "My car. Queen Charlotte's hospital, right?"

"An ambulance."

"Do what I say!"

Ethan fumbled his way along Isabella's clothes rail, unseating outfits until he found her silk dressing gown. He looked at it, about to ask if this would do.

"Give it here!" Zack yelled. "She got a bag?"

From the look on Ethan's face his brother might have been speaking a foreign language.

"An overnight bag!"

Isabella waved a hand at it.

"Hold her," said Zack and went to get it.

As he stooped to pick up the suitcase his eye fell on Isabella's laptop. It was open on a small nest of tables.

He would come back to it. He slammed the suitcase into Ethan.

"You take that, I'll get her down the stairs. Go!"

For the briefest moment he wondered where the brother he had grown up with, known to be so clever, so abrasive, so capable and, yes, so good in a crisis, had disappeared to. Was it just the booze, the weed which the attic reeked of, or had Isabella robbed him of... something else? He stopped thinking, and with his arm tight around her waist half carried Isabella down the stairs and out to his car.

In the ten minutes it took to reach Queen Charlotte's, Isabella vomited just once and had another contraction, liquid still pouring out from between her legs. As he glanced at her in the rearview mirror, Ethan telling her to breathe in all the wrong places, Zack was thrown off balance a little. He fancied he saw, for the very first time, the human being within her. She was petrified. Even the tears were real.

* * *

An hour later Zack returned to Ashbury, having phoned Amy and asked her to meet him there. She arrived within the hour, fresh from a morning spent being a rodent at Freebooter Studios. Fleshing out the details of Isabella's labour he added that she would be hospitalised for at least a week and Ethan would doubtless spend most of his time with her. He took a flash drive from his pocket and held it up with a smile.

"Follow me," he said.

"Where?"

He pointed above his ahead, then led her out of his

room and stomped up the creaky stairs. No need to tread softly. He opened the attic door with a flourish and gestured Amy to enter ahead of him.

Isabella's future son or daughter hadn't given her time to close her computer, though to Zack's annoyance it had logged itself out. He placed it on one of the chests of drawers, powered it up again and waited. The screen wallpaper was the panoramic view of Estancia Sobromente in all its grandeur. It settled and then asked him for a password.

"Fuck!" he said, and slapped the chest harder than he meant to. "I knew it was too good to be true. Bloody password."

He turned away, still swearing, but Amy grabbed him by the arm.

"Try Balcarres167," she said. He looked at her. "Balcarres167. I watched her type it in one day when she was in the kitchen 'working from home'. I shouldn't have been spying but..."

Whereas the Lawlors, whenever two or three of them were gathered together, indulged in banter and competition, Amy watched, listened and filed away. She spelled out the password and he entered it. Balcarres? It sounded Spanish enough, he thought. The granny smith apple hove into view and Isabella's computer burst into life.

Not that there was much to see on the desktop. There were folders containing her coursework, mostly to do with her modern languages degree, but the more personal folders were unpromising: a sparse email box, a few photos, a lacklustre contacts file. Her Safari search history had been wiped, the bookmarks were nonexistent, but ever hopeful, Zack loaded anything he could onto his flash drive. Amy watched and in time laid a hand on his shoulder and said, quietly,

"Type Balcarres167 into the Spotlight Search."

He did so and it produced a single file. He opened it gingerly and a moment later turned to Amy with a smile. His first impulse was to ask her, jokingly, to marry him. It was smothered by the fear that she might accept.

"If my old man doesn't do something about this, then I will!" he said, triumphantly. "Let's go."

He led the way downstairs to the front door from where he yelled for Amy to hurry, assuring her that he hadn't switched things on, opened windows or unlocked the back door. Finally she believed him and they left the house.

As they walked to his car, a taxi pulled up in the middle of the road and a late middle-aged woman with sun-wrinkled skin and grey hair stepped out of it and checked the house numbers. She reached back into the cab for her luggage, a hefty suitcase on wheels, the sort people trip over in airports and railway stations. She opened her shoulder bag, took out a pile of postcards, sorted through them and showed the driver one.

"£25·50," he said in response to it.

The woman rummaged for her purse and Zack, ever gallant, went to assist.

"Can I help you?" he asked the driver, icily.

"She owes me £25·50."

"Where from?"

"Battersea."

It sounded about right. With the woman's consent, Zack extricated three ten-pound notes from her purse and told the driver to keep the change. When the taxi departed, the woman reshuffled her fistful of postcards and produced one that said in bold felt tip, "Hallo, my name is Maria Santos."

"*Buenos dias,*" said Zack, none the wiser.

Maria pointed at herself. "*Niñera, niñera.*"

She rocked her arms from side to side, as if holding a baby. Zack stared at her.

"Jesus, she's hired a nanny!"

Maria looked at Amy and frowned. "Signora Morales?"

"No, she's in hospital. It's not our baby."

Amy wanted to say more but felt there was little point. Zack turned back to the house, unlocked the front door and carried Maria's suitcase over the threshold.

***

It took an hour to set Maria up in the downstairs back room, achieved with smiles, a great deal of nodding and a cup of tea. As Maria sipped it Zack called his brother to say that a nanny called Maria had just arrived. Ethan didn't know what he was talking about and asked him to repeat it. He still didn't know but at least he was calm... calm in a cannabinoid way.

"I'll text you a photo," Ethan said.

"What of?"

"Rafael Henry Lawlor. Born at 11:52."

Zack smiled. "Congratulations."

"I'm sending it to everyone, to the whole bloody world!"

Zack's mobile pinged a moment later. The photo was of a fragile, blotchy and peeling baby, with tubes in every orifice. He weighed four pounds two ounces and was lying in the care unit, motionless with a grumpy look on his face, no doubt annoyed by what had gone on that morning. Zack showed the photo to Amy and she dissolved gently into tears.

-29-

That night Zack phoned Golden Meadow to tell his parents about Balcarres167. Teresa answered and began effusing about her beautiful new grandson and the delightful photo she had been sent. Ethan had also invited her to drop in at Queen Charlotte's the next day to meet Rafael, even though it would be through a glass window. She then turned slightly and began to fret about how small and frail he was. She turned again and chided both sons for not telling her that Isabella had gone into labour. Zack apologised on his and Ethan's behalf, then asked to speak to his father.

"Dad, I want you to write this down."

There was the usual scuffle to find a pencil and pad before Zack spelt out Balcarres167.

"And what is that exactly?" Marcus asked.

"It's the password to Isabella's computer. And much, much more."

He explained what he and Amy had discovered and outlined the implications of it. Marcus listened in respectful silence and then said,

"Do you mind saying all that again? I'll put you on speaker so that your mother can hear."

Marcus had clearly been shocked and probably needed

to hear it a second time in order to absorb it. Zack went through the main points then offered to accompany Marcus the following day. Marcus considered the proposition and declined it.

"Nice of you to offer, mate, but I think I can handle it." He turned to Teresa. "I think I *should* handle it."

Let me know if you change your mind."

There was just a hint in Zack's tone that Teresa wasn't the only one who had qualms about Marcus's attitude towards Isabella. Here was his chance to set the record straight. He finished the call and said,

"Early start, I think. Better let them know at *Salter's Edge*."

He called the production assistant to say that he wouldn't be available for a few days. There was an understandable silence from the other end but no argument. The filming would have to be rearranged, the poor girl said, but in the grand scheme of things no one would suffer as a result of his absence. It was a curious moment to realise that for the first time in many months he could write his own schedule, minute by minute, rather than have a production flunky present him with it, cut and dried. He went on from there to wonder if he'd become slightly afraid of being autonomous, having spent so much time playing figments of someone else's imagination, always under a third party's direction. Tomorrow would be very different.

* * *

Marcus's friends had often teased him about the car he drove, a fifteen-year-old Ford Focus with a hundred thousand miles on the clock. They wanted to know why a man who had been so successful hadn't bought himself a decent car, even a flash one. Was it inverted snobbery? After all, he enjoyed people recognising him, despite his protestations to the contrary. True, he admitted, but he wasn't keen on being recognised by anyone on a motorway.

He left Golden Meadow at six o'clock the next morning with Teresa wishing him the best of luck. He headed towards the M6, a motorway which he quite liked, if a strip of tarmac can be said to inspire affection. He took the toll road around Birmingham, mainly because that's what he had always done when hauling The Others up to The Lake District. There was a decent service station halfway along it with edible food and clean toilets. His mother had always said that you can tell the state of a place by the cleanliness, or otherwise, of its toilets.

It was years since he'd been to Scotland. The last occasion had been twenty years previously to appear as Macduff in an oddball production of *Macbeth* at the King's Theatre. It was a run of three months and Marcus would have stayed longer, had he not been aware of a growing political iciness towards Sassenach invaders. His father had counselled him to take no notice, especially of a handful of critics who had praised his performance and then asked why a Scottish actor hadn't been chosen for the role.

As he approached Edinburgh he knew roughly what to expect, at least in terms of bricks and mortar, since he had given himself an induction course on Google Earth, pinpointing at street level the very place he was bound for. Balcarres Street. It lay south of the city centre and was once an endless stretch of Victorian grimness evoking the sound of rolling carts, the clink of hobnail boots and the voices of too many children. Fog would have clung to the stonework in the mornings, whipped away as the day went on by a biting wind from the North Sea. But at five o'clock on this balmy twenty-first-century afternoon the sun was shining on a row of refurbished tenements, the price of a flat within them rising daily as a consequence.

Marcus parked on the more manicured side of the street where postwar semis sat high on a steep grassy bank, behind them an extensive park where mothers pushed toddlers on swings and coaxed them down silver slides. He crossed over the road and, right beside where he'd expected to find number 167 a square archway led through to a courtyard. Four small businesses occupied converted stabling. One of them claimed to manufacture the finest stained glass in Europe, another sold raw pet food, the third belonged to an upholsterer, the fourth was a car body shop.

The scream of a cutter and the smell of scorched metal and oil drew Marcus towards the open double doors, beyond which he saw a figure stooped over a bench, a tall, angular man in stained dungarees. A visor was pulled down over his face to shield it from sparks. As the off-cut dropped to the floor it clanged and echoed on the concrete. Beyond him two other figures were at work, one of them lying on a wheeled trolley beneath an old Hillman.

The cutter spotted him, lifted his visor and removed the helmet. His face was the right one for the tall angular body. It was thin and bony, drawn into an expression of sadness. Dark hair, lots of it, and widely set, sunken eyes. He didn't recognise his visitor and for once Marcus was grateful for that.

"Help yer, pal?" he asked in an accent more Glasgow rough than Edinburgh smooth.

"I'm looking for 167 Balcarres Street."

The man took a moment to ponder the English accent so far from home, and came towards it. He nodded out to the nearest tenement, the one right beside the arch.

"Who y'after?"

"Juan Morales," said Marcus, carefully.

The man shook his head. "Nearest you'll get is John Morrison, but not... whatever you said."

"Does John Morrison live at 167?"

"Why d'you wanna know?"

Marcus held out his hand and asked quietly, "Mr Morrison?"

Morrison removed a leather gauntlet and the two men shook hands, guardedly.

"Favour to ask," said Marcus, adopting Morrison's clipped style.

He took out his phone and opened the photos app. First to appear was a snap of Isabella, taken the night of Imogen's 21st birthday.

"Recognise this young woman?"

Morrison looked at the photo, then at Marcus again.

"Something wrong? You police?"

"No, no, she's fine... safe and well. Who is she?"

"My daughter. Isabel."

They stared at each other until Marcus gestured towards a windowed-off corner of the workshop. It was kitted out as an office with a desk, phone, computer and a snowfall of untouched paperwork. Morrison nodded and led the way into it, where he scooped up piles of paperwork from the only chair and gestured for his guest to sit, first placing a copy of the *Daily Record* on the oily padding.

It took Marcus just under an hour to explain what he was doing there and at no point did John Morrison show the slightest emotion. He simply leaned back on the desk, staring down at the floor and retreating behind his folded arms as he listened to the story, beginning at Imogen's 21st birthday, ending with Rafael's birth just two days ago. As Marcus reached Isabella's elaborate fantasy in which she had replaced her modest upbringing with that of being the daughter of a wealthy Argentinian cattle baron, Morrison raised a hand. He did so not to halt the narrative, but to absorb the idea of it, maybe even to take a breath at the pain it was causing him. He gestured for Marcus to continue. The theft of money from friends, the purloining of first editions from Jack Relph's library, the fake job, they all seemed slightly trivial to both men in the light of her overall determination not to be herself. So too did her manipulation of the Lawlor family, for what end they had only guessed at. Marcus finished his account and opened his hands for Morrison to speak. Eventually he said,

"She was always a strange lassie."

If it had not been so heartfelt it might have sounded comical. Morrison paused before carrying on, searching for words that wouldn't sound disloyal yet at the same time would tell the truth.

"She realised early on she was clever, smarter than her mam and me, so she started organising life the way she wanted it." He smiled. "Sometimes it felt this wee girl was running the place. We gave her all we could. The one thing I couldn't do was move us away. I could nae afford it. She held it agin me."

He pointed vaguely in the direction of the tenement beside the archway.

"Third floor, so it's not green fields and open spaces. Nor is it downtown Kabul. We sort of became passing strangers, but when she needed to she could wind me round her little finger."

"Did she have friends?"

Morrison looked at him, as if it were a trick question.

"They came and went, almost scared of her. The ones she liked she made a fuss of, but they never stayed. Just when I thought she was... you know, smoking, drinking, drugs mebbe, and boys... boys, boys, this teacher stepped in. Peter Chalmers. Girls loved him. He saw something in Izzy and said if I gave him the chance he'd make sure she went far."

"Oxford," said Marcus.

Morrison nodded. "That's when we lost her. I knew she'd gone when she didn't come to her mother's funeral. Five years ago now."

"She came home at Christmas, right?"

"Aye, but we didn't talk much." He looked up. "How d'you find me?"

Marcus smiled. "The password on her computer. Balcarres167. In a list of prompts to help her remember it she'd written the letters 'M & D'. Somewhere else there was a picture of the street. So maybe you haven't lost her completely?"

"You got a picture of the bairn?"

Marcus flicked through his phone and found the picture of Rafael which Ethan had sent to everyone he could think of. Morrison smiled for the first time.

"Bit of a scrap, huh? What've they called him?"

"Rafael. Do me a favour, John? Come down to London with me tomorrow, the hospital she's in..."

"Why still there?" he asked anxiously.

"The baby came early. Five weeks. They're both fine though."

Morrison nodded. "Come with you why?"

"If we face her with everything she's done, what would happen? Would it make her see how wrong she's been? Sounds ambitious I know, but... motherhood? Maybe we can pull her back? New start?"

* * *

Early the following morning, Marcus phoned Teresa from his hotel room in order to share what he had discovered. It was an odd conversation, one where Teresa kept wanting, expecting to hear more, though more of what she didn't know. An explanation, perhaps, as to why Isabel had turned into the person she was? Some dark family secret that could be blamed? The whiff of a horrendous upbringing in a drunken, drug-fuelled, abusive home? Marcus couldn't say for sure, but didn't think any of that was the case. All he knew was that he had startled awake several times during the night, hearing the voice of one or other of his children declaring they were no longer part of the Lawlor family, no longer his child. Their words had a finality to them, a sense of there being no return from the view they held. They blamed him for his cruelty, his insufficiency and the preferential treatment of one child over another. It had taken him a good fifteen minutes on each wakening to fully restore his peace of mind and drift back to sleep. John Morrison had no such luxury. His daughter, his only child, had acted on her resentment and denied his very existence. In doing so she had robbed him of the joy and pride an only child should have brought.

Marcus checked out of the hotel early and drove to Morrison's workshop to find him giving instructions to the elder of the two mechanics he employed. He was dressed, rather uncomfortably, in dated and sober clothes, a tweed jacket and grey cotton slacks. There was a shine on his freshly shaven face, and his hair was slicked back. They shook hands and Marcus led him over to the Ford Focus. Morrison had expected it to be a big Merc or a tank-sized Range Rover, from the way the man had spoken. Posh, confident, with something vaguely familiar about the look of him. He put his suitcase in the boot, uttering the single word,

"Thanks."

They said virtually nothing more to one another for a hundred and fifty miles, each of them lost in his own apprehensions. Eventually Morrison asked if Marcus wanted him to drive for a while. Marcus accepted the offer gratefully and turned in to the next service station for breakfast.

-30-

Ethan woke earlier than usual and began to bask in the euphoria that follows the birth of a first child. The second not so much, an old hand visiting the maternity ward had told him. The third even less. The fourth was almost run of the mill. Ethan had smiled. Maybe being 'run of the mill' explained all Imo's nonexistent problems. He would call her today, invite her over to Queen Charlotte's to meet her nephew. Jane Sillitoe as well. Why not? They were all one family now. Having sent Carla a photo he would compose a bygones-be-bygones text and end by enquiring after Matt's health.

Zack and Amy were downstairs in the kitchen with the morning news on the radio. They had left a note the previous evening saying they had been called to Freebooter for a couple of hours, which meant they could visit the hospital later and wax gaga over Rafael. My son, Ethan would say to people who may or may not have been interested. I'm sorry, I can't hang about today, my partner has just had a baby. He's called Rafael. Rafael. It's Spanish, you know. His mother is from Argentina. He's my son.

And then, as he kicked back the duvet and lunged himself out of bed, so the dream followed and crash-landed on the floor. The midwife, a vast Jamaican lady who had delivered literally hundreds of babies, had taken him into her office the previous evening, sat him down and worried him.

"Dear, you know what PND is?" she asked with a faint Caribbean lilt. "No, I can see from your face that you don't. Postnatal depression."

"I've heard of it," he replied.

"It is early days, not 36 hours even, so I could be mistaken but she hasn't touched her baby once."

She held up her hands lest he suddenly panic. He looked the sort who might.

"All I'm saying is this – I'm sure Isabella's a warm, loving person, but you need to keep an eye. Did you both attend antenatal classes?"

"She did. I went once, but..."

"Is her mother still with us, her father?"

"They're in Argentina, but my own mother will help."

"I'd like to meet her, but as I say, nothing... nothing to worry about."

The very words 'nothing to worry about' propelled Ethan into a state of high anxiety. Trust Isabella, he thought, to garner the best of all possible options. First she gave birth, a dramatic enough business in itself, to his son, Rafael Henry Lawlor. He arrived early, putting everyone on high alert, though Ethan could hardly blame Isabella for Rafael's timing. And now there was PND. If there was any drama to be wrung out of that Isabella would find it, if only to make sure that he didn't sit back and enjoy the experience of becoming a father.

He got dressed and went down to the kitchen. His

delight was surfacing again, enough that he barely noticed the reserved expression on Zack's and Amy's faces. Maria was seated at the table, her very presence echoing the implications of the midwife's words, her warning that he should keep an eye out. Would Maria take Isabella's place permanently, Ethan wondered. On the positive side, however, by employing a nanny Isabella had recognised her own shortcomings and that was halfway to solving any problem with bonding.

He smiled at Maria as she spooned her way through her porridge. Amy had made a huge pan of it and Ethan helped himself as he wished them good morning.

"I'm a dad," he said, suddenly. "A father. You're an uncle, Amy an honorary aunt."

"I like his name," said Zack, to fend off more paternal silliness.

"Strong, isn't it, and if it gets shortened it'll be to Rafa, which I also like." He paused. "You're working today?"

"Leaving at half nine."

"Any chance you can go via Queen Charlotte's, drop me off?" He turned to Maria and raised his voice. "Maria, I'm off to..."

"She doesn't speak a word of English," Zack reminded him. "Or so she says. Or rather *doesn't* say. Where's she from?"

"Madrid, I believe." He smiled at Maria. "Madrid, yes?"

Maria nodded and smiled back, uttering the one English word she had learned. "Yes, Madrid. Yes."

Come nine o'clock, with a flurry of arm flinging and pointing, they managed to get across to Maria that she was to stay here while the three of them left. In the end it was uncertain as to how much of the sign language she understood but they left her to it all the same. They then waited while Amy checked the windows, lights and gas hobs in her usual way.

Zack dropped Ethan off at the hospital and in a sudden pang of guilt, stepped out of the car himself and embraced his brother for no apparent reason. He got back in the driving seat and headed for Freebooter. He felt treacherous. Clearly, Ethan knew little about the real Isabella and instead of sharing their latest discoveries, Zack had betrayed him by keeping silent.

* * *

It was almost dark when Marcus reached Queen Charlotte's with John Morrison, and he led the way to the hospital cafeteria. It was surprisingly busy, given the late hour, but the presence of other people was something of a blessing for Morrison. He seemed to merge into the crowd rather than stand out from it.

Zack and Teresa rose from their table to greet him and he twitched with embarrassment and uncertainty. Teresa fancied that he was questioning the wisdom of having come to London, yet at the same time knew he would have regretted not doing so.

She smiled. "Mr Morrison, John… I'm Teresa, this is my… other son, Zack. I'm so glad you could make it. This is your first grandchild, right?"

He clasped and released his rough hands and cleared his throat before responding. He spoke in a small voice for such a large man.

"Aye, 'tis. First. Only child, see..."

"Ours too."

"You've met him... so to speak?" asked Marcus.

Teresa smiled. "And he's beautiful."

She took each man by the arm, as if to guide two terrified children across a busy road, and led the way out of the cafeteria and down two flights of stairs. She opened the doors to the neonatal intensive care unit and guided them to a window. She stopped and gestured through it to an elaborate cot which seemed, at first, to be a mass of tubes and pumps surrounded by flashing monitors and of itself would have been unremarkable but for the tiny human being lying on his back, gently hooked up to all the technology.

For Marcus there was something of the wide screen about his first sight of his grandson. A drama was going on beyond the glass, with Rafael not exactly fighting for his life but struggling to keep up. How would the story end, he wondered. With a cliffhanger to keep them all guessing? Or something more final? Knowing Isabella it would be a twist no one had foreseen. He suddenly wanted Rafael to break through the screen, walk towards him and shake his hand with Lawlor panache. Rafael kept on sleeping.

Morrison reached into his pocket for a piece of kitchen towel and dabbed both his eyes, then sniffed.

"Sorry, sorry," he asked. "How long's he there for?"

"Nine more days," said Teresa. "But he's thriving."

"Have you held him?"

She smiled. "Not yet. Are you ready?"

He nodded and Teresa led them along the corridor and

peered through the porthole in a door. There were four new mothers in the ward, two with babies in cradles beside them, a third on her feet, stretching her back. Isabella was propped up in a corner bed, dozing, the hair spilling down either side of the barrage of pillows. A nurse had offered to pin it up, or at least contain it in a bandana. Isabella had declined. Ethan was stretched out in a chair, gazing at her as if ready to receive the next instruction. He looked up when his parents and Zack entered the room.

"Dad!" he whispered, struggling to his feet. "Mum, Zack, guys, how's it going?"

He smiled at Morrison who stayed close to the door, as if at any second he might turn and run. His eyes were on Isabella and Ethan took him to be some hospital jobsworth who would need boxes ticked. Isabella surfaced slowly, sleepily. Teresa watched her for the slightest hint of recognition as Morrison took a step towards the bed and said quietly,

"Hi, Izzy, how are you, sweet?"

She opened her eyes wide and frowned.

"Who is this man?"

"Izzy, please don't..."

"Who *is* he?" she demanded to know, in a panicky voice.

Ethan turned to his father. "What's going on, Dad?"

"This is Isabel's father, Mr John Morrison."

Ethan stared at Morrison who reached out to shake his hand.

"Keep away!" Isabella screamed. "Don't bring him near me! I've never... I've never..."

"I've just brought him down from number 167 Balcarres

Street," said Marcus. "Where you grew up… Isabel."

"And where the hell is that?" asked Ethan, closing on them.

"Edinburgh."

Isabella stepped away from the moment and watched herself kick back the bedcovers and stand up, quite steady on her feet, no discomfort from the long suture. She went to her suitcase, flicked it open, and from the lid took out the nail file, the thin, steel nail file. She held it in a clenched fist and turned to Marcus, who smiled. She reached up and plunged it into the side of his neck. She pushed until the file met bone. The blood fountained. He clapped a hand to the wound and gradually crumpled to the floor. Blood began to pool beneath his head in a purple halo. Morrison, Teresa, Zack, Ethan, all were frozen, powerless, as they watched Marcus bleed to death. The first fly came in through the window and started on the feast.

Isabella yelled angrily, "Edinburgh?! Ethan, call security."

She began to hyperventilate. Without further effort to gain his daughter's acceptance Morrison turned and walked out of the room.

"Go after him, Zack," said Marcus. "He's got no car. See what you can do."

"What the hell are you playing at?" Ethan demanded.

Marcus held up a hand. "I'll call you tonight."

He turned and left the room, Teresa following. The door closed behind them but was immediately opened again and Ethan ran towards them. His face was marble white with fury.

"What the fuck is this?" he yelled.

"Later..."

Ethan caught him by the shoulder and turned him. "This woman has just given birth! Have you forgotten what that does? He's in the care unit, for Christ's sake! What, what... you bastard! You think I'll turn against her over some made-up name? Is that what you hope?"

"You know what else she's done?"

"Oh, don't spoil your day by keeping it to yourself. Tell me."

"She has lied on an industrial scale."

"The whole *world* lies." He roared with anger, then clamped his hands over his ears, voicing some angry jingle as he turned and went back to the ward. He barged open the door and let it slam behind him. Marcus turned to confront the two breathless security officers who had been summoned by wide-eyed staff.

"Alright, guys, it's over," he said, quietly.

He took Teresa by the hand and strode past them.

***

Far from spending the next few days in the limbo of postnatal depression the midwife had predicted, all Isabella could talk about was Marcus and his cruel attempt to exploit her vulnerability. He had wanted to belittle her, she insisted, to frighten her, to paint her as a liar, a fake, a troublemaker. She didn't understand why. She summoned Maria to the hospital and for the rest of the week Ethan watched in bewilderment as this middle-aged woman he knew nothing about became nursemaid to his son. She sat in the corner of the ward, seemingly transported to another world, as she performed the tasks that Isabella should have been desperate to do.

"What did they think they were *doing*?" she asked one evening, for the umpteenth time. "Marcus, Teresa, Zack and no doubt that pathetic, simpering, squeaking... Where are they, Amy and Zack?"

"Her flat."

She glared at him. "Don't tell me they've hooked you. God, your mother's hated me ever since she clapped eyes..."

"I spoke to my father the other night." He smiled. "You're not from Argentina, Bella, and that's not even your name. Estancia Sobromente is the size of an allotment. The website's phoney. All the photos are from magazines. The email address for Juan Morales leads to your inbox." He began to laugh, nervously. "Nice touch. Had them going." He paused and lowered his voice. "You still need to answer some questions."

"I don't *need* to do anything!"

"Put it this way. Would you please make one or two things clear for me?"

She closed her eyes and changed her attitude. The attack in her voice became the quiet defence of a struggling victim and she reached for the box of tissues on the bedside cabinet. She leaned back against the pillows and winced to remind him that she had just given birth.

"You're right," she said. "You need to hear it from me. Where shall I start? The job with M & S..."

Her voice faltered.

"What about it?" Ethan asked.

"It doesn't exist. I needed an excuse to be near you."

He reached out and took her hand. "I should have

guessed, all those days you spent 'working at home'. Phone calls to the office?"

"Harmless enough."

"My father disagrees. He also says you think you're related to Diego Velazquez. What the hell is that about?"

"Most of your family makes a living doing that. Telling stories. Does it hurt anyone? No. Does it make me feel good about myself? Yes! Or it did, given that it's all over now."

The whine in her voice carried a twist of blame. Marcus had brought her inoffensive fantasy crashing to earth.

"They reckon you drove Carla and Imo out of the house."

"That isn't true, I tried to help," she argued.

"Then made a pass at Zack, hoping he'd leave?"

She closed her eyes, tightly, desperate to be understood. "It's you I want to spend the rest of my... Why? Why would I drive them away?"

He wanted to agree with her. After all, had any of her actions caused irreparable harm? Her scheming and her deceits could also be seen as mere vanities. Had they changed anyone's life for the worse? Had her stealing impoverished anyone? He let go of her hand.

"The man who came to the hospital, John Morrison. He was your father, right?"

She smiled, ruefully. "Yes and no."

"Believe me, I don't care who he is. I just want to know who *you* are."

"My name was Isabel Morrison. I changed it by deed poll to Isabella Morales. It cost me fifteen quid. Yes, he's my biological father, but do I think of him as my dad? Never." She whimpered again, apologetically. "I'm sorry, sorry...

really I am, but he and I have nothing in common. He's dull, he's boring, he's colourless. I know you think that's awful of me, but you weren't there in that stultifying flat! 167 Balcarres Street might have been a lodge at the gates of hell." She paused. "And then I met Peter Chalmers."

From the way she brought his name into the conversation he could have been anything from a mentor to a serial rapist, Ethan thought.

"He was a teacher at the school I went to." She answered his silent question. "Yes, I fancied him like mad, but nothing happened. He saw something different in me and that made him more of a father than John Morrison ever was."

"You can't just shrug off your dad..."

"I'm just saying I made choices, like now, with you." She gripped his hand excitedly and steered him away from the subject of John Morrison. "We can use Rafael as our fresh start, turn things around, lead a different life."

He remained silent for a moment or two, then asked with a smile, "The days you didn't go to work because there was no job, where *did* you go?"

She laughed. "You mean did I have a secret lover somewhere? Zack, maybe?"

"Zack's a carbon copy of my father. Too wrapped up in himself for the odd fling."

She shrugged. "Museums, galleries, exhibitions, things I'd never dreamed of in Edinburgh."

"Where did you get the money? For *any* of it? Rent, coke, clothes...?"

"Borrowed from people. Didn't pay them back." She paused. "And the books."

"Books?"

"The library at Golden Meadow. All those first editions just sitting there, smiling down so smugly, begging to be cashed in."

He laughed. "You nicked some?"

"I owed so much to so many friends, I just..." She looked at him, with an honest face. "I took *Pride and Prejudice* right after Imo's twenty-first birthday. Did anyone miss it?"

"That isn't the point, surely."

From his softening manner she sensed him falling into line.

"Please don't be cross. Just believe that Rafael's put an end to all that and he's the only thing that matters now." She reached up and touched his face. "Why don't we leave Ashbury? Find a place of our own out of harm's way."

"You don't think we should get married, do you? For the baby's sake if nothing else." He nudged her, almost playfully. "Let's just do it. You, me, Rafael, Maria and a registrar."

She looked down at him. For the baby's sake? Why? Half the people she knew had parents who were either divorced or had never married in the first place.

"No rush," she said.

Ethan nodded across the room at Maria.

"Where did she come from, by the way?"

"I advertised in a Spanish magazine, the equivalent of *The Lady*. She's a widow, needed a break. I gave her one." He laughed again. "But I paid my bills, didn't I, paid my rent?"

"Bella, you borrowed from your friends and didn't pay them back!"

She chuckled. "I tried to. Some wouldn't accept, others had moved away."

"And at least three of them set debt collectors on you."

She shook her head, bewildered by his insistence. "God, it is only money, Ethan. Whatever I earned I shared with you. I did it for *you.*"

He looked at her in something akin to awe and then smiled.

"Christ, Bella, you are some piece of work. If you could put it to good use, the world wouldn't stand a chance."

***

In a moment of wishful thinking, Teresa wondered if Rafael could wield the mystical power of a newborn child and bring her family back together again. She reached forward in her mind a year hence, to when Rafael would be up on his hind legs, even talking a little, a human being in his own right brimming with personality and curiosity. It was a long shot, admittedly, but maybe, just maybe, time would have reduced his mother's assault on the Lawlor family to aggravated mischief-making. Immature, spiteful and petulant, but hardly terminal. There was even a possibility that Isabella herself would be as mystified by her past behaviour as anyone, thanks to the timely distraction of raising a small child.

There was only one thing standing in the way of this idealised return to sanity. Teresa herself. Throughout her life she had forgiven many of the wrongs done to her, but she had not forgotten a single one. They formed an indelible hit-list of hate and periodically she toyed with the notion of revenge.

She called Zack the day Isabella was due to leave hospital and in the wooden style of phone messages asked if he had seen them yet. He phoned back half an hour later to find his mother either excited or highly anxious. He wasn't sure which.

"You got my message?" she asked.

"Yes. And no, I don't think they're back yet."

"They should be. What time is it?"

"Six. Have you phoned him?"

"He's blocked my calls. All I want to know is if Rafael's fit and well, if Isabella's okay and if Maria is doing her job."

"I'm sure yes, yes and yes."

"Has anyone checked this nanny's credentials or looked into her past? Why has she left Madrid and come to England, do you know? One hears such terrible stories of abuse, abduction... worse..."

"Mum, come down off the ceiling."

She took a deep breath and descended. "Pop upstairs and see if they're alright, will you? I know you say you haven't heard them, but..."

"Okay, Mum, I will."

"I'll hold on?"

"No, I'll call you back."

He abandoned the beer he was drinking and made his way up to the attic, having first located the spare key. He didn't need it. The door was unlocked. He knocked on it and called out. There was no answer, and only at that point did his adrenalin surge. He opened the door and froze. The place was empty, hollow, almost echoey. No clothes, no shoes, no books. No piles of dirty laundry. The kitchen and bedroom were the same. No duvet, no sheets, no pillowcases, just a bare mattress on the bed. The only sign that Ethan and Isabella had ever been there was the huge picture of Estancia Sobromente, still on the wall as if to mock whoever came looking for them. In a short burst of rage Zack lifted it off the wall and ripped it into five pieces.

He closed the door behind him and went back to his own room, wondering how he would put his brother's moonlight flit to Teresa. As he considered his options she called him.

"Something's wrong," she said.

"They've gone," he replied, gently.

"Gone where?"

"They've left the house."

"But where are they?"

"I don't know, Mum."

"No forwarding address?"

He sighed with frustration. "Don't be daft."

"Well, what about social media? Surely you can find..."

She stopped quizzing him, put the phone back on its cradle and went down to Marcus's office. The door was half open and he was at his desk making notes on the play script of *Dangerous Corner*. She watched him until he became aware of her presence and turned to her.

"We went too far," she said, icily.

"Pardon?"

"He's gone. She's taken him and our grandson. After all I've said to you about losing him, you just had to zoom off to Edinburgh, to prove a point..."

She broke off, realising that what she was saying made no sense.

"And now we've lost him," she mouthed.

She slumped back against the desk, hands to her face. The sight of her in tears forced Marcus to his feet. He put his arm around her shoulders and kissed the top of her head. It was an odd moment to realise that he hadn't seen her cry for years.

-31-

As the weeks went by with no message from Ethan as to his whereabouts, so Marcus and Teresa began to retreat into their individual worlds. In the run-up to rehearsals for *Dangerous Corner*, which was scheduled to open before Christmas, he found it comparatively easy to back-burner his son's disappearance, though it flared up during conversations with Teresa. Ashamed though she was to admit it, her family had become her reason for being. The disappearance of one of them was like a death. Unfairly, she blamed Marcus. He adored his family, no question, but the downside to that had always been his unwillingness to engage with their problems, let alone to ever chastise them. That's where it had all gone wrong. When discipline had been called for he had always delegated the task to Teresa. And twenty years on here she was, for the first time in her life, with a problem she couldn't solve and a husband whose main obsession was himself.

In time they were forced to communicate, usually to discuss the practicalities of day-to-day living. Occasionally, if the atmosphere warmed a little, they would speculate wildly even as they realised how absurd their guesswork was. Where could Isabella have taken Ethan and Rafael?

Argentina, if that had been her fantasy? Edinburgh, now that her true identity was revealed? Australia, America, Canada...God only knew. Even Henry, who could turn tragedy into comedy with a mere look or gesture, was at a loss to lift anyone's spirits.

By contrast his new wife was annoyingly optimistic in her belief that Ethan would return. She didn't know when, how or why, but meantime they would all have to be patient and loving towards each other. If any of them had heard the sentiment voiced in a television drama they would have hurled rocks at the screen.

* * *

Isabella walked into the police station and stood looking round. She had expected it to be bustling with lowlifes but there were no more than half a dozen people in the seating area, two of them plainclothes officers, she imagined, talking to a couple with young children.

This must be how Marcus felt when he walked onto a stage at the beginning of each performance, she thought. How will I be received? In his case the audience numbered hundreds: in hers just one. He sat caged in a security den the size of an old telephone box, with a slot in the mesh through which members of the public could feed him their woes. He was early thirties with short hair that oozed gel down across his forehead. His face was shaven almost raw, and with it being such a warm day she fancied that he would smell like a mixture of sweat and cheap deodorant. She winced and turned away as if to head for the exit and in doing so drew his attention.

"Can I help you, Miss?" he called out from his lair.

She stopped and took a deep breath as if to steel herself against the finality of reporting an event she couldn't later deny. She went over to the officer and blinked rapidly, nervously.

"Sorry?"

His voice became more personal. He even smiled. "I said, can I help you?"

She hovered before deciding to answer. "I'd like to report a crime."

"What sort of crime?" he asked, flatly.

"A sex crime. Against me."

The words had captured his interest and he looked her over. She seemed defeated, the hair was a mess and almost hiding her face. She wore no makeup. The clothes were passable, he thought, but the blouse, buttoned so tight to her throat as if to strangle her, needed a wash.

"When did this take place, Miss?"

"Two years ago now. I've been wondering ever since…"

He put a finger to his lips and nodded at the other people in the foyer to prevent her sharing any details.

"If you take a seat, someone'll come and talk to you."

"A woman?" she asked, anxiously.

He nodded reassuringly. "Specially trained in this area. She's at her desk today so we're in luck."

She wanted to take him up on his use of the word 'luck' but decided against it. She backed away from the cage, over to a bench seat beneath a wall crowded with posters about crime, how to report it, how to claim compensation if you had suffered it, how to complain if the police had let you down. The largest poster was a sign that told visitors not to smoke here. She pulled back a smile, changing it to a wince of fear.

* * *

Marcus had called his father three times that week seeking his advice on the character of Robert Caplan in *Dangerous Corner*. How would Henry tackle this typical Priestley prig whose wife had been having an affair with Robert's more exciting brother who had recently committed suicide? God, he thought *he* had problems! Henry quoted Laurence Olivier's advice to Dustin Hoffman. "Try acting, dear boy."

Autumn was certainly in the air, but with it being a sunny day Henry took his coffee into the garden and settled in the wicker armchair. Normally he would have devoured the morning papers but today *The Times*, *The Telegraph* and even *The Spectator* had been replaced by *Loot*. He had read the play several times since being offered it and relished its lack of reverence, its unmasking of hypocrisy and social humbug. His new wife had made no comment about the play, though he was certain she didn't approve of him appearing in it. But Henry was looking forward to playing someone venal, ruthless and crooked.

Jenny came out into the garden carrying a cardigan of Henry's over her arm. She sniffed the air and complained that the sheep in the meadow beyond the hedge smelled. He looked up and smiled.

"Of course they smell, my love. They smell of sheep because they *are* sheep."

They had been there when he and Margot had bought the cottage, not the same sheep, of course, but their forbears.

Forty years ago now: a country retreat in the Welsh Marches which few people had then heard about and certainly didn't consider near enough to London for a daily commute. These days the place seemed to be overrun.

"I'm nipping into Ludlow." Jenny said.

"Yes, yes, my dear. Take your time."

"I'll bring us back a treat for supper. If it turns chilly, put this on, won't you?"

She folded the the cardigan over a chair, kissed him on the temple and left him to the bad influence of Joe Orton.

It must have been an hour later when Henry heard a car pull onto the drive and assumed it would be Jenny returning. He stayed put, somewhere in the middle of Act Two with Truscott saying:

"Good. I shall proceed to bring the crimes to light. Beginning with the least important."

To which another character asks, "What is that?"

"Murder," says Truscott.

Henry turned to see two men rounding the side of the cottage, both in shirtsleeves, the older man with his jacket slung over his shoulder. Henry called out to them as he rose from the armchair.

"Good morning, gentlemen. How may I help you?"

"Sir Henry Lawlor," said the older man, more statement of fact than question. "Detective Sergeant Hewitt, sir, and my partner D.C. Clay."

They came over to him, offering their warrant cards as proof of who they were. Neither of them took a good photo in Henry's opinion. The younger man was pinched and greasy with bullethole eyes, while his sergeant was too heavy for the forty-year-old Henry took him to be. He was also sweating around a receding hairline and he reached into the jacket for a wad of tissues to wipe his brow. Each man then leaned forward, deferentially, and shook Henry's hand. Henry made a note to self to wash his hands as soon as they had departed.

"Sir, might we ask you a few questions?"

"By all means."

He gestured for them to settle on the garden chairs while he retook the armchair, first laying the script of *Loot* face down on the table, open at the page he was reading. He crossed one leg over the other in a relaxed manner that he sensed was disconcerting to his visitors. Hewitt lowered his voice to a confidential level.

"I report to a superior officer, rank of Commander in the Met, who has asked me to chat with you about an allegation made against yourself."

He was watching Henry's face as he spoke, hoping for the downward dive in the latter's confidence that might reasonably follow such an opening line. Henry held the man's gaze and smiled.

"An allegation of what?" Henry asked.

"Sexual assault."

"Goodness me," Henry purred eventually. "How distressing for you."

Hewitt cleared his throat. "I consider it all in a day's work, sir, following up allegations of this kind, seeing if there's any substance to them."

"A worthy necessity." Henry smiled at each man in turn. "My wife will be back within half an hour. Would you care for some coffee then?"

"Well, that would be very nice."

"She's just popped into Ludlow."

He was either too cool for words or hovering on the edge of dementia, Hewitt thought, and gestured to Henry for permission to continue. It was given graciously.

"Do you know a young woman by the name of Isabel Morrison?"

"As a matter of fact I do," said Henry, without hesitation. "I also knew her as Isabella Morales. You obviously don't know the story and I won't bore you with it. Suffice to say that she is the partner of my eldest grandson."

"Ethan Lawlor."

"That's the man. They've just had a baby – Rafael Henry Lawlor."

"Have you seen Rafael?"

"No, I haven't yet."

"Why would that be?"

"I haven't the faintest idea," he said. "Have you?"

"No, no, we haven't," said Hewitt, quickly.

"You're not saying that Isabella is the one who has accused…" said Henry, more surprised than horrified. "Good grief, you are!"

"She claims that on August 21st two years ago at your granddaughter's 21st birthday party, you assaulted her."

Henry raised his eyebrow, a television performance as opposed to a stage one. Smaller gestures.

"How and where does she allege this occurred?"

Hewitt was beginning to see what his wife had meant when she said there was something seductive about this man. It wasn't simply his remarkable good looks, which had survived into his seventies, it was an inexplicable force which drew those in his presence towards him. Near enough to rape them, he wondered?

"The where is your son's residence, Golden Meadow in Aston Merrick, Buckinghamshire. The how?" He frowned. "I'm not exactly sure what the question..."

"What exactly am I supposed to have done?"

Hewitt took a small notebook from his jacket pocket and turned the pages with fat fingers which had dirt under the fingernails.

"She alleges that you, quote, 'forced yourself on her, kissed her, restrained her and then penetrated her'."

Henry shook his head, sympathetically. "You must get so tired of language like that, Mr Hewitt. Restrained and penetrated? Surely you mean held her down and fucked her?"

Hewitt was taken aback by Henry's directness. "Whether it tires us or not, sir, is hardly the issue. That is her accusation."

How prescient Joe Orton had been, Henry thought. This man Hewitt spoke in the same way Truscott did, as if from a badly written police report about a lost dog.

"Did you?" Hewitt asked.

"Did I what?"

"Did you penetrate... rape her?"

Henry chuckled. "I believe you know that I did not, Sergeant. Do carry on though, if there is more to carry on about."

"The assault allegedly took place in an attic room at your son's house."

Henry held up a kindly hand. "A slight inversion, if I may. You mean the *alleged* assault took place in an attic room, according to Miss Morrison."

"Sir, with respect, this isn't a word game."

"No, but I'm a stickler."

Hewitt tried to become even trickier. He leaned back in a bad impersonation of confidence.

"You don't seem surprised by the allegation," he said.

"On the contrary, I am horrified that anyone should think me capable of such an act."

The considerate stone, D.C. Clay, came to life. "Your reputation precedes you. Famous actor, string of women."

Henry smiled. "I'll pretend I didn't hear that." He turned to Hewitt. "The young, so ready to make a name for themselves."

"Is that a threat?" Clay asked.

"I don't see how a simple observation might be construed as a threat. Would you care to enlighten me?"

"A name for myself, how?" Clay asked. "When you sue for libel?"

"It would be slander, not libel. And I never sue." He turned to Hewitt again. "You were saying?"

"The weekend of your granddaughter's 21st, you spent a considerable amount of time talking with Miss Morrison. Alone."

"That would have been quite a feat, Sergeant, considering there were two hundred guests at the party."

"But you don't deny talking to her at some length?"

"I spoke with many of the guests. It would have been discourteous to ignore them."

"What did you talk about?"

"Cabbages and kings, I expect. In truth I don't remember."

"Do you recall what she was wearing that evening?"

"I'm afraid not. My main impression was of hair. A magnificent display of it. I'm sure you noticed it yourself."

"I haven't actually met the young woman in question, but..."

"May I offer you a piece of advice, Sergeant. Find out all you can about Miss Morrison before you go any further with these inquiries. Pay particular attention to the dual nomenclature. It may point you in a certain direction."

"Leading where, sir?"

"To the unarguable fact that she's a fantasist. Or, as most people would say, a liar."

Hewitt rose from his chair and replaced the notebook in his jacket pocket. He held out his hand to Henry, who shook it reluctantly.

"You won't stay for coffee then?"

"Thank you, no. I'll simply say that you may be contacted again for further questioning." He looked down at the copy of *Loot* on the table. "My wife – she's an amateur dramatics buff, local group and all that – she tells me you're appearing in this, sir."

Henry twinkled mischievously. "Yes, I'm playing the policeman, Truscott. He's bent as a nine-bob note."

Hewitt smiled and led the way round the side of the cottage and back to his car. Henry went into the house to wash his hands.

* * *

"What do you reckon?" Hewitt asked his younger partner as he drove them away from the cottage.

"Arrogant old bastard," said Clay.

"Did he rape the girl, is what I meant."

Clay shrugged. "Not this one, maybe. Others, I wouldn't mind betting."

"So this winds up NFA?"

"Men like that old bastard have been getting away with it all their lives."

Hewitt laughed. "And denied you a share. You haven't got the looks for it, mate. Or the charm. Or the money."

"I still think it's worth throwing it to the jackals, see if they go for it."

Hewitt nodded. "Mind you don't get bitten."

-32-

Within a week of rehearsals for *Dangerous Corner* starting, Marcus and Charles Burgoyne had locked horns and their differences seemed irreconcilable. Marcus was casting round for a modern interpretation of his character. Burgoyne didn't think one was possible and suggested he stop trying to be trendy and rely on the words Priestley had written. They had a colourful slanging match, at the end of which neither had shifted his position, indeed, each had dug his heels in even deeper.

After a calming weekend Marcus arrived at the rehearsal room somewhere in the bowels of Covent Garden to be greeted most oddly by fellow members of the cast. As a rule they acknowledged each other's appearance with a quip or a wave and then carried on competing. That morning when he entered, they fell silent, their eyes trailing him with anticipation. What did they want, what had happened, he wondered. Had they turned against him? Had Hortense Farraway decided that his opinions about Priestley would jeopardise the entire production? Surely not. Hortense knew that out of the high-wire tension of rehearsal would come a better than average run.

The assistant stage manager brought him his usual coffee

from a café round the corner, smiled quickly and looked away. Charles Burgoyne approached him, eyebrows drawn down in his all too recognisable worried look. He had put on weight since *An Inspector Calls*, Marcus thought, and his shirt was straining at the midriff. His complexion under the grizzled beard was rough and red. He gripped Marcus's free arm and looked him squarely in the face.

"I am so sorry, my dear," he said.

Certainly they had exchanged harsh words the week before, but nothing that warranted an apology.

"For what?" Marcus asked.

Burgoyne swallowed, loudly. "Christ, you haven't heard." He turned to the rest of the cast. "Ladies and gentlemen, shall we take ten minutes?"

The cast began to slither from the room.

"Stop, everyone!" said Marcus. "Heard what?"

"Your father," said Burgoyne, quietly.

"What about him?"

Tom Slinger, who was playing Charles Stanton in the production, came over to them and handed Marcus a tabloid newspaper, the front page of which bore the headline: *Henry the Eighth*.

Below it was an unflattering picture of Sir Henry with accompanying text. Some smart-arse journalist claimed that Henry was the eighth celebrity to be accused in a recent roundup of historical sex crimes. It was a sharp way of implying that Henry was as guilty as hell without actually saying so.

Marcus felt his throat tighten as anger radiated out from the pit of his stomach. Slinger had the good sense to take the coffee from him and lead him over to a tubular steel chair at the side of the room. Marcus slumped down in it, grabbed the paper and read the front page – fifty of the most devastating words he'd ever encountered.

"A 25-year-old single mother yesterday accused the acting legend Sir Henry Lawlor of a sexual assault. The young woman alleges the incident took place two years ago during a party at the country home of Marcus Lawlor, Sir Henry's son."

He stopped reading and looked up. "Jesus, a sexual assault is always taken to be rape. My father is supposed to have raped her?"

There was a long silence which no one dared to fill.

"This *fucking* girl!"

He punched the front page, buckling the gory details and in a count of one, two, three he saw his father's career, his own career and those of Zack and Imogen descending into oblivion, leaving behind their single claim to notoriety. The head of their dynasty, Henry Lawlor, had once raped his own grandson's partner. Isabella Morales had taken her revenge for being exposed as Isabel Morrison, liar, thief and fantasist.

His first thought was to call Teresa, to warn her of what to expect – reporters at the gate to Golden Meadow, incessant phone calls, delighted neighbours invigorated by the possibility of a scandal.

"You want to talk?" asked Burgoyne. "The two of us, go somewhere..."

"Not today," said Marcus, turning to the rest of the cast. "I'll be here tomorrow, everyone – usual time, usual mood, argumentative as ever ahead of a full day's work. Today, I'm needed at home."

He handed the paper back to Tom Slinger and left.

* * *

When he reached Golden Meadow the usual suspects were gathered at the five-bar gate at the end of the drive: a bevy of young reporters and a photographer or two. Marcus wasn't sure why they had descended so rapidly, but in the distance he could see Henry's new wife's car parked on the gravel and assumed that his father's presence had drawn them here.

When Marcus approached in his car, they rose from their settlement on the verge and crowded the driver's window as he pressed the handset to open the gate. As he waited he slid down the window and a babble of catcalling questions poured in, a camera nudged the heads aside and clicked, clicked and clicked again.

"Mind your feet under the tyres," said Marcus. "I would hate one of you to be run over."

He drove up to the house and the gate closed behind him. It wasn't just Jenny's car on the drive. Zack's was there too, parked beside Carla's Mini Countryman. He slapped his steering wheel a couple of times to applaud his understanding of human nature. He had always known that Carla would rally to the family's side in a crisis. He just hoped that she had left Matt at the boat. As he switched off the engine he heard the first normality since reading the paper's front page, the dogs barking at his arrival.

In the living room the entire gathering rose to its feet, even his father, and turned to him as if he had brought with him a one-step solution to their current problem. They went to him, but he eased them aside and held out both arms to his father. For a fraction of a second he noticed that Henry looked… elderly. The illusion fled as the two men embraced.

"What the hell has happened?" Henry asked with a smile.

"We've been shafted by a lunatic, Henry. All of us, one way or another, the latest victim being you."

Henry shrugged and turned to Marcus. "And the next move is?"

"I think we should call your solicitor."

"Mary Talbot," said Henry. "I want you all to know two things. One, I did not assault this young woman. Two, I am for the first time in my life devoid of any witty remarks, which must mean that I am shocked and a little alarmed, perhaps."

He sat down in the armchair and told them about the visit he'd had from the police, which even Jenny didn't know about. Carla leaped in to ask why he hadn't shared it.

"Because, my love, there is now absolutely no doubt as to who leaked – dear me it sounds so urinary, doesn't it – leaked this lie to the press. Isabella herself or Sergeant Hewitt and his sidewinder, D.C. Clay, as in feet of."

"No witty remarks, Grandad?" said Zack.

Henry smiled. "The occasional dig."

"It still doesn't help us," said Marcus. "The bugger of an allegation like this is it falls to the accused to prove their innocence. And mud sticks."

"That sounds remarkably bleak," Henry whispered.

"So what do we do about it, Dad?" said Zack.

"I'm not sure. The first few days'll be the worst. We'll ride them out and then make plans."

-33-

Throughout the day Marcus tried to define the mood which had settled on his family, but it kept shifting, from outrage and anger to despair, acceptance and then suddenly surging forward to being laughable and of no consequence. Absurd, even. No one in their right mind could consider Henry Lawlor a rapist. That evening, Imogen arrived, full of sound and fury, signifying not much at all save incredulity that Isabella would stoop so low. And where was bloody Ethan, she wanted to know. Shouldn't he be here, apologising to everyone for bringing a monster into the family?

By the time Teresa realised that the invasion of people would need feeding Marcus had detected the one good thing to have come from the allegations against his father. His family, with the exception of Ethan, had been brought together and were speaking with one voice. Jenny, the only person in the house who wasn't a blood relative, clearly acknowledged her exclusion though tried to not let it show. She was breathing fire about the trollop Isabella and expressed it by madly picking fluff from Henry's lapels, primping and tidying him until quite out of character he let rip.

"For the love of God, woman, leave me alone!"

It was a brief admonition but delivered in a voice which

rang through the house. Even Marcus, who was in the shower at the time, heard it through the sound of running water and chose to think of it as a call to arms. When he came down the stairs, dressed but still drying his hair with a hand towel, he paused in the exact same place that, all those years ago, he had recognised Jack Relph as Professor J.D. Relph, the world famous entomologist. Odd how useless details insist on being recalled in stressful times. His father's new wife emerged from the library dabbing her eyes with a handkerchief.

"Jenny, are you...?" he began.

She waved his concern aside and hurried away to the kitchen where a horde meal was being prepared, spaghetti bolognese. Through the open door Marcus could see his father, seated in one of the reading chairs, a copy of *The Spectator* on his knee, unread, unopened. As he entered, Henry tossed it onto the table beside a pile of the day's tabloids, all ablaze with the accusation against him.

"Hello, my dear boy," he said, trying to rally.

Marcus gestured back in the direction Jenny had departed.

"She's upset by the latest development," said Henry. "My agent's just called. The board of the Sherborne in their wisdom have decided to 'back-burner' the production of *Loot*."

Marcus went towards him. "Oh, Dad..."

"It did occur as a possibility. I mean, who wants a bent copper who might also be a rapist?"

Marcus shook his head. "Please stop that."

Henry smiled weakly. "It's all bravado on my part, surely you can see that."

"You're such a great actor it's difficult to tell."

Henry looked out of the French windows and through the gap in the box hedge to where Zack, Carla and Imogen were seated on the lawn beside an ancient birdbath.

"I just hope it doesn't rebound on them in any way. Or on you." Then he added in a surprisingly thin voice. "Why did she do it, Marcus?"

"Retaliation. Listen, I have a sort of a plan. I know we're at the mercy of the police and then the CPS, but I dare you to get in touch with some of your old flames and have them vouch for you being gentlemanly."

It was the first time they had acknowledged Henry's infidelities. It had taken over 30 years to get there, and Marcus proffered the idea as much to ensure that his father had been the considerate, courteous lover he had imagined him to be: that there was no sliver of truth in him being an abuser.

"I would gladly do so, but I fear most of them have gone the way of all flesh."

Marcus smiled. "You mean hip replacements, bad facelifts and dyed hair?"

Henry shook his head and turned away to the French windows. Marcus went after him, took his hand and turned him back into the room.

"I won't have it, Dad. Capitulation to events. This family depends on you. Everything we are derives from you. Give up now and we're all dog meat."

"You've appeared in too many soap operas, dear boy."

Marcus raised his voice. "I won't have that taken away from them, from me, from the business we both love. So, spend a few days feeling sorry for yourself and then get back to being you."

"Will anyone employ me, though?"

"Of course they bloody will. You're Sir Henry Lawlor."

He wasn't sure if voicing that made it true, but it sounded right. He opened the windows and stepped out onto the patio. The garden had changed very little in the time the Lawlors had been at Golden Meadow, indeed, the same man who had tended it for Jack Relph was still doing so. His wife was 'helping Teresa in the house'. Marcus had a problem with the word 'cleaner', or rather its application to the gardener's wife. The notion that someone should be employed to clean up after him and his brood was vaguely shameful.

* * *

Carla, Zack and Imogen didn't hear their father emerge from the library and as he went towards the gap in the hedge something alerted him. It was to do with the way they were clustered together, talking in low tones. They never did that. They always shouted across distances. When he was close enough to hear their conversation he stopped, breathing gently. They were halfway through a discussion which was developing by the word.

"You think Grandad assaulted her?" asked Imogen.

"No way," said her sister.

"How can you be sure?"

"He's the kind of guy who never had to step out of his own way to get laid," said Carla. "You've seen the photos of him when he was young? Christ! Why would a man who can have it any time of his choosing suddenly get violent?"

"What are our options?" asked Zack.

None of them seemed to know at that point in the conversation. Carla felt that they needed prodding into action.

"She's busted the family apart, she's seen Gemma, Anna and Billie off like stray cats – sorry Imo, but that's what she did. Lied, cheated, fantasised, stole, manipulated. On the one hand we can do nothing. On the other hand…?"

There was a slight pause.

"If you were standing on the edge of a cliff, Isabella beside you, would you… or wouldn't you?" asked Zack.

"If no one was looking, I hope I would," said Carla.

"I certainly would," said Zack. "And I'd relish every moment."

"Hang on, guys," said Imogen in a panicky voice.

"If nothing's done she'll be with us for the rest of our lives," said Zack.

Marcus stepped out from behind the hedge and walked through the gap towards them. They turned immediately, each trying to determine if he had overheard their conversation. From the angry, hard-set face he certainly had.

"So, who's in favour of pushing her off a cliff?" he asked. "Killing her?" He looked from one face to the other while they tried to avoid his stare. "Nobody? Right. I'll attribute the exchange of ideas I've just heard to the stress of the situation. But in this family we do not resort to violence in order to solve our problems."

"No need to be self-righteous, Dad."

"Shut up, Zack!"

"Okay then, tell us what you're going to do, Dad,

because so far it's been fuck all."

"I said shut up!" Zack looked down at the ground and fell silent. "But to answer your question, I have no idea yet."

The possibility of further argument was forestalled by a sound which rocketed them all back to childhood. Unsure of where they were in the ten acres or so, Teresa had gone to the front door with the handbell and rung it vigorously. At the first clang Imogen burst into tears.

***

It was exactly ten thirty in the evening when Ethan arrived and it was deliberate timing. For as long as he had known them his parents had switched off the television at that time and begun to make tracks for bed.

Troy and Cress struck up their warning duet as Ethan pulled onto the gravel and recognising the particular sound of his car soon dissolved into yelps of delight. He entered through the kitchen door and greeted his mother coldly as she rose from filling the dishwasher. He asked, offhandedly, how things were going, opened the fridge door, leaned in and began to graze from the contents.

"Can I make you something?" Teresa asked.

"No, I'm okay, thanks."

He turned and embraced her and over her shoulder waved once at his siblings as they entered from the hall and fanned out like lions at the start of a hunt. Marcus followed them shortly, wearing a dressing gown he had bought 30 years earlier. He had started doing that of late, dating trivial items that he owned. "God, this is x years old," he would say in amazement. His family would burst into a chorus of 'Happy Birthday' to the item.

"Do you want to dive straight in and talk about it?" said Ethan.

"I'd first like to know how Rafael is," said Teresa.

"He is bouncing, as they say."

"When will we be able to see him again? Where are you living? Hey, why don't we all go into the library…"

He sucked in air through gritted teeth. "As you can imagine, things are a bit topsy-turvy…"

"Is that code?"

"No, Mum, it means Isabella's a little wary of this family at the moment. I take it Henry's in bed, sound asleep, no doubt?" He broke into a bad imitation of his grandfather's voice. "The face, my darlings. An early night. I promise you'll keep your looks for as long as I have."

"Is Maria still with you?" asked Teresa

"If you mean has Isabella bonded with her new baby yet…"

"Why are you here?" asked Carla. "Did you come of your own accord? Or did Isabella send you?"

Ethan glared at her, then pointed upwards. "You don't think there are things that need discussing? Possibilities?"

"You mean did my father try and rape your girlfriend?" said Marcus.

"Henry's been notorious throughout his life. Maybe his bloom is fading, maybe they don't fall over him as readily as they used to and maybe, just maybe, he's been forced to try and take it where he can."

"Henry would never be that crass."

"You mean as long as it's done with good manners

and charm you can stick your hand up anyone's skirt?" He softened a little, almost pleading them to believe him. "Why would she lie about something like this? Isabella Morales would, but not Isabel Morrison. You have to see the difference. She's changed."

"Since her visit to the nick?" said Zack.

Ethan closed his eyes tight, as if to conjure up somewhere on the planet he would rather be. "When you get found out, unmasked, you start again and part of that is to put things behind you. Some stuff you can't. You need closure."

"That stupid, meaningless word," said his father.

"Your dislike of it doesn't make it any less true."

"So you believe Henry did that to her?" said Teresa.

"I just know I have to support her. She's the mother of my child."

"Make sure she doesn't abuse *him*," said Imogen.

He flared. "What does that mean?"

"She'll use him against... poor little thing'll be a bargaining tool, an emotional sledgehammer."

"My sister the dyke speaks. Let's see what the police find out, shall we?"

As Imogen launched herself at him, Zack caught her round the waist and held her. They turned as Henry came into the kitchen from the hall, his presence seeming to enter before he did. They stared at him as if he were a stranger. In a way he was. He was wearing a tattered dressing gown, the sweep of hair fell either side of his face, the eyes were bleary. They had never seen him so dishevelled. He looked across at Ethan and said in a strangely small voice,

"I did not."

Inevitably, Jenny was right behind him. She took his

arm and guided him away, as if helping a blind man to get his bearings. Ethan headed for the door.

"At least let us know your new address," Marcus said.

Ethan turned back into the room. "What for, Dad? So that you can come and visit us? Give me some fatherly advice? What would that be, I wonder? How to make sure your family never spoils your image, never ruffles your self-esteem, never shakes your legendary self-confidence?" He glared at Teresa and pointed at Marcus. "Yes, Mum, half the blame for that falls on you. He doesn't need protecting, he needs his eyes prising open. So fuck you both. Fuck the lot of you."

In the breathless silence which followed they heard the front door open and slam behind him, and a moment later his car roared away down the drive. Zack stretched out his arms to his mother but she eased them aside and went over to Marcus.

"Why *did* he come?" Marcus asked her. "To finish with us, to explain, to gloat, to see if we were okay, to ask for help?"

She stretched to her full height and let rip, spittle flying into his face like sparks from a grinding wheel.

"Whatever the reason, you will do *nothing*!"

Zack dared to breath in, as if about to protest. His mother flung an arm in his direction.

"You bloody actors! Everything is about you." She jerked her head back towards Marcus. "Even now, when she, she, she, this tenement tart accuses your own father of rape, you'll still do nothing."

With her energy spent, she headed for the door through to the hall, slamming it behind her. Beams that had been in place for three hundred years shook at the force of it and a chunk of brick fell down the chimney in the next room and landed on the metal stove.

-34-

Mary Talbot had an office that neither Henry nor Marcus could have worked in for more than a day. It was oppressively small, the walls lined floor to ceiling with shelves. Between the usual collection of law books were jammed folders, journals, reports and bundles of curling correspondence.

Mary was searching for something in the chaos of the shelves, turning occasionally to her clients to say that she wouldn't be a moment.

"May I ask what you're looking for?" said Henry.

"Money, ducky."

Marcus and Henry exchanged a bewildered glance.

"I earn seven figures a year, they tell me, but I can't find a twenty-pound note to save my life. I left my handbag in a taxi this morning and there's cash tucked away here for such an emergency."

"What emergency?" Marcus asked.

"Coffee. I want the girl to pop round to Starbucks for some."

Henry opened his wallet, took out a fifty-pound note and handed it to her. Mary went to the door, opened it slightly and fluttered the fifty. "Zena, sweetie, three lattes soon as you can."

She sat down at her desk opposite them. Henry had warned Marcus that she had a characterful face, his euphemism for plain. It was a hatchet face, sharp at every feature, with steely gray eyes. At certain angles, due to the powerful lenses of her glasses, they appeared to double in size and shrivel whoever she was looking at. She dressed expensively but unremarkably in solicitor dowd with sensible shoes on her feet. Her one vanity was her hair. It was dyed ash blonde and permed close to her scalp in tight waves.

"So, this Isabel Morrison strolls into Walworth nick and reports a sex crime, naming you. Ten years ago the Crown Prosecution Service would've had a field day, on the strength of your celebrity."

"Can you make it go away, Mary?"

"Depends what you mean by that. What happens is this. The old bill floats allegations to the press, to social media. Some scummy little journalist picks it up and runs with it. Others follow, naming names. What the cops want is another Isabel Morrison to come out of the woodwork and claim you slid your hand up her skirt in 1968 and her life has never been the same since. If one woman comes forward, then two, three, half a dozen might follow." She leaned forward on her elbows. "Which seems a good point at which to ask if there's anything in your past which could leap up and bite us in the neck." Henry looked at her. "I'm waiting. Is there?"

"Nothing," he said. He lowered his voice to a stage whisper. "People do lie, though."

"You say that as if you've just realised it."

"Not that being declared innocent would help.

The allegation itself is enough. The mud sticks, the stench hangs around and in some cases it's been sufficient to kill the person accused..."

"Spare us the purple monologue, Henry."

"It's just that I have a... reputation."

Marcus laid a hand on his father's arm to quieten him. "What do we do next?"

"Nothing whatsoever," said Mary. "From this moment on I don't want to hear a whisper about this business from either of you. No interviews, no tweets denying it, no catcalling questions answered, nothing some brat can make a story out of. And that applies to your excitable family, Marcus. Zilch, zero, zip it. Is that understood?"

"Perfectly."

"It's still a waiting game, but eventually, when no one has come forward, we'll turn the tables on Miss Morrison and get her to retract. Then we'll sue any bastard who might have stalled your career meantime, e.g. the Sherborne. I was looking forward to your bent copper in *Loot*. Where's that coffee?"

She sprang out of her chair and went to the door.

* * *

Zack didn't so much ignore Mary Talbot's advice as give way to his emotions.

He was filming opposite an actor who had taken an instant dislike to him on the grounds of his success in *Conshie*, made all the more complicated by rumours that Phillip Bray would soon be leaving the cast, for health reasons, and Zack Lawlor's character, Charles Mantle, would take over as the lead.

The scene they were due to shoot took place on a 1940s allotment where Mantle goes to meet the descendant of a man shot for desertion during the First World War. After the first four setups a break was called for coffee. At the catering van the other actor sidled up to Zack and asked him how things were going with his grandfather. Had he really done what that girl accused him of? Zack paused to absorb the insult and, as if a switch had been thrown, the world turned red. All he could see clearly was the speaker's face. He punched it and blood sprouted from the man's nose as he staggered back and fell into a row of plastic cabbages. He lay where he landed, dazed and terrified, blood still pouring out of his nostrils. A production assistant got between the two men and hollered for Zack to back off. The rest of the day's filming was cancelled.

* * *

The following morning Zack was called to the production office. It soon became clear that the producer couldn't make up her mind whether she fancied him all the more for what he had done or endorsed the general view that he had been grossly out of line. In her ambivalence she handed over the meeting to the director who had cast Zack. He didn't mince his words.

"What the hell did you think you were doing?"

Zack opened his arms wide. "You *know* what I was..."

"I don't mean did you or didn't you take offence at what was said. I mean there's you, a here today, gone tomorrow bloody actor with the chance of a lifetime to join the Netflix elite and you balls it up! I have had to crawl like a slug for two hours this morning to keep you in this show. The two cowgirls who run this ranch are all for slinging you out."

"Well, they can't, not without cancelling the show."

"Arrogant twat! Actors with real reputations have been recast in big budget films on a bloody whim. You broke this poor little devil's nose. You're lucky the cops aren't all over you."

"I'm sorry. Really."

The director leaned back against the wall and took a deep breath or two.

"I'm out of steam," he said, quietly. "We've lost a day and half, thanks to your temper. And the damned clocks go back next week so we're pushed for daylight. Start being nice again." He paused. "How is your grandfather, by the way?"

Zack looked at him before saying, quietly, "Different."

The director nodded. "Tomorrow morning we reshoot the allotment scene, different actor. Be there, ready."

Zack nodded and left.

The news of him having punched a fellow actor never came to light. It was widely believed that the man was paid, by a friend of a friend of Mary Talbot, to get his nose straightened and to keep his mouth shut. The problem with Jenny Ballard was not so easily dealt with.

The incident took place in a small restaurant in Oxford. A much reduced Henry, or so his new wife described him, was seated with her at a corner table when a middle-aged woman came over to them and spat in Henry's face. Quite how he would have handled it had he been alone was anyone's guess, but Jenny instantly threw an americano over the woman. By a strange quirk of prurience, the rape allegations were overshadowed by the 'horror, scandal and outrage' of Ms Ballard's 'vicious and unwarranted' attack on the 'widowed pensioner who was recovering from a recent operation in the John Radcliffe'. Jenny held her own throughout it all. Her court appearance was set for 10 weeks thence and she set about losing the unwelcome half stone which had recently gathered around her hips.

She was also delighted by the 'respeck' which Zack, Carla and Imogen accorded her for defending their beloved grandfather.

-35-

When Zack and Amy decided to leave Ashbury Road and buy a flat in Richmond, on the strength of their now considerable earnings, Teresa swore she would never visit the house again. It represented the catalogue of devastation Isabella had wrought, a list which kept turning over and over in her mind. Her family had been set against each other, if not downright estranged; her father-in-law had been accused of rape and was now an object of scorn and suspicion over his attitude to women. Her grandson was unlikely ever to be part of her future.

Those were the broad outlines. The details were too painful to keep mulling over, but in the middle of the night they would startle her awake, demanding to be considered. There were visions of the tearful Gemma Blake, the unrequited Anna Macey, the sidelined Billie, Carla's anguish at her brother's vitriol, the stolen books, the friends who had lost money.

And at every turn she blamed the man sleeping beside her for not having waved a magic wand and made Isabella disappear. Why hadn't she done something herself, then, she wondered. The answer to that lay in a single word: what? What could she, or Marcus come to that, do that would solve the problem of Isabella, or rather Isabel? Exposing her as a liar, thief and fraud had had no effect. She had retaliated by taking Ethan, and Teresa's first grandchild, from their family and persuading Ethan that she was a maligned victim of her own impulses, not simply… an evil cow. How odd, Teresa suddenly thought, that she had hesitated, even in her mind, over describing Isabella as 'evil'. It was a word that she had always applied sparingly.

***

Events took their toll on Marcus as well, and halfway through November *Dangerous Corner* opened to less than dazzling reviews. Politeness and a barely concealed sympathy coloured the first-night celebrations, which Henry and Jenny attended. Henry was unrecognisably subdued, even ignored by one or two fellow thespians who three months earlier he had considered to be friends. On top of that, first-nighters held that, while it was a good, workmanlike production, it lacked that certain something which Marcus Lawlor always brought to a part. A purple-prosed critic went overboard with 'Mr Lawlor failed to imbue Robert Conran with the air of menace and the magnetic volatility we have come to expect from him.'

Marcus wasn't entirely happy to lay the blame at Isabella's door. He had known actors who had used adversity, even personal tragedy, to give their performances a very definite boost. Why hadn't he been able to put all the hurt, all the anger, the helplessness into Robert Conran? To begin with he thought the answer could be found in Teresa's disappointment with life, with circumstances…

and with him. Even though she admitted there was little he could have done, she still blamed him for having stood by and watched Isabella wreck their family. For some reason, which he couldn't fathom, that took him in a straight line to Jonas Kemble.

On the opening night Jonas Kemble had been hovering in Marcus's dressing room for at least two hours before curtain-up and for the first time in a while Marcus pondered their relationship. He knew where Jonas fitted into his life, but what did Jonas Kemble think of *him*, he wondered. Marcus could hardly ask him outright. To start a conversation, essentially with himself, would smack of madness. But... what would Jonas say if, in some obscure dimension, it was possible to ask one part of you what it thought of the other? The answer was uncomfortable. In Jonas's opinion it was all well and good to call on a bolder, braver, 'magnetically volatile' version of oneself when it came to a performance, be that on stage or screen, in a restaurant, a supermarket, at a party or at the school gate... anywhere there was an audience. But where am I in your real life, Jonas wanted to know. Am I just a tool of your trade? Have you ever considered that I might have a larger purpose?

When five minutes to curtain-up was called, Marcus left the dressing room and made his way to the stage left wings. As he waited there he was distracted. As an actor, albeit with the help of Jonas Kemble, he was impressive, purposeful, reliable... even slightly dangerous. As a husband and father he might... God, how difficult it was to even think it, let alone write the words on the slate of his mind... he might be seen as insipid, indecisive, ineffectual.

His cue to enter was imminent. It was a line from a character called Betty Whitehouse. "You're beginning to look purple in the face and bloated – a typical financier."

As she uttered the words Marcus turned to Jonas Kemble and was about to beckon him. He wasn't there.

***

It was a grim Sunday when Marcus drove his father to visit Hamilton Gray. He had borrowed Teresa's car for the journey, and soon after picking Henry up he asked him if there was a particular reason for this visit.

Henry smiled. "I thought you were going to ask why I hadn't driven there myself."

"That too."

"The answer is fear. I'm afraid to walk into a place like Bungay in case they won't let me leave. I'll need you to rescue me."

Marcus laughed. "Safer not to go, perhaps?"

Henry shrugged. "I need to step back into the past, or at least contact a friend who won't see me as a creature from the lagoon. If, like his son said, Ham's not the man he was he may not even remember me. He won't have heard about the hideous crime people think I've committed."

"You haven't committed a crime, Dad. I think I know you well enough by now."

Was that really true, Marcus wondered. As a child and teenager he and his parents had lived in a London town house overlooking Richmond Park. Margot had struggled to make it a welcoming home for Henry to return to after filming or touring. A labour of love, undoubtedly, and just after his 18th birthday Marcus discovered the real reason his father spent so much time away from home.

One evening he had taken a girlfriend to Sadler's Wells Theatre where, from up in the gods, they saw a tinny production of *Rigoletto*. Shortly after the overture Marcus spotted, in a box with three other people, the unmistakable profile of his father. It was remarkably similar to the one beside him now in the passenger seat, thirty years later, the main difference being the hair: white now, but then a sweep of rich dark brown. According to Margot he was working in Hollywood, playing the eternal Englishman in a New York society romp, but there he was, in plain sight, in the company of a well-known actress. There was no mistaking the affection they had for each other.

It wasn't until the second half of the opera that Marcus caught his father's eye, albeit in the half-light of the auditorium. The two stared at each other and then Henry smiled and turned away, as if his son had been a complete stranger. They had never spoken of the incident and were unlikely ever to do so.

In spite of his philandering, when Margot died Henry wept like a child for weeks on end. Marcus had never seen him reduced to tears and in an ungilded conversation a month or so later Henry spoke of his many conquests, some of whom had attended the funeral. Much as he had admired them, Margot was the only woman he had ever loved. Marcus hadn't believed it then, but with the softening of time he was more inclined to do so.

Marcus had expected Bungay Hall to have much in common with the hospital portrayed in *One Flew Over the Cuckoo's Nest*, but nothing could have been further from the truth. As he crawled down the gravel drive he was confronted by a truly magnificent house dating back to the fourteenth century. Over time it had been battered by rough weather and countless wars, but its restoration in 1695 had lasted to the present day. Rising from the slated roof, an octagonal bell tower jostled with a dozen or more tall chimneys. Beyond a vestigial moat were spectacular gardens which not even the greyness of the day could detract from.

As they got out of the car Henry hung back and gazed up at the building, as if glimpsing his own future in such a place. A small part of him was inclined to turn tail, to abandon the visit, but having spotted the warning signs, Marcus said,

"Come on, Dad. Best foot and all that."

Henry straightened up, adjusted his demeanour, and marched towards the front entrance as if he were about to commandeer the place.

They were greeted in the hall by the matron, a middle-aged woman in a white uniform and butterfly hat who introduced herself as Mrs Goatwell. She recognised them instantly but doubtless had seen so many famous faces that a couple more was neither here nor there. Marcus could see his father searching for beauty in Mrs Goatwell's face, but it wasn't there. Her features were podgy, her skin was beginning to blotch with age. Her manner was cold and businesslike as she ushered them into the office. What was she thinking about Henry, Marcus wondered.

She gestured for them to sit in two armchairs while she leaned back against her desk, arms folded as she addressed Marcus.

"You're aware of Mr Gray's health problems?"

Marcus smiled. "I wouldn't say we were totally up to speed. In fact it's a while since he and my father last saw each other."

She nodded. "He is suffering from Alzheimer's, as I'm sure you know, so he may or may not recognise him. Like the rest of us he has good days and bad days. I'm afraid today is a bad one."

Henry shifted in his chair. It had never occurred to him that such a magnificent voice as Hamilton Gray's would one day fall silent.

"I'll take you through to the day room."

It was set out like an old-fashioned club, leather armchairs and low oak tables bestrewn with newspapers and magazines. It was a pleasant enough place in which to spend your declining years, Marcus thought, but nothing could fend off the air of finality about it, a sense of it being the last but one stop on the journey home, and but for the localised snoring and snuffling it might well have been the dying room itself. Mrs Goatwell gestured to a bay overlooking part of the garden. Gazing at it from an armchair was a skeletal being, dressed in clothes which had once fitted him perfectly, but now hung around his frame.

Henry stepped towards his old friend and reached down to take his hand.

"Hamilton, good to see you!"

Hamilton Gray turned, looked up at him and eventually smiled.

"It's Sir Henry Lawlor," said Mrs. Goatwell.

"I've brought my son Marcus. Do you remember him?"

The eyes moved slowly towards Marcus and the body began to tremble, hands reaching out for a walking stick.

"My pleasure, my pleasure," said Hamilton.

Henry and Marcus turned to Mrs. Goatwell. "He parrots the usual courtesies," she said.

"Does he recognise me?" Henry asked, softly.

"I don't think so," she replied.

At that point an extraordinary change came over Hamilton as the door opened at the far side of the room and a fragile lady in a long skirt and voluminous cardigan entered, pushing a walking frame. Her name was Antonia Bickerstaffe and both Marcus and his father, if called upon to give an opinion, would have said she was long dead. She made her way towards Hamilton and stopped. He rose from his chair, as Antonia smiled sweetly and reached out to take his hand.

"What man art thou that thus bescreen'd in night so stumblest on my counsel?" she asked.

"By a name I know not how to tell thee who I am," Hamilton replied. "My name, dear saint, is hateful to myself, because it is an enemy to thee; had I it written, I would tear the word."

Antonia shook her head slightly. "My ears have not yet drunk a hundred words of that tongue's utterance, yet I know the sound: art thou not Romeo and a Montague?"

"Neither, fair saint, if either thee dislike."

"How camest thou hither, tell me, and wherefore?" asked Antonia. "The orchard walls are high and hard to climb, And the place death, considering who thou art, If any of my kinsmen find thee here."

"They do this often," said Mrs Goatwell. "Once they start it seems cruel to stop them. Their *Macbeth* is quite something."

Henry turned away and headed towards the door. Marcus and Mrs. Goatwell followed.

"Alright, Dad?" Marcus asked, when they reached the foyer.

"Yes, yes. What have we just witnessed?" Henry asked.

"The core memory at work," said Mrs. Goatwell.

***

Soon after leaving the nursing home, Henry broke their silence and asked in a subdued voice, "Is that how we end up? Actors? Reciting the entire Shakespeare canon but unable to say please or thank you on our own behalf? Is that all we *ever* were, echo chambers for some other man's thoughts?" He smiled to try and take the curse off the proposition. "Said King Lear to Richard Salter."

"Would you rather we hadn't gone to see him?"

"Not really. Hamilton Gray was important to me. Whenever we met, we'd carry on talking from where we'd left off. A sign of true friendship, I believe, and God knows ours is not a profession where friendships thrive."

"We prefer effusive acquaintanceships," said Marcus.

Henry chuckled at the description, but then his mood suddenly dipped.

"Seeing those old duffers hasn't helped the present situation, though. I'm sick of it. Police loitering in the background, waiting for a chance to heel me into the ground. Don't tell Mary Talbot I said this, but sometimes I wonder if perhaps I made some… remark to Isabella which she misinterpreted, mistook for an invitation she couldn't refuse and I crossed the line. You think that's possible?"

"I refer you to my previous answers to that absurd question."

Henry reached out and patted him on the thigh.

"Thank you. How is John Morrison, by the way? Odd that I wake up in the night thinking about him."

"I'm not sure, to be honest. I rang his workshop. No answer."

"I couldn't bear it. To lose a child to some impossible fantasy." He turned to Marcus. "I don't know what I'd do if you suddenly weren't there."

They drove another mile or so before Marcus had the courage to say, "Dad, I've been meaning to ask you this for quite a while now. Years, in fact. When you perform anywhere does a sort of... *alter ego* go on stage with you?"

"No."

"Oh."

There was a lengthy pause before Henry added, "However, I never go on alone."

"Oh."

"Other vowel sounds are available, you know."

"Who goes with you?"

Henry glanced at him. "Your mother, of course."

-36-

November gave way to December and winter gales stripped the last leaves from the trees at Golden Meadow. The meadow itself had been spruced up and cleared of encroaching nettles, its leaning fences made upright, its hedges relaid. Bigg's Cave was still an eyesore, though to be fair it couldn't be seen until the onlooker was standing right over it. Much of Marcus's idle thought was given over to picturing the tree that would soon be planted in it and dominate the field. He had received an email from a conservation company in Belgium. They had been monitoring the construction of a new housing development near Liège, where the only casualty was to be an English oak. They had heard that he was looking for such a thing. Theirs was eleven metres high and they could deliver it to him next year before it started to leaf. Was he interested? In spite of the long wait he would have to endure, he wrote back to accept their offer. It would be his Christmas present to himself.

Christmas was destined to be a subdued affair. There was no sign of Ethan and consequently none of Rafael, not that at three months old the occasion would have meant much to him. Even so there was a cardboard box the size of a house in the corner of the library, filled with baby clothes, soft toys, mobiles, all the landfill a grandmother might buy for her first grandchild. There it would remain, Teresa declared, waiting for happier times. Imogen showed up on Christmas morning, without Jane who was 'knackered from appearing in a risqué pantomime'. She sent her apologies, Imogen said, and assured them that it wasn't the risqué element that had worn her out, but the sheer hard work. Even Matt and Carla showed up for lunch but left before the Queen's speech, citing that as a reason not to stay. Zack and Amy were there too but left in the afternoon to travel down to Herne Bay to look in on her parents. Henry and Jenny tried to make the best of the occasion with long, distracting walks in the blustery weather, which tired them both out and saw them napping in various parts of the house.

The only good thing about the occasion was the renewed reception to *Dangerous Corner*. It was one of the few occasions, Henry noted, when the critics had succumbed to the view of the audiences. The latter had been astounded by the lukewarm reviews whereupon a handful of critics went to see the play again and agreed that Marcus Lawlor was back on form... along with his 'magnetic volatility'.

On Sunday January 5th Marcus woke at 11:00 a.m. He would remember the date, day and time forever. He was alone in the bedroom, save for the knight on his white charger and the damsel still gazing up at him, not a sign of age in her face, not the slightest hesitation in his determination to rescue her.

He struggled into his dressing gown and flapped his way downstairs to the kitchen, where he fussed the dogs until they settled. He ground some coffee beans and only then saw the note Teresa had left on the coffeemaker. 'Waitrose. Gone there. Text me if you think of anything. BTW, see *The Stage*. Ringed."

The Stage was a bone of contention between Marcus and Teresa. It dropped onto the doormat once a week and was read, cover to cover, by her but never by him. He had cancelled it on several occasions down the years, only for Teresa to reinstate it each time. He took his coffee to the kitchen table and drew the latest edition towards him. It was open at the obituary page and Teresa had circled the one she thought would interest him.

'Zoltan Damiani, who died on January 2nd, aged 93, will be remembered by his students as a brilliant and colourful teacher. What few will know, however, is that in 1957 at the height of the the Hungarian revolution Damiani escaped from a Soviet military encampment near Budapest just two days before a show trial which would surely have seen him executed...'

No matter the circumstances of someone's passing, when learning of it Marcus always felt a sense of relief. Regardless of any grief which might follow, the deceased had been set free and so it was with his old RADA tutor. There was slightly more to it, though, in Zoltan Damiani's case. He was the only person in the world to whom Marcus had confided the name Jonas Kemble. He had made him promise not to tell anyone and was certain his tutor had honoured that, which meant that from January 2nd onwards, Jonas Kemble was known only to his creator. Not another soul. And given the plans Marcus had for him, that was just... perfect.

Back in their bedroom he went over to the walk-in

loft and paused for a moment, as if on the verge of some milestone in his life's journey from which he would never return. He opened the door and stepped in, breaking a vast cobweb. A spider the size of a hand scuttled upwards into the rafters. Marcus smiled and saluted the memory of Jack Relph. He felt for the light switch and turned it on. On the rare occasions he had ventured into this space, the first thing he always noticed, after the spiders, was the cold. Then the stillness. Then the smell of old timber and dust.

Not surprisingly, the most recent junk, the fallout from twenty-odd years of family life, was piled close to the door. More dated rubbish was farther back in a section off to the right. He ducked beneath a crossbeam and went to a stack of boxes containing school reports, tax returns, correspondence and theatrical bric-a-brac. He found himself being drawn to a leather suitcase. He lifted it by the handle, the dust fell away and he carried it back through the boxed-up family history, switched off the light behind him and stretched up to his full height again.

He sat down on the bed and flicked open the suitcase at his feet to find that inside it was as fresh and clean, the purple lining as bright, as the day it was last closed, 23 years ago. It contained the wig he had worn in a highly forgettable production of *Julius Caesar*. He had played two parts, the first an also-ran, the second the inessential character of Livius. Mousey-haired Livius marked him out from the chestnut pleb he had been for the bulk of the play.

He lifted it from the stand it was stretched on. The texture of the fake hair was indistinguishable from the real thing, though God knows it was only made of nylon. People at the time had said how real it looked, how they hardly recognised it was him wearing it. People always said that. He smiled as he recalled his father's words. "If people compliment a hairpiece over and above your performance, you are in deep trouble."

He took the wig through to the bathroom, applied gel to his hair, then pulled on an unused wig cap liner. He looked in the mirror and his instinct was to look away again, but he held fast. He dabbed a few spots of stage glue around the edge of the cap and secured it with Teresa's hair grips, two at the front, one either side of his neck.

He turned to the full-length mirror and wondered how the image he saw would dress. It certainly wouldn't be in the style of Jonas Kemble, in trendy, expensive jackets, embroidered shirts and tailored jeans, or handmade shoes that fitted like a glove. The disguise would need to be the exact opposite of that, and with a touch of embarrassment Marcus remembered a complete outfit from years ago, wrapped in a bin liner and marked by Teresa 'Old clothes, Oxfam'. Thankfully, they had never made it to their destination.

He found the ensemble and put it on. A checked shirt and beige chinos, suede shoes for the feet – not even blue, just brown. Over it all went a grey, cottony jacket and then a quilted navy blue anorak. Would the total impression benefit from glasses? They were always definitive, the first thing people remembered about a face. There was a dusty pair of readers in the drawer of his bedside cabinet.

***

Marcus let a few days pass before testing the disguise. It was one thing to be sure in his own mind that it was foolproof, quite another to test it on the Acton locals. To help him dispel any doubt, however, he recalled a recent television series where a fellow actor, one he even knew slightly, had managed to fool him. The series was called *The Americans* and the two central characters were Russian spies, living in the US as man and wife. They were often required to use physical disguises in order to carry out their work and in one episode Marcus had simply not recognised the male lead, so careful, so perfect, so subtle had been his new persona.

During the run of *Dangerous Corner* Marcus had taken to staying several nights a week at the Royal Overseas League in St James's Street. On one occasion he left the hotel the following morning, instantly recognisable as Marcus Lawlor with a sports bag in his hand, and drove to the now empty 19 Ashbury Road. In the upstairs bathroom he carefully morphed into his disguise, applying the gel and the cap, and fixing down the wig. He touched in a smattering of pale makeup, stepped into the unremarkable clothes and then checked himself in the mirror. An ordinary bloke, he concluded, who would never stand out in a crowd, on a train, in a pub.

At the front door he waited for Jonas Kemble to join him before stepping out onto the pavement. He made his way down the hill towards the local shops, only to find that it was market day, the road was closed off to traffic and stallholders and shoppers alike were making the most of the kind weather. Hurrying in between them, rush-hour locals were heading towards buses and the local station. Hundreds, hundreds of people were in flow, not one of whom gave Marcus a second glance. When an hour later he settled in a café where the pace of life had slowed, nobody gave a damn about the man in the blue quilted anorak reading the *Metro* and sipping a latte. And given that he was about to play the most dangerous role of his career, he was uncharacteristically pleased about that.

* * *

There was an obvious problem to the next stage of the unfolding drama. Neither he, nor anyone else in the family, had the faintest idea where Isabella and Ethan had moved to. However, when Mary Talbot revealed that Isabella had made her allegations to the police in Walworth, Marcus realised it must have been her local station. It was certainly worth a gamble. He consulted a Google map of the area and saw that there were three or four patches of green marked. Larger than any of the others was Kennington Park.

On his third visit there his hunch paid off. It was eleven o'clock and his only problem, as far as he could tell, was that he was becoming a regular. He would buy a coffee from the Starbucks nearby and take it into the park, where he would read *The Guardian* from cover to cover. With the prospect of spring being just around the corner, the park was soon busy with people walking their dogs, office workers taking their lunch breaks, mothers pushing prams…

He saw Maria enter through the iron gate on Kennington Road. She passed within three feet of where he was sitting, even glancing at him and looking away as he returned to his coffee and newspaper. A hundred yards farther on she parked the pram, reached in and with grandmotherly delight, lifted Rafael out into the sunshine and sat him on her knee. Maria was clearly as thrilled with him now as the day he was born. She pointed to everything – birds, the buds on trees, passing people, other children. She even exchanged greetings with a young mother she clearly knew who sat beside them and introduced her own child to Rafael. Marcus reached for his phone, then decided against it. A middle-aged man taking photos of children in a London park? Such things were easily misinterpreted.

Maria left the park about an hour later and Marcus followed her. He kept well back, much farther than he had often done as Richard Salter. He watched as she reached a set of traffic lights on Kennington Road, crossed over and doubled back on herself. She paused outside the end house of an Edwardian terrace, five stories tall, once yellow brick, now gray and be-dieseled. It was too far away to read the number, not that it mattered. It had a bright blue front door.

Maria lifted Rafael from the pram and went up the dozen or so steps, apparently explaining to him all the way what was happening. Marcus was swamped suddenly by a wave of sorrow. That should have been Teresa, strutting through a London park, showing Rafael off to other women, nattering to him inconsequentially, returning him to loving parents. It was a year of Rafael's life that should have been Teresa's by right, not given away to this stranger from Madrid. As Rafael and his nanny entered the house Marcus turned and walked away.

When he returned a few days later he brought with him a cheap pair of binoculars. The girl in Starbucks was beginning to recognise him and greeted him with smalltalk about the weather. He decided to transfer his affections to Costa from then on. Once in the park he settled on a bench with a distant view of the blue door and waited.

At around 8:15 a couple in their early thirties came bickering down the front steps, the man tapping his watch irritably, the girl hurling defensive abuse back at him. A small Mercedes had already drawn up to the kerb and was being hooted by other drivers. It was a colleague of the pair, most probably, taking them all to a place of business.

Ten minutes later a young woman emerged from the house. She was dressed for a London office: a secretary or PA perhaps. She carried a heavy bag over one shoulder and, like many of her age, appeared to talk to herself constantly, directing her words to a microphone in her lapel.

Eventually Ethan appeared, baggily dressed and smoking a cigarette. He hurried off in the direction of the bug-eyed Lambeth North tube station, presumably to take the underground to… where? Had he found another job? If so, he didn't seem overly keen to start the day.

At around eleven Maria bumped the collapsible pram down to the pathway and opened it out. She went back into the house to fetch Rafael, treading sideways down the steps with him in her arms. She settled him, all smiles and baby talk, before strolling to the traffic lights. She crossed the road and entered the park.

Isabella never appeared.

After three more days of reconnoitring, Marcus decided to take the plunge. He arrived at Kennington Road the next day, went up the steps to the blue door and turned to the panel of buzzers. He made a mental note of the names – James and Lister on one of them, the squabbling young couple, no doubt, the other one Donaldson, the muttering single girl. He pressed Lawlor and waited. For a moment

Jack Relph revisited him, the day they had first met at Golden Meadow when Marcus had rung the bell only to fear that no one was at home. If he hadn't been, would life have turned out so very differently?

The panel crackled and Isabella said, "Who is it?"

He looked round and lowered his voice. "It's Marcus Lawlor."

There was a pause. "What the hell do *you* want?"

His voice quivered as if he were summoning the courage to speak. "Bella, please, I have to say all this or spend an age regretting that I never did."

He had pitched it exactly right, enough to gain her interest.

"Sounds very dramatic," she said. "You can't come up here, though."

"That's fine. The baby, yes?"

"The baby is out with his nanny. Give me five minutes. Is it cold?"

"Fresh. Bring a cardigan or jacket."

The crackling ceased abruptly. Marcus went down to the front wall and leaned back against it. Isabella's five minutes became ten, then fifteen and when she finally appeared at the front door he went to greet her. For a moment she didn't recognise him, then laughed, a hand flying to her mouth.

"What's all this?" she said of the wig, the clothes, the glasses.

"I'll tell you..." He leaned forward as if to kiss her on the cheek, but pulled back. He looked round again, nervously. "There's a Costa just beyond the park."

She smiled. "I thought you and coffee shops were at war. 19 pence bean to cup, £4·50 cup to lip?"

He laughed. "Ethan told you that? Where is he?"

"Work. Ethix Films."

"How is he?"

"He's fine. I won't say he's enjoying fatherhood, but men get used to it, I'm told." She smiled. "Don't they?"

He nodded. "Let's go."

She was dressed to attract inappropriate remarks, in hooker boots, as Teresa would have called them, and a patchwork coat of many colours, no doubt with a golden lining. The hair hung down her back, past her waist and was loosely tied with a red silk scarf. Her matching lipstick was freshly applied. Marcus hoped that people they passed wouldn't assume he was her client.

At the Costa Coffee, which was huge but packed, they ordered lattes and retreated to a corner table in the comparative gloom. She removed her coat to reveal a cardigan, yes, but worn over a tight blouse which was straining at the neck. She leaned forward and said,

"Do you think Clannad drank coffee here?"

She nodded at a black and white print of the ancient group on the wall behind him.

"They didn't drink coffee anywhere. If they had their music would have been livelier."

She laughed. "So why the disguise?"

"I couldn't tell you what I need to as... me." He laughed breathily, avoiding her eyes. "And if you take it badly, if you scream and shout and I have to run for it, no one'll say, 'There goes Marcus Lawlor.'"

She smiled. "Unless I tell them."

"In which case they'll say you're mad and I'll be halfway down Kennington Road." He paused and forced himself to look at her steadily. "I didn't want all this to happen, Isabella. I didn't want to never see you again."

She was puzzled. "You mean never see Ethan and Rafael, surely?"

"No. You." He sighed with relief at having made the confession. "See, I don't think you're the person some people believe. And even if you are, I'm not sure I care. Like father, like son."

She shifted in her chair, but kept her eyes firmly on him.

"You'll have to give me time to get used to that," she said.

"Teresa might have wanted..." He slapped the table, annoyed with himself. "I promised myself I wouldn't be disloyal, but the truth is she never liked you."

"And you did?"

"From the very first. That night at Imogen's 21st? As for some of the things that've happened since, some of the fantasies, the lies you've told, well... I tell lies for a living!"

"Books I'm supposed to have stolen?" she asked, warily.

He smiled. "That old fool Jack Relph... a pile of books worth a fortune just sitting there."

"What about Henry? Don't you care about that?"

He flicked the question aside and said flatly, "Of course I care, and part of me is angry and wishes you hadn't done it. Truth be told, he's been playing with fire all his adult life. He treated my mother appallingly, screwed every woman he took a fancy to..." He broke off suddenly. "There, I'm doing it again. The disloyalty thing. But I think of what you did as a kind of karma. It was bound to happen."

"You sound almost pleased that it did."

"It's difficult being the son of such a man. We've been

in competition ever since I started acting. How are you two… three getting on?"

She rocked her head slightly. "We're okay. Ethan seems to like working for Ethix, this project about the coast."

Marcus laughed. "I haven't spoken to him for a while."

"I can't really say I have either."

He nodded. "Newborn babies, they change things more than they've a right to. Is Maria good with him?"

"She likes babies in general and, well, you either do or don't, I suppose. I joined the NCT. You know them?"

He smiled, wryly. "National Childbirth Trust."

"The women there were mostly daft about kids. One or two felt the way I do, but didn't dare admit it. So I left."

"Teresa once told me, long after we'd had The Others, how bored she was talking all day to two-year-olds."

Isabella nodded in sympathy. "It's the monotony I couldn't stand. The routine. Every day wake up, change, feed, sleep, wake up, change, feed, sleep, wake up, change…"

He gestured round the café. "You fancy doing this again?"

She laughed. "You mean a weekly trip to Costa Coffee? There's a devil in you, Marcus Lawlor…"

"We could go places. Exhibitions, galleries, a film, shopping. For shoes."

She smiled and at last reached out a hand to touch his arm. "Sounds good. I'd have to be careful about price tags. I mean, we're supposed to be living on Ethan's wages and some cash my dad sends, but it doesn't go far."

"How is he? Your father?"

"I've no idea." She smiled feebly, pretending to be ashamed.

"But he still sends you money. Do you owe people?"

"I owe Maria, I know that." She gazed into his eyes, wondering just how generous she could persuade him to be. "Nine hundred pounds."

He nodded. "I guess she doesn't have a bank account in this country. Why don't you open one for her? Let me have the details." He smiled. "Fancy a walk? Nice day, park right across the road."

She smiled. "Let's."

They strolled slowly towards a large, irregular shaped pond and stood by the side of it. Farther along the path a middle-aged man crept up behind a much younger woman, slipped his arms round her waist and kissed her on the top of her head. She smiled and flopped back into him. The pair might have been lovers, father and daughter, brother and sister. Whatever the case, Marcus took it as a cue, turned and smiled at Isabella.

"So, when… next time, I mean?" he asked.

"Why don't you text me?"

The last thing he wanted was a digital record of any contact with her. "Let's make a date now. Friday afternoon, Covent Garden for lunch."

"Beralini's?"

"Not on your life. I know the head waiter too well."

"You think he'll see through your disguise?" she said, teasingly.

"There's a place opposite Beralini's. Fish restaurant. Friday, twelve thirty. Shopping afterwards."

She wriggled with pleasure at the prospect of an assignation. It appealed to her weakness for taking risks, she said. And her love of power. She could tease him endlessly about his disguise, threaten to blow his cover at any moment.

"And persuade you to buy me anything," she squealed with delight. "Oh, and who are you, by the way? I mean, does your disguise have a name? What is it?"

Marcus smiled. "Jonas Kemble."

"I like it," she said.

* * *

Back at Ashbury Road Marcus went up to the bathroom and removed the wig, the cap and the thin line of glue using eyelash remover which Imogen had left behind.

The meeting with Isabella had gone to plan, but he couldn't help wondering if she had really fallen for it. Did she really believe that he would turn on his wife, father, children, just to be in her company? On the other hand every scrap of research he had done assured him that people like Isabel believed so firmly in their power to manipulate a situation that basic doubts were irrelevant. She would go along with it just to see where it led. He wasn't sure how long it would take him, perhaps as much as two months from hereon. His only slight fear was that, during that time, he would come to understand and sympathise with why she had tried to destroy three generations of his family.

He took off his clothes, hung them in the bathroom cupboard, then stepped into the shower and began to wash off whatever remained of the day.

* * *

They usually met at Craft's, the fish restaurant in Henrietta Street. On the fourth or fifth visit they were recognised by at least one of the waiters, who clearly didn't rate them as a married couple. Their routine was to have the most expensive lunch on the menu and then stroll hand in hand to wherever took Isabella's fancy.

Only once did Marcus fall prey to a massive bolt of doublethink. She had asked that they visit the Natural History Museum. He considered it an odd request and her reaction, once they entered the building, was even more alarming. Like a child of ten she rushed from exhibit to exhibit, never stopping long at one, always anxious to move on to another. She gestured him frantically to keep pace and within an hour he was exhausted. Had her interest been real, her curiosity genuine? He couldn't tell, but it made him wonder if he'd made a grave mistake, if maybe there was an Isabella not far beneath the surface who none of them had known. If they could just coax it out.

As they rested in the museum café he asked after Ethan and Rafael. Her answer was the usual one. They were both fine, and as for Maria, since being paid by Marcus she had become more of a housekeeper than just a nanny. He took the hint to offer more money to secure her services.

The time had come, he decided right there in one of Britain's most famous buildings. If she had changed, even slightly, from Isabella to Isabel, she would refuse his offer. If she was still the self-serving deceiver he had first met at Imogen's 21st, she would accept. He reached across the table, took her hand and gazed into her eyes.

"Shall we go away somewhere?" he asked.

"Where?"

"Oh, I don't know. Just for a night or two."

She laughed. "Somewhere you can be the man you really are? Underneath?"

He smiled, awkwardly. "I know there's Ethan to think about and what you'll say to him."

She responded with harsh enthusiasm. "I can handle Ethan."

"The baby?"

"Maria will be in seventh heaven."

He shifted, uneasily. It wasn't a question of morality, he was sure of that, but was this really such a good idea? Here he was, playing fast and loose with his entire future. If this escapade went wrong, that would be the end of his marriage. His children would never forgive him. Was it worth risking those things? And what of his career? That was usually the first thing he thought of, though not today. All the same, she could ruin it on a whim, just as she'd ruined Henry's. All it needed was a photo, a recorded conversation, a fingerprint, a scrap of DNA. If her past was anything to go by she doubtless had some of that in the bag already. So why didn't he do what those in the know always advised? Just walk away?

"You're so sweet, you really are," she said, giggling. "How about Florence? Or Amsterdam? New York, maybe?"

"I was thinking more of the Cotswolds," he said, apologetically. She groaned. "Somewhere I used to know in my youth."

"Before Teresa?"

"Of course."

"When? When shall we go?"

He smiled, relieved that she had accepted his invitation.

"How about Saturday? I mean right after the performance of *Dangerous Corner*? The logistics will need to be looked at."

She roared with laughter. "Logistics?! If I know you, Jonas Kemble, you've taken care of those already."

"You're right and I'm sorry I'm such a coward." He reached out for her hand. "It won't always be like this, me in disguise. Let me work on it. Be patient."

She whispered, stagily. "As long as you take that wig off before you get into bed, I'll fit in with any plan you've made."

-37-

Teresa had delayed selling 19 Ashbury Road for longer than good sense dictated and eventually decided to make two lists, for and against getting rid of it. The two columns were parallel on a dead page in her A4 diary and the 'for' list had won by a dozen points.

She drove into London that Thursday morning to meet the estate agent who would value the house. She parked her car and looked up at the place, noticing, unsurprisingly, only its faults: a loose gutter down the left-hand side, a slipped tile, the front garden, and presumably the back, overgrown. She hurried inside to put them out of her mind. As she closed the door behind her and the background noise of Acton at large faded, melancholy and regret took its place. Her attempt to give the house a new lease of life by moving The Others into it had failed. Ideally, they would have lived there until they decided to move on. That decision had been taken out of their hands by a usurper and the house had returned to being an archive of her bleak childhood. Her mother and father seemed to be everywhere, hardly speaking to one another, while she herself was the ghost on the stairs, creeping up to the attic, hoping against hope that the next time she emerged from it life would be brighter, gayer, more deserving of being lived.

She scoured the house from top to bottom and found very little evidence that The Others had ever been there. The odd picture hook was still in place, a spattering of tacky plastic where posters had hung, the odd scuff on the paintwork, but that was about it. As she stood at the bathroom sink she noticed the small hand towel on the rail beside her. She held it to her nose and thought she recognised the faint perfumey smell it gave off, but couldn't place it.

She looked carefully round the room. The airing cupboard door was slightly ajar and she eased it fully open. To her surprise, hanging on the makeshift rail was a navy blue quilted anorak. One of the boys had left it behind, no doubt. On a hanger beside it there was a checked shirt and a pair of chinos; on the floor a pair of suede shoes, neatly placed as if trying to hide themselves away. At the back of the cupboard was a battered leather suitcase which seemed vaguely familiar, but as with the hand towel she couldn't place it. And then suddenly she could, as her eyes fell on a set of number plates leaning against the wall in the farthest corner. VK56 DFP. They were Marcus's plates and belonged on the crumbling old car he drove round in. The faint smell on the towel was his cologne, Penhaligon's Bayolea. The leather suitcase had been in the attic at Golden Meadow.

She set it down on the floor and snapped it open to find a mousey brown wig stretched over a stand, with a packet of cap liners beside it. There was hair gel, hair grips, a selection of theatrical makeup, a bottle of stage glue and its antidote. Trembling now ahead of half a dozen explanations, she tried to make sense of what she was looking at. She sat on the toilet lid and ran them through her mind. Was she terrified by her growing belief or invigorated? It was difficult to say so soon after finding the stuff, but in the end she replaced everything exactly where she had found it. She even left the airing cupboard door slightly ajar.

She had an hour before the estate agent was due and went into the kitchen to make tea, using a kettle which, being Teresa, had been on her day's list of things she would need for the London trip. Kettle. Two mugs. Milk. Teabags. Spoon. Biscuits.

-38-

Ethan returned from Ethix with a preoccupied look on his face and Isabella asked, dutifully, if everything was alright. Yes, yes, he replied, rattily, and immediately asked for the daily update on Rafa. How was the cough that had been bothering him for days now? Had Maria fixed it? Yes. She was putting him to bed at this very moment and Ethan should resist the urge to go and cuddle his son. He nodded, and made to kiss her on the lips, but she turned her head at the last moment.

He dropped into the chair at his desk and let out a stifled groan. He had work to do before tomorrow. He needed to plug a hole some moron had left in the second episode of the documentary.

"Oh, dear. The same moron as last time, or a different one?"

"Same. Vigo Johnson."

Had it not been for Rafael's presence in the next room, Ethan would have screeched the details. He kept them to a whisper. Vigo Johnson, the historian fronting the coastal documentary, had written a piece on Hastings.

"By which I mean the battle thereof."

"What's he done?"

"One of the most well documented moments in British history sounds as if a four-year-old's written it. Why they asked the twat to write the commentary for the entire project, God knows. He regurgitates it in a patronising, condescending style with grammatical errors, repetition, the lot. And I found out today that his first name isn't Vigo, it's Bert!"

He sat down at the table, took out his laptop and fired it up.

"Did you ever meet Grace Drayton?" Isabella asked. "She was at Somerville with me."

"Doesn't ring a bell."

"Only she's having a reunion. Girls only. She called this morning."

"When is it?"

"Tomorrow. In Bristol. I'll stay over, I think."

He looked up at her. "You think that's appropriate?"

"What do you mean?"

He nodded towards the nursery. "He's less than a year old. I don't think you should leave him. Even for one night."

"That's what Maria's for." She was raising her voice beyond baby level. "Stepping in. Helping."

He patted down the air to quieten her. "Fine. Go if you want to."

"You've had a bad day," she said gently. "Would a glass of wine help? There's some from last night."

"Please."

That was the first time he'd ever disapproved of her plans. Sure, he'd whined and whimpered occasionally, but he had never, ever had the guts to cross her. She went through to the kitchen, found the half-drunk bottle and filled two glasses.

She stepped away from the moment and watched her hand reach down into her bra for the tiny glass phial. She removed the stopper and tapped the powder into his glass. She held it up to the light and swirled it round, then took it through to Ethan. He nodded his thanks and sipped from the glass as he carried on working. She began to count in her head. In time he put a hand to his stomach and tried to ease away the pain. It got worse. He doubled up and began to retch. He fell from the chair and started to writhe on the floor, spewing red from his mouth. He looked up at her and knew what she'd done by the smile on her face...

Isabella put an arm around his shoulders and kissed him on the cheek.

"You want to get on, I can see."

"Sorry, yes."

She nodded. "And don't worry. Rafa will be fine."

* * *

The next day she caught the four o'clock train from Paddington to Stroud, just as Marcus had suggested. She disliked train journeys at the best of times and on this occasion the weather was less than sympathetic. The world beyond the carriage was obliterated by rain streaking down the window.

She turned her attention to her fellow passengers, themselves an unprepossessing bunch, many with laptops throbbing away on the tables in front of them, others deformed by smartphones trapped between cheeks and shoulders as they shared their most trivial thoughts with friends they had called.

Directly opposite Isabella sat a married couple in their mid-fifties. The man had flat grey hair, his wife a motionless perm with a dead straight fringe just above her eyebrows. They were dressed in anoraks and walking boots and spoke little for the first half-hour of the journey. They held hands discreetly and stared straight ahead of them into that no man's land of train journeys, one metre away. The woman kept refocussing to glance at the hair which Isabella had unleashed from its rain hat when she took her seat. The woman was dying to comment on it, Isabella thought, so she gave her the chance to do so.

She fumbled with her phone and dropped it on the carriage floor, propelling it forward with her foot. It was as though someone had fired a starting pistol and a panic of activity ensued, even from people across the gangway. The rambling couple dipped out of sight to retrieve the phone, the husband getting to it first and handing it over to Isabella.

"Thank you," she said breathily, patting herself just below her throat. "It's like dropping a small child. You wonder if you've damaged it for life."

"The power of technology," said the husband. "It has us all by the throat."

"I was trying to find out what time the train arrived in Stroud," Isabella said.

"17:52. By which time the weather is supposed to have improved."

"Do you live there, work there, are you just visiting?" the woman asked in a croaky voice.

Isabella smiled. She was on the verge of coyly confessing

the affair she was having with her father-in-law. He's a famous actor. Yes, of course you know him. Reeling him in has been one of the easiest things I've ever done. Too easy, perhaps. And tonight I'm going to… well, I'm going to fuck him to bits. Who wouldn't! Shall I tell you who he is? Please ask me. And keep on asking till I crack…

"I'm meeting my uncle," she said. "We don't hook up very often but I always look forward to it. Hearing the latest gossip."

The man twinkled slightly. "About whom?"

Isabella fiddled with her throat as if trying to swallow what she had just said.

"His colleagues in Westminster."

"He's an MP? For Stroud?"

Isabella had a feeling that he knew the name of Stroud's MP and probably that of every other MP in the country. She laughed.

"You know, I really shouldn't have said that. I mean, I've been brought up to keep trade secrets. Where are you two bound for?"

"A few days tramping round the Cotswolds before the clocks go back."

His wife seized the opportunity while it lasted. "Forgive my forwardness but your hair is truly glorious."

"Thank you," said Isabella, as if no one had ever paid her such a compliment.

"If only!" said the woman, ruefully considering her own grey bonnet of the stuff. "Mine was always dormouse brown, now it's off-white."

"You sound like a D.I.Y colour chart," said the man.

"Enjoy it while you can," said the wife.

Isabella had finished with them. She smiled and returned to her phone.

At Stroud station the husband lifted down his own and his wife's rucksacks and Isabella's travelling case. He found himself carrying it as far as the ticket barrier before handing it over.

The husband had been right about the weather: such people usually are. The rain had petered out, but the wind was freshening. Out on the station forecourt Isabella walked over to a taxi, addressed the man standing beside it and handed him her case. He placed it on the front passenger seat, opened the rear door and all but bowed as she climbed in.

-39-

After the performance of *Dangerous Corner* that evening Marcus fell in with Charlie Burgoyne's invitation to join the cast for 'surprise' drinks at the Cross Keys, the excuse being that it was Tom Slinger's birthday. Tom wasn't that keen, but, mainly to give himself an extra alibi, Marcus jollied him into being agreeable. Who would believe he was off to a late night assignation, in Stroud of all places, if he had chosen to party with colleagues ahead of it?

Marcus drank a single glass of wine and Burgoyne mocked him for it, as he did most people who couldn't down a full bottle every night. It was the cirrhosis talking on Charlie's behalf, forcing him to make his own habit seem normal and other people's freakishly modest.

***

It was nearly midnight before Marcus left the Cross Keys. He had intended to grab a bite near the theatre before the journey to Stroud, but with time against him he went straight to Ashbury Road, showered and changed into the disguise. He would grab a sandwich at the garage on the A40, he promised himself, a warmup exercise for his new creation. His steps from the pumps to the cashier would be slighter than his own, the movements quicker, the gaze less confident. He would choose a bog-standard ham sandwich and takeaway tea, pay with cash and then continue the drive to Gloucestershire.

As he left London behind him the rain gradually eased off, and on reaching Painswick he made his way down Beech Lane. At the bottom he pulled into the ungated field he had discovered a few days earlier, oddly drawn to it now as if he had known it all his life. He got out of the car and listened for a moment to the background sound of the breeze and far-off traffic, the foreground sound of silence. Would he lose his nerve when the chance arose? Would Marcus Lawlor lay a hand on his shoulder at the last moment and bring him to his senses? He pulled the collar of the quilted jacket up as far as it would go, locked the car and set off up the hill towards the Falcon.

It was an imposing building, an old coaching house fashioned from local stone in the eighteenth century. The cars parked on the forecourt spoke of money – not fortunes, but comfortable living.

One of the double doors of the place was closed when Marcus reached it. Through the secondary glass door he could see a pale-faced boy tidying the foyer ahead of locking up and leaving a notice on a stand outside that asked late arrivals to ring the bell to attract his attention. The young man was an underfed, under-slept undergraduate making a few extra pounds a week by manning the front door while he sat at reception and checked his coursework.

Marcus entered and approached him with a lighter voice than his own and informed him that his name was

Kemble. The boy pointed up the stairs.

"Mrs Kemble is expecting you, sir."

He smiled. "Annoyed, I expect. Bad traffic."

"Room 7, top of the stairs and straight ahead, end of the corridor." Marcus turned to the stairs. "Your bag, sir?"

Marcus paused and snapped his fingers in irritation. "Dammit," he said. "I've left it in my car."

"You want me to...?" the boy began.

"No, I'll fetch it. Let me just make my apologies."

The stairs were a recent vanity, far too ornate for the original building. The banister was carved mahogany, spring flowers and woodland creatures. Who had the owners let loose on it, Marcus wondered, or was it a B & Q special? The wall was staggered with tinted prints of birds of prey, including the obligatory falcon.

At the end of the dimly lit corridor he knocked on the door to room 7 and, as he entered, Isabella stirred from the bed. She had fallen asleep while watching a film. She switched off the television and came over to him.

"You said... when did you say?"

"Eleven. I know, I'm sorry."

She draped her arms round his neck and hung there looking into his eyes, then stepped back for a moment.

"Makeup?" she asked. "It makes you look younger, but not nearly as... sexy."

She reached up and kissed him on the lips and he played the distraction of a man who has forgotten something vital.

"My bag. I've left it in the car."

"Well, go and get it, silly boy."

"I've parked some way off, I'm afraid."

"Why on earth...?"

He squirmed a little. "Well, I know it's not a car that stands out, but..."

She laughed. "God forbid someone recognises it and asks what the famous actor in disguise is doing with a woman half his age?"

He smiled. "Something like that."

"Take off your wig," she said with a commanding jerk of her head.

He backed away and pointed out of the door with his thumb. "Just let me..."

"Oh dear, please tell me you're not having second thoughts."

He smiled just as he had smiled numerous times at leading ladies, seconds before the bedroom door closed and denied the audience the next scene.

"I promise, promise. Hey, why don't you slip on a pair of shoes and come with me?"

"I think I should," she said, playfully. "If only to make sure you don't escape."

He helped her into an anorak that would have been more at home in the King's Road than in deepest Gloucestershire. She locked the door behind them and they made their way down the stairs. The undergrad was already in position behind the reception desk, his laptop open at his latest essay, and greeted them cheerfully.

"Would you like a hand, sir?"

"No, no, we're going to get some air first. Won't be long."

"Ring the bell when you get back."

He watched them as they left, the woman smiling and nudging at the man, who seemed embarrassed. No way were they husband and wife.

They set off down the road, Isabella with her arm through his and, once free of the security camera's gaze, Marcus straightened up a little. Farther on he removed his glasses and folded down the anorak's collar. Isabella squeezed his arm.

"You will let me know, won't you?" He turned to her. "When you've become the man I'm here to have a raunchy weekend with."

He nodded. "I will."

"I mean, the car parked a ten-mile hike away? The wig, the glasses, the funny walk, the throwback clothes?"

"It's hardly ten miles."

It had turned into the perfect night for an assignation, if romance was all he had wanted. The stars had appeared in number, the light from the full moon was casting long shadows. Marcus had wanted it to still be cloudy, misty, dark. The BBC's weather app had assured him it would be. It had forecast persistent rain. Ground-softening rain.

"You know, I never come to this part of the world without thinking the ghost of Laurie Lee will appear."

"*Cider with Rosie*?" she said, in a long-suffering voice. "I did it for at school."

"My father was in a BBC production of it, back in the mists of time."

"Who did he play?"

"Uncle Ray." She nodded, not in the least discomfited by mention of Henry. "He describes the book as the most sumptuously overwritten novel in the English Language." He stopped and turned to her. "Did he really try it on with you?"

She smiled. "I so wanted him to."

"Is that why you did... what you did to him?"

She looked at him and hesitated, as if about to make a confession. Or even to apologise.

"I never meant to be nasty," she said, in a quiet voice. "I went to counselling once, five years ago now."

"What for?"

"There was a man once who looked just like a younger Henry. I wanted to be everything he desired."

"What happened?"

"People around me pretended they knew what love was. I tried to copy their emotions. I tried to make them my own, until I realised I could fake anything, even love, but never feel it. So it fell apart. He left me." She smiled. "I ended up sleeping with the counsellor."

He laughed. "That doesn't really answer my question about Henry."

She shook her head. "I did it simply because I could, just like I can do this."

She reached up and kissed him on the mouth, then raised a hand and with her finger and thumb opened his lips. She pushed her tongue into his mouth and pressed her body hard up against his. He could feel her shape, her legs, hips, breasts, and as she pulled him towards her she ran a hand down the front of the chinos and smiled.

"Well, I never, the divine Marcus Lawlor is as much an animal as anyone. I knew I could bring it out in him."

She reached out and he took her hand. It was a child's hand, feeling for warmth and comfort as they walked on in silence. When they reached a dip in the lane he pointed to the entrance to a meadow. His car was parked just inside the gate. A breeze suddenly rattled the branches above them and made him flinch.

"You really are frightened we'll be caught!" she said in a stage whisper. "You know something?"

"What?"

"I've never made love in a car. Have you?"

"No."

"Would you like to?"

"Yes, I think I would."

She smiled. "Well, don't sound so excited about it!"

He laid a hand on the side of her face and caressed it. He drew her towards him, arm around her waist. He kissed her on the lips.

He had thought about this moment many times in the last few weeks, broken it down into its gruesome parts as if rehearsing a stage fight or a film stunt. Would Jonas Kemble stand by him now? Would he give the steel to tighten his grip and drive her head back at an angle with all the strength he could muster? It wouldn't sound like a tree branch breaking underfoot, or a pistol shot, or any other worn-out comparison. It would be a dull snap, the sound muffled by the flesh in her neck. Her head would loll back, her eyes would open wide. She would collapse as she concertinaed into his arms. He would fold her lifeless body into the boot of his car and drive away. It was the perfect murder, committed by someone who didn't exist.

-40-

Marcus arrived back at Golden Meadow the next day, prepared for a few questions from Teresa about how the play had gone the previous evening and if anyone they knew had been in the audience. She might even ask where he had spent the night. She was seated at the kitchen table, a full house of Sunday newspapers in front of her: some had bothered to report the leak, others didn't consider it to be newsworthy. The Crown Prosecution Service, who would ultimately decide on Sir Henry Lawlor's fate, had received no less than fifty letters from well-known actresses, and other women he had known intimately down the years, each one describing him as a perfect gentlemen. The deluge had been orchestrated by Henry's new wife, of course, who had taken courage and got in touch with many of his old paramours. They had responded magnificently. Jenny had been on the phone, apparently, and Teresa had made the mistake of asking her,

"What about those who didn't respond?"

"To hell with them!" Jenny had said. "Fence-sitting bitches. If they've anything to say that'll damn him, let's hear it!"

Her ferocity had been endearing and Teresa had

apologised for suggesting there might be an alternative view.

Marcus stood over the highlighted paragraphs, read a few of them and nodded. "Good. That's good."

"Will it help, though?" Teresa asked.

He smiled. "It's great timing. That was always his forte."

He slumped down at the table, then stared at the coffeemaker. Teresa took the hint and went over to make a fresh pot.

"Did you stay at the Overseas League?" she asked. "Only your phone was switched off."

He smiled. It was something else Richard Salter had taught him. Never leave a GPS trail if you plan to murder someone.

"There was a bit of a do for Tom Slinger and I came away the worse for wear."

"Better now?" she asked casually.

"Fine. How about you? You alright?"

She waited before answering. "I miss my children."

"I know, but..."

"I don't mean I want them back here, aged ten. I just wish I could pick up the phone and talk to them, meet up for coffee. And how can I miss a grandchild I met once for five minutes, a few hours after he was born? Is that stupid of me?"

"Not at all," he said, gently.

"You're being mysterious."

"Because I agree with you?"

She took a deep breath. "We need a few things. I'm going to Waitrose."

He poured himself some coffee. As he drank it he heard

her car crunch across the gravel, reach the tarmac drive and fade away. He waited five minutes or more before going into the living room and taking a handful of firelighters from the coal box beside the grate. Matches as well. He settled the dogs and went out to his car. He opened the boot, took out the big carrier bag and checked the items it contained against the list in his head: puffer jacket, chinos, three shirts, shoes and socks. Then he reached back for the leather case. He placed it on the ground and opened it, snap, snap. Wig, wig stand, skull caps, hair grips, stage glue, solvent. He closed it again, locked the boot and made his way round to the back of the house to the hedged-off vegetable garden. In one corner of it was an old cast-iron incinerator, the metal blackened with years of burning cardboard packing, oddments of wooden furniture and garden rubbish. He shook out the contents of the bag and the case, placed the firelighters strategically and set light to one of them. He stood back and watched it burn.

He returned to it the following morning after a shower of rain had rendered the ashes a black treacly mass, which he scooped out of the incinerator with a shovel and transferred to a canvas sack. At one point he wondered if he had fallen victim to a surfeit of television detail – documentaries, drama series, even reported instances where a pinhead leads down a chain of forensic evidence to the bad guy, the perp, the villain. There were bits of the disguise which hadn't burned: the zip on the jacket, two press studs at the cuffs, the hook on the trouser waistband, shards of glass from the solvent bottle. Some ultra-bright spark would need just one of those items to lead them straight back to Marcus.

Later on he took the dogs for a walk down to the river

Thame, two miles from Golden Meadow and fast flowing now because of the rain. He paused halfway across the tractor bridge, kneeled down and emptied the contents of the sack into the water. The dogs looked on, one at either side of him, innocently unaware of his purpose. The ash flowed away, breaking up as it went; the metal and glass sank to the bottom.

* * *

It was early Wednesday morning before Ethan phoned his mother to say that he was worried. Isabella had been missing for three days. Teresa suppressed the immediate surge of hope that it wasn't just a temporary flit on Isabella's part but a longstanding wish finally granted. She had gone. Ditched her child and her husband and moved on to fresh opportunities. It seemed too good to be true. There would be other explanations. She glanced at Marcus, afraid that he might be able to provide one. She put the phone on speaker so that he could hear.

"When you say missing…?"

"Saturday afternoon she went to see an old friend from uni who lives in Bristol, Grace Drayton. Only she didn't. And Grace Drayton doesn't exist. I've been onto Somerville, there's never been a woman of that name."

Marcus pulled a disinterested face and gestured to Teresa, asking if she wanted him to make toast. She shook her head.

"You've tried her mobile?" Teresa asked.

"Of course I have!"

"Have you called her father?"

"Mum, I can't work out if you're pleased or genuinely concerned. No, I haven't been in touch."

"Ethan, I never panic but I am worried. Did you fight or something?"

"No!" he shouted.

"I see. What about Rafael?"

"He's fine."

"Does he see a health visitor occasionally? Do they still have such people?"

"For fuck's sake, Mum, Isabella, Rafael's mother, has gone missing! That is priority." He could be heard taking a few gulping breaths, which somehow calmed him. "I'm sorry. It isn't your fault. What the hell do I do, Mum?"

She warmed to the apology, to say nothing of her delight that he had asked her advice. "First thing, you phone her father. If he hasn't heard from her, call the police." She lowered her voice. "And can I make a request? Keep an eye on Maria."

"What the hell…?"

"Don't ask me to elaborate, just watch her. If you've any doubts, bring Rafael out to Golden Meadow."

"Right, right. What do you think has happened?"

"I'm just hoping it's one of Isabella's little quirks. She fancied a few days off, disappeared without telling you." She could hear Ethan about to protest. "Phone John Morrison, then get back to me."

They finished the call and Teresa turned to Marcus.

"I put some in anyway," he said of the toast.

She watched him as he ducked into the fridge for the butter dish and marmalade and didn't close the door properly. She went over to it and finished the task.

"Do you think she's gone? For good?" she asked, carefully.

He smiled. "We can always hope."

-41-

Two months later, in spite of the Missing Persons Unit's best efforts, there was still no sign of Isabella.

Teresa accepted an offer on 19 Ashbury Road and the contracts were exchanged just before Christmas. It sold for one point three million pounds, a house which her father had struggled to pay £23,000 for. She banked the money with a mixture of gratitude, guilt and regret.

As for The Others, Imogen was still living in Greenwich with Jane Sillitoe, 'partnered up' as she described it. Carla was still living aboard the good ship *Landmark* with Captain Matt, back at Paddington Basin for December. How happy either of her daughters was Teresa couldn't say, but at least they were talking to her and, indeed, visiting their parents on a regular basis. Zack and Amy turned up occasionally, not as often as Teresa would have liked. They were busy, if not with work then renovating the house they had bought in Windsor.

The centre of attention, during nearly ever waking moment, was Rafael who, with his father, had gone to live at Golden Meadow. Maria was sent back to Madrid, albeit in floods of tears, and her place was taken by a retired Norland Nanny. Louise Lavender lived in the next village and had stopped working six years ago, intending to concentrate on her garden. However, when Teresa's advert appeared in the local paper, she couldn't resist the prospect of the easy journey to work, to say nothing of the generous pay offer. She was a young looking 60-year-old, fit and witty, and she came with the added bonus of wanting to go back to her own house every evening.

It was a wise move to employ her. It meant there was no push-pull between Teresa and Ethan about how to bring up his son. They could defer their private opinions, or any cause for argument, onto Louise. Nanny always knew best. Unsurprisingly, Louise generally agreed with Teresa. Ethan should concentrate on his career and leave the business of seeing Rafa through his first few years to others.

With *Dangerous Corner* still playing to full houses, in spite of what Marcus referred to as its 'mind-numbing mediocrity', he gave what little spare time he had to Rafael. The latter's power to charm those he clapped eyes on, even with the soft focus of babyhood, was quite in keeping with the Lawlor magic. Teresa thought she could already see in him the confidence, perhaps even the roving eye, of Henry and occasionally the darker, uncharted side of Marcus. She kept the opinion to herself.

As Easter approached it was overshadowed by the lingering sadness of a visibly diminished Henry. Unnervingly he seemed content not to be the life and soul of any party. He was comfortable in his own shell, his new wife insisted, secure in the knowledge of his own innocence. Even so, a certain fire in him had been beaten out by the ever present threat of a charge against him. For attempted rape. It showed itself in his reluctance to flirt with every woman who came into view, in some cases to even acknowledge their presence. He had felt an iciness from neighbours in Burford, those he passed when out for a walk or as he indulged that most old-fashioned of habits, posting a letter. Their guard was up. Wasn't he the actor who had been accused recently of trying to rape his granddaughter-in-law? Hadn't it been all over social media and the papers?

Mary Talbot finally justified her exorbitant fees and received a response to her badgering of the Crown Prosecution Service. She had argued that since her client was accused of the attempted rape of Isabella Constanza Morales, not one woman had come forward to say she had a similar story to tell. On the contrary, he had received no less than 87 letters of support from women he had known. Make of the word 'known' what you will, Mary had said. Not all of them were from famous actresses. Two were from Members of Parliament and one from a peeress in the House of Lords. The CPS wrote back to say there would be no prosecution. They minced their words, citing lack of evidence and the fact that his accuser could no longer be found. Mary Talbot rose up to her full five feet two inches and made them change the letter to read: "There is absolutely no evidence against your client in this matter and the case is therefore closed. We regret any distress caused to Sir Henry." Mary left it at that. It was as close to a full apology as Henry was likely to receive and she blasted it across every media platform she could think of. Within days, the artistic director of the Sherborne called Henry to ask how he felt about giving the Joe Orton revival another go. Henry laughed at the man's ham-fisted delicacy.

"Thanks to your decision to cancel the project, due to

unforeseen circumstances, I now fear that I look too old for the role of Truscott."

It was a perfect cue and the artistic director picked it up shamelessly. With a barrage of obsequious waffle he assured Henry he wasn't too old for anything.

So it was that an unremarkable production of a new play was sidelined and a revival of *Loot* staged in its place. The publicity was immense. No one could accuse the Sherborne of failing to cash in on its star's fame and lingering notoriety. Marcus prepared his father for possible brickbats. There might be detractors lurking in the wings, rats behind the arras, hoping that Sir Henry would give a less than brilliant performance.

The first night arrived with what felt like unseemly haste and the theatre was packed. When the lights went down and the play began the audience had only half a mind on the opening scenes, the setup of the story. They were waiting for the appearance of Truscott, the retired bent policeman. As his entrance grew ever nearer those who knew the play began to shift a little, clear their throats, and then all of a sudden there he was. Henry entered from the left and paused for a moment, as he always did, to get a feel for his audience. He was about to speak his first line when he was interrupted by a man in the front row, who rose to his feet and began to clap. He was followed by a second person, farther back in the stalls, then a third, a fourth, fifth, sixth... until the entire audience was on its feet applauding, along with members of the cast.

Henry turned to the auditorium and came downstage. He smiled and looked round, appearing to take in every face. The applause went on for thirty seconds and would have lasted longer had he not raised a hand and stepped back. He turned to the actors on stage as Truscott again and said in a London copper's voice,

"Good afternoon."

"Good afternoon," said the character of Fay. "Who are you?"

"I am attached to the Metropolitan Water Board. I'm on a fact-finding tour of the area. I'd like to inspect your mains supply."

-42-

It was delivered to Golden Meadow by helicopter direct from Liège, where the previous day it had been lifted from the ground. It dangled upright in the air, suspended by a web of ropes and an enclosing net, its root ball swathed in canvas to prevent the crumbling earth from falling. It arrived at exactly 12:13 and the entire family, together with respective partners, was there beside Bigg's Cave ready to greet it. They cheered as it came over the horizon, hovered and then began its slow descent. The contractors on the ground moved the family back, away from the intense noise of the blades, and as the oak seemed to feel its way into Bigg's Cave and the main holding rope was dropped, they applauded.

Rafael gurgled with them but wasn't sure why. His grandmother stooped down to his pushchair to explain what was going on. The big tree coming out of the sky was being planted in Nana's field so that all the dickie-birds would have somewhere to live, she said in a voice that irritated everyone. Except Rafael.

The helicopter drifted away to the edge of the meadow and landed. The people on board joined the contractors, climbed into the pit and began to unwrap Marcus's present to himself. Before Carla could prevent him from doing so Matt had asked how much the whole operation had cost. Marcus smiled at him.

The team foreman warned them for the umpteenth time to stand clear and signalled one of his men to start the bulldozer, which began shifting recently delivered topsoil into the space around the roots. He himself climbed the rear ladder of a water tanker parked close by and with its outsize hose he washed the soil into place around the oak tree.

From start to finish the whole business took a couple of hours and eventually Marcus was able to take stock of his new purchase. The trees in the wood were already covered in the green haze of oncoming spring, but the oak looked as dead as a doornail. Not that he could reach the tips of any branches to check. The tree was forty odd feet high and the lowest bough several feet above his head. The foreman said, in answer to his simple enquiry as to whether it was dead or alive,

"He lives, my friend! He will live a thousand years!"

His assertive tone and the Belgian accent somehow made his pronouncement utterly believable.

"Tomorrow I come back with more water. Water is the key. I come back till I think it safe to leave. You understand me?"

Marcus nodded and they shook hands. He asked if the team would care to join them in the house for tea and the foreman declined on their behalf. Marcus stood and watched the helicopter reel in its ropes and take to the sky. The workforce piled into the cab of the tanker and followed the bulldozer to a side gate that led to the drive. Alone with his tree, Marcus gave it one instruction.

"Grow!"

As he strolled back to the house he saw a small car turn in from the lane and crawl slowly up to house where it parked on the gravel. The young woman who stepped out of it was tall with an auburn tint in her dark hair. She wore businesslike clothes, inexpensive but smart, a navy blue jacket over a cream dress. She reached back into the car for a shoulder bag and as she came towards him Marcus tried to guess at her ethnicity. Middle Eastern, he thought.

"Hallo!" he called to her.

"Hallo, sir, I'm Detective Constable Nilou Gilani."

They shook hands and he smiled.

"Marcus Lawlor."

Her mother, a fan of *Salter's Edge*, was right. A handsome man, she had said. Like his father. Be careful. And try to get an autograph. Gilani offered Marcus her warrant card, but he waved it aside.

"How can I help?"

"Actually, it's your son I need to speak to. Ethan Lawlor?"

Unlike most police officers of her age, her face was unblemished by cynicism and obligatory world-weariness. She might have been a schoolteacher or a young doctor.

"He's in the house. We've just had an oak tree delivered."

He gestured back across the field to where the oak stood recovering from its sudden displacement.

"Capability Brown style," Marcus went on. "Came in by helicopter, not horse and cart, though."

"How wonderful," said Gilani and appeared to mean it.

"Come and join the celebrations. Help us with some of the food. My wife always makes more than we need."

Marcus led the way into the house via the back door and the dogs did their usual figure of eight around the newcomer, making her nervous. Marcus told them to settle.

"Ethan!" he yelled as he took off his boots and lined them up with others in the back porch. "Someone to see you!"

Ethan came through to the kitchen from the living room, where the celebrations were taking place. He raised a glass of cranberry juice to his father.

"You bellowed, my lord?"

"DC Nilou Gilani," said the visitor, leaning forward to shake Ethan's hand. "I can see my timing leaves a lot to be desired."

"Nonsense," said Marcus. "You've caught us all in a good mood. Don't tell me you're about to put the mockers on that."

"I'm from the NCA's Missing Persons Unit."

"Good God," said Marcus, quietly. "Don't tell us she's turned up?"

"No, no, that's not why I'm here," she said, hurriedly.

She set her shoulder bag down on a chair and took a pair of reading glasses from it. They altered her face. She went from being almost beautiful to snipey and severe as she read from a page of handwritten notes.

"You reported your partner missing at Walworth early last year."

She turned as Teresa entered the kitchen.

"Mum, this is DC Gilani. From the Missing Persons Unit."

"Isabella?" said Teresa, eyes darting from one face to the other.

"Her father," said Gilani. "A Mr..."

"We know John Morrison," said Teresa.

"He believes that we've washed our hands of the case and since there were no grounds for a formal investigation he's conducting his own."

There was a slight pause.

"Good for him," said Marcus. "Has anything come of it?"

"As a matter of fact, yes. A student living in Gloucestershire saw the photo of Isabel on a news website and recognised her. According to him, on the night she disappeared she'd been staying at a hotel he worked in. The Falcon, Painswick."

She looked at them to gauge their reaction.

"Where is Painswick?" Marcus asked.

"Near Stroud. She was in the company of a man called Kemble – indeed they booked in as Mr and Mrs Kemble."

She took a folded photo sheet from her bag and passed it to Ethan.

"It's from the hotel CCTV. Grainy and he's facing away from the camera, but it's the best we have. Apart from the student's description. Do you by any chance recognise the man?"

Ethan studied the photo and eventually said, "I'm afraid I don't."

He passed the sheet to his father, who looked at it and slowly shook his head.

"That's Isabel alright but I can't help you with the man. What did you say the name was?"

"Kemble. Early forties. Five feet ten. Light brown hair. It's bound to be a false name but he may have used it before. I'll leave it with you and perhaps you'd be kind enough to show it to friends? Ask them if it rings any bells?"

Teresa took the photo and looked at it. Quilted jacket. Chinos. Fair hair. Early forties? Gilani handed Ethan a card.

"Please get in touch if anything occurs to you."

From the next room Rafael gave a piercing scream and Ethan apologised before hurrying off to deal with the upset.

"So you're taking this seriously?" said Teresa of the photo.

"Of course."

Gilani removed her glasses, put them back in her bag and zipped it up. "I've taken up enough of your time."

"Are you sure you won't stay for some cake or a glass of wine?" Marcus asked.

She smiled. "No, thank you. But I would love to see your new oak tree."

Marcus shrugged. "By all means. I'll walk you over to it."

"No, no, stay and enjoy your family."

Marcus and Teresa went to the window and watched Gilani cross the lawn and enter the golden meadow. She made her way to the oak tree and on reaching it began to circle it, gazing up into the branches. Then she stopped, looked down at the ground. She dug at the loose, wet soil with the toe of her shoe and wondered. She glanced across at the house, then back at her foot. Teresa laid a hand on her husband's shoulder and asked in the shorthand of marriage,

"Did you?"

He looked at her and smiled. "You know me better than that."

* * *

Two weeks later, Marcus entered the kitchen one morning with wet dogs and Teresa groaned. He apologised quickly and took out his phone.

"Look, look at this," he said, with childish delight.

He turned his phone towards her and showed her the photo he had taken five minutes earlier.

"A leaf. It's alive!"

END

Printed in Great Britain
by Amazon

83602818R00215